THE DEADLY NEIGHBORS

OTHER ZOE HAYES MYSTERIES

The Nanny Murders

The River Killings

THE DEADLY NEIGHBORS

MERRY JONES

THOMAS DUNNE BOOKS
ST. MARTIN'S MINOTAUR
NEW YORK

This is a work of fiction. All of the characters, organizations, and events portrayed in this novel are either products of the author's imagination or are used fictitiously.

THOMAS DUNNE BOOKS.
An imprint of St. Martin's Press.

www.thomasdunnebooks.com
www.minotaurbooks.com

ISBN-13: 978-0-312-35621-7
ISBN-10: 0-312-35621-8

First Edition: December 2007

10 9 8 7 6 5 4 3 2 1

To Robin, Baille and Neely,

and the memory of Sam

ACKNOWLEDGMENTS

I was maybe two-thirds of the way through the first draft of this book when, suddenly, my mother and favorite woman ever fell violently and gravely ill. For a good six months, she hovered between life and death. Family gathered around her in Chicago; my Miami-based sister and I took turns flying into town; my daughters, brother-in-law, a niece and two nephews, aunts and cousins and uncles and friends joined us at Mom's side during her seemingly endless struggle.

During that time, of course, work just didn't happen. Which meant that this book didn't get finished on time. My editors at St. Martin's Press, Thomas Dunne, Marcia Markland and Diana Szu, and my agent, the fabulous Liza Dawson, were not merely understanding about the delay; they were supportive, reassuring, patient and generous, allowing me to take time out for my family without worrying about the timelines in our agreements. For that, as for the opportunities and encouragement they've given me with all the Zoe Hayes books, I am extremely thankful.

Also, I need to express deep and special thanks to:

Detective Chuck Boyle of the homicide division of the Philadelphia Police Department for sharing his valuable time and insights on the inner workings of the Roundhouse and police procedures.

Lanie Zera, Sue Solovy Mulder, Sue Francke, Ruth Waldfogel, Mike and Jan Molinaro, Steve Zindell and Leslie Mogul for being close by always, no matter where we are.

Janet Martin, Nancy Delman, Jane Braun and the rest of my

family—I can't list everyone—for being consistently encouraging and dependable through good times and bad.

Dr. Ned Zelig for caring and persisting.

Coach Gabi Cipollone, for reasons only she will understand.

Our late sweet corgi, Sam, for keeping me company, lying under my desk as I wrote until he died one morning while I was with Mom.

Our new corgi, Jack, who is the devil incarnate.

My daughters, Baille and Neely, who are joy incarnate.

My beloved, brave husband and merciless in-home editor, Robin.

My sorely missed late dad and brother, Herman S. and Aaron N. Bloch.

And my miracle mom, Judy Bloch, who fought her way back to us by sheer strength of will and determination, and who, even in the worst parts of her ordeal, remained a lady.

THE DEADLY NEIGHBORS

ONE

THE HOUSE LOOKED SMALLER THAN I REMEMBERED. SMALLER, and much more forlorn. Standing at the curb surveying the property, I half-expected to see myself at six, bursting out the door and running down the hill to the stream, or burying myself in mounds of crisp fallen leaves. Or at ten, hiding in secret shaded spots in the garden where no one could find me. Or at sixteen, sneaking out on crisp fall nights to meet Kenny Birch, the high school track star who lived next to the gated property on the corner. Who, it turned out, cheated on me with that trashy redhead in my trig class, Stephanie Laing.

Oh, Lord. Why was I remembering all this? I hadn't thought about any of these people in decades. But now, from all sides of the street, memories came swirling. Old Dr. Hennigsman, who lived across the street and always wore a three-piece suit, even when taking out the trash. Professor Hogan, who smoked nostril-searing, pungent tobacco while sitting on his porch swing, arias charging full-throttle from his window. Hilda, our plump housekeeper, her waist-long caramel-colored hair coiled into a gravity-defying knot, trimming rosebushes in the side yard. And my dapper dad, eyes twinkling, rushing off somewhere magical with a cheerful kiss and dazzling smile.

Stop now, I told myself. Don't revisit the past; those times are gone. You're here to deal with the present. I closed my eyes and took a deep breath, steeling myself for the walk up the path, reminding myself that I was not a child anymore. I was a grown woman, no longer vulnerable to the house or to the demands of the man who occupied it. Years had passed since I'd lived here. Decades. I had my own life now, my own home and family, a second child on the way. Being here was no reason for my stomach to churn or my hands to go clammy. What could happen? After all, he was just an old man.

Molly let go of my hand and raced up the path to the veranda steps. Six years old and high-spirited, Molly had little tolerance for standing around. "I'll ring the bell," she called.

Fine, I thought. You ring it. Because if you don't, we'll have to stand here while I get up the nerve. Which might take days. Weeks. Oh, Lord. What were we doing here? Why had we come? Yes, okay. We'd come because my father was a widower, alone and eighty-three. And Molly was his only grandchild. And I was his only daughter. But still, I hadn't seen or spoken to him in years. I hadn't wanted to and still didn't. Our complete estrangement suited me fine. In fact, I tried my best never even to think of him. Life was easier, more normal, that way.

Of course, there had been times—entire years—when I'd thought of him ceaselessly. His handsome, contagious smile; his twinkling, playful eyes. His deep reassuring voice. His boundless promises. His endless lies.

Eventually, I'd stopped spending energy on him. With the help of an interchangeable stream of sitters, housekeepers and maids, I'd managed to survive my mostly motherless childhood, had finished college, married, divorced, adopted a child. I'd built a career, gotten engaged again, become pregnant. Hell, I was forty-plus-one-or-so years old. I bore no resemblance whatever to the skinny, self-conscious, apprehensive and often disappointed kid who'd once lived here and unconditionally, usually at her own peril, adored her father. Through long years of repeated disillusionment, I'd turned so far away from my father that when I'd been making a list of wedding guests, I'd automatically omitted his name. I'd never even told Nick, my fiancé, that my father was still alive, let alone that his house was only a twenty-minute drive from ours. I'd acted as if I'd had no father. And that had been fine.

Until now. Somehow, despite my strongest survival instincts, here I was, at my father's door, my six-year-old daughter at my side. A warm October breeze rattled the brilliant leaves of a dozen ancient trees, sounding like applause. As if the trees were clapping, welcoming me home.

Molly pushed the buzzer, removed her finger and immediately pushed again. And again. And again.

"Molls—" I grabbed her hand before it could make another jab. "Don't ring so many times. It's rude."

"But Grandpa's waiting. He's expecting us."

Grandpa? She'd never met him, yet she seemed instantly comfortable with the concept. Grandpa. She was going to visit her grandpa, as if it were a normal thing to do. I wondered what she expected, how she pictured him. How would she greet him? And how would he react? Would he scoop her up in still strong, suntanned arms, charming her with a broad grin and baritone laugh? Would he lure her with a jangle of gleaming gold coins and silver dollars?

"Wait a minute." I squeezed her hand. "Give Grandpa a chance to get here. He might be upstairs."

Her eyes turned to the door, waiting. And my mind wandered. Somewhere close by, dogs barked furiously, cloyingly. Across the street, a large buffed man in a black T-shirt and jeans stood under a weeping willow tree holding a huge dog, maybe a mastiff, on a leash. Was he watching us? He seemed intent, staring at the house, eyes darting away when I looked at him. But why would he be watching us? He wasn't; he was just a man walking his dog, gazing across the street while waiting for it to sniff a tree trunk. So, where was my father? Why wasn't he answering the door? And, when he did, what would I say to him? How should I greet him?

My stomach fluttered and wrenched, and I put a hand on my belly, as if reassuring the baby. I didn't want to be here. When Dad's next-door neighbor, Lettie something—Kinkaid? Yes, Lettie Kinkaid. When she'd called, I should have told her that she had the wrong number. That I'd never heard of Zoe Hayes or her father, Walter Hayes, or any Hayeses at all, ever. Or that Zoe Hayes had moved away, leaving no forwarding address. Or that she'd died; that, in fact, I'd buried her myself.

But I hadn't said any of that. Instead, I'd asked what was wrong, what had happened. She'd pointedly asked when I'd seen my father last, and I'd felt my face get hot, embarrassed by her chastising tone, a stranger's assumptions. She must have wondered what kind of daughter I was, neglecting an old widower. She must have thought I was an ingrate, a self-absorbed superficial brat. Living so close, not seeing him at all. Ignoring the poor man in the winter of his years.

Afterward, I'd considered pretending that the call had never come. That I didn't know he was ailing. But in the end, I'd been compelled to listen to the stranger who lived next door to him imply that it was my fault that my father hadn't been eating, had become fragile and occasionally disoriented, had been ill with the flu much of last spring and hadn't played cards in months.

"No cards?" I'd repeated.

"Not even with his usual guys, hon. Not a single game."

My father was avid about few things; one of them was cards. Any kind of game that he could bet on gave him pleasure, but card games were a way of life for him. He'd play anything. Gin. Poker. Blackjack. Even Canasta. So when Lettie'd said that he'd not played a single game, I knew the situation was serious. Emotions became irrelevant; the duties of blood prevailed. It was time to go home.

And so here I was, waiting for the door to open. We waited. And waited. The neighbor's dogs kept barking, fraying my nerves. Fidgeting, Molly pushed the buzzer again. Then she climbed the stone railing that ran along the long veranda, jumped down and ran beneath the weeping willow branches on the front lawn. I watched her, recalling my early years, and gazed beyond her along the street of aged rambling homes, the gold and red hues of century-old trees, the mix of color and shadow.

Mount Airy was hilly and overgrown with foliage. Overripe. Stone houses hunkered under the shadows of leafy branches; the ground was dotted with moss and freckles of light that penetrated the shade. The people here were racially and economically mixed, an eclectic population of all professions, educational levels, religions and cultures. There were even some authentic hippies, still around from the sixties, still running a food coop. My father hadn't selected the community; he'd landed here by chance. After his gambling binges had finally left us broke, his grandmother died and left him the house in her will.

As a child, I'd thought the house immense. Now, though, I realized that its formality, not its size, was what had made it seem formidable. Corinthian pillars lined the porch running along the sides of the house. On the south side, a wide, once flawless lawn sloped down to a wooded creek. I knew the terrain well, remembered darting among those pillars as a child, pretending, as a teenager, escaping from life. I'd climbed up and dashed down the hill, splashed on slippery rocks. Now the pillars were chipped and cracked, the porch sagging, the garden overgrown. The wood on the shutters was rotting and the lawn neglected, bursting with weeds. My father had completely let the place go. I wondered if he'd cut me out of his will. Or if someday all this—the massive decaying house, the large untended property and the responsibility to care for it—would be mine. I shook my head, dismissing the thought.

Where the hell was he? What was taking him so long? I'd called the day before to confirm the visit. I was sure I'd made the time clear. Mentally, I replayed the phone conversation.

"It's Zoe."

"Zoe?" He'd sounded hoarse and baffled. Well, it had been years.

"Yes."

Silence. Apparently he hadn't been any more thrilled to hear from me than I'd been to call.

"What can I do for you?"

What could he do for me? As if I'd want anything from him. "I thought I'd stop by and see you tomorrow."

No response.

"How's the morning?" I suggested. "About eleven?"

A pause. "Eleven o'clock?" I could hear him breathing. "Okay."

And that had been the extent of it. No "How are you?" No "What's new?" Not a word of happiness or shock or horror that, after years of silence, I'd suddenly called. Just a casual okay, agreeing to see me at eleven o'clock. So, it was ten past eleven. If he was expecting me, where was he?

I stepped off the porch into the untrimmed hedges and peered through smudged front windows. No sign of movement.

What was going on? Maybe he hadn't heard the bell. Or maybe he was outside, in the back. Or on the phone. Or lying dead in the bathtub, or on the bathroom floor, paralyzed from a stroke. I'd once heard of a woman who'd lain like that for days until someone found her. By then, she'd died of dehydration, not of the stroke. Stop it, I told myself. Dad is perfectly fine. Okay, I argued back, if he's so fine, why isn't he answering the door? Obviously, something was wrong. Besides, Molly was running out of patience. We couldn't stand there waiting indefinitely. It was time to move.

So, holding hands, we set out on the slate path that circled the house, overgrown foliage tickling our legs. We passed the neglected vegetable garden, thigh-high with weeds. I tried to open the mudroom door, the hidden door off the driveway, the elongated windows along the porch. All were locked and rusty. No sign of my father. Finally, dreading the descent, I led Molly to the always damp and moldy rear stairwell and started down, hoping she wouldn't have time to notice how slippery the walls were.

"Eww," Molly declared. "My sneakers." Her favorites, the yellow pair, had already squished into mud coating the steps.

"Careful. Don't slip."

"Mom, this is gross."

"I know. Try not to think about it." We descended another step.

"Yuck."

Clutching her hand, trying not to slip, I led her downward, remembering the squirming clump of worms I'd once encountered at the bottom of the stairwell near the drain. A single ray of light bounced off the wet concrete wall; the rest was shadow and slime, smells of mildew, damp earth, decay, something rotting. What the hell were we doing here? Why didn't I just take Molly and go home? An image flashed in my head: my father lying unconscious on hard linoleum; and I knew we had to go on. Stop whining, I scolded myself. Just keep moving. I took another step down. One foot, the other. Molly followed slowly, reluctantly. Four, five, six steps down.

At step seven, Molly simply stopped. "I'm not going, Mom." Her voice was firm. Even in the shadows, I could see the finality in her eyes.

I squeezed her hand and gave it a tug. "Molls, we can get in the house this way. Come on. It's just a few more steps."

"No way." She stamped her foot as an exclamation point, splashing my legs with slime. Perfect, I thought. So far, it was a fabulous homecoming.

"Molly, please." I was begging, sounding pathetic. "There's a way to get in down there."

Her jaw was set. Immovable. "I don't want to get in. I want to go home." She stamped her foot again, splattering more muck.

"Molly, we have no choice. We have to look in on Grandpa. Then we'll go home. I promise."

She stood her ground, refusing. Molly was strong-willed and persistent; arguing with her would get me nowhere. So, as I had when she was a toddler, I reached out, scooped her up and carried her down the steps, praying that my feet wouldn't slide out from under me, wondering if the worms were still there and if we'd land in a soggy, writhing mass. Carefully testing each step, I held on to Molly, ignoring the chorus of her whines and the repeated thunk of her wet sneakers against my khaki capris.

Finally, we reached the bottom. The air around us clung

clammy and dank; the sunlight had disappeared. Something thick and moist was sucking my shoes, and I didn't dare look down. Shadowy webs and encrusted cocoons coated the basement door. I took a breath, balanced Molly on my hip and, praying that my father hadn't removed it, remembering briefly Whopper, our long-deceased golden retriever, I kicked the spot where the doggie door used to be. It swung open easily, soundlessly, not even rusted. I knelt, tentatively balancing Molly's weight on my thighs, and pushed the panel open again. Molly clutched my neck, gaping in disbelief.

"Molls, it's not as bad as it looks. I used to go in this way all the time." I didn't mention the dread evoked by that memory.

She tightened her grip. "I'm not going in there."

I looked at the doggie entrance, the muck surrounding it and the darkness beyond. Frankly, I didn't blame her. I didn't want to go in either. Still, we had to get into the house, and, without breaking a window, this was the only way I knew of. But I didn't want to force her to go in. I couldn't. Instead, I gave her a choice. "Okay, here's the deal. I've got to go find Grandpa to make sure he's all right. But you don't have to. If you want, you can wait outside."

"What—out here?" Molly glanced back up the dark, mucky staircase, then down at the door. "By myself?"

I was about to say that I'd take her back upstairs and that she could wait on the porch, but before I could say another word, she dived forward and flew through the opening. All I could see of her were the muddy soles of her bright yellow sneakers.

TWO

AND SO, MUDDIED, DISHEVELED AND MORE THAN A LITTLE DISconcerted, I'd come home. Molly had been unable to unbolt the lock from inside, so I'd had to crawl through the muck and slither through the doggie door after her. Finally inside, I got up off my knees, brushed crud off my legs and hands, gave Molly a quick hug and flicked the light switch. One dim bulb came on at the far end of the basement.

Molly scowled. Apparently, her visit was not going as planned.

I didn't blame her. The basement air was chilly and mildly rank. Rotting garbage? Dead rats?

I squatted beside her in the shadows, wiping smudges off her face with soiled fingers, making them worse. "Molls, I'm sorry. This visit is all messed up. Hang in there a little longer, okay? We'll go—I'll take you for ice cream as soon as we find Grandpa."

"I don't want to find him. I don't like him."

"Well, we still have to find him and see how he is."

"I don't care how he is. I hate him."

Oh dear. I wondered if I'd traumatized her, if she'd forever associate the word "Grandpa" with dank slimy stairs and chilly dark basements. Actually, to me, the description didn't seem far off.

"Mollybear, Grandpa's an old man, and he might not be feeling well. We have to make sure he's okay."

She glared, defiant. But she let me take her hand, and together we started across the expanse of darkness under my father's house. The basement was an open underground space, unbroken by walls. We stepped around support columns, piles of newspapers, stacks of cartons, mountains of luggage, mounds of old clothes. We passed hunkering silhouettes—the water heater, a tangled mass of pipes, the furnace. The guts and bowels of a big old house. I told myself that I was imagining the crawling sensations on my arms. No spiderwebs were clinging to my face, no whispers tickling my neck, taunting me with secrets I couldn't quite remember. No shadows flickered in the dark corner near the cedar closet. I hurried Molly through the clutter, around discarded furniture and broken appliances, barely escaping the grip of a familiar uneasiness I'd thought long forgotten. By the time we reached the stairs we were almost running, and near the bottom of the staircase, afraid to look back, I felt certain we were merely two steps ahead of some deathly embrace.

My mouth went dry. I clutched Molly's hand and sped up the steps. Panicking about something nameless and unseen, telling myself I was being childish, I literally dragged Molly up the steps. We flew, but, as in a nightmare, the staircase seemed to elongate before us, each step seeming steeper and farther away, harder to climb than the last. With each step, Molly got slower, her breath faster. She was upset and tired; I was being insensitive, expecting too much of a six-year-old. I forced myself to slow down, grasping her hand until, finally, we made it to the top of the narrow, creaking steps, and, relieved to escape the basement, I pushed open the kitchen door.

Even before we'd stepped onto the fading linoleum, though, I'd stopped breathing, stunned first by the sight of my father, then by the knife and the widening pool of blood.

THREE

INSTINCTIVELY, I STEPPED IN FRONT OF MOLLY, TRYING TO PROtect her, to block her view. But that was futile. We stood at the basement door, gaping.

I took it in quickly, but in a jigsaw of pieces. A giant bottle of orange soda. A bowl of potato salad. White paper napkins. A jar of mayonnaise. I saw each item separately, in close-up. Cabinet doors, hanging open on loose hinges. A parched philodendron beside the window. A broken platter in shards near the trash can. Dishes of dog food and water. Slices of white bread peppering the floor. A woman in a floral housecoat, spread-eagled on the floor near the refrigerator. My father, unshaven, thin, his white hair long and unkempt, crouching over her, his hands dripping red, gripping a carving knife, slicing her neck.

Suddenly, events blurred. I was in the air, flying, plunging across the room, over chairs and countertops, landing on my father, knocking him over and sending the knife soaring from his grasp, clattering to the floor. Somebody yelped; someone howled. Angry and spry, my father shoved me away, pounced to retrieve his weapon and grabbed it by the blade, cutting deeply into his palm. Righting it swiftly, he began brandishing it over my head, mindless of the bleeding gash. My father's face was gaunt and he looked frail, but, even wounded, his body was wiry and his movements surprisingly swift. We circled each other warily, and, suddenly he gazed over my shoulder, behind me, to the left. I turned to look; his bloody fist struck the side of my head. Light flashed white and green, and I sank to the floor, dazed. He crouched beside me. Both of him. Raising two right arms, each with its own scarlet-stained knife. Great, I was half-conscious and seeing double, apparently about to be carved by my maddened father.

"Dad—don't!" My voice was raw, a whisper. I grabbed at his wrists, yanking them. The knives glittered. He fought with all his strength, his mouths coated white with thick saliva. Insane.

"Dammit, Dad," I croaked. We were caught up in a breathless struggle. Father's weight and will were pitted against mine. I tried to focus, squeezing double images into one. My hands clutched the slippery red wrist that held the knife; the gnarled fingers of his free hand worked at unfastening my grip, nails digging, scratching, clawing. His face was a portrait of wild desperation; mine of disbelief. Eyes locked, attention riveted, I wondered how many ways this man had damaged my life. How many times he'd snookered me. Well, not this time. This time, my father would not prevail. Twisting his thin wet arm, I withstood the pounding blows of his free one, endured the blood-drawing scrapes of his fingernails, absorbed the raging fury in his eyes. This time, for all the times I hadn't, I stood up to him, and we battled silently, a wasted old man and a wobbly, pregnant fortyish woman, each refusing to cave in or concede to the other. We slid across the bloody floor, twisted our torsos, bent forward and back, grunted and panted and pushed and jerked until, finally, I became aware that the small voice I was hearing was not inside my head.

"Mom? Grandpa? Stop it!"

Molly. "Molly—" I grunted, wanting to tell her something calming, but my father jabbed me and we fought on, rolling through warm crimson clots, grappling and grabbing, clawing and slapping, kicking, twisting, punching and panting, until finally he slipped, his head thunking first the counter and then the floor, gouging an impressive hole in the side of his head. The knife slipped from his hand, and as soon as he hit the ground I straddled his belly, settled all my pregnant bloated weight onto his cadaverish frame, pinning him, nauseous from the smell of blood and something sweet, like rotting leaves. Molly watched from the doorway as he lay spent, heart racing, cursing.

"Goddammit, get off me—" He growled. He wriggled. He fought with every gasping breath. My father was maybe thirty pounds lighter now than he'd been when I'd last seen him, and his whiskers had gone completely white. But his jaw was still strong, and his dark eyes glowed like cold polished stones. No question, even distraught, skinny, bleeding and unkempt, he was still disarmingly handsome.

"Settle down, Dad." I was still panting.

"Get me the knife—before it's too late!" His fingers stretched toward the weapon.

I looked down at his feverish eyes. "It's over, Dad. Settle down."

"Let me up—dammit." He craned his head frantically, blinking, straining to turn toward the woman. "At least check her pulse—is she dead?"

For the first time, I looked closely at the woman on the floor. She was solid, sixty-plus, her hair dyed pinkish blond, clipped in a short curly perm. Her features were strong, symmetrical, her lips full, her eye shadow iridescent blue. She lay motionless, gray eyes open wide, mouth stretched into a tortured grimace. Her neck glistened red, no longer spouting.

"Beatrice?" my father wheezed. "Bea?" He waited, repeated her name, got no response.

I stayed on top of him, alert, waiting for the fact of her death to settle in, afraid he'd start swinging again. But he didn't. When he realized she was gone, he simply covered his eyes with bloody hands.

I climbed off him. "You okay, Molls?"

She nodded, wide-eyed. But I couldn't go to her yet. First I had to check Beatrice. She wasn't breathing. I felt her wrist, her slippery throat for a pulse. There was none. My father crawled to her slowly, on hands and knees. He knelt beside her, running his hands through his silver hair, leaving crimson streaks. "Damn," he finally said. "Look what you've done."

I blinked, baffled. "What *I've* done?"

"You killed her."

"Dad. You slit that woman's throat."

"What choice did I have?"

I studied him, wondering how long ago he'd lost his mind. "Besides cutting her jugular?"

"That was her only hope." He stared at her. "Her last and only hope."

Obviously, he wasn't rational. I was a therapist; somehow my professional side kicked in, and I spoke to him slowly, calmly, as if to a child. "It's all right, Dad. Come sit down."

"How is it all right? Beatrice is dead. Don't be foolish, Louise."

Louise? Louise had been my mother's name. She'd died a few weeks before my sixth birthday. Did he think I was my mother?

Dad stood and began pacing. "Mother of God. Why did they have to kill her?"

They? Maybe he was delusional. Gently, I took him by the arm and led him to a chair. "Sit."

But he wouldn't sit. Bereft, close to tears, he paced and tore at his stringy white mane. "She ran over here. Choking. Her face was purple. The Heimlich didn't work. Something was stuck in her throat—"

I closed my eyes, erasing the image of spurting blood, finally understanding. "So you cut it open?"

He blinked rapidly. "I tried to dig it out, but it was too far down. A tracheotomy was her only chance."

And so, with a carving knife, on the kitchen floor, my father, who'd had no medical training whatsoever, had decided to perform delicate throat surgery.

"I was opening her airway. I was doing fine until you knocked the knife out of my hand." He regarded me with a withering glare. "Dammit, Louise. You as good as killed her."

There was no point in arguing that the woman had died because he'd sliced into an artery and she'd bled to death. Or, for that matter, that I was not Louise.

My father knelt beside Beatrice, his knees in her blood, cradling her head. "Beatrice. Stupid, stupid Beatrice." He caressed her bloody cheek. "Why the hell didn't you listen?"

He scolded her, questioned her, drifting in conversation with a corpse. I put the knife on the counter, safely out of his reach, and finally went to Molly, who still hadn't moved or spoken. She was standing by the basement steps, wide-eyed, watching, twisting a ringlet of hair with her fingers.

"Molls? Are you all right?"

She nodded silently and stood still as I hugged her, then allowed me to usher her away from the blood and the body. When I turned back to him, my father sat dazed on the kitchen floor, watching Beatrice as if unaware that we were there. Cuts and scrapes from our struggle dripped blood over his face and arms. He needed to go to a hospital, get examined. A wound on my forehead rained blood into my eyes, a painful lump was rising on the side of my head, and a chunk of skin was missing from my chin. I took a paper towel from the counter, an ice cube from the freezer, pressed them against my sores. Then I retrieved my purse from the floor, took out my cell phone, and called Nick.

Nick Stiles was my fiancé, the father of my unborn child. He was also a homicide detective for the Philadelphia Police Department. But he wasn't there. His voice mail answered. "This is Detective Nick Stiles . . ." Cool and professional, it asked me to leave a number and promised to return my call. Damn. Why wasn't he there? Trembling and cursing, I dialed 9-1-1.

As my call went through, I tried to piece together what had happened. Who was Beatrice? A neighbor? A friend? And how in touch with reality was my father? He'd confused me with my mother; had he also been confused about Beatrice's choking? Would he be arrested? Charged with killing her?

A voice interrupted, calmly asking how it could help, and as I explained that someone was dead and that we needed an ambulance,

I was distracted by another, smaller voice. “Don’t worry, Grandpa,” it promised. “It’s okay.”

I turned to see Molly taking hold of my father’s blood-crusted hand. When he didn’t respond, she climbed onto his lap and rested her head against his chest. His eyes didn’t move, but his hand rose on its own, gently supporting her back.

FOUR

THE REST OF THE DAY PASSED IN A DIZZYING FRENZY. WHILE WE waited for the police, a woman's head suddenly popped up at the kitchen window, a drowsy puppy in one hand, cigarette in the other. Fit and petite, skin weathered by the sun, Lettie Kinkaid radiated energy. Racially mixed, her hair the color of straw, her eyes gleaming with specks of gray and red, gold and green, she might have been thirty-five, might have been sixty. She stood outside exhaling smoke through the screen, a chorus of barking dogs backing her up.

"Walter?" Her voice was a baritone, deeper than my father's. "Are you in there? Hey, Walter—I know you're home—open up, handsome. I gotta talk to you." She began rapping on the window frame.

Awkward and dazed, aware of an unfamiliar tightness around my middle, I went to the window and waved her away through the screen, making excuses, explaining that we were busy at the moment. But she wouldn't leave. "You're the daughter?" She assessed me through the screen, insisting on seeing my father. "Tell him Lettie's here. I need to see him a sec."

Finally, I went to the adjacent mudroom to open the door. Before I could ask her in, though, Lettie had readjusted her puppy and yanked the screen door, bursting inside, brushing past me to get to my father.

"Hey, Walter? Have you seen Bea—" She stopped cold, struck speechless at the sight of Beatrice's blood-drenched body.

I knew I should say something, but my voice didn't seem to be working. Words wouldn't come. I watched mutely as Lettie's eyes moved from Beatrice to my bludgeoned father and back to Beatrice, her hand rising to her cheek.

"Oh my God, Walter. God Almighty. What have you done?" Her voice was gravelly, tobacco-stained. She wore lots of blue eye shadow and a powder-blue sleeveless sweater over bright yellow capris. Her small frame was draped with lots of loosening leathery skin. Her puppy blinked sleepily, indifferently as Lettie shook her head, gawking at the body. "I knew it. I said he wasn't right, didn't I, girlfriend? On the phone? See what I was talking about?"

"Can I pet him?" Molly had wandered over to look at the puppy.

Lettie blinked, seemingly confused first by Molly's presence, then by her question. "Huh?" She gaped at Molly, her cigarette ashes falling onto the floor.

"Your puppy," Molly explained. "Can I pet him?"

Lettie's dazed eyes moved from Beatrice to Molly, to the puppy, to my father, to me. "Oh. Not a good idea, dollface. I'm training him to be a guard dog."

Molly pouted, confused.

"Nobody but his owner should pet him." Lettie paused, watching Molly's face. "Oh, what the hell. Just this one time, go ahead."

Molly reached up and tentatively stroked the puppy's head. "What's his name?"

But Lettie didn't answer, distracted. In the distance sirens wailed, announcing the approach of an ambulance and the police. Lettie sidled back to the mudroom. "I'll let you handle this by yourselves. Better to keep it simple with the cops—but I'm not running out on you. I'm right next door. You need anything; you let me know."

On her way out, she turned to me. "Call me, hear? I mean it. Christ Almighty." The mudroom door slammed behind her as the sirens peaked.

Within minutes, gawking neighbors lined the sidewalks. Dogs barked restlessly, relentlessly. Police rushed in, trampling the overgrowth along the front path. An ambulance pulled up, then the coroner's wagon. Uniformed officers asked our names, our relationship to the victim. One of them asked what had happened here. I heard myself give out information; my voice had returned and seemed to function independently, answering questions on its own. Molly clung to me, hanging on my arms. But my father became unresponsive. He sat staring with hollow eyes at Beatrice, apparently oblivious to the crowd of strangers invading his home.

FIVE

Nick showed up sometime later. I felt him enter the house, a wave of pulsing energy. He scanned the room, his eyes lingering nowhere, taking in details. I actually felt an electric jolt as his gaze landed on me, lingering, checking to see if I was all right. Thank God, I thought, Nick's here. Nick's going to take charge now. We'll be okay.

The detectives who'd been assigned to the case came over to fill him in, formed a tight triangle. But Molly was undaunted. She burst away from me and barreled over to him, dodging police officers, throwing her arms around his waist. "Nick, know what? My grandpa killed that lady."

Nick knelt to speak to her as his eyes drilled into mine. Boosting Molly into his arms, he carried her back to me, his bagged shoes avoiding blood puddles and smears. A uniformed officer tagged along, hanging on Nick's ear, still trying to fill him in on what he'd learned so far. I waited, too depleted and bruised to move, until Nick set Molly down beside me. Then, relieved and ready to be rescued, I reached for him. But Nick didn't embrace me, didn't place even a perfunctory peck on my cheek. Instead, he gently lowered my hands and stood back, studying me, his head bent, listening to the officer. I felt my face heat up, embarrassed, not sure about what. When the officer finally finished, Nick's pale blue eyes examined me, tenderly touching the sore spots on my face, assessing my injuries.

"You're hurt." Nick finally spoke; the unscarred half of his face was tense. Alarmed. He knelt beside me, gently cloaking me in his arms.

"I'm okay." I was, as long as he was here, holding me. But his embrace was tentative, too short.

"What the hell happened here?"

I shook my head. "I'm not sure, exactly—"

"Is it true the old man's your father?"

I squirmed, sort of nodding. "Yes."

Nick said nothing. His eyes settled on me, waiting for me to continue. I was aware of his breathing, steady, heavy. Impatient?

"Nick, I . . . I'm sorry. I have a lot to tell you."

He exhaled, holding on to my hand. "First, you need to see a doctor, get checked." Why was he scowling? Did I really look that bad? Was he worried about the baby?

"I'm okay, Nick. The baby's fine. I see the doctor Thursday for my regular appointment. I've just got some scrapes and bruises." All I wanted to do was go home, curl up on my purple velvet sofa beside him. Eat some mocha-almond ice cream.

He shook his head, dominant and protective. "You're going to the ER, Zoe. No discussion. You'll give your statement later. Molly's going, too."

"Why? Molly's okay."

"Maybe. Maybe not. Sit here a minute; I'll get you a ride." He watched me for a moment, but that was the end of our conversation. Nick's fingers carefully grazed my cheek, and his lips brushed my forehead. But he didn't hold me again; he whispered no more private words. He went about his business, speaking in hushed tones to the officer beside him, giving instructions, assigning tasks. I reminded myself that this was a police matter. I would have to wait. Nick had to do his job. But my skin still tingled where he'd touched it, and I ached to be wrapped up in his arms.

"Nick—" My voice surprised me, calling him on its own, sounding needy.

He turned, still moving away, distracted. And something else. Angry? He waited; his eyes definitely looked disturbed.

"Nothing, sorry." I backed off. "Never mind."

Uh-oh. What was wrong? What was bothering Nick? And then: Bam, the answer hit me. Nick's feelings were hurt. Of course they were. I should have expected them to be; I'd be hurt, too, if I'd met his father only because of a homicide at his home. But I told myself that Nick would be okay; I'd explain why I hadn't ever mentioned my father, tell him that I'd never meant to hide anything from him. As soon as he knew the facts, he'd recover. I'd talk with him as soon as we had a moment alone. Meantime, I had to be patient. Nick had to talk with the other detectives. The scene had to be processed, and Beatrice's body had to be removed. And my father . . . What would happen to my father? Oh, Lord. Would they put him in jail? No, he was in no condition for jail. Nick would take care of him.

Under Nick's influence, the scene bustled. My father resisted, accusing the medical team of being kidnappers. He turned to me for help, still addressing me by my mother's name. Even so, they lifted him onto a stretcher bound for Germantown Hospital. I was not permitted to go with him; technically, he was in police custody. Instead, Molly and I were assigned to the care of Officer Cal Hollister. He was to drive us to the Emergency Room in our car and to stay with us until we were released, when a police car would pick him up. Nick and his colleagues were efficient, taking care of everything. I tried to get Nick's attention as we left, but he didn't look my way. He was busy, I reminded myself. It was best not to bother him. We'd have time to talk later; it didn't really matter whether or not we said good-bye.

SIX

BY THE TIME WE GOT TO THE HOSPITAL, MOLLY WAS TIRED AND cranky. I was edgy, exhausted. I wanted to go home. In the waiting room, I felt trapped. Officer Hollister couldn't sit still; apparently he hadn't been thrilled at his baby-sitting assignment. Pacing, he drank coffee from the vending machine, repeatedly wandering to the triage desk to chat up the nurse, urging her to have us seen promptly. Time blurred as it does in waiting rooms. Molly whined and hung on me for moments that dragged on, tiresome and endless, until she became too lulled by boredom even to complain. I watched the clock or the walls, trying not to stare at the others in the area: the preteen boy icing his elbow, his weary mother leaning her head back against the wall, eyes closed; the obese couple, rasping in tandem, seated side by side like corpulent mirror images; the impatient mustached man with jeans hanging low enough to expose a substantial section of his hairy hindquarters, pacing from the waiting room to the hall, the hall to the waiting room. We were caught in a timeless loop, a community of strangers, waiting without any idea of why or for how long. Molly leaned on my arm, clung to me, occasionally whining that she hadn't had lunch, and I struggled to ignore the pain in my skull and the blood-drenched images in my mind until, finally, we were called to an examining room.

It was pale green, with stark neon lights that hurt my head. A flimsy white curtain separated us from the hallway. The space was stacked with sterile bandages, bedpans, miscellaneous monitors and machinery, tubing and packaging, instruments of unknown purpose. Our move revitalized Molly. She began talking again, asking what each item in the area was for, why we had to wait so long, when we could eat, why we were there, when we could leave. An endless singsong lament. Eternity, it seemed, was to be spent in small increments, in waiting rooms or behind white curtains.

Finally, a harried young doctor looked us over and basically pronounced us fine. When he asked Molly what had happened, she said she'd just met her grandpa for the first time. Other than that, she said she was hungry and bored and wanted to go home. He checked the baby's heartbeat, cleaned my scrapes, prescribed an ice bag for my emerging lumps, told me I had a mild concussion and should rest, and had me sign a paper. We were released. Free to go.

Amazingly, the outside world remained unchanged. When we stepped outside, bright daylight still gleamed, as if not eons, but only a couple of hours had passed. The warm city air welcomed us, embracing us with soot and car exhaust, replacing the sterile chill of the hospital. Officer Hollister left in a police cruiser and I drove us to our town house in Queen Village, and for the rest of the day, for Molly's sake, I tried to be cheerful, to act normal, fix lunch and follow our routine. But I couldn't, not even almost. A dull pain rolled inside my skull, separating me from those around me, preventing me from thinking clearly. When the phone rang I didn't want to answer, couldn't bear to make conversation.

"Mom, the phone," Molly announced, as if I couldn't hear it. "I'll get it—"

"No, Molls. Don't. Let the voice mail pick up."

"But maybe it's important. It could be Grandpa—" She looked around the kitchen, ran into the hall. "Where is it?"

The fact was I had no idea. The cordless was always disappearing, traveling on its own. It could be anywhere, and I was grateful when it stopped ringing before Molly could locate it. The bump on my head throbbed, and every muscle in my body ached. Thoughts of Nick, of my father, of Beatrice, of shadows I couldn't identify and questions I couldn't articulate rattled around my head. I fought them off, keeping busy. While Molly soaked in the bathtub, I threw our clot-covered clothes into the trash bin, wanting never to see them again. I took a long shower, scrubbing away basement grime and crusted blood. It was after eight when, feeling faint and vaguely nauseous, I remembered we hadn't eaten dinner.

"Mollybear, want a hot dog?" I hoped so. It was about all I had the energy to cook.

Molly wasn't thinking about food, though. She'd spotted the clothes toppling out of the trash can. "Mom, are those my clothes?" She looked mortified.

I nodded. "Mine, too."

"You threw out our clothes? Why? Mom, why?" She repeated the question, trying to make sense of the inexplicable.

"They have stains, Molls."

"So? We can wash them." She stood at the trash can, staring.

"Some stains don't wash out."

"But you didn't even try." She reached into the can, removing a bloody yellow sneaker.

"I didn't have to try. I know those stains won't wash out."

"Why won't they wash out? We can use stain remover."

Why did she have to know so much? "It's blood. A little blood might come out. But not that much."

She was digging deep into the trash, anyway, retrieving what she could. "But my sneakers—my yellow sneakers."

"Molls, they're ruined. I'll get you another pair."

"I don't want another pair. I want these." She held them up. The sneakers were caked with dark brown splotches.

"The new ones will be just as good."

"No, they won't. These are my favorites."

I stood beside her, taking the grisly items from her hands and dropping them back into the can. "Molly, please. Leave them there."

As fast as I replaced things, she pulled them out again. "No—it's my stuff. You can't just throw it out." She was indignant, her arms filled with bloodied clothes.

She was right. The clothes were hers. I stopped grabbing and let her hold a sneaker and a blood-smeared T-shirt. Slowly, she looked them over.

"Mom." She looked up at me, her large eyes welling with disappointment. "My sneakers are ruined."

I sighed, stooping to face her. "I know. Sometimes stuff gets ruined, Molls. If you can't fix it, you just have to let it go."

Her eyes widened, accepting the awful truth. Then, somberly, slowly, she dropped her clothes one item at a time back into the trash. "Good-bye, yellow sneakers. Good-bye Dora T-shirt. Good-bye daisy socks." She stood at the can, mourning, addressing each item.

"We'll get new stuff. I promise."

She nodded soberly.

"I have an idea." I stood, struggling to sound cheerful. "How about we order a pizza?"

She stopped her farewells, silent for a while. Then, in a soft, serious tone, she uttered, "Pepperoni?"

Somehow, a pepperoni pizza lifted her spirit and restored her faith in life, and we made it through the evening. By the time she went to bed, Molly was chattering about her soccer team practice and teacher, Mrs. Kellen, and her friend Hari's dog, Lucy, who was about to have puppies. Amazingly resilient, she seemed already recovered from the crises of the day.

Unlike her mom. For me, the upheaval, like the night, was just beginning.

SEVEN

I WENT INTO THE LIVING ROOM AND CURLED UP ON MY PURPLE velvet sofa, waiting for Nick to come home, remembering the trouble in his eyes, preparing for the inevitable conversation. Nick would be steady and controlled, never admitting that he was hurt. But I could see him almost as if he were in the room with me, his gaze accusing me of being a hypocrite. After all, hadn't I been the one who'd insisted on unflinching honesty and openness? Hadn't I hesitated to get involved with him because I wasn't sure he could be completely forthcoming? Hadn't I been concerned about the secrets in his past, about his former "work" relationship with a sexy forensic psychologist, about his role in his former wife's death? Hell, hadn't I been alarmed that Nick hadn't volunteered the truth about the scar on his face, that he'd neglected to mention that the bullet that had paralyzed half his face had been fired by his own late wife? Hadn't I preached to him about the virtues of honesty and openness? And now, after all my preaching and probing, hadn't I proved that I was just as guilty as he was of keeping secrets?

I listed Nick's imagined accusations, accepting my guilt. It was true, all of it. I'd kept secrets. For all my insistence on full disclosure, I had held back a number of significant facts. I'd told him that my mother had died, but left out the circumstances of her death. I'd skimmed over details of my motherless childhood, had barely mentioned Hilda, the housekeeper who'd helped raise me. I'd only vaguely referred to the string of holidays I'd spent with friends and college roommates, only hinted at the dread I'd felt at having to return home. And I'd omitted telling him anything at all about my father.

How could I defend myself? What could I say that would explain? No doubt, Nick would accuse me of walling myself off, not exposing my weak spots, not trusting him, not being capable of trust. Would I have a defense? Was there one?

The fact was that all of those accusations were accurate. I didn't know if I was capable of fully revealing myself to anybody. It wasn't just Nick—it was everyone. I hadn't told even my closest friends about my childhood or my father. But that wouldn't wash; Nick wasn't just anyone. He was the man I was about to marry. The daddy of the child I was carrying. The man I loved. Presumably, Nick was closer to me than anyone. Shouldn't I have clued him in on the fact that his future father-in-law was alive and residing a few miles away? Shouldn't I have explained the reasons for our estrangement, told him why Dad's name wasn't on the wedding list?

Okay, yes. I should have. Definitely. So, instead of defending myself, I would simply admit my mistake. Apologize. Pledge never to withhold again. Swear that I had no other secrets. And Nick would probably forgive me, or at least pretend to. After all, he was pragmatic, and he had to deal with the pressing issues first. The circumstances of Beatrice's death would take priority; the murkier issues of our relationship would wait until later and, with any luck, they'd fade away without further conflict. I practiced my lines—my description of my father, my abridged family history. I rehearsed assurances that my father wouldn't disrupt our lives any further, that I had no desire to maintain a relationship with him. Good. I was ready to face Nick. But Nick was working nights, still wasn't home.

I turned on the television but couldn't focus. The images flickering on the screen transformed into a dark basement, a blood-spattered kitchen, an old man brandishing a carving knife. A gaping wound in a woman's throat.

Eleven o'clock came and went, then twelve. Nick still wasn't home, hadn't called. I got up, ate another pizza slice. A banana. Swallowed a glass of milk. I waited for Nick in every room of the house. I logged on to the computer to check e-mail, shut it down even before entering my password, distracted. I kept seeing my father poised over Beatrice's bleeding neck, and I watched myself fly across the room, knocking over furniture, fighting him for the knife. Scenes replayed on an endless loop in my mind, and I lamented that alcohol was verboten to pregnant women. I longed for a big fat Scotch on the rocks. Or maybe a tall cold vodka with cranberry juice. Anything to ease my aches and shut down my mind.

When Nick finally came in, it was after one. I was in the bedroom lying down, revising my speech. But I didn't want to face Nick lying down. Lying down was too vulnerable. So I got up and went downstairs, meeting him in the kitchen.

He was rooting around in the refrigerator. He looked wiped out. Wilted. He made no move to kiss or hug me. He glanced over his shoulder. "You're still up?"

Of course I was. How could I sleep? I went to kiss him; he accepted my lips automatically, without energy. Maybe he was too tired to respond? He took a swig of orange juice, right from the container. I tried to remember my speech. How did it start again?

"You okay? They checked you out?"

"Fine. We're fine."

"Your father's in the psych ward. He's getting a complete psych workup as well as a physical. The works."

The psych ward. Was my father actually crazy? "Okay. Good." I didn't know what else to say. Nick drank more juice. Something was off. He kept his distance, his eyes avoiding mine.

"Did you have dinner?" That hadn't been how I'd planned to begin my speech.

"Cheesesteak about eight."

I nodded. "Want me to fix you something? Or there's leftover pizza—"

"No, I'm good." He took the half gallon of mocha-almond out

of the freezer. Good, I thought, eyeing the carton. We'd cuddle and talk over ice cream. Nick took spoons from a drawer and offered me one, but there was a shadow in his eyes. Reflexively, I shook my head—no, thanks—backing off. Damn. What was wrong with me? Why was I holding back? Why didn't I go to him, grab the spoon, lean against his chest? It was my own guilt, I told myself. Nothing else.

Nick replaced my spoon and sat across the kitchen on a stool, casually, as if nothing were wrong. He opened the ice cream and dug in. I could almost taste it. Change your mind and ask him for the spoon, I thought. Or get it yourself.

"Turns out your dad was right." He sucked on a cold mouthful. "The victim, Beatrice? She was choking, just like he said."

Choking? I'd been completely focused on bittersweet mocha; it took a few seconds to digest what he'd said. "Is that what killed her?"

Nick nodded, swallowing. "Her windpipe was completely blocked off."

So my father hadn't killed Beatrice, after all. She'd choked to death from swallowing too much or too fast. Maybe she hadn't chewed long enough—I made a mental note to warn Molly about that. Remember to chew each mouthful until it's mush. The ice cream on Nick's spoon gleamed softly, promising to require no chewing at all. "So what was she eating?"

"Thing is, she didn't choke on food. Her throat was stuffed with paper."

Paper? "She swallowed paper?" Why?

"Wads of it. Small pieces, crammed down her throat." He swallowed ice cream. "Each piece had a name and some numbers on it. Dollar amounts." He licked the spoon. "Looked like betting slips."

Betting slips? Good God. I sat down, suddenly queasy, Nick's words clanging in my head. Betting slips. She'd choked on betting slips. Oh, man. Not possible. Memories buzzed inside my skull, dangerous as angry bees. Betting had been my father's true love, his mistress and passion. He'd bet on everything traditional—horses, cards, games, sports of all kinds. But he'd also make bets on random events. The date of the year's first snowstorm. Whether or not passing strangers would return a smile. How many noodles were in a plate of spaghetti—and, to the nanny's chagrin, he'd have me count them. My father would bet ten dollars on the length of the pastor's sermon in church, or how many times his sermon would contain the word "evil." Early in my childhood I'd been captivated and delighted by my father's antics. He charmed and enchanted me, as he did many others. But gradually, my father's endless gambling became less attractive. It had brought his downfall, and our family's. And so, when I heard "betting slips," I had to sit. There could be no coincidence. If there were betting slips in Beatrice's throat, my father had to be involved somehow. Oh, God. What had my father gotten into? What had he done now?

"She choked on betting slips?" My voice was a croak. "That's what killed her?" In a way, I supposed that was good news; at least she hadn't bled to death from a slit throat.

"Looks that way."

But why would someone swallow betting slips? "Was she trying to get rid of them? Why wouldn't she burn them? Or flush them down the toilet?"

"Zoe." Nick spoke slowly, patiently. "She didn't swallow them on purpose. It's a homicide. Somebody stuffed them down her throat."

Oh. Of course. Obviously. I pictured strong fingers, thrusting, forcing small tidbits into a moist gaping hole, recalled stuffing a Thanksgiving turkey.

"Look, I can't say any more about it. I shouldn't even have said that."

Of course he shouldn't have. It was amazing that he had. Nick revealed the absolute minimum about his work; less if possible. But why would someone kill Beatrice with betting slips? How was my father involved? Obviously, he had to be. Where there was gambling, my father couldn't be far away. I knew I should tell

Nick about my father's history, but I hesitated, not ready yet to face the implications.

"Anyhow, that's pretty much all I know. Because, officially, I'm not involved in the case." He dug out yet another spoonful of glistening ice cream. "My relationship with you gives me a conflict. But I'll stay in the loop; keep my eye on him. Don't worry."

His tone was kind but cool, almost professional. He hadn't really touched me since he'd come home. Normally, Nick and I were physically magnetic, almost inseparable. What was going on? If he was hurt or angry, why didn't he say so instead of being distant? Where were the questions about my secrecy, the resentment about my duplicity?

I inhaled, remembering my speech, bracing myself to begin. "Nick—"

"So, are you really feeling all right?" He cut me off, sliding a glistening ball of ice cream into his mouth. "You got pretty banged up today."

"I'm fine." Why had I said that? Why couldn't I admit I felt miserable?

He watched me tenderly. "Good. I guess you look worse than you feel."

Did I? I had a mild concussion, a blue-green lump on my head, stitches above my right eyebrow and a swollen red scratch on my chin, but did I look that bad? I hadn't realized. I smoothed my hair back, lifted my shoulders, and watched ice cream glide through Nick's lips. Rich and enticing, it offered soothing, cool comfort. I stared at his mouth, thought about how slippery it would be, how sweet it would taste. Stop it, I told myself. Focus.

"Nick," I started my speech again. "I have to say something. About today."

He looked up, biting on an almond.

"I'm sorry. I was wrong."

His head tilted. His eyes lit up, curious. Maybe hopeful.

"I should have told you about my father a long time ago." Good, I told myself. It was a start.

Nick's eyes retreated, disinterested. Or disappointed? He sucked the spoon clean, didn't say anything. He didn't ask a question, didn't make an accusation. He jabbed the spoon back into the ice cream. Go on, I told myself. Explain.

"My history with my father is . . . complicated. Until today, I hadn't seen him in years. He was out of my life, permanently, for a thousand good reasons. Until yesterday. Yesterday, his neighbor called to tell me he wasn't doing well, so I had no choice. I had to look in on him. It was very last-minute. I wasn't, I mean . . . it wasn't like I was keeping him a secret from you." Despite all my planning and rehearsing, I sounded defensive. Pathetic. But I couldn't stop. "In fact, I was going to tell you about him afterward—"

"Don't worry about it. Not a problem."

What? How was it not a problem? "But Nick, I don't want you to think I was hiding him from you—"

"Relax. It's cool."

How was it cool? "But I shouldn't have kept him—"

"It's no big deal." His voice was too easy, stinging me with indifference.

"It's not?"

"Of course not. It's not my business if you have a father or a sister or a cousin or an ex-husband or a hundred other relationships I don't know about."

It wasn't? "It isn't?"

"Why would it be? You're a grown woman. You have your own life. Your own past. Your relationships with your family or anybody else are your own business. They become my business only if you want them to."

Oh. Okay. Suddenly, painfully, I got it. I felt it like a jab in the gut. Nick was clever, using this situation to draw up rules, set guidelines. After all, if he didn't claim a right to know about my relationships, I could hardly complain when he didn't reveal much about his.

"Nick, we're getting married. We should know about the people in each other's lives—at least the important ones. I was wrong not to tell you about my father. I'm sorry."

"No need to be." His tongue darted along the spoon, glib and easy. Snakelike. "Really. You don't have to talk about it unless you want to. It's fine."

How could he say that? Why was he being so amenable? What was that subtle edge in his voice? "How is it fine? You have a right to know. We need to be open with each other. I didn't talk about him, but it wasn't that I was keeping a secret from you. It had nothing to do with you. It was that I didn't want even to think about him—"

"Zoe. Let it go. It's not a problem."

Lord, he was infuriating. Letting the issue go. Accepting my behavior. Agreeing with me. Not getting angry or hurt. How could he be so goddamned pleasant? Didn't he care about me at all?

Go ahead, I told myself. Tell him how awful you feel, how much you need him to want to know and accept your past. Tell him you want him to hold you. Admit that you're so tangled up inside that you can't begin to express it.

I stood silently, wondering why I couldn't speak. Something about Nick was different, holding me back.

"It's been a long day," he offered. "You should go to bed."

"I'm not tired." I was exhausted, aching to snuggle up beside him like normal and sleep.

"Last chance. Sure you don't want any?" He held out the spoon, his eyes teasing, waiting for me to grab it. Stainless steel beckoned, promising smooth, creamy cold mocha.

"No, thanks." I resisted, still not sure why.

The half of his face that wasn't paralyzed lifted into a knowing smirk, and he took a fresh spoon from the drawer. Container in hand, he led the way to the living room. I followed and sat beside him on the sofa, eating ice cream from the carton in silence. Slowly, comforted by his closeness, I began to relax. If Nick was upset that I hadn't told him about my father, he wasn't going to admit it. Probably we wouldn't discuss it further; we would simply move on, silently learning from the experience. He'd relax and warm up again in a day or two. For now, I'd have to give him some space, let him absorb the fact that I had some secrets, too. Relieved, sated with ice cream, I leaned against Nick. He sat with his arm wrapped around me, but his body felt oddly stiff, not our usual snuggle. I gazed up at him. Nick's jaw was tight.

"What, Nick?"

"What do you mean, 'what'?"

"You're angry."

"I'm not angry."

Then why did he seem distant? "Nick, what's going on?" I shifted so I could face him and waited.

Finally, he answered. "Okay, Zoe. Maybe you're right. Maybe I am angry. I'm trying not to be. I'm trying not to be controlling. But what you did today was beyond me."

"I said I was sorry—"

"About your father. But I'm not mad about your father or family secrets or your privacy—"

I sat up straight, defensive. "Then what are you mad about?"

He sighed loudly, shifting his weight, sitting up straight. "Okay. Let's do this. Let's get into it. You took Molly to meet her grandfather today, right? And while you were there, she watched a violent struggle and saw a murder victim."

Right. She hadn't had a great experience. "You're angry about Molly? Molly's tough. She'll be okay. I'll explain—"

"You'll explain? Zoe, she's a kid—how are you going to explain this stuff to her?"

I couldn't, of course. No one could. "I'll just be honest, Nick. Molly will be okay—"

"How do you know? How can you be sure about what's going on inside her head? How much violence do you think a kid can look at before it takes a toll on—"

"Wait, so what are you saying?" I got defensive. "That it's my fault? That I should have prevented it? How was I supposed to know that there would be a corpse in my father's kitchen?"

His eyes pierced mine. “It’s not just about that one corpse, Zoe.”

It wasn’t? Then what was it about? What was he talking about? Oh, great, I thought. The past. Nick was going to list every traumatic event that Molly had ever been exposed to, implying that I hadn’t protected her well enough. That I wasn’t a good mother? Well, maybe he was right; Molly at six had witnessed more violence than most people would in their lifetimes. In the last year alone, she’d seen the work of a local serial killer and a murderous slave cartel. No question, she’d been exposed to far too much danger and gore. But I couldn’t change that. I was monitoring her closely, watching for signs of emotional damage. And Molly seemed, so far, to be incredibly fine.

I braced myself for a tirade. But Nick didn’t bring up the past. In fact, he didn’t speak at all for a while. He sat quiet, brooding. Nick seemed very un-Nick-like. Uncertain. Unsteady. When he finally spoke, his voice was almost a whisper. “When I walked into that house today, I saw you collapsed on a chair, covered with blood. Zoe, do you have any idea what I thought?”

Oh, Lord. I hadn’t, no. How stupid was I? How self-centered? Why had it not even occurred to me? Nick must have thought I’d been stabbed. That the blood was mine. I leaned over and touched his face, reassuring him. “Oh, God—Nick. You thought he’d cut me? I’m sorry—I should have known. But I’m fine, Nick. Really—”

He watched me, his jaw tightening again. “Zoe. That’s not quite the point.”

It wasn’t? “Then what? Tell me.” I sat up straight and faced him. His eyes had darkened, turned steel-gray, and the scar on his cheek gleamed jagged and purple.

“Christ, Zoe. How is it that you don’t see it? Don’t you get what could have happened today?”

I began to blither an answer. But Nick wasn’t listening. He continued slowly, his voice low, like distant thunder. “It wasn’t just you and Molly who could have been hurt.”

"Nick, I was trying to prevent a—"

"Someone else was there, too."

I stopped speaking mid-sentence; my mouth hung open, silent. I finally understood.

"You put the baby at risk. You could have hurt our kid—"

I blinked as if he'd slapped me; my face went hot. "Nick, I would never—"

"But you did. You wrestled like a thug. You fought over a carving knife. You got off easy with some scrapes and a concussion; it could have been a lot worse."

"But the baby's fine—the doctor said so—"

"Then we were lucky, weren't we?"

Yes. I supposed we were. I blinked, refusing the tears that blurred my vision.

Nick's eyes drilled through my skull, penetrating my aching brain. Oh, God. What had I done? Nick was right. Trying to save a stranger, I'd risked our baby's life. I'd jumped on my father and fought without hesitation. What kind of mother was I? How could I be so irresponsible? What could I say? I wanted to run, to dissolve into the night.

"Look, I know you didn't mean to hurt the baby. You acted out of sheer instinct. But I've got to wonder, what about your maternal instincts? Where were they? Why didn't your children's safety come first?" Nick's gaze seared me; I could almost smell burning skin.

"Nick, it went so fast. I had no time to think. Of course, the kids come first. Nothing's more important than they are." Didn't Nick know that I'd do anything for Molly or our baby? That I'd throw myself in front of a train for them?

Nick's eyes thawed a little; his shoulders relaxed. "Well, today's over. Nothing we can do. We all survived. Let's put it behind us and move on. Come to bed. Let's get some sleep." He offered his hand, but I didn't take it. I couldn't move. I couldn't even look at him. I was ashamed, hating myself.

Nick watched me for a moment. "Zoe?" Then, leaning over, he

kissed me, his lips forgiving me, and lifted me, his arms guiding me to my feet. Silently, he led me upstairs, leaving the remainder of mocha-almond to melt in its box. I went along passively, my head throbbing, and got into bed, where I clung to him, spooned against his familiar body, and stared at the darkness until sometime near morning, when I must have fallen asleep.

EIGHT

THE DREAMS BEGAN IN THAT PREDAWN STILLNESS, LIKE CLOCK-work, acknowledging my father's reappearance in my life. In my sleep, I recognized his basement steps and felt a clammy, familiar dread, anticipating what lay ahead as I descended the steep and narrow staircase. The banister was as high as my shoulder, hard to hold on to, and I shivered, wanting to turn back, continuing anyway, having no choice. Some part of my mind reasoned that, maybe, this time it wouldn't unfold badly. Maybe it would end well. Or maybe I could control the outcome; after all, it was my dream. But, even with that contradictory awareness, I was compelled to continue, passively following some script of my unconscious mind, searching for something long lost. Darkness stretched ahead, distorting the walls, concealing obstacles, and the air smelled moldy and dank.

Don't go on, I told myself. Turn and go back upstairs. My feet, of course, wouldn't obey, couldn't stop, and I proceeded silently, seeking I didn't know what, barely avoiding a gaping hole in the floor, sidestepping shadows, straining to remember what I was searching for.

And then, past the hulking furnace, beside the cedar closet, I remembered why I was there. Run now, I told myself. Run while you can. I forced myself to spin around, but it made no difference. The woman was there, in the corner, digging up the floor. Then she wasn't in the corner anymore; she was at my back, chasing me—not running or walking, but floating effortlessly above the concrete floor. I glanced behind me and, at eye level, I saw a row of polished pearls, ten of them, round and iridescent, her toes suspended in the air. I ran, breathless, tripping, falling, but before I hit the floor, of course, I sat up, sweating and suddenly awake.

And I stayed awake for the rest of the night, listening to Nick's soft snoring, touching his chest for reassurance, hanging on to the arm that he'd unconsciously wrapped around me. Unable to shake the terror of my dream, I watched the sky out the window, waiting for rays of sun to rise and deliver me from darkness, if not from dread.

NINE

SUSAN STOPPED KNITTING HER SWEATER AND GAPED AT ME IN disbelief. "Wait. Back up. You went to Mount Airy why?"

I swallowed with a dry mouth. "To see my father." My voice sounded small and tired.

"Wait," she said again. "Excuse me. I must have heard you wrong."

"No. You heard right. Molly and I went to see my father." I looked away, watching a gaggle of girls, including Molly and Susan's youngest daughter, Emily, scamper across the soccer field. It was the next day, Sunday, and we sat under a tree near the bleachers in Fairmount Park, watching the kids' mini-team play an away game of soccer. Nick had been gone when I woke up; weekend mornings he rowed his shell on the Schuylkill River. I'd called the hospital to check on my father, but by 8 A.M. he was already off the floor for tests, and they said he'd be gone most of the day. So, as I always did when I needed grounding, I'd turned to Susan. I needed to tell her what had happened to my face, but she cut me off right at the start.

"Your father." She said it as if it were an accusation.

I nodded, exhausted, dreading having to make yet another explanation.

"You're telling me that you have a father, right here in Philadelphia. And you never once in all the years we've known each other mentioned him?"

Bingo. Correct. I hadn't.

"And while you were hiding your family from me, I completely let you into mine. You've been to all the holiday dinners. The barbecues. The Christmas extravaganzas. And you've seen our dirty laundry: my dad passing out after too much bourbon; all four of my brothers' ugly divorces; Uncle Bill's transvestite lover; Aunt Sybil's hypochondria . . . You even have my nana's recipe for roast duckling with drunken cranberry sauce—not that you ever use it." She was indignant, sputtering, but she stopped to breathe and forced herself to resume her knitting, trying to appear calm. "Then again, maybe I'm not being fair. A person can't be expected to remember everything. Probably, you just forgot to mention him. I mean, it's not like he's important or anything. He's only your father."

I took the punches without flinching. What could I say? She was right. "Susan, please. It's not like I deliberately kept him secret—"

"No, of course not. It was an accident. You accidentally, never in over a decade, thought of mentioning him. It's totally understandable." She closed her mouth and counted stitches, completing her row. When she was done, she set the knitting down on her lap and put on her sunglasses, staring out at the field. Shutting me out. Angry.

Great, I thought. First Nick, now Susan. Everyone close to me was mad at me, and all because of my father. Susan was hurt that I hadn't told her about him. But why was that such a serious offense? It wasn't as if I'd deliberately hidden him from her. We'd simply had no relationship. He hadn't been part of my life, so I'd never talked about him. I'd had no reason to. Besides, given what I'd been through in the last twenty-four hours, couldn't she cut me some slack?

Of course I knew the answer: No slack. Not an inch. Not a smidgeon.

And, in a way, I understood. Susan Cummings was my best friend. We shared just about everything. Openness was a given. Our friendship had grown and thrived on admitting the truth to each other, no matter how harsh. And I'd grown to depend on that unflinching friendship. Susan balanced me; I spent almost as much time at her house as at my own. Unlike mine, hers always smelled like fresh-baked banana bread or simmering marinara sauce or some other fragrant comfort food. The place literally buzzed with the sounds of children and vacuums and food processors and phones; it pulsed with the tensions of her criminal law practice and the never-ending, always competing demands of her various roles and relationships. Susan was a wife, mother, lawyer, housekeeper, decorator, hostess, daughter, cook, community leader, bargain hunter, recipe collector and loyal friend, not necessarily in that order. Her life was a cyclone of activity, a carnival act of juggled priorities. She made potato salad while on the phone with prosecutors, sorted laundry while rehearsing closing statements. And, although every project she undertook seemed chaotic, disorganized and subject to unpredictable interruptions, Susan managed miracles. Her children and marriage were robust, her clients usually satisfied. And her friends were always welcome, especially in moments of crisis. But now, she was closing me out. She was hurt, thinking that I'd violated the tacit terms of our relationship by keeping a hugely significant secret from her.

But, damn it, my silence about my father hadn't been secrecy; I hadn't intended to hide him. I hadn't lied about him. I'd simply walled him out of my mind for a decade or two. And that had worked fine, until he had suddenly rematerialized, knife in hand, chopping my life to pieces. Couldn't Susan understand? And if not, couldn't she get past some petty slight? I took a deep breath, felt a warm October breeze stroke my face.

Around us, parents on bleachers and folding chairs stood and began to cheer, waving their arms. "Go, Tigers—Run! Go!"

A man a few feet away bellowed, "T-I-G-E-R-S! Go, Tigers!"

The Tigers were the other team. We were the Rams. I looked out onto the field, where a tall, lean Tiger was taking off with the ball, closing in on our goal. I held my breath, suddenly realizing that my little Molly was in the heat of the action, fearlessly storming the much larger girl who controlled the ball, heading in to intercept just yards from the goalie. Even in her soccer gear, with knee pads and protective clothing, Molly looked tiny and fragile, but she stormed the large girl without hesitation. Suddenly, the Tiger was swinging her leg at empty air while little Molly darted away, the ball spinning safely away from the goal, successfully passed to a Ram teammate. Gaping, the crowd of Tiger parents stopped screaming, sat down again, silent.

"Yes! Go, Rams." Beaming, unembarrassed, I got up and clapped and yelled with Susan despite the glares of the home-team Tiger parents. I was relieved that Molly was having fun, that she was seemingly unscathed by the shocks of the day before.

"Unbelievable." Susan stopped cheering, sat down again and reached for her knitting. "I didn't even see Molly coming. Man, she's quick."

Yes, but not quick enough. The ball came back to her and, as she began to move it down the field, mammoth Tiger girls closed in from all sides, cutting her off. Molly tried to swerve, but swiftly, deftly, a large Tiger stuck her leg out and blatantly tripped her. Molly went flying, sprawling to the ground, about to be trampled by the other team. Tiger parents pounced to attention, roaring encouragement. The referee watched, did nothing.

I was on my feet, ready to jump onto the field and rescue my daughter, but Susan restrained me, shaking her head, ordering me to sit down. And before I could get free of her grip, Molly had bounced up again, back in the game, apparently unhurt. There was no danger, no harm. The girls were merely playing a sport, kicking and running and passing and panting. I was overreacting, still on high alert. My head ached where a purplish lump had risen, my stitches throbbed, and I hadn't slept much. I was worried about my conversation with Nick, upset about my father, shaken by Beatrice and her death by betting slips, haunted by my dream. I slumped back onto the folding chair, wanting comfort. But Susan resumed her knitting, stiff and distant. Her feelings were hurt; she was punishing me with silence and feigned indifference. I closed my raw eyes, saw the red glow of sunlight through my lids, and the red liquefied, became Beatrice's blood.

I opened them, but too late. The memories had begun. Again I saw the draped body being lifted into the coroner's wagon. And, for the hundredth time, I tried to sort out the events of the day before—the mess of blood, the fury in my father's eyes, the flurry of commotion as the police arrived. Betting forms clumped, swirling and bloody, in my mind. Lord, what had my father gotten into?

The thoughts chilled me, even in the October sun. I shivered despite the warmth of the day. No, I wouldn't dwell on yesterday. Would not revisit it. I'd watch a mini-league soccer game and enjoy myself with other parents.

"Okay. You might as well tell me the rest." Apparently, Susan's curiosity outweighed her pique. "What happened? Who was that woman—what was her name again? I saw it in the newspaper—"

The paper had covered the story briefly, on page five.

"Beatrice. Beatrice Kendall."

And so, despite my resolve, I did revisit the day, after all. While the girls kicked and ran and the sun beamed, I sat beside Susan under a tree, gushing out events like water, or maybe like welled-up tears.

TEN

My telling wasn't very coherent. Ever since I'd stepped onto my father's porch, I'd been squelching memories, holding back feelings. Finally, as I began talking to Susan, I began to lose control. Events blurred with emotions, emerged out of sequence, but I blurted out the basics. Finding my father as he was cutting into Beatrice, struggling for the knife, realizing Molly had seen it all, calling the police. Facing Nick and his concern. Finding out about the betting slips in Beatrice's throat. Hating myself for endangering the baby.

"Here." When I finished talking, Susan took a sweating insulated mug from her cooler. "Have some iced tea."

Her mothering instincts were resurfacing; she was forgiving me. I drank, felt cold, minty liquid slide down to my belly, wondered if the baby could feel it.

"Nick's never really been mad at me before." I couldn't get him off my mind. His reserve.

"Oh, please, Zoe. What did you expect? A man learns that his future father-in-law is alive and living five miles away only because there's a homicide in said father-in-law's home? Of course he's mad. You kept a big fat secret from him. You shut him out."

I shrugged, not ready to explain that the secrecy hadn't really been what upset him. Nearby, the bleachers erupted in a rousing cheer. Apparently, the Tigers had scored. We paused, scanning the field, instinctively looking for Molly and Emily, finding them unscathed.

When the playing resumed, Susan pushed hair out of her eyes. "Zoe, I have to say this: I don't get it. Why didn't you tell us? What's the big deal?"

How was I supposed to answer her? How could I condense into a coherent sentence or two a lifetime of broken promises and disappointments, my mother's fatally broken heart, my father's incessant gambling, his compulsive lying, our gradual complete estrangement? For years, I hadn't let myself think, much less talk about any of it. And now, with Susan, just as they had with Nick the night before, words failed me. Circuits locked down in my brain, refusing access to the unbearable, protecting me, rendering me speechless. I floundered.

"After my mother died, Dad was gone a lot. He couldn't handle her death and didn't have a clue about how to raise a kid. He hired a widowed woman to take care of me."

"Hilda?" Susan recalled; I'd mentioned her now and then.

I nodded. "She pretty much raised me, and over the years my father and I . . . drifted apart." Fabulous. That sounded like a dodge, even to me.

Susan squinted, waiting. Caring.

Be specific, I told myself. Give her something concrete. Go ahead and blurt it out. "Look. My father's a gambler. Big-time. On the surface, he's charming. Witty, charismatic. But under his smooth façade he's a sociopath, a liar, a compulsive, addicted gambler."

Susan nodded, waiting, as if there had to be more.

"His gambling is pathological. He can't help himself. And sometimes he loses. When I was a baby, he apparently lost everything. He kept our family broke and my mother miserable until she finally died. Thank God, he inherited the house from his grandmother—otherwise, we'd probably have been homeless. It's a long, ugly story. I left it—and him—behind a long time ago."

Susan's eyes had softened. Maybe I'd been forgiven? "Well, you may have tried. But it didn't work. He's back."

Oh, Lord. Yes, he was.

She lifted her mug with a smirk. "Well. Here's to family reunions." She chugged iced tea. I wished I could have something stronger. But I was thirsty and took a swig of iced tea despite the toast.

"And so, those betting slips. You think your father's gambling had something to do with the murder?" She kept knitting, didn't miss a stitch.

Of course I did. "I don't know. He's probably not gambling anymore. He's over eighty, for God's sake."

She nodded, quiet for a while. I stared at running children. "So, what about Nick? You said he was mad."

Oh, Lord. What about Nick? Exhaustion or pregnancy was getting to me. I felt woozy, leaned back on my aluminum chair.

"He'll get over it," she decided. "The man is nuts about you. And besides, he hasn't always been exactly open—Nick's in no position to be mad because you didn't tell him something."

She was right. Nick's past was full of question marks. But last night, openness hadn't been the issue.

"He's not mad that I kept a secret. He's mad that my father and I got physical. Because of the baby. I could have harmed it." I swallowed, choking on the words.

Susan pushed a lock of shiny hair behind an ear. "You can't blame him, Zoe. He's about to commit to you for life, and, understandably, he's scared. Add to that the fact that you're carrying his baby. His first kid. And you went six rounds in a bare-knuckle fight. You scared the crap out of him. Men like Nick don't do well with scared. They get mad. They're more comfortable with mad—they understand it."

Maybe. I appreciated the theory. Maybe Nick was just scared. After all, his life was changing, too. Marriage might scare him—his last marriage had ended badly when he'd tried to leave. His wife had died after shooting him in the face. Years had passed, but still, the prospect of having another wife—especially a pregnant one—might be scary to Nick. Oh, God. Maybe Nick was looking for a way out. Maybe my recklessness would give him an excuse to escape. I leaned back in my folding chair, looked up into a tangle of tree branches and dying leaves.

No, I told myself. I was simply off balance, overly vulnerable. In a single day my entire life had turned upside down. My father was back in it, involved possibly in illegal gambling and definitely in murder. Nick was upset. Susan was annoyed. And who knew how Molly was affected? I held the cold mug of iced tea against the lump on my head and closed my eyes.

"Give him some time." Susan touched my arm. "Tonight, I bet he'll be all contrite and lovey-dovey protective. Tim's like that, can't stay mad for long. Nick's a marshmallow. You'll see. He'll feel guilty and protective and melt all over you."

I wasn't convinced, but the image of melted marshmallows drowned the other thoughts in my mind. Suddenly, the problems with Nick and my father seemed minor; what really mattered was lunch. I was famished. Probably that was why I felt light-headed. I hadn't eaten since the cereal I'd toyed with at breakfast, and it was past one. Even if I weren't, the baby growing inside me was hungry, demanding to be fed.

ELEVEN

In the end, the Tigers won, 7–5. Molly had scored two of the Rams' goals. The coach and team members praised her after the game, and Emily, a year older, was jealous, pretending not to care.

"Let's get some lunch." Susan tried to console Emily, smoothing her hair.

"Whatever." Emily shrugged.

"Can we get Chinese, Mom?" Molly was a fan of chicken with broccoli.

"I hate Chinese." Emily sneered.

"You do not," Molly argued. "You love Lo Mein."

"That was a long time ago. I outgrew that."

Ouch. Emily was pulling the "I'm older than you are" string, trying to make Molly feel bad. "Okay, so where would you like to go, Emily?" I tried to cut her off.

"I don't care. Anything but Chinese." Emily could be a brat at times.

"How about pizza?" Susan put iced tea mugs back in the cooler.

"Yeah—let's have pizza!" Molly looked at Emily.

"Not again," Emily whined. "All we ever eat is pizza."

"Don't whine, Emily." Susan frowned.

"Then what do you want, Emily? You pick." I'd had it. I wanted food. Any kind of food. And I wanted it immediately.

Emily avoided my eyes. "Oh, fine. Chinese. Whatever. I don't even care. I'm not even hungry." She pouted, martyr-like.

"Good. Chinese. Let's go." I helped Susan fold up the chairs while Molly and Emily headed to the car, carrying the cooler.

"So. What now?" Susan pushed her sunglasses up on top of her head.

"I guess we have Chinese."

"I don't mean about lunch. I mean about your father."

Oh. "They're doing a workup. He'll be in the hospital for a few days." I riffled through her knitting bag, hoping to find a granola bar. Even a cracker. Nothing.

"But what about afterward? You'll have to find a place for him."

A place?

"What is he—you said he's about eighty?"

"Almost eighty-three." We followed the girls toward the car.

"Well, assuming the DA doesn't charge him with anything, it might be time for him to move out of the house. You said he was unkempt. He might need to live somewhere he can get cared for."

Like a nursing home? I'd have to move him? The idea stopped me cold. I hadn't yet decided that I would see my father again, much less that I would find a place for him to live. But Susan wasn't finished. She kept listing things for me to do. "In that case, you'll have to assess his belongings, maybe sell some or give stuff away. And you'll need to get power of attorney. That way, you can sell the house. What shape is it in?"

My head was spinning, trying to absorb what she was saying, to comprehend what would have to be done. Visiting nursing homes. Moving my father. Packing up his house. Figuring out his finances, taking care of his bills. Getting the house in shape to sell. Susan was still talking.

". . . But it's got to be strange. All those years with not a word, and suddenly you're in charge of the man's entire life. His future is in your hands."

Oh, Lord. I covered my eyes with my hands. Why had I gone to see him? Why had I answered the phone when Lettie Kinkaid had called? Why hadn't I simply ignored her and stayed at home?

"But look at the bright side." Susan smirked. "All the grudges you have against your father? Now's your chance for revenge."

I kept walking, suddenly cold. Susan was kidding, but in fact there had been years when I'd longed to get back at the man. The idea didn't seem funny.

"And revenge, they say, is sweet."

I supposed it could be. But it didn't feel that way. "Well, they're wrong. Revenge is overrated. The truth is, sometimes when you get what you want, you don't want it anymore."

Susan unlocked the car, and the girls climbed in. Nearby, a young woman ran down the sidewalk chasing a toddler. When she caught him, she tried to pick him up; he arched his back, shrieking, trying to slip out of her grasp. Watching them struggle, I wondered how I'd manage to keep up with a little one. I was over forty, a lot older and more tired than she was. I rested a hand on my swelling belly, wanting food. Susan and I got into the car, and she continued my to-do list as she pulled out of the parking spot.

"The most important thing is to find him a good home. He has to live somewhere."

No matter how I tried to deny it, she was right. If my father was, in fact, unable to care for himself and the house, I was going to have to take charge of his life. Make his decisions, handle his affairs, secure his future.

"Look, Zoe. You can't manage this on your own, especially with the baby coming. You're going to have to make use of all of us—me, Nick, your other friends. I'll make a list of what you have to do—the real estate, finances, medical stuff—remember, I had to do all this with Tim's mom."

I was reeling, light-headed. Already, I was over my head decorating the baby's room, looking at bassinets and playpens and mobiles while working full-time. How was I to take on my father's affairs, too? And where was the restaurant? I was ravenous.

"Mom, are you talking about Grandpa?"

"Yes, Molls."

"Emily," she continued. "Guess what? I went to see my grandpa yesterday."

"So?" Emily was unimpressed. "I go to my grandpa and nana's condo all the time. Except in the summer, we go to their house down the shore."

"Yeah," Molly bragged. "But yesterday my grandpa killed a lady."

Emily paused. "No, he didn't. You're making it up."

"Emily," Susan interrupted. "Let it go."

I closed my eyes, wanting to disappear.

"No, I'm not making it up," Molly insisted. "He killed her. I saw it myself."

"Liar."

"I'm not lying—ask my mom." Molly turned to me, indignant. "Mom, tell her: Didn't Grandpa kill that lady?"

Susan glanced my way, frowning.

"W-we don't really know what happened, Molls," I stammered.

"Grandpa killed her," Molly insisted. "Right in his kitchen."

"The lady was in the kitchen. And she was dead," I began. "But that doesn't mean that Grandpa killed her—"

"So?" Emily, ever competitive, was not to be outdone. "That's nothing. My pop-pop was in the war. He killed lots of people—hundreds . . . a thousand. Didn't he, Mom?"

Susan didn't answer. She pulled into a parking spot near Wing Yee's Restaurant in Chinatown. "I'm up for some hot and sour soup." She backed into a spot, looking over her shoulder. "And a big fat spring roll." She turned off the engine. "Last one out's a ninny."

Seat belts came off instantly, and with a bunch of happy chatter, as if their argument had never occurred, the girls burst out of the car and ran toward the entrance holding hands, best friends ready for lunch.

TWELVE

SUSAN WAS RIGHT ABOUT NICK. WHEN WE GOT HOME FROM SUSAN'S early that evening, Nick greeted us, his arms wide open for hugs, and as I accepted mine, I saw that the ice in his eyes had thawed, melted to mush. Nick's eyes were uncertain and tender. And he touched me gently, protectively, as if even his hands were sorry. He had shopped and planned a feast for dinner, preparing it himself. Steaks, pineapple slices, corn on the cob and portobello mushrooms grilled outside on the patio. He'd made fresh lemonade and set the table with a centerpiece of tiny pumpkins and bright orange lilies.

We devoured our meal, but Molly was so tired from the long day of soccer and playing at Emily's that her eyes rolled and her lids drooped as she chewed. As soon as we finished dinner, Nick carried her up to bed, and together we tucked her in. Then, with dishes still on the table and leftovers sitting out, Nick and I fell onto each other. We didn't talk about what had happened. Neither of us mentioned issues of child safety or parental behavior; nobody referred to trust or honesty or openness or secrets. The topics of my father or Beatrice or gambling or her murder did not come up. In fact, Nick and I didn't speak at all. Silently, without a need for conversation, we concentrated on what was really important. Nick held me closely, preciously. His touch told me everything I needed to know; words would have been weak and redundant. His hand stroked my belly, caressing both the baby and me. His lips brushed my neck, his bristly whiskers skittering, tickling my flesh. My fingertips, my kiss told him I was sorry; my hips declared how deeply I treasured the life I carried. Slowly, gently, our bodies blended so completely that it was difficult to tell where one stopped and the other began, which leg was mine, which thigh his. We rolled together over waves, our bed a raft in the ocean, and we hung on to each other desperately, carefully, as if for our very survival.

Afterward, Nick lay back, eyes closed; I thought he'd dozed off. "What about Vanessa?" he said.

Who? "Vanessa?"

"If it's a girl. Or Gabrielle?"

"Gabriella?"

His eyes opened. "No, Gabrielle."

Gabrielle? "So we'd call her Gabby?"

"We'd call her Gabrielle. I thought we should name her something unusual. Distinctive. I like Skylar, but it might be too trendy. Sibyl's too witchy. What do you think of Meredith? It means 'guardian from the sea.' Or Shoshana?" He was on a roll.

"You've been reading name books."

Nick half-smiled. "Well, skimming through them."

I nodded.

"Actually, I've been making lists."

How adorable. I was impressed.

"So what names do you like?" He propped himself on an elbow, waiting. "If you want something more conventional, how about Hannah?"

I'd been thinking about names for weeks, searching through name books, reviewing names of people who'd meant something to me. I couldn't bear to name a baby after my mother, Louise. Or after Hilda. "Maybe Susan."

"Really?" Nick frowned. "But there are a million Susans."

"It's simple. Basic. Strong. My best friend's name."

"You want simple for our daughter?"

"You don't like 'Susan'?"

He shrugged. "For simple, I kind of like Judy." He repeated it, doing an awful impression of Cary Grant. "Judy. Judy. Judy."

"Okay, no Susan, no Judy." I sighed, resting on his shoulder, and we lapsed into cozy silence. "We'll keep on searching."

"And if it's a boy?"

"Molly's set on Oliver."

"I know. I think we're stuck with it."

"Oliver? You're serious?"

"That's why there are middle names." Nick chuckled.

"Speaking of middle names, what's yours?"

He winced. "No, uh-uh."

"Come on, Nick." I began to tickle him. "Tell me. Out with it—you know mine."

"That's not fair." He was laughing. "You don't have one—stop—" He was doubled up, protecting his ticklish spots, but I climbed onto him, keeping it up until, breathless, he belted out, "Okay, okay—Ambrogino."

"What?" I stopped tickling.

He repeated it. Nicholas Ambrogino Stiles. "It's Italian." He felt the need to explain.

"Well." I lay back, releasing him. "I guess Oliver's not so bad, after all."

We chuckled together, lying limbs entangled, imagining our future.

"Maybe we should name him after one of my brothers."

I'd never met his brothers; all I knew was that he had three of them scattered across the country.

"What do you think of Eli, Samuel, or Anthony?"

I considered the series. Odd set.

"Or my father's name, Solomon."

"Solomon?"

"I told you. We're half Italian, half Jewish. My parents took turns naming us." Half of Nick's face grinned. "They took turns at everything—one year, we'd have Christmas and Easter; the next year, Hanukkah and Passover. Well, some years, we'd have both."

"You're serious?"

He was. "Two of us had confirmations; the other two had bar

mitzvahs. Looking back, I guess it was odd. But it didn't seem that way. To us, it was normal."

His eyes gazed into his past, his childhood. They seemed pleased with what they saw. Nick turned, facing me. "So, we're committed to Oliver?"

"I don't know . . ."

"Eli Oliver. Anthony Oliver. Samuel Oliver. Oliver Solomon—or Solomon Oliver—"

I pounced, planting a kiss on his mouth to silence him. We laughed, rolling in each other's arms, filled with joy and jitters, both acutely aware that picking a name was a heavy responsibility, loaded with repercussions. And that it would be merely the first of many such responsibilities on our imminent parental trek.

THIRTEEN

THE NEXT MORNING THE SKY SWELLED WITH DARK CLOUDS THAT hung heavy and gray. Monday. The phone rang early, while I was getting dressed, and it took me a moment to identify the crusty voice. "How's it going, girlfriend?"

Lettie's unmistakable gravelly voice was checking on my father. "The whole neighborhood's alarmed, girlfriend. Especially our Town Watch group. Beatrice was one of us, and we want to help out any way we can. People like Beatrice are rare to come by. Treasures. I always told her, 'Beatrice, there isn't anything in this world that will ever come between us. Nothing can tear apart our friendship. You and me, we're friends for life.' For life, I told her. 'Til death us do part, just like a married couple. That's how I do my friendships, girl. You'll see. For life. So, have they arrested Walter? Because nothing was in the paper about an arrest. He wasn't even mentioned by name."

I was in a hurry to leave, but Lettie persisted, darting from one topic to another, asking if she could do anything for me, if little dollface was okay, going on about children and how they are God's gifts. Asking, by the way, if I'd heard anything about the status of Beatrice's body or funeral because nobody seemed to know anything about it, as the police had taken her away. Insisting that I stop by for coffee and cake next time I came over; she'd made fresh lemon poppy seed cake just that morning, which wasn't easy anymore with her arthritis acting up like it always did before a storm. Dogs barked in the background, at times drowning her voice out, and I was desperate to get off the phone. I assured Lettie that we were all right, thanked her for calling, promised to be in touch and to have coffee with her, and hung up abruptly, trying to escape her raspy questions and the images they stirred up. I had no desire to bond with my father's neighbors or to gossip about the brutal murder found in his house. I had to get away from all that. To work, to concentrate on my own life.

Outside, the air held still, cloudy and chilly, promising an October storm. I put aside thoughts of Lettie's call, but the memories she'd stirred merged with the dark sky and damp air, unsettling me. The cabdriver who dropped me off on the circular drive to the Institute warned that it was going to pour; just like Lettie, he knew because of his rheumatism. It never failed. He could predict the weather by his joints.

Even the Institute seemed to foresee a storm. The sprawling bulk of the building seemed to lie low, as if trying to conceal itself among the trees and vast landscaping that surrounded it. Without sunshine, the place seemed more melancholy than usual, its Victorian red brick and stone facade dour with gloom.

For over a hundred years, the Pennsylvania Psychiatric Institute had housed people afflicted with diseases of the mind. Their voices still echoed there, lost within its walls. My task was to help those voices express themselves, finding solace and direction through art. So I pulled open a heavy cut-glass door and, despite the ominous skies, put on a positive, professional smile and entered the marble-floored, elegantly domed rotunda, ready to face the day.

As usual, Agnes, the receptionist seated opposite the double doors, ignored me. She stared through her reading glasses at the newspaper splayed out on her desk.

"Good morning, Agnes," I chirped, purposely antagonizing her with cheeriness. There was, as always, no reply. Agnes and I were not friends. Due to her thirty-plus years at the Institute, she regarded me and other relatively junior staff members as interloping newcomers, and she pulled rank whenever possible. She didn't greet me, but I felt her spectacled, critical eyes follow as I passed her desk. I felt her stare as I crossed over the marble floor, under the elegant brass-and-crystal chandelier, along the intricate mosaic murals that covered the walls. As I finally entered the long hallway that led to the art studio, I almost skipped, glad to have escaped Agnes's line of vision.

"Oh, Ms. Hayes," she sang out, her voice echoing through the domed atrium. "There's a note for you."

I turned and looked back; Agnes held out a folded white paper. Agnes had a color-coded system for messages, and she was always revising it, posting memos about what each color signified. Blue, pink, green, lilac, yellow—each meant something different: outside or internal calls, high or low urgency, call back or don't. She waved the piece of white paper, waiting for me to walk back across the foyer to get it. I would have ignored her, but I couldn't remember what white meant—was it urgent? Could it be about a patient?

Agnes had deliberately waited until I was almost out of sight to call me to come back. The woman never sacrificed an opportunity to assert her piddling amount of authority. Annoyed, I started back across the foyer. But just then, Bertram Haggerty sailed through the front door. Seeing Agnes waving the paper at me, he snatched it from her with a smile and a "Good morning, Agnes. I see that you're a ray of sunshine as usual. Is this for Ms. Hayes? Here—I'll give this to her."

"It's confidential," Agnes croaked. "I'm supposed to deliver it personally." She bolted out of her chair and grabbed Bertram's wrist with mottled, arthritic fingers. Was she going to fight him for the paper? Their eyes met in a silent duel. The chandelier rattled with tension. And then, amazingly, Agnes backed down. She released his arm and sat, huffing.

"Thank you, Agnes." Bertram was already heading my way.

"Just a minute, Dr. Haggerty. There's one for you, too." She held it out as he went back for it, but she didn't grace him with eye contact.

Bertram Haggerty was even newer to the Institute than I was, but he was a brilliant renowned psychiatrist, so Agnes treated him with minor deference. In his late thirties, despite his professional stature, Bertram was a man who, outside of work, I'd never have noticed. No one would. He had the kind of face that blends invisibly, undistinguished, into a crowd. Short, balding, wiry, splay-footed and pale, he had small, shiny hands and glasses with clear plastic frames. Within the Institute, however, Bertram was a man of impressive stature. Known for his quick mind and cutting-edge research, he was the youngest department head on staff, in charge of Dissociative Disorder Research. I'd met him only recently, but I found him more approachable, less arrogant than most of the Institute psychiatrists. He walked my way, bouncing briskly, the toes of his brown cowboy boots pointing outward, his charcoal pants, like all his slacks, expensive but cut slightly too short and too tight. As he handed me my note, he eyed my bruises, wincing. "Zoe, what happened to you? Get hit by a truck?"

"In a way."

I took the paper, preparing to explain. But Bertram didn't want an explanation; his mind had already moved on, scanning his memo.

"What's this?" His already pasty skin turned ashen. His free hand rose to his chin, rubbing nervously. "Shit. Holy effing shit."

"What?" I unfolded the paper. The letterhead announced the Board of Directors. Bertram had stopped walking. He stood still, massaging his chin, blinking rapidly.

"They can't do this—I just opened the new wing. They promised me five years—they gave their word—" He ranted, cursing, turning in circles, running a hand through the few hairs remaining on his head. "They approved my five-year plan—this can't be happening. It's got to be a mistake."

I skimmed the letter, took in key phrases. Board meeting. Trustees. Budget deficits. Funding crisis. Uh-oh. This was serious. I slowed down, reading more carefully: Government funding had dried up; private contributions and special grants were down . . . Managed care covered limited costs . . . I skipped ahead to the bottom of the letter, to the part that said, "Therefore, to maintain the superior quality of care and service to patients of the Institute . . ." blah blah blah . . . Bottom line: Over the next few days, reallocations would be announced. Reorganization would be under way. Unessential programs would be eliminated. Resources streamlined. In other words: Programs were going to be cut and people were going to get fired. Damn.

Of course the memo didn't give details. It simply announced that communications had been issued about individual positions. And it confirmed that the rumors that had been flying through Institute corridors for months were true. The Institute was in deep financial trouble. Staff was to be reduced. But which people, what positions? What did they mean by "unessential programs"? Was art therapy "unessential"? They'd probably think so. But hell if it was. What about all the patients I'd worked with, the progress they'd made? What would happen to them if the Institute dropped the program? And not only that—what about me? I'd worked hard here, built the program up myself, accomplished amazing results. And I had a child—no—two children—to support. We needed my income. I needed my job. This was unbelievable. Was I going to be fired? What was I going to do? Suddenly I was dizzy. Light-headed. Unable to walk. For a moment, I couldn't breathe. I swayed, holding my middle, closing my eyes, wondering why I felt dizzy.

"Zoe? Are you okay?" Dr. Haggerty had stopped arguing with his letter. He was watching me, a little alarmed.

I nodded, but couldn't answer. I stroked my belly, trying to breathe until the tightness passed.

"This happen often?" He eyed my swelling middle and held on to my wrist, taking my pulse.

"No, it's nothing." It had happened only a few times before, though not as decisively. "I'm just tired." I assured myself more than him.

He watched me, eyed my middle, waiting for me to say more.

"So," I changed the subject, walking on, "what about this?" I rattled the letter.

His eyes widened. "Hell. I don't know. Are we supposed to just give up and walk off into the sunset? Fade away?"

I shrugged. "I guess."

"Well, that's not going to happen. If they try to cut my program, believe me, they'll hear from my lawyers. It'll cost them." He sighed, hopeless, aware that his words were bluster.

"How bad do you think it'll be?"

"Bad," he answered. "If the Institute goes the way of other mental health facilities, it might shut down altogether. And even if it doesn't, it's going to provide bare-bones care to far fewer patients."

"So I guess I'm a goner, then."

"In reality? I'd guess we both are, unless we can raise our own funding."

"How?"

"You know—private sources. Grants. Endowments and such."

Endowments? For my arts and crafts program? Not likely. We walked on silently toward the elevator, neither having much to say. My head felt light, and I was still dizzy. Near the elevator I missed a step and wobbled against Bertram's arm.

Bertram eyed me cautiously as he pushed an elevator button. "Zoe, you know, for women your age, pregnancy can be complicated."

Did he think I was brain-dead? In the past four months, I'd read about a million books and articles on middle age and pregnancy.

He held up his memo. "Stress like this can't help."

I agreed. No, it couldn't.

"Well, you don't have to be passive, you know. There are things to do about it."

Like what? Was he going to suggest unionizing? Going on strike? I pictured the Institute staff, a bunch of therapists and shrinks marching down Market Street carrying placards, chanting slogans. "Don't shrink our staff." Or "We're crazy about our patients."

He looked at his watch. "Tell me. When's your first session?"

I had about half an hour.

"Perfect. Let's stop at my office and talk." Bertram held on to my arm and led me into the elevator, insisting. I assumed that he wanted to discuss the memo, what steps we could take to protect our jobs. Before I knew it, I was in his office, seated in a plush leather chair, realizing that I'd been absolutely, completely wrong.

FOURTEEN

"HYPNOSIS?" I WAS SKEPTICAL.

"Basically, it's controlled, extreme relaxation. It's not magic. But it can help reduce stress and possibly decrease your episodes of dizziness."

I shook my head. "Thanks, Bertram. I don't think so."

"May I ask why?"

I smiled. "Frankly, I doubt I can be hypnotized."

Bertram nodded knowingly. His massive ego had undoubtedly convinced him that he could hypnotize anyone. "Well, it's up to you, of course. But think about it. If it doesn't work, what have you lost?"

Nothing. He was probably right. Still, I was reluctant. I looked around his office, noted the expensive furnishings. Bertram sat on a modern designer leather desk chair designed to protect the spine, beside an elaborate antique escritoire which seemed to match a towering mahogany grandfather clock. The walls between bookshelves were papered with original art—including a Calder and an Eakins—and dozens of certificates, awards, framed degrees. Bertram's office, like his wardrobe, was eclectic, uncoordinated. But everything in it, individually, was high-end. Expensive. Papers, books, files and journals were stacked neatly on a table beside a sleek computer screen, yet Post-it notes were stuck almost everywhere, dotting surfaces like blemishes, inconsistent with the expensive furnishings.

"So? It's worth a try, isn't it?"

I shifted on the upholstered leather cushion. "What's involved, exactly? Do I watch a swinging pendulum?"

"No, no. It's pretty informal. First, I'd have you relax. If we were to try it, I might have you breathe evenly, from your diaphragm. Here. Like this." He pointed to his midsection, demonstrating.

I began to breathe deeply, following his lead.

"Then I'd ask you to think of a place where you feel perfectly safe. A place where you feel completely at peace."

My mind traveled. I pictured a lake in New Hampshire, surrounded by green mountains. Cold, calm water beneath a blue sky. A lone cloud drifting overhead. I was floating, lying back on an inflated raft.

"Then, while you envision yourself in that place, still breathing deeply, I'd suggest that you relax your body, limb by limb, muscle by muscle, beginning with your toes, working your way along your feet, your heels, your ankles, your calves. Relaxing each muscle, one at a time, slowly, up to your knees, your thighs, your hips and your pelvis."

Bertram's voice was soothing, guiding me through steps, but the idea was ridiculous. I was wary of his suggestions and techniques, of everything he said. Despite Bertram's good intentions, there was no way he could hypnotize me. It was time to go. I had to get to work.

"Thanks anyway, Bertram. I'm not sure this hypnosis stuff is for me; I doubt it would work on me."

He smiled again in his smug, superbly confident way. "And why is that?"

"I guess I'm too conscious. Or too stubborn. Don't get me wrong—It's not about you or your abilities. I just don't think I can be hypnotized."

"I see." He watched me patiently. "Okay, then. It's just an idea. Let me know if you change your mind."

I nodded. I would.

He swiveled his chair around to face the files on his desk. "Oh, by the way," he added, "you can put your arm down now."

My arm?

I looked at my arms. The left one was suspended weightlessly in the air, straight up over my head. As I watched, on its own, it dropped down to my side. What was going on? I looked at Bertram, confused.

He was smiling, amused. "Apparently, you' re wrong about your ability to be hypnotized. In fact, you're a very compliant subject. I merely suggested that your arm was lighter than air, and up it floated. It's been there the whole time you were under hypnosis."

Wait—what? I'd been under hypnosis? Not possible. "But I haven't been under. I remember everything—"

Again, that knowing smile. "Do you? Or do you remember everything you want to remember?"

What was he talking about?

"Zoe, listen. You are highly suggestible. I'm convinced that hypnosis might be quite helpful in reducing your stress, even in easing your pregnancy. Think about it and let me know. I'm here, and I'd be happy to work with you. But now, you better hurry. Your session begins in about a minute."

A minute? I looked at the antique grandfather clock. Thirty minutes had passed since we'd sat down. I blinked, confused.

Bertram handed me some tissues. "Here." He dabbed my cheeks. "You'd better freshen up before you go."

What was he talking about? I glanced at the tissue; it was soaking, blotched with mascara stains. And my face was wet. Tear-stained.

"What—I was crying?"

Bertram blinked rapidly, his expression kind. "Yes. A bit."

"Why? What was I crying about?"

He watched me. "Zoe, while you were under, I told you to remember what you wanted and to forget what you wanted."

"But half an hour went by—why don't I remember it? What did I say?" I was alarmed, stunned. "What was I so upset about?"

Bertram leaned forward and gently took my hands. His were small and hairless, and his nails were shiny. I noticed his Rolex watch. "Like I said. If you don't remember what we talked about, it's for your own reasons. Ethically, I can't tell you what you said. If and when you're ready for them, the memories will come to you on their own."

He released my hands. I felt naked, as if he could see parts of me that I hadn't intended to expose. That I might not even know about myself. I was angry, felt invaded.

"Bertram. I'm not comfortable with this. I didn't agree to this. Whatever I told you, I didn't intend it—and, frankly, I'm not happy about this whole conversation—" I wasn't articulate, but he got the point.

"Relax, Zoe. People don't submit to hypnosis unless they want to. And once they're under hypnosis, people don't do or say anything they don't want to. Clearly, you wanted to be hypnotized. And you must have wanted to say what you said. I didn't force you to talk to me; you volunteered."

What the hell had I talked about? Nick? Molly? The baby? My father? What?

"Don't worry." He scratched his thinning hair, shedding some flakes. "I'm a doctor. You can trust me; what I've heard is confidential. And seriously, let me know if you want to continue. If we work in conjunction with your obstetrician, we should be able to ease your pregnancy and, down the road, your delivery. Meantime, we can reduce the effects of all this job stress." He waved a piece of paper in the air. Oh, right. The memo. I'd forgotten. We might all lose our jobs.

Somehow, in the light of our career crisis, Bertram's efforts to reduce my stress seemed helpful and well-intentioned. I stifled my anger about having been hypnotized unwittingly. In fact, I thanked him and told him I'd think about his offer. Then, already late for my session, I hurried to the art studio, wiping away tears I couldn't remember shedding and didn't understand.

FIFTEEN

In the studio, on my own turf, I kept thinking of Bertram and what had just happened in his office, trying to remember what I'd said under hypnosis. At the same time I couldn't stop worrying about the memo and my career, picturing what would happen to the patients I worked with if the art program was suddenly eliminated. One by one I saw them, their hands bound, their mouths gagged. Art, for some patients, was the most effective mode of expression, and without my program they'd be virtually cut off from communicating. I told myself to focus, to get to work. I couldn't do anything about the Institute's policies at the moment, and I set out materials for my first session, telling myself to keep my mind on my patients.

In moments, orderlies arrived with group members, and before I knew it, the session was under way. The first group worked on collages made of a zillion small colored paper tiles I'd cut up the week before. Kimberly Gilbert, a thirty-two-year-old schizophrenic, had her usual difficulty with organization. With determination and focus, she glued paper bits in patternless, random positions without borders, both on and off her poster board. I worked with her, urging her to attach the pieces onto the board, but as soon as I left her she'd wander, gluing tiles onto the table, her clothing, her chair, and the back of Frank DiMarco, the person sitting beside her.

Frankie was a muscled twenty-nine-year-old, the lone survivor of a gas explosion that had killed his co-workers. He suffered severe depression and chronic post-traumatic stress disorder. As usual, he didn't react to Kimberly or the papers she'd glued to his body or clothing. He stared silently at his blank poster board for a long time before attaching a single black splotch to its middle. Meantime Hank Dennis, a handsome forty-year-old, recently readmitted for a setback in his compulsive disorder, looked on. A few weeks ago, he'd have been distracted, frantic about Kimberly's disorganized behavior. Now, he repeatedly glanced her way, but without comment or disruption he managed to return to his own project, arranging pieces of paper into groups by color, gluing red ones side by side in an unbroken, perfectly even line. The pieces were unevenly cut, so his effort was tedious and frustrating. Still, Hank worked diligently, trying to fit incongruent edges seamlessly together.

Samantha Glenn, twenty-three, arms coated with scars, wrists healing from her most recent suicide attempt, concentrated quietly on creating what seemed to be a pink oval cloud, occasionally gazing up at Frankie, eternally trying to catch his eye. Gloria Swenson, her features and body distorted by an addiction to plastic surgery, created a simple, puny flower—a skinny, disjointed stem with an asymmetrical red-and-purple blossom. And Jeremy Wallace, schizophrenic and new to the group, unable to focus for any length of time, alternately sat in his chair and marched around the table in circles, his body still adjusting to his medications.

The session passed unremarkably, even calmly. I moved from person to person, observing their work, talking to them, jotting down case notes. But as I made the rounds, before my eyes Kimberly's spatter of blotches transformed, became the clutter of a dark, neglected basement. Hank's row of red began to run like the straight trail of Beatrice's blood. The dark spot in the middle of Frank's poster stared like an eyeball in shock, unblinking. And Samantha's pink oval lay swollen like my belly, bursting with child.

Knock it off, I told myself. You're a professional. You're supposed to look at patients' work in the context of their lives and problems, independent of your own. Still, images emerged from poster boards, reminding me that, without question, my father was back in my life. I saw him, felt his presence everywhere I looked. I'd hoped to escape him by delving into familiar routine, but pretending that nothing had changed was like ignoring an earthquake. The upheaval was internal, but the ground under me shifted, and my world shimmied and shook. I told myself not to overreact. I would adjust. My father would be cared for, and life would proceed normally again. Meantime, I had to get a grip. But I couldn't. Worries juggled in my brain. My father. My job. The baby. Molly. Beatrice. Nick.

By the end of my first session, my head was swimming, and the muscles in my lower back were twisting like wringing dish towels. I went to my cubicle of an office, light-headed, needing a break, and saw a pink envelope lying on the blotter. Pink? I stared at it, hesitating to touch it. Did they really write pink slips on pink paper? Slowly, I picked it up and opened it. My hands trembled as I read it. Then I set it down, looked out at the studio, the tables and easels, the creations of patients on the walls. In a haze, I canceled the rest of the day's sessions and started to leave. But I stopped at the door, came back to call Bertram and make an appointment. Hypnosis might not solve my problems, but it couldn't hurt.

SIXTEEN

UNTIL FURTHER NOTICE, MY JOB HAD BEEN CUT TO HALF-TIME. Half a job. At half a salary. Treating whom? Half-patients? Stunned, I drifted past colleagues in the hall, seeing them as if they were memories. I wandered past Agnes's desk without a glance, unwilling to face her smug expression. I left the Institute, but I didn't know where I was headed. I didn't want to call a friend, didn't want to talk. I couldn't face going home, wasn't ready to sit alone and mope, thinking about my patients, the impact the program cuts would have on them.

When the cab pulled up, I got in without knowing what my destination would be. But my voice surprised me, announcing without hesitation where it wanted to go. Great, I thought. Visiting my father would be the perfect way to continue this already miserable day.

By the time the driver deposited me at Germantown Hospital, the dark clouds had expanded, ready to burst. I stood outside in chilling air, regretting that I'd come, hesitant to go in. Raindrops were starting to fall, but I stayed at the curb, watching the doors slide open and shut, simultaneously swallowing and belching people, fighting something that felt like panic.

Go inside, I told myself. It's about to pour. But my feet didn't budge. My pulse raced, ringing out alarm. Why? I'd never been afraid of hospitals before.

Are you kidding? I asked myself. Get real. You know why. It has nothing to do with hospitals.

It didn't?

Think. Why are you here?

Oh. Of course. Obviously. My nervousness and hesitation were about my father.

Thunder rumbled; wind picked up and the cold raindrops thickened. The storm was here. Go in before you get drenched, I told myself. Get the visit over with. So, drawing a last deep breath of wet, raw air, smelling traffic and tasting soot, I closed my eyes and thrust myself forward through the hospital doors.

Instantly, the flesh contracted all over my body. The air felt frigid, refrigerated. I was damp from the rain, shivering. Nurses walked by, looking greenish under neon lights. People in aqua scrubs conversed, parading past. I bit my lip, smelled antiseptics. Keep going, I told myself. It's just a damned visit.

At the information desk the receptionist fiddled with her computer. I cleared my throat, but she didn't look up. I wondered about receptionists, why they seemed to ignore me. Did they communicate among themselves about whom they liked or didn't? Had Agnes phoned ahead?

"Excuse me," I interrupted.

The woman rotated to face me. Her long black lashes were probably false, and they rose gradually, revealing large brown irises outlined with irritation.

"I'll be with you," she drawled, "in a minute, ma'am."

I breathed hospital air, throat tightening, fingers fidgeting, and waited. Doctors walked by in crisp white coats draped with stethoscopes. A man hobbled by on crutches. A woman and a young boy passed with a bouquet of balloons. An orderly approached, pushing a wheelchair carrying a woman and her tiny new baby.

And, boom. My mouth got dry. My heart threw itself against my ribs, and I pivoted, watching her chair rolling to the door. Studying her. Wanting to ask her questions I couldn't voice. Her hair was limp, matted. Her posture slumped. Her eyes outlined in dark circles. Oh, God. Five more months. In just five months, I would be her, the woman in the wheelchair. Would my hair be matted like that? Would my eyes be hollow with exhaustion, devoid of joy? An image flickered in my mind—someone, a woman I knew, her eyes hollow. Who? But it was gone before I could define it.

Outside, lightning flared and thunder rattled, a spotlight and drumroll introducing the truth. The dread I'd felt outside the hospital hadn't just been about my father. It hadn't merely been a delayed reaction to the news about my job, either. More than anything else, it had been about the delivery—about having the baby. I hadn't admitted it even to myself. But here, in the hospital, there was no denying it: I was afraid. Don't be a wimp, I scolded myself. Settle down and deal with it. But questions and unknowns battered my mind. What would labor be like? How bad would the pain be? Would it come and go, or persist? Would it be sharp and jagged? Searing? Would medications help? And Nick—was he too macho to be patient? Could I count on him as a childbirth coach? I felt helpless, out of control. And I wondered who the baby would be? Would it be healthy? Oh, God, what if something went wrong—

Stop it, I scolded myself. Women and children have made it through childbirth since the dawn of time; the baby and I would, too. Still, there were no guarantees. What if the umbilical cord wrapped itself around the baby's neck? What if the baby had some congenital heart problem? Or difficulty breathing? Or a complication of any kind? The possibilities were endless, terrifying. I studied the woman at the desk, her sculpted nails clicking briskly on computer keys, gold rings sparkling on each of her slender fingers, bracelets clinking on her long tawny arms. I watched the jewelry scamper and hop as she typed, and I rubbed my own arms, shivering, scolding myself. It was only a hospital, and I was not here to give birth, but to see my father. I had to deal with one issue at a time. Focus. But I couldn't help imagining the hospital nursery. A row of cribs filled with pink or blue bundles, one of them labeled "Hayes-Stiles." Oliver? Leah? Oh, Lord. How would we ever pick a name?

Finally, the woman swiveled her chair around and faced me, smiled warmly as if seeing me for the first time. Some machine to the left buzzed and whirred contentedly. I asked for my father's room number. In an eyeblink, the woman wrote it down and drew a map of the shortcut through the old section to the new wing.

I followed the map to the elevator and got in. The doors began to close, but an arm shoved itself between them, pushed them apart. They opened, and an orderly rolled a gurney into the car. I stepped back into the corner.

A young woman lay on the gurney, withered and open-mouthed, staring at the lights. An IV bag swung from its pole, dripped into its tube. Backed against the wall, closed in by the gurney, I ignored a bothersome tightness in my belly and reminded myself that, despite the upheaval at work, nothing was irreversibly wrong. The baby was fine. I would be, too. I'd see my doctor in a couple of days. I drew a breath, repeating the mantra. I am here to see my father, just to see my father.

SEVENTEEN

THE CORRIDOR WALLS OF THE NEW PSYCHIATRIC UNIT WERE BEIGE and covered with oil paintings, the windows large to give people a view. I rang a bell to be admitted, and walking down the hall, heard my father before I saw him. His voice resounded, listing complaints. But when I entered his room, I saw that he was alone, talking to no one. His head and one hand were bandaged. He was standing near the closet, his hospital gown hanging open in back, a catheter tube swinging between his legs. Why did he need a catheter? I had no idea. But there it was. He held the catheter bag in one hand, his IV stand in the other. Apparently, he was on his way out. Leaving.

"Dad?"

"Thank God. You're here. Where the hell are my pants?" The question was general, not directed to me. "Someone's taken my trousers." He eyed the empty closet, began hobbling toward the door.

"Dad, what are you doing?"

"What does it look like? I'm getting out of here. I have responsibilities to take care of." He kept walking.

"But—let's call a nurse—"

"What?" He glared. "Why? These people here—they talk baby talk to me. Do I look like a baby? They're idiots."

Dad was wild-eyed, unshaven, his silver hair standing in disheveled clumps. His dark eyebrows formed an angry V.

"I want my pants," he went on. "And then I'm getting the hell out. Jack's got to be looking for me." He stopped at the dresser and yanked drawers open, searching.

Jack? What was he talking about. "Who's Jack?"

"Move. Let me pass." He shoved me.

I placed myself between him and the door. "Dad. You can't leave. The police put you here."

"The police? What the hell are you talking about?"

"The police sent you here. You're in the hospital because of what happened to Beatrice."

He looked baffled, as if I made no sense. "Beatrice? Why would I be here because of Beatrice? She didn't hurt me—it was the other way around. I was the one who broke it off. She moaned and whined, but she knew why, believe me."

I paused, trying to make sense of his response. Was he pretending not to remember that Beatrice was dead, or just avoiding the topic? I started over, trying to steer him back toward his bed. "Dad, tell me. What happened to Beatrice?"

"Never you mind. It's not your affair." He tried to move around me, but I took his arm, made him face me.

"She choked to death. On papers, Dad. On betting slips." I waited, letting the words sink in. He frowned. "Do you have any idea where she would get betting slips, Dad? Or why they might be in her throat?"

"Beatrice choked on betting slips?" My father's right eyebrow raised and his frown deepened. "For real? How would you know that?"

I met his eyes. "The medical examiner found them. A detective told me."

He shook his head, digesting the information. "Beatrice was a good woman. But, to be candid, I've seen tree stumps that are smarter." He removed my hand from his arm and headed toward the door again.

I stepped in front of him, blocking his way. "Dad, don't play games with me. Don't play confused, forgetful old man. I know you too well. You can't fool me."

"What the hell are you talking about?"

"Tell me the truth—are you gambling again? Did you have

anything to do with those betting slips?" Shards of memory sprinkled my mind, echoes of my mother confronting him. Probably I sounded just like her.

He stopped again and stared at me, puzzling over the questions. "You seem to think you already know. So why don't you tell me? What do you think? Twenty bucks says you think I'm gambling." His eyes twinkled sadly.

"Tell me, Dad. I'm serious. What have you gotten into?"

He looked away, gazed out the window. "You know? It's difficult to say. There's so much to remember." He stopped at the closet again, opened and slammed it. "Dammit. I tell you, somebody stole them."

"Nobody stole them, Dad. They probably had to throw them out because of all Beatrice's blood. I'll bring you another pair tomorrow."

"Never mind. Hell with it." He grabbed hold of the IV pole and started for the door again. Tubes dragging, liquids sloshing, he tried to pass me. I stepped ahead of him.

"Dad. I told you. The police put you here. You can't just leave."

His mouth closed tight. "Can't I? Ten bucks says I can."

I stood in the doorway. He raised the fist holding his catheter bag like a club, ready to slug. "Get out of the way. I'll douse you if I have to."

I still had bruises and a concussion from the scene in his kitchen; I remembered how he'd pounced and pummeled, and I knew he wouldn't hesitate to pour a bag of urine on me. My eye on the bag, I took a step back. Holding on to his IV pole, my father made his way out of the room. I looked around for help. The hallway was deserted, the nursing station empty. I stayed beside him, jabbering, trying to slow him down, pressing him for information. "Tell me about the betting slips, Dad. Are you gambling again? Was Beatrice gambling, too?"

"For the last time, let me pass."

"Did she owe her bookie money? Did he have her killed? And what about you?" I kept it up, hoping to distract him from his trek down the hall. "Are you in debt again? Are they going to come after you, too?"

He stopped for a fraction of a second. "You know what? If anybody kills me, it won't be any bookie. It'll be you."

Me? How was any part of this my fault?

My father, unshaven, uncombed, undressed, yet still somehow remarkably handsome, peered at me with wizened, narrowed eyes. Smelling like the hospital, he leaned into my face. "I'm here because of you. Except for you, everything would have been fine. You couldn't leave things alone. Showing up again, back from the dead. Bringing little Zoe into it. Putting her in the middle. I have my faults, but I'd never put that child in the middle of our troubles. Get out of the way, Louise, or I swear, when they kill me, I'll come back and haunt you. I mean it."

I faced him and met his eyes, determined to reason with him. "Dad. I'm not Louise. I'm Zoe. And you are completely safe here. No one is killing you."

"Says who?"

"Says me."

"You? You never knew anything. Listen, Louise-who-thinks-she's-her-own-daughter. You're confused. It's not the way you think it is. You don't even know who you are. Trust me, I know what I'm doing."

This was crazy. Why was I bickering with a stubborn, cranky eighty-three-year-old man who'd lied to and disappointed me all my life? And where was the hospital staff? Why wasn't anyone stepping in to help me?

"If not for you," he went on, "I'd be home in peace."

No argument there. He was right. Again, I regretted that I hadn't ignored Lettie Kinkaid's call. I should have left him there, should have let our estrangement stand, even if it meant he'd have rotted in that house.

"I'm sorry that you feel that way." Good, I congratulated myself. I wasn't fighting with him anymore. I was responding like an actual adult.

"Who the hell takes a man's pants?" he grumbled, clutching his pole like a walking stick. "Jack needs me," he insisted. "Get out of my way."

Father pushed past me, making his way down the hall, his gown open in the back, exposing thin white thighs and a pale drooping butt. I went after him, running interference, a basketball guard in slow motion. He dodged; I scooted. He scooted; I dashed. But my father was determined. Slowly but surely, he made it to the doors to the psychiatric unit.

"Nurse? Somebody?" My call was desperate.

Where was everyone? If I didn't get help soon, my father could soon be strutting down Germantown Avenue waving his urine bag. Breathless, I blocked the doors with my body.

"You can't get out. These doors are locked, Dad." Where was the staff?

"Locked?" His eyes narrowed. "Okay," he growled. "I get it. I see. I'm a prisoner here." He stepped forward, pushing me against the doors. "Why don't you just kill me yourself? That's what you want, isn't it? Isn't it? Are you a sissy? You need them to do it for you?"

His eyes narrowed, furious, and the urine bag swung from his raised fist, ready to strike. "Move away." He snarled.

I moved, but not by choice. Suddenly the doors opened behind me, and I stumbled backward into the sleeve of a white coat. The coat supported me while I regained my balance. Then it released me and, joined by two staff members, the doctor who wore it led my father back to his room.

Seething, I stormed to the nursing station, now fluttering with personnel. Before I could speak, a nurse raised an eyebrow and barked, "What do you mean, miss, taking Mr. Hayes out of his room? That patient is here by police authority—"

"But I didn't take him out—"

"In fact, that patient has a head wound and is supposed to remain in bed." The nurse puffed herself up, managing to look down at me, even though we were about the same height. "You can't just waltz in and interfere with hospital policy—"

That was it. I'd had it. Emotions surged, and I blasted her, declaring that no one had been at the station, that I'd tried to get help, that if she'd been doing her job, my father wouldn't have left his room. Lord knows what she said to me. Nose to nose, voice to voice, we ranted, neither listening to the other. I watched her jaws flap around her large, impressive mouth, slapping my words away, rebounding them right back at me. Still, I couldn't stop. I exploded enthusiastically, with increasing volume and rapidity, spitting out my frustration, spewing my pent-up worries and despair. My voice was alive, a creature beyond my control.

Gradually, I felt my face heat up. Helpless, embarrassed, aware that people—staff members, nurses and visitors—were staring, I waited for my anger to exhaust itself. Finally, even as the nurse yammered on, I heard my voice cease its purging and collapse, silent and spent. Mortified, face burning, I hurried away, escaping the nurses' station before my voice or my temper could gather a second wind.

I paced outside my father's doorway, flushed and actually shaking. The nurse was a moron, but she wasn't the problem. The problem was my father. I didn't need to tolerate him or his hostility and accusations. With everything else going on in my life—the baby, my job, Molly, my upcoming marriage—I really didn't need another responsibility. And after all he'd done to me, to my mother, did I have to deal with his irrational behavior? Worry about his gambling again? Get involved in his financial, legal and emotional messes? No, I did not. And I would not. In fact, I would not go back into his room. I was finished with him, finally. Finished. I'd have some ambulance service move him back home, and let him survive somehow on his own. Or not. I was done with him forever—

"Excuse me, madam? You are Mr. Hayes's daughter?"

I nodded without enthusiasm. His name tag read "M. Habib." He spoke with an accent, something Middle Eastern.

"I've given your father an injection that will make him sleep." Dr. Habib took me aside and opened my father's chart. He had a few questions for me. Here we go again, I thought. No, I had no idea when his symptoms first manifested themselves. Or what kind of diet he kept. Or how he slept. Or how long he'd had trouble with urination. Or what medications he was on. Or whether he'd ever had a stroke. The doctor looked puzzled, maybe shocked; once again, I was Zoe the irresponsible, neglectful daughter.

"My father has . . . kept to himself over the last several years," I explained.

"Secretive?" he asked. "Would you say he's been secretive? Possibly agitated or hostile?"

Why not, I thought. Clearly, Dr. Habib wanted me to agree. "I suppose. Maybe."

"Well, that would make sense, actually. He's most probably been deliberately hiding his symptoms from you. But I don't think he has Alzheimer's. As of now, although the results aren't all in, I suspect that he's suffered a series of small strokes which have had the cumulative effect of temporarily and recurrently disorienting and confusing him. The symptoms are similar to those of dementia, and understandably he's upset and most probably angry and frustrated. So it won't be surprising if he behaves somewhat erratically, even irrationally, or even with bad temper at times. People often take out their anger on those closest to them, after all, which usually means on their family members."

Dr. Habib went on, his words flowing past in a liquid stream. I caught phrases, chunks of information. Father's condition was not unusual among people his age. The prostate problem could be managed; the other problem was more ambiguous. It was not immediately life-threatening, but would undoubtedly worsen with time. Father should rest. He should not live alone. He would require only minimal care for now, and most of the time he'd be perfectly lucid. But that could change anytime, with further small strokes. So far, his vision had been slightly affected, as well as his short-term memory. Maybe other functions, as well. He might have incidents in which he became lost in time or space, when he would not recognize familiar people or even common objects. He might try to cover up his confusion, might lash out in frustration. But, inevitably, maybe rapidly, maybe not, he would continue to deteriorate.

After the doctor had left, I stood in the hall, absorbing what he'd said. It sank in gradually, but I finally got the message. Quite simply, my father was dying.

He was propped up in bed, his dark eyebrows contrasting with his shock of white hair, still striking even now. All the years of conflict and turmoil, all the bitterness and anger and loss had led us to this moment. The charming, elusive rogue was finally at his end. He lay in bed, growing helpless and dependent and slowly dying. Nothing had been resolved. Neither apologies nor truces had been made. The conflict had simply ended. Nobody had won.

I sat on the chair beside his bed. His dark eyes wandered in my direction and, seeing me, he raised a finger, motioning me closer.

"Zhoeee . . ."

Wait. Had he said my name? Did he know I was there, not my mother?

"Zhoeee . . ." He said it again, pausing, struggling to go on.

"What, Daddy? What is it?" I leaned forward, straining to hear, wondering what wisdom he was urgently trying to impart.

"Zhoee . . . gemmy . . ." He stopped to draw in some air and continued. "Pants . . ." he exhaled.

Then his lids dropped, and he drifted away.

EIGHTEEN

NICK PULLED ON HIS BEER, RESTED HIS FEET ON THE COFFEE table and released a belch. "In a way, half a job might not be a bad thing." The part of his face that wasn't paralyzed smiled, as if what he'd just said made sense.

But it didn't. In fact, it stung. It felt as if he thought my job and career weren't all that important. I didn't know how to reply, so I didn't. Instead, I leaned away from him, sinking into the cushions of my purple velvet sofa, staring at the flames that crackled in the living room fireplace. It was about nine o'clock on a rare evening when Nick wasn't working; lately, he seemed to be out on cases half the night, every night. Molly was upstairs, sleeping, and we'd been talking. I hadn't gotten to the part about my father's failing health yet. I'd started with the Institute, the cutbacks, the impersonal mass notifications, the apparently arbitrary decisions about which jobs would be slashed, the insensitivity to patients and staff members alike, the frustration I felt at having no recourse. Nick sat beside me, watching me in the dim, glimmering light, listening without interrupting, and when I'd finished, he'd lifted his bottle of Yuengling and sucked more lager before making his comment that half a job might "not be a bad thing."

Was he serious? "Are you serious?"

He swallowed, nodding. "Think about it."

"So, wait. If your job got cut in half, would that be a good thing, too?" I resented his implication that my job was expendable. Or at least half-expendable.

"My job has nothing to do with it."

Of course it didn't; his job was far more important than mine. He was a big-shot homicide detective in a city with more than one murder a day. His job was essential; people's lives and safety depended on it. By comparison, he must think what I did—making papier-mâché daisies with mental patients—was trivial. "So exactly what are you saying? That my job's not important? They can just cut half my hours, no harm done, no big deal?"

Nick sat up and set his bottle on the coffee table, half-smiling. Why was he smiling? Was he laughing at me? "Calm down, Zoe. You're pissed off, and that's understandable. But think clearly for a minute."

So now I was too emotional to think clearly?

"Right now, you're mad, and no question, you have reasons to be. The MBAs running that place are managing from their assholes. But, luckily for us, the cut might work out to your advantage."

"Really." I was baffled. "My advantage? I must have missed something. To me, it looks like I'll be losing salary, job security, health benefits, development funds for the art program, control over my patients' therapy—"

"Yes, you're right. All those things are true. Even so, in some ways the change might be good for you personally. At least, right now."

"Nick. We have a baby coming. We need my income—"

"Exactly. We have a baby coming. And we don't need your income as much as you think; why do you think I'm doing so much overtime? I'm pulling in a lot of cash for when the baby comes. Forget about money. Point is you might appreciate having some time to yourself before the baby comes. This way, you'll have more time to spend with Molly and prepare her for her sibling. Time to relax and fix up the nursery. Time to talk about our wedding—"

Oh, yes. The wedding. It kept getting postponed, was now tentatively planned for late December, when I'd be as big as a whale. I closed my eyes, covered them with my hands, overwhelmed.

Nick was still talking, listing more things that, without a full-time job, I'd have time for.

". . . So you don't need to worry about losing your medical insurance. Once we're married, my benefits cover you, Molly and the baby."

Nick seemed chipper and bright, finding a dozen positive sides to my career disaster. But I was exasperated. Did he think that, since I was pregnant, I should be fat and happy, just sit around and study bride magazines and pick the baby's window treatments?

"What's wrong, Zoe? Talk."

Talk? Okay. "Fine. You want to know what's wrong? What's wrong is you're patronizing me."

He looked baffled. "How am I patronizing—"

"How? You've just dismissed my work as if it's completely irrelevant. Expendable. I'm not a stock boy at the supermarket. Believe it or not, my work is important—"

"Of course it is. I never said it wasn't. Don't be defensive." His tone was gentle, firm. Unapologetic.

"I'm not being defensive—"

"All I'm saying is that, if your hours have to be cut, the timing couldn't be better. You can relax. Get your life organized. After all, your father's going to add to the mix—"

My father? Wait, I hadn't told him about my father's condition, but Nick was already assuming I'd have to take care of him. Suddenly I was hot, short of breath. I broke into a sweat. "Trust me, Nick. I don't need to take time from my profession to manage my personal life. And certainly not to attend to my father. I am not, nor will I ever be his caretaker." How could Nick suggest such an idea?

Nick shrugged calmly, not rattled by my reaction. He repeated himself slowly, as if speaking to a child. "Zoe, calm down. All I'm saying is that the half-time thing isn't a complete tragedy, at least not right now."

I crossed my arms, blew steam out of my ears. Instead of validating my frustration and sympathizing with my plight, Nick was hell-bent on tenderly, lovingly insisting that my job cut was good, possibly even fabulous. He took another swig of beer. How could he be so infuriatingly unrattled?

"You don't get it, Nick."

"I get that you're very upset. And I get that you're stressed out. And I get that you're a pregnant woman whose hormones are charmingly out of whack—"

Okay, that was it; I exploded. I was on my feet, blasting. "So now I'm upset because of my hormones? You're saying that my concern for my career is a 'female' problem?"

Nick shook his head. "No. Come on, Zoe." He reached out, grabbed my arm and pulled me back to the sofa. "Sit."

I was breathless and hot. And actually, a little dizzy. I wanted to sit down again, but I wouldn't. I was too stubborn and mad.

Nick released my hand, leaned back and ran a hand through his hair. His eyes were tired, bloodshot. In the last two days, he'd worked thirty-odd hours chasing a serial rapist/killer through Old City. Probably he wasn't thinking real seriously about my job problem. Probably he was trying to quiet me down so he could go to bed. Poor guy was exhausted. Why was I being so hard on him? It wasn't his fault my job was fizzling out. He was only trying to cheer me up.

"Dammit, Nick." I sat again. "This is not about hormones. If your job were cut, you'd be upset, too. Of course, being you, you'd be all silent and macho and never let anyone know how you felt. But I can't help it. I'm pissed off and I don't care who knows. I've worked damned hard to build this job and this life for Molly and me. And now, suddenly, in a heartbeat, my job's dissolving, and the baby's coming, and after a dozen years my father reappears and the doctor said he's dying, and everything I've built—it's all coming apart, and there's nothing I can do about any of it." Tears streamed unexpectedly, flooded uncontrollably from my eyes. My voice was gulpy and high-pitched, didn't sound like me. I was imploding, overwrought.

Nick sat quietly, patiently, probably assessing my hormone

levels. When I finished, he remained still, watching me with hesitant blue eyes. The silence grew until, drained from crying and embarrassed, I stood to leave the room. Nick was on his feet, reached out and stopped me, held me tight, his breathing uneven.

Even in bed, he didn't continue the discussion, didn't mention my job situation again. When the lights were out, though, he gently touched my face.

"I didn't know Walter was dying." His voice was a dark whisper. "No wonder you're upset, Zoe. You have every right to be. I'm sorry."

I didn't answer. There was no point trying to explain. Nick assumed that my father, not my job, was the real reason I was upset. The idea was absurd. I'd been estranged from my father for years, wasn't the least bit affected by his health. But my eyes already burned from crying, and I was spent from the events of the day, finding it difficult to stay awake. Nick kissed my forehead good night, his arms encasing me. In moments, he was snoring. Or maybe, my nose puffed up and swollen from crying, the droning snores I heard as I dozed off were my own.

NINETEEN

THIS TIME, MY PARENTS WERE DANCING. WALTZING LITHELY through the hallway, around the dining room floor. They didn't notice me as I sped frantically through the house, searching, looking in cabinets, in the closet under the front staircase. They didn't look my way as I tossed sofa cushions, tore paintings from the walls. While they glided together, gracefully in step, I ripped through the house, needing to find—what was it? My baby? Yes. I was looking for my baby. It was there, lost somewhere in the house—in peril. Oblivious, the couple dipped and turned, spinning, smiling and indifferent as I cried out, wailing, calling for my child.

In the nursery, I found an empty crib, and knew I was too late. I wailed so loud that Nick thought I was having a miscarriage.

"Zoe—" He shook me, lifting the blankets, probably checking the bedsheets for blood. "What? What's wrong?" Alarmed, he sat up, apparently ready to leave for the hospital.

I apologized for waking him and got up to use the bathroom, trying to shake the nightmare from my mind. It was after five, and I doubted I could fall asleep again. Quietly, letting Nick sleep, I went to check on Molly. I stood in her room, listened to her even breathing, rearranged her covers. Then I wandered down the hall to the room that would be the nursery. It was mostly empty, the walls bare. Molly's old crib was there. And our old cane rocking chair. And my ton of pregnancy books, in a heap on the floor. I sat there in the almost empty room, rocking, and my mind wandered again through the halls of my nightmare, recalling the desperation I'd felt, the sense that I'd lost my child. Ridiculous. Actually, the dream had simply reflected my anxiety, my general sense of being out of control and vulnerable. That was all. My parents and their house had appeared simply because my father was back in my life, reviving all kinds of unresolved issues, for no other reason. The dream had been a typical hodgepodge of memory and emotion, just a regular dream.

Feeling calmer, I rocked in the darkness, my hand resting on my swelling belly, cradling the tiny foreigner who boarded there. Watching the streetlight pour through the still undraped window into the vacant crib, I considered how much work I had to do before the baby arrived. The walls had been painted yellow in September, but I still had to finish the detail work, add a strip of wallpaper patterned with baby ducks and chicks. And I had to clean up Molly's old baby furniture, polish the wood of the crib and the dressing table, the armoire. Get a new stroller and high chair, a car seat, a playpen. And toys. And a layette. Diapers, and a bag. Oh, man. I began to remember the houseful of equipment that infants generated. Bottles, bibs. Pacifiers. Teething rings. Blankets. And I wanted one of those strappy thingies so I could carry the baby around like a papoose. There was so much to do, and the baby was due in just five months. How was I going to get everything ready in time?

Nick's voice echoed in my mind, cheerily declaring that having half a job wasn't a tragedy. That losing my hours at work might be a good thing, that I could use the time.

The truth was that he was right. I could use some time to get ready for the baby. And to be alone with Nick and Molly before the baby was born, while we were still just us. No question, right now, our family would benefit from me being available, close to home. Much as it irritated me to admit it, I was lucky that my hours had been cut. So why had it bothered me to hear Nick say so? Again, I heard his voice: "Your hormones are out of whack."

And I got insulted all over again. Resented his knowing, understanding, patient attitude. What was going on with me? The very thought of Nick made me weak in the knees. I still swooned when he walked into the room, still found myself paralyzed by his gaze. But half the time, lately, I bristled at every word he said. Why? What was wrong with me? Damn. Could he be right about my hormones? Medically speaking, were they out of whack? For sure, the rest of me was. Nothing felt normal. My feet swelled in my shoes. My breasts burst out of my bras. My body had been taken over by a tiny alien, and my form changed daily, magically knowing all on its own what to do to bring that little being to life.

I rocked for a while, thinking about the baby. Would it look like Nick? I smiled, picturing a tiny baby with Nick's rugged face. And imagining the room smelling powdery soft, sweet like baby skin. I gazed out the window at the row houses across the street, the view the baby would have from the crib, and I patted my belly, wondered if the baby was awake, if it could sense my attention. For a moment, amazed, I thought that the baby was responding, pushing back at my hand. Then, slowly, I realized that the pressure wasn't a tiny push. It wasn't local; it expanded across my waist, around my back, and it increased, squeezing until I was dizzy. And then, as I leaned back, panting in the rocker, it eased, leaving me breathless and chilled in the almost empty room.

The moment passed, and so did the sensation, but I stayed there, wondering what had just occurred. A cramp? A contraction? Oh, God. Was I going to have a miscarriage? For a long while, I didn't move. I sat still, as if moving might cause me to lose the baby. Finally, I reached for the stack of books beside me, poring through them, trying to find an explanation that I could accept. In a pamphlet on home birthing, I read that the female body prepares itself for delivery throughout the pregnancy. Its muscles practice for the work of labor, starting months before they give birth. That was it, I told myself. No big deal. My body's practicing, getting itself ready to give birth, nothing more.

The sun was up when I got back into bed. Without opening his eyes, Nick covered my belly with an arm. We lay there, my arms crossed beneath his, layers of limbs covering, protecting our small, precious stranger.

TWENTY

SO FAR, NO CHARGES HAD BEEN FILED AGAINST MY FATHER. SO, given his medical condition, on Thursday morning, before my doctor's appointment, Nick and I moved him and the four new shirts, six pairs of socks and underwear, two sweaters, navy blazer, and two pairs of pants I'd just bought him into Harrington Place, a posh high-rise retirement home near the art museum and Fairmount Park. Susan's mother-in-law had spent her last years there, and Susan had pulled strings for Dad to get a spot in the assisted care unit, sharing a two-bedroom suite with another man. The facility offered varying levels of medical care, as needed, as well as a broad spectrum of social, cultural and recreational activities. Dad would be taken care of there, and I was relieved.

Nick had taken over the logistics of the move. Susan had her firm draw up power of attorney forms, and, somehow Nick had convinced my father to sign them. All I had to do myself was some Medicare and insurance paperwork in the administration office, and after I finished filling out forms, I went to my father's suite. The place was well furnished, decorated in neutral tones. A living room with a blue-cushioned sofa and two matching easy chairs, a coffee table, a television. Two bedrooms, each with its own bath. I looked into one, saw my father sound asleep, apparently exhausted from the move.

"Let the man sleep. He's tired out."

A round, white-haired man with a bulbous purple nose had joined me at my father's door.

"I'm the roommate." He stuck a soggy unlit cigar into his

mouth and held out his hand for a shake. "Name's Leonard Parks."

White stubble coated Leonard's face. His brown slacks, the waist pulled up to his ribs, were unbuttoned; his belt hung open. "So, this new guy." It was a sentence. "You're the daughter? You ought to get him a haircut." His face asked what was wrong with me, letting my father get so shaggy. "He got any other kids?"

"Just me."

"Any grandkids? I got seven. Three in Seattle. One in Pittsburgh—his father's my youngest, an architect. My middle son's a CPA. And my eldest—he's in real estate—his kids are all grown now, out of the nest. He's in Kenya now. Wait. Let me get the itinerary." He pulled a crumpled paper from his pocket and set reading glasses on his nose while he opened the page. "Let's see. Yes. Today, he's on safari. In Kenya. Next, he'll be in South Africa, in Cape Town." He held up the list for me to see. "He's on a trip around the world. Writes me every day, keeps me up-to-date, doesn't want me to miss a beat. See, I'm staying here while he travels. Just for a few months. But listen, who can begrudge him? He's earned it, my son. He's worked hard, raised his family. Now it's his time to enjoy. When he gets home, of course, I'll go live with him and his wife at their home out in Malvern. I'm only here for a short time, for the interim." He folded the itinerary, carefully put it away. "That's probably why they put us together."

I didn't follow.

"Walter and me." Leonard gestured into my father's room. "He's here for only a short time, too."

"He is?" I must have misunderstood what Leonard meant.

"Sure, he's going home in a couple weeks, back to his own place. Says a guy named Jack is there, waiting for him. That's what he said."

Damn. Didn't my father get it? Nick and I had each explained that he was going to live here now, but apparently we'd have to go over it again. Maybe lots of times. Dr. Habib had warned that the strokes had damaged his short-term memory.

"So, we're both just temporary." Leonard tugged at his pants, hefting them up even higher.

I smiled, looking around toward the door, wondering where Nick was.

"It's not a bad place, don't get me wrong. But not a place you'd want to stay permanently unless you have to. Some of the people here, they have nobody who cares about them. So they end up here. Thank God, I've got my sons. And Walter has you."

I blinked, excusing myself, saying how nice it was to meet him and that I'd come by later, and, before Leonard could go on, I backed out of the room.

TWENTY-ONE

I FOUND NICK WAITING IN THE HALLWAY BY THE FRONT OFFICE.

"Your dad fell asleep," he told me. "The move wiped him out. And we have a small problem: He thinks he's here on vacation, to rest for a while. He's decided this place is a resort."

I didn't want to talk about it. "Give him time. He'll figure it out."

"Who's Jack? He says he has to go look after Jack."

"I don't know." Leonard had mentioned Jack, too, and Dad had talked about him in the hospital. But I had no idea who he was. For all I knew, Jack was long dead like my mother. "Can we go get lunch?" I changed the subject.

"Sure, how's Le Bus?"

Le Bus was a casual restaurant in Manayunk, which was a Native American word meaning "place we go to drink." Formerly a mill and factory neighborhood, Manayunk had been built along the Schuylkill River above Philadelphia. Now gentrified, its Main Street had become a trendy high-end shopping center, a narrow road lined with designer and fashion boutiques, high-caliber bars and eateries. Le Bus was not one of the fancy spots, just a place for reasonably priced hearty meals featuring home-baked breads and buttery mashed potatoes. Le Bus was a fine choice, but I managed only a mild, less than enthusiastic, "Okay." I was hungry, but more than that, I was disturbed. My father, his deteriorating health, his ambiguous role in Beatrice's death and, now, his declared plans to return home had darkened my mood, and I remained quiet until we were seated at the restaurant facing a basket of fresh warm bread.

"Don't worry. He'll be okay there, Zoe." Nick took a piece of pumpernickel.

I slathered a slice of pumpkin-seed bread with melting butter.

"While you were doing the paperwork, Walter was chatting people up, joking around. He was real sociable."

"Dad's a real sociable guy. In a real sociopathic kind of way."

Nick took a bite of bread. "Just out of curiosity. Why are you so mad at him?"

Oh, God. Did we have to talk about that? I gulped raspberry iced tea.

"Who said I was mad at him?"

"Zoe, he's just an old man, not a monster." He said that as if it were true. A given that everybody knew for certain. Nick spread butter on a roll; it melted instantly. "Look, you're a grown woman. Whatever happened in your childhood, it's long over with. Shouldn't you move on?"

I looked into Nick's eyes, determined to ignore the disturbing shadows flickering in my mind.

"I've got to tell you, Zoe, Walter's growing on me. I kind of like the guy."

Damn. I put down a slice of pecan raisin bread. "Oh, please, Nick. Don't tell me you're letting him con you. You're too smart for that."

"Just because I like him doesn't mean he's conning me. What did he do that was so terrible that you can't forgive it in his old age?"

I closed my eyes, glimpsed the dangling hem of a nightgown, refused the image, concentrating instead on the shiny butter knife in Nick's hands.

"I don't know where to start."

"Just anywhere."

I squeezed my water glass and took a deep breath. Okay. I'd talk about it. Fine. Why not? While we're at it, why didn't I just take that butter knife and slice my veins open? "Dad's a gambler. He used to borrow from loan sharks to pay off his bookies. We'd have to hide from the loan sharks because he couldn't pay them back. He was always in debt, and we never knew who would come knocking at the door to collect. My father's a gambling addict who cares about nothing more than the game. He'll swear that he's stopped, but he never stops. That's why, when I found out about the betting slips in Beatrice's throat, I knew my dad was involved—"

Nick blinked. "Wait, what?"

"She was his friend—she died in his kitchen. He had something to do with it. It's no coincidence that her death involved gambling."

Nick looked skeptical. "Your father's eighty-three years old. I doubt he had anything to do with her murder—"

"You don't know him, Nick. He charms people. He lies to your face. He promises to stop gambling, but he doesn't stop. My childhood was a series of high-stakes card games and junkets, and a whole lot of hiding from gangsters. Don't tell me he's a likable guy. That likable man broke my mother's heart so many times that, by the time I was six, she was dead." My voice was too loud. I felt stares from all directions.

For once, Nick didn't jump to defend my father. He reached for my hand, waiting for me to calm down. "If your mother was unhappy, why didn't she leave?"

Why didn't she leave? Well, in a way, she did. Again, I pictured her, an angel's face, pale in death, imagined her floating, drifting nowhere, ghostlike above the ground. "She might have, but she died first." I took a sip of water.

Nick studied me. "Okay. So you blame him. You blame your father for your mom's death."

Bingo. The guy was a genius. "Nick, can we please—"

"I finally get it. It makes sense." He put what was left of his roll down, reached out for my other hand. "Zoe, sorry. I don't mean to play shrink with you."

Then don't. Please. "Okay."

"And I don't pretend to know everything—I wasn't there."

No, you don't and you weren't. "But?"

"But you're the therapist—you should be able to see what's happening here. You were a kid when all this happened. And kids tend to confuse cause and effect with sequence. Your mom's unhappy with your father; then she dies. So . . . maybe little Zoe's mind connected these events. However illogically, she thought her dad must be responsible. Maybe she's held that against him all these years. Is that a possibility?"

Definitely. Absolutely a possibility. "I guess."

"But all this time later, you must see the fallacy there. Granted, your father was a bad parent—a miserable one. A gambler. An incorrigible liar. A complete cad."

The list was too short, but so far, I was with him.

"But that doesn't mean he caused your mom's death. You see that, right?"

Oops. He'd lost me.

"So maybe, if you recognize all that, you can let go of some of your anger. I mean, I spent only a little while with him, but I'm a pretty good judge of character. And, to an outsider like me, your dad doesn't seem so bad. He's feisty. Spry. Funny. Likable."

Oh, no. Likable? Spry? Please don't tell me that. My father had gotten to Nick. Already. "Okay. Thanks. I'll think about what you said."

"Now you're upset." He shook his head, leaned back in his chair. "Why? Because I brought this up?"

Upset? Me? "No. I'm actually glad. We need to be able to talk about things." Even fetid, infested things.

"I only want you two to have some peace while you still can, Zoe. After all, he's eighty-some. And Walter doesn't have that much time left."

Did he think I didn't realize that? Again, I heard Dr. Habib warn that my father could go at any time.

"And besides, he's going to be my father-in-law."

Oh, God. Were they going to bond? Hang out and watch Sunday football?

"Nick, don't worry about me and my dad. We'll be okay."

"Really?" He was still holding my hand; now he squeezed it.

"Really." Can we change the subject now? Please?

He half-smiled. "Then why are you still scowling?"

I wanted to scream. "Talking about my father makes me scowl."

"Okay. Then let's change the subject." He half-smiled again.

"Fine. What do you want to talk about?"

"How about your mom?" His eyes twinkled.

Was he serious? "What is this, Nick? Why do we have to talk about my family? I don't like talking about them—"

"I don't like to talk about my scar, either. But I told you about it the first time we had dinner together. It's called 'confiding.' It's what a person does to let someone else get close."

I didn't remind him that he'd left out major details in telling me about his scar. Like the fact that the woman who'd given it to him had been his wife. Or the fact that he'd been suspected of killing her afterward. Instead, I reassured him. "We are close, Nick." I squeezed his hand. "I'm having your baby."

"Thai turkey salad and a charbroiled cheddar burger." The waitress smiled as she placed the plates in front of us. "Anything else? Can I get you more to drink?"

"No, thank you." Nick politely returned the smile, but his cool blue eyes remained on mine.

The waitress nodded, moved awkwardly away.

I stiffened, anticipating what Nick would say. I expected him to say that I put walls around myself, that I didn't let anyone close. I could hear the words before he said them. Not that he didn't have his own walls—in fact, I knew almost nothing about his family or his childhood. All I knew about his brothers was their names and their unconventional religious training. But then, Nick's background wasn't the issue at the moment. Mine was. And he was right. I needed to trust him and open up.

"Okay." I tried to dodge the spat. "I don't remember much

about my mom, but I can tell you what I do. What would you like to know?"

He shook his head. "What I want to know isn't the point."

It wasn't? "It isn't?"

"We've been through this before, Zoe. The point isn't what I want to know—it's what you want me to know. What do you want me to know about your family? Anything?"

"You already know my family. As far as I'm concerned, Molly is my family, my entire family. My mother's been dead since I was a kid, and my father's been out of my life until now. He's been a non-relationship, completely irrelevant."

"Irrelevant?" Nick's eyebrows dropped into a doubting frown. "How? He's your father."

"Only technically."

"Bullshit. You're the shrink here. You know that family gives us our foundations. It teaches us how to care for others."

"So?"

"So, according to you, you grew up without one. A dead mother and an irrelevant father."

My mouth went dry. It sounded so cold. I thought of Hilda, the chubby, pink-cheeked German housekeeper who'd pretty much raised me without ever really speaking English.

"So maybe you never learned how to be part of a family. Maybe you don't want to be part of one." His eyes narrowed.

"I can't help how I grew up, Nick."

"But you can help what you do about it."

"Meaning?"

"Meaning"—he met and held my eyes—"that just now, you said that Molly was your whole entire family. What about me? Am I not your family?"

Damn. "Oh, come on, Nick. Of course—"

"What about the baby? Is the baby not your family?"

"Nick, stop it. Of course it is. And so are you. You're twisting my words."

"Am I? Or am I simply repeating them?"

I could hear his thoughts. Is Zoe capable of letting down the walls? Is it possible to be close to her? Did her first marriage fail because she couldn't manage the intimacy? Was her parents' marriage so bad that she feels unable to succeed at her own? The questions pummeled me, even unasked. Nick studied my face.

Damn, I told myself. Tell him you're insanely in love with him, that you consider him closer than family, that you adore his baby the same way that you adore Molly—that you'll say anything he wants and do whatever it takes to make him blissfully happy for the rest of time. Maybe even talk about your parents.

"I'm sorry." I was. I didn't want friction or fights. I wanted peace.

"All I'm saying is . . . you're always on edge lately. In your eyes, I can't do anything right. I'm on your nerves all the time—"

"No, you're not—"

"I've got to wonder if you're feeling trapped. Maybe you're having second thoughts about us—"

"Not at all—"

"I love you, Zoe. And I know having your father around is confusing the issue, opening a lot of old wounds. I don't want to interrogate you. I just want to understand what's going on. I don't want us to get messed up, that's all."

"Neither do I, Nick. You've got to know that." Didn't he?

He waited, watching me with a look I couldn't read. I had to stop this conversation, couldn't take any more. Mercifully, Nick relaxed. "Good. Then let's eat."

Amazingly, he bit into his burger and moved on as if nothing were wrong. He talked about the retirement home, the posh lifestyle it offered. How you could get concert and sporting tickets right there on the premises and they had free bus service to everything. They had a movie theater, an Olympic pool and spa, a visiting-lecturers program, a library, a beauty salon, a boutique. I picked up a forkful of turkey and noodles and chewed. Washed them down with iced tea. Took another bite. Repeated the process until my plate was almost empty. Trying to be normal, worrying that the scars of my childhood were going to ruin our marriage even before it began.

Finally, lunch was over. We walked to the doctor's office hand in hand, but all the way there, I felt uneasy and guilty. And very much alone.

TWENTY-TWO

"GOOD. THE BABY'S HEARTBEAT IS STRONG."

Dr. Martin moved the ultrasound probe over my swollen abdomen. Watching the monitor, she pointed out the various parts of the small person living in my belly. Nick craned his neck, trying to see. His fascination, his delight glowed in his eyes. I was suddenly overwhelmingly fond of him again.

"That's the heart?"

"Yes." She pointed a rubber-gloved finger to a tiny pulsing blot on the screen. "And there's the head. The spine." She went on naming body parts, and I stared at the shape, trying to comprehend the amazing fact that I was watching a being take form inside me. Someone was living, growing there, day by day.

"Can you tell the sex?" Nick asked.

"Well, it's early. Are you sure you want to know?"

Simultaneously, I said Yes, and Nick said No.

We began debating, both listing our reasons, but Dr. Martin interrupted. "It's just four months into the pregnancy. You have time to decide. Think about it and let me know." She was clearly busy, didn't have time for our debate.

Nick shrugged and squeezed my hand. But I didn't squeeze back. I wanted him to give in. I wanted him to do things my way; after all, I was the one giving birth. And I wanted to know everything I could about the baby—I didn't want to have to call it "it." I wanted to be able to say, "He's kicking," or "She's asleep." I wanted to consider appropriate names. And pick out clothes and wallpaper.

"Look—the baby's stretched out on your bladder. Lounging."

We had to laugh. Dr. Martin was right. The baby seemed to be posing like a tiny movie star. Smiling, the doctor turned off the monitor. The ultrasound was over. She wiped gel off my belly. "So, you're four months along, into the second trimester. That part is usually a breeze, the best part of the pregnancy. Women tend to feel good, energetic. Glowing. It's a peaceful time, for the most part. Morning sickness is generally over—yours is gone, right?"

I nodded. Other than gagging over a woman's corpse, I'd stopped sucking down saltine crackers and hadn't been nauseous at all. Just a little light-headed.

"How are you feeling in general?"

I glanced at Nick. He watched me, his eyes adoring and warm. I didn't want to worry him. "All right. Fine."

Leslie Martin was perceptive. She hesitated. "Well, good. Get dressed. Nick, can you take these to the front desk?" She held out the billing forms.

Obediently, Nick took the papers, and after squeezing my hand, stepped out of the room. When he was gone I took a deep breath. I told myself it was nothing. But I had to ask about the recurring waves of dizziness and the sensation of tightness around my belly.

When I did, Dr. Martin frowned. Not a good sign.

"The tightness. Was it like a cramp?"

I nodded. Kind of like a cramp, only higher and wider.

"It's probably Braxton-Hicks. All during pregnancy, the baby's body is preparing to be born and your body's preparing to deliver. Braxton-Hicks contractions are your body's way of practicing for labor. They're normal."

That was what the book had said. I released a long breath. I was normal.

"But sometimes the early contractions occur too frequently or too intensely. Then we have to take precautions."

Precautions? I folded my hands, swallowed. "How do I know if they're normal or not?"

"Well, to begin with, you need to keep track of them. So far, you're just reporting an occasional incident. It's probably nothing. But if the tightness recurs, pay attention. How often does it occur? How long does it last? How intense is it?"

Not all that often. Sort of long. Kind of mildly intense. "I don't know, exactly."

"Well, you're just in your fifth month. It's early to have a lot of these." She advised me to keep a log of contractions. She said I should take naps. She told me not to strain myself physically or emotionally, to avoid stress at home and work and told me to see her the following week instead of waiting until our usual appointment.

"I take it that your husband doesn't know about this?" She raised an eyebrow.

My husband? I loved how that sounded. We'd never explained our marital situation to the doctor. "Not yet. I don't want him to worry."

"Well, if your contractions worsen, be sure to tell him. He needs to be prepared, too."

Prepared? Oh, God. "For what?"

She spoke slowly, gently. "It's possible that you could develop premature labor."

I bit my lip. I'd read about that. "You think the baby will come early?"

"Not necessarily. Lots of women have premature labor and don't deliver early. Most hold on until close to their due dates. We have treatments that are usually quite successful."

Usually? "By treatments, you mean drugs." I'd read articles about premature labor.

"There are medications that help. And, if necessary, we'll put you on bed rest."

Bed rest. I'd been afraid she'd say that. The articles had

described women who'd lived in bed for weeks or even months, controlling early labor. "For how long?" My pulse raced at the thought. I couldn't stay in bed. I had Molly to take care of. And I still had half a job—patients who relied on me. A wedding to plan. A nursery to decorate. I was breathing too fast; my stomach was flipping.

"Zoe. Don't get ahead of yourself. We don't know that any of this will happen—you've had only . . . how many? One or two significant contractions?"

"But if it does—"

"If it does, we're ready to deal with it."

I thought of Bertram Haggerty, his offer. "What about alternative medicine?"

Dr. Martin raised an eyebrow. "Like what exactly?"

"Hypnosis?"

"Hypnosis?"

"A colleague at work has offered to work with me. He says it might help."

Dr. Martin folded her arms. "To be honest, Zoe, I don't know of any valid research indicating that hypnosis can affect premature labor. But, then again, hypnosis is really just extreme, controlled relaxation. And in general, the more relaxed you are, the better. So, I doubt it can hurt, and—who knows? It might help. I say go for it if you want to."

I closed my eyes, feeling lost.

"Zoe, listen. Right now, your baby's fine. What you need to do is to take it easy. Avoid stress. Keep track of your contractions, and call me if they become more frequent or intense." She covered my hand with hers. "Taking care of yourself is the best way to take care of your baby. Eat well. Rest. Take walks. I'll see you next week."

I watched her smiling and talking, heard her voice make rhythmic, soothing sounds. When she left, I took off the gown and looked down at my belly. It was firm and a little plump, but not all that big yet. I held my hands against it, trying to feel a sign of the life inside. But feeling nothing but my own skin, I got dressed and met Nick in the waiting room across the hall, where he greeted me with a bear hug and a completely unsuspecting kiss.

TWENTY-THREE

FRIDAY. MY LAST FULL DAY OF WORK. MORALE AT THE INSTITUTE had nose-dived. Even Agnes seemed muted as she ignored me when I passed her desk. Not everyone was directly affected by the cuts; many psychiatrists had private practices and teaching positions; their work at the Institute was mostly for prestige. But staff members like me—various therapists and social workers—and researchers like Bertram, we depended on our jobs for livelihoods, and we were gloomy and dour, passing one another zombie-like in the halls, allowing our moods to penetrate the walls, pollute the air.

Not surprisingly, patients were affected. In my art sessions they were increasingly agitated, unfocused, not willing to concentrate on projects. Friday's first session was private; I worked one-on-one with schizophrenic Evie Kraus, who refused to participate. She sat silent, ignoring me, staring into the air for several long minutes. When I handed her a paintbrush, she responded by letting it fall to the floor, then knocking several jars of acrylic paints over, creating large puddles of ocher and cadmium on the linoleum. An orderly intervened, and Evie shoved him; the orderly slipped in the wet paint, knocking over the easel, covering his pastel-green uniform with puce. I was trying to calm Evie, but the orderly called for assistance, and before Evie could react to me, another orderly and a nurse rushed in. Startled, Evie tried to run, but the three surrounded her and, ignoring my protests, forced her into a jacket and wheeled her out of the studio. Just eleven minutes into her session, it was all over. The studio was empty and silent, and I was alone.

I thought about cleaning up Evie's mess, scrubbing red and yellow stains off the floor. But I didn't, couldn't. They were Evie's way of screaming, her reaction to the changes that were shaking her world, so I left them there, a sign of respect. But I was trembling, shaken by the outburst and the violent scuffle that followed. I needed to get out of the studio, wandered to the lounge, made myself a cup of tea, dumped it out, walked the halls and finally found myself at the door to Bertram's office. I stood there, not knocking, hesitating. Why? I felt guilty, as if by being there I was doing something wrong.

That's ridiculous, I told myself. Go ahead. Knock. You have nothing to feel guilty about.

But maybe I did. After all, I hadn't yet told Nick about Bertram's offer of hypnosis sessions. Hell, I hadn't even told Nick about my early contractions, the reasons for the sessions. Shouldn't I talk to Nick before proceeding? Was I keeping more secrets, putting up more walls?

No, I told myself. This was not about walls. This was private. Bertram wanted to work with me on my personal issues and stress levels. Those didn't concern Nick; they were mine alone.

And so, without further debate, I knocked. Bertram answered, pleased to see me. He welcomed me into his office even though we had no appointment. I sat in the same chair as last time, relaxed just being there. At his suggestion, I pictured myself floating on my New Hampshire lake, watching a sunset in my "happy place." And the next thing I knew, it was eleven o'clock. Almost an hour had passed; it was time for my next session. My mascara was smeared with tears, but I felt lighter and, magically, able to get through the day.

TWENTY-FOUR

SATURDAY MORNING DAWNED BLUE AND SUNNY. NICK TOOK Molly and Emily to the zoo, giving me time to go sort through the mess at my father's house with Susan. Susan had insisted on helping, on the condition that I buy her breakfast first. She ordered chocolate-chip pancakes with bacon. All I wanted was a toasted bagel.

"You need to eat more." She placed a napkin in her lap.

"And you could probably eat less."

She glared at me. "I'm stressed. You know I eat a lot when I'm stressed."

"What's going on?"

"Just the usual. My life is stress. My kids don't do anything that even rhymes with 'help.' My husband thinks helping me means asking a thousand questions, so that it's easier for me to do whatever he's helping me with myself than to answer him. And I've got too many cases. Including one that should have pleaded out easily, but hasn't because I'm dealing with Doug Morrison, a moron ADA who has to be the most arrogant, incompetent lawyer in the DA's office, if not in Philadelphia—maybe in the world—"

The waitress interrupted, offering coffee.

"Anyhow, I'm fine. Same old same old." Susan poured sweetener into her cup. "But you should eat more. Especially calcium. And vitamins."

"I take vitamins."

"Order a glass of milk."

I hated milk. "I'm having cream cheese. It's okay." I asked about her cases. Why she was so angry at the ADA.

"Let's not talk about it. I'll get an ulcer. The guy just has his head up his behind." She gulped coffee, eyeing me, changing the subject. "So are you feeling okay? Physically?"

Except for possible early contractions and the threat of bed rest, yes. "Fine."

She studied me, concerned, and I realized how little we'd talked about pregnancy. Susan was experienced. She'd given birth three times. Wasn't it odd that she never talked about it?

"So." Why did I feel so awkward asking? She was my best friend. We talked about everything. "What was it like?"

"What was what like?"

"Having babies."

She looked into her coffee cup. "I survived. Not a big deal. Why?"

Why? Was she kidding? "I'm doing research for a PhD."

"Zoe, it doesn't matter what it was like for me. It's different for everybody and for each delivery. You never know what to expect."

Great. Thanks.

"So you're nervous?"

I poured cream into my decaf, trying to act nonchalant. "Not really."

She smirked.

"Just a little." I sipped decaf, tried to dodge her probing eyes.

"Well, that's completely normal."

Was it?

"Why are you chewing your lip? What else is wrong?"

I'd have to say something or she'd keep nagging. "I don't know why, but Nick's on my nerves a lot. It's not his fault, exactly. I'm just irritated."

Susan's shoulders shook. She was laughing.

"What's so funny?"

"Sorry. It's just that—Zoe, that's *so* typical. Pregnant women are hell to live with. Men cannot please us, no matter what they do. When I was pregnant, I contemplated murdering Tim on a daily—no, an hourly—basis. No matter what he did—especially if he tried to please me, he annoyed me. Being irritated by your mate is part of the deal. Nick will live through it. You both will."

A gangly waiter with a huge Adam's apple stepped over and refilled our cups. I waited for him to leave, grateful for a chance to change the subject, but Susan persisted.

"By the way, Tim and I have a video of Lisa's birth. You should watch it." The waiter swallowed; his Adam's apple rose and fell. "It would be good for you to see a delivery."

Oh, God. No way did I want to see that. The waiter fled, and I gulped fresh decaf. Too hot. Burned my tongue.

"Thanks. I'll let you know." Would she serve popcorn and soda? I squirmed.

"They aren't really relevant, but I can tell you about my deliveries if you want." She fingered the handle of her coffee cup. "I mean, if you're sure you want to hear."

Oh, God. Was it going to be detailed?

She leaned forward, her tone confidential. "People say you forget the labor and the pain. That's bullshit. I remember every damned second of it."

How delightful. "It was bad?"

"I don't want to scare you."

"How bad?"

"Not bad. It wasn't 'bad.' "

I exhaled, relieved.

" 'Bad' doesn't touch it. It was more like all-consuming. Like being eaten alive and burned at the stake all at once. From the inside out. Listen to me, Zoe. Go for the drugs. My labors didn't last long enough to get the epidurals going. My body spits babies out. Emily came in less than two hours. But those two hours were sheer undiluted hell."

Oh.

"Screaming pain."

Okay.

"Worse than words can describe."

I got the picture.

"But, like I said, that was just me. It's different for everybody."

Right.

"I mean, it hurts. You'll want it to be over with."

I didn't say anything, too scared to move.

"Actually, though, it's not a big deal. You're having a baby, not a heart transplant. It's what women do. They'll get it out of you, and that'll be it."

Lord. Didn't Susan see any magic in childbirth? "Sounds like you're talking about a kidney stone." I was irked.

"It's no kidney stone. A kidney stone comes out and it's gone. Once the baby comes out, it's just the beginning. Life as you know it will be gone for good."

"Pancakes?" The waiter set an overflowing plate in front of Susan. "And a bagel." His tone seemed disdainful of my breakfast choice.

"It can't be that bad, Susan." I watched her slosh butter and syrup onto her stack, found myself salivating. "I have Molly, and she hasn't interfered with my life. You have three kids, and you still run your law practice and travel—"

"But it's not the life I used to have. Truth is I'd die for my kids; you know that. But, in a way, I don't have to—it would be redundant. I've already sacrificed myself for them."

I shook my head, eyeing my paltry bagel, her sultry stack.

"I'll spell it out. You were single when Molly came into your life. This time, you're not. This time will be different. You and Nick will never have a moment alone ever again. The baby will cry on cue whenever you want to eat a meal, take a bath, sleep or, God forbid, talk on the phone. And without exception, it will cry whenever you even think about having sex. The baby will also generate fifty thousand times its weight in paraphernalia—cribs, car seats, prams, high chairs, not to mention diapers, tote bags, pacifiers, sippy cups, teething rings, cuddle toys, clothes, blankets, wipes—whatever.

You'll have more expenses than you ever imagined, and therefore no money for yourself or your spouse. So even if you want to get away together, you won't be able to until college is paid for. And I'm just skimming the surface."

Wow. I had no idea Susan was so bitter about motherhood.

"Sorry. I don't mean to sound so negative."

She thought that sounded negative? "Not at all."

"I'm sorry, Zoe. What kind of friend am I? This is one of the most exciting times in your life, and I'm making it sound like a complete disaster. I don't mean to. Kids are great. They are. And babies—you know I can't resist them. It's just that I'm constantly stretched thin. I never feel like I do enough for them. To me, coming here and going with you to clean out your dad's house feels like a vacation. It's a break from the never-ending drama at home. Lisa's a teenager and boys are coming around, drinking, hooking up. She has a hickey on her neck, and we find empty beer cans, cigarette butts out back. And Julie does whatever the crowd does; she thinks that who she is gets defined by what she owns, so she always needs more—designer jeans or handbags or whatever her friends have. And Emily's so demanding and bossy—"

"They're great kids, Susan."

"But they soak up every ounce of energy and time and money and emotion that I have. There's nothing left."

I didn't know what to say. To me, Susan was a natural nurturer. Her kids glowed, and her family seemed to thrive. I didn't have a mother; Susan had become my model of what a mom should be. But apparently I'd missed a few details. We were quiet for a while. She munched her pancakes; I ate my bagel. It was dry, tasted like cardboard. I eyed her pancakes, coveted them, considered digging my fork into them.

"So are you going to find out the sex?" Cutting syrupy mouthfuls, she began listing pros and cons, as if I hadn't already thought of them.

The sex? I wondered. What would it be? I put a hand on my belly, wondering who was inside. Was it a girl or a boy? I tried to imagine its face, but couldn't. Nor could I conjure up the feel of the baby's flesh against mine or the smell of its new skin or the sounds of its coos or cries or the sight of it in Nick's arms or in Molly's. I had no idea who this new person would be, and though I doubted it would shatter our lives as Susan predicted, I felt a wave of unexpected sadness, an awareness that time was limited, that our cozy threesome was about to be forever lost, invaded by a tiny stranger, name, face and gender unknown. And I knew then that the fear I felt wasn't just about childbirth or pain, bed rest or premature labor. My apprehension was also about change, about the unpredictable results of adding another person to our family, molding it from a triangle to a square.

"So, I think you were smart about the color," Susan insisted. "Yellow is good for both. And it's cheerful."

Yellow? I'd lost her.

"But don't buy that Bugaboo stroller. That's going to be our gift." She beamed.

"Really?" I smiled. "Thank you."

"Tim and I want you to have the best." She looked at the remaining pancakes on her plate. "Want some? I can't finish."

Before she finished the question, I'd taken her plate and forked up a wad.

"Have milk with them," she scolded. "Take care of yourself while you can."

I didn't answer, didn't listen. I merely inhaled the remainder of her breakfast, as if I were feeding a starving beast.

TWENTY-FIVE

THE POLICE HAD FINISHED THEIR WORK DAYS AGO, AND WE'D removed the remaining yellow tape from the door on our way inside. Susan stood in the foyer, wide-eyed, scanning the domed ceiling and the grand front staircase.

"You grew up here?" She seemed baffled.

"After I was four or five. Yeah." Oh, Lord. Was Susan going to grill me about my childhood? Was she going to press me like Nick?

"Neat." She shivered. "Very homey. If your name is Munster. Or Addams."

"It wasn't that bad."

"Zoe. It looks like a freaking haunted house."

She was probably right. "Well, it wasn't so bad back then."

A memory, too fleeting to catch, flew through my mind. The house when it was spotless. The scent of my mother's perfume, the rustle of fabric as she swished by.

I followed Susan through the domed foyer down the wide hall, passing the tiny storage closet under the staircase. I remembered playing there as a young child, hiding, huddled in that secret place, but I couldn't linger on memories, made myself keep walking. We wandered around the cluttered and dusty first floor. Cobwebs drooped from the dining and living room light fixtures. Paint crumbled off ceilings; faded paper curled on the walls. Wooden furniture was unpolished and brittle, and on the sideboard, my grandmother's silver tea set had long since tarnished to black. Clearly, Dad had let everything go untended for a long time. In the kitchen, the ambulance crew had uprighted the table, but the mess was basically still there. Congealed blood had dried on the floor, thick and cracked.

Susan sighed. "Well, let's get at it." She opened a cabinet, frowned, closed it again. "Where should we start? How do you want to do this?"

How? Oh, God. I had no idea. In fact, I really didn't want to do it at all, dreaded the entire process. Cut it out, I told myself. Deal with it.

We stood in silence, breathing in shadows. I must have looked as lost as I felt because Susan took over, managing, delegating. "Why don't we start by getting rid of all the trash?"

With that, she produced a box of trash bags and began throwing things out. She emptied the refrigerator in a flurry, started on cabinets, setting usable items on the counter, dumping the rest.

I watched, fascinated, appreciative and completely useless. I was trapped in a crisscross of dimensions, a hodgepodge of time and space where moments in the kitchen slipped, colliding with the past. I was caught up in a thousand vague impressions of breakfasts and after-school snacks, roasting turkeys and simmering soups. Of Hilda making pots of hearty stew; or baking apple strudel, asking me to test it to make sure it was good enough. Or not of Hilda—of my mother, her slender hands rinsing dishes, handing the small ones to me to dry. Of my father sauntering in like a movie star, a celebrity, spewing boasts and promises. Of a plate shattering against a wall, or someone wailing . . . My mother's voice? Or mine?

Maybe Nick's concerns were justified. Maybe some childhood experience had crippled me emotionally, making me ineligible for intimacy. Maybe I was permanently impaired.

But there was no point worrying about that now; there was work to be done. I opened a cabinet and faced my mother's mixing bowls, rolling pins, a cheese grater, and a kettle. Props of a woman's life, used by others, outlasting her by decades. I don't know how long I stood staring before Susan noticed.

"Those bowls are chipped. I'd toss 'em if I were you." She handed me a fresh trash bag.

I touched a bowl but couldn't manage to throw it out. Somehow, I'd regressed, become childlike, a person with neither the authority nor the capacity to make decisions about any of the items in the room. Susan, however, had no trouble. Chipped saucers, dented utensils, old food—a cyclone of stuff clattered into the sacks.

"Zoe, come on. This is junk. Get rid of it."

"Sorry." I couldn't explain, didn't understand myself. "You're right."

"Okay." She stepped to my side. "What's going on?"

"I don't know. I'd forgotten about all this stuff."

"Oh, great. You're getting sentimental about spatulas and saucepans?"

Damn. Was she going to scold me again? Lecture me on how I should behave, how I should let go of these valueless, material connections to the past? I braced myself, checking my temper.

"Because, if you are," she went on, "it's completely understandable. Especially since you've been out of touch with all this stuff for so long." She put an arm around me, and her tenderness ambushed me. My eyes suddenly flooded; tears spilled down my cheeks.

"Oh, Lord," I said. "Sorry."

"For what?" She gave me a hug. "Look, it's normal to be upset. What we're doing isn't easy. Aside from the fact that you're confronting your past for the first time, we're dealing with major life issues here. Let's face it, it's big-time stuff. Nothing less than life cycles. The actual *M* word."

The *M* word? Mother? Murder? Menopause?

"Mortality," she continued. "We're dealing with passages here. When Tim had to do his mom's place, he curled up on her rocker and bawled like a baby."

I pictured Tim. Paunchy, middle-aged, pipe-smoking Tim, sobbing in a fetal position. Not pretty.

"So," she went on, "is there anything in the kitchen you especially want to save?"

"No, nothing." I wiped off my face.

"Then, look. I have things under control here. I'll save anything questionable. Why don't you go to your dad's room and pack his personal things. Stuff he'll want to have with him."

Good plan. But I didn't move. I watched her throw out a dented colander, a bent and blackened cookie sheet. "What about when it's us?" I asked. "When it's our turn, will our kids have to do this? Can you see Emily and Molly sifting through our stuff?"

She dumped an entire odds-and-ends drawer into a trash bag. "It's not going to be our turn. Our generation's different. We won't age the way people do now. We're healthier, more active—"

"Right." I headed for the stairs. "But, for the record? If you're lucid enough when it's my turn, tell Molly and little junior here to toss it all. In fact, tell them not even to look at it, just burn—"

"Hey. What's this?"

Susan held up the empty drawer. A large manila envelope was taped to the bottom. She peeled it off and held it out to me. I took it, turned it over, examining it. It had no label, no writing. It was just a blank sealed envelope. I stared at it, confused.

Susan rolled her eyes, hovering, unable to contain her curiosity. "Zoe, my God. It's not going to bite you. Just open it."

"Okay. I'm opening it." I slid a cautious finger inside the corner, ripping the paper carefully. Why were my hands shaking? A fleeting image tickled my mind—someone sneaking into the kitchen, hiding something. Was I imagining it? Remembering it? No matter, the image was gone, and the envelope was open. At first glance, it seemed empty. No papers. No writing paper or letter. Puzzled, I turned it over, upside down, and shook it. And, gently, delicately, the contents tumbled out, drifting to the ground like autumn leaves. Five bills—a hundred, two twenties and two fifties—landed softly on the floor.

TWENTY-SIX

"SOMEBODY'S SECRET CHRISTMAS STASH?" SUSAN GUESSED.

"I guess." More likely, somebody's secret gambling stash.

Susan gathered up the cash. "Here."

I looked at it.

"Take it."

I didn't move. "I don't want it."

"Why not?" She looked at me like I was nuts. "Well, what do you want me to do with it?"

I didn't know. It wasn't mine. "Just leave it on the kitchen table." I didn't wait for more questions or more discoveries. Before Susan could speak, I grabbed an almost full trash bag and dashed out through the mudroom door. I wouldn't dwell on hidden money or its meaning. I would take the trash out. Then I would get my father some fresh clothes.

Dogs barked on the other side of the hedges, and I glanced over, saw Lettie in her backyard with two muscled young men in tight black T-shirts and huge protective gloves who worked with a couple of large dogs. Training them, no doubt. Something dangled from a tree branch, and the dogs yammered to get to it but held back as commanded. Lettie walked in my direction, and I looked away, hoping to pass unnoticed, not wanting to make conversation.

My trash bag wasn't heavy, just bulky. I moved along, lugging it down the overgrown, weedy path toward the alley, thinking about the hidden money, besieged by fleeting memories. In one, my parents were dancing in the living room. Maybe the fox-trot. They whirled happily, avoiding the coffee table and the sofa, gliding into the hallway as I watched. But that memory faded away, replaced by a darker one: A woman—or was it a man? sneaking downstairs in the dark. I tried to freeze the image to see it more clearly. But, abruptly, it was gone. I closed my eyes, trying to recreate it, and saw a shadowy form dashing down the basement stairs. Or through the kitchen. Or along the hall. I couldn't recall, couldn't hold on to it long enough to see. Had I watched one of them hide money from the other? Probably. But which one? And what did I care? It didn't matter anymore.

"Morning—" a deep voice rasped. "How're you today?"

I spun around toward the voice. And faced a chest-high mastiff standing inches away, alongside the shed at the edge of the alley. I stepped back, instinctively lifting the trash bag for protection. The dog was huge, slobbering. A beast.

"Stan Addison," the voice declared.

I blinked, assuring myself that the words had not come from the dog. Ridiculous.

"Don't be frightened. Larry's gentle as a rabbit. Sit, Larry."

Larry sat, giving me a view of a skinny fiftyish mustached man with thick oil-slicked hair standing beside my father's toolshed. He wore a white undershirt, several gold chains around his neck, bright-magenta madras shorts. Not an easy sight to miss. I must have been so absorbed in my thoughts that I hadn't seen the two of them walking along the alley. The man walked around his dog, and I saw pale freckled legs, white socks, black-laced shoes. His ensemble was complete.

"I don't mean to intrude." Stan Addison reached a hand out. I had to put down the trash bag to shake it. "But I'm with Town Watch. Part of the patrol team. We keep an eye on what's going on around the neighborhood. We look out for strangers, suspicious activity, the like."

"Nice to meet you." I didn't give my name.

Stan Addison's eyes darted around, looking down the vacant alley, up my father's gnarly walkway. "Not to get in your business, but I saw you and another lady going into the Hayes house." He eyed my trash bag. Did he think we'd been robbing the place?

"I'm Walter Hayes's daughter. I'm here with a friend. No need to worry." I didn't explain further. I opened a trash can and dropped the bag in. Larry's muzzle nudged my rib. The dog weighed at least as much as I did.

Stan's chin lifted, and he gazed down his nose as if sizing me up. "That's good, that Walter has family looking after him. How's he doing?"

"He's coming along, thanks."

'Well, it's tough on all of us. Beatrice getting killed. Especially tough for me—she was my Town Watch partner. Mind you, I don't believe for a second that your father had anything to do with it. Not intentionally. The whole neighborhood feels that way. But everybody's on edge this time. Town Watch Patrol is on red alert."

Red alert? I imagined my father's neighbors scurrying around wearing bike helmets, carrying flashlights and binoculars. "Good." I didn't know what else to say.

Larry nudged my arm, left a trail of foamy saliva. Stan leaned closer, confidentially. "I don't know if Walter's filled you in on the neighborhood. Our problems. The area's changing. Getting more violent."

I had no idea what he was talking about.

"Did he tell you about Gavin?"

"Gavin?"

"The other murder?"

Other murder?

"Back in July, not three months ago. Right over there." He pointed diagonally across the alley.

"What happened?"

"He didn't tell you? Probably didn't want you to worry."

I followed Stan's gaze across the narrow gravel alley, through lush green shrubbery, past the stillness of trees and hot haze. Not even a rustling leaf disturbed the quiet. The neighborhood seemed calm and peaceful, but I'd grown up with Walter Hayes. I knew not to trust appearances.

"Broderick. Gavin Broderick. An accountant. Young guy, twenty-eight years old. Murdered. So were his bulls."

"Bulls?"

"Both of them. His dogs."

Oh. Bulldogs. "Somebody killed his dogs?"

Stan gazed in the direction of the dead man's house. "He found them on the front porch, gutted."

Good Lord. I bit my lip, tasted blood.

"Like freshly killed deer."

Larry nuzzled my rib cage. I put my hand on his head, partly for support.

"My guess is the dogs were his final warning."

Warning? From whom? About what?

"But, even after that, he must not have paid up. Because a few days later, he was dead, garroted."

I closed my eyes, saw Beatrice, her mouthful of betting forms.

Stan shook his head. "So the neighborhood had to get organized. Band together. Unite. This is Town Watch territory. We're in charge around here. Some of us patrol. Others donate equipment like cell phones, flashlights, printed materials, T-shirts and hats, pepper spray, cash. One neighbor breeds guard dogs and she's giving some away free of charge to elderly folks and single women."

Did he mean Lettie? "Lettie Kinkaid?"

"You know Lettie? Sure, of course you do. She lives right here, next to Walter. She's one of the Town Watch founders. An angel, giving those dogs away. Four, so far."

Larry slobbered on my arm. I stroked his head, mostly to push it away.

"You know"—Stan's small eyes narrowed—"about the only one who wouldn't join us was your father. Walter wanted no part of Town Watch, wouldn't even give his ten-dollar donation."

I wasn't surprised. By all accounts, Dad had been cutting himself off from people. Isolating himself. He wouldn't be likely to join a community organization. Then again, in his undershirt, gold chains, white socks and madras shorts, Stan Addison didn't seem to be my father's type. Dad had let himself go of late, but he still had discriminating taste; Dad's refusal might have been a mere fashion statement.

Stan leaned forward, whispering. "Between you and me, my guess is that Walter didn't join because he was into a gang for something."

A gang? "Excuse me; what?"

Again, Stan leaned too close, as if speaking confidentially. His breath smelled sweet and meaty. Liverwurst? "You know. Into some locals. I'm betting he got in over his head."

"Wait. You think my father's involved in—"

"Slow down, ma'am. It's not like your father's an actual gang member. But, see, around here, the gangs control a lot of stuff. Drugs. Loans. Weapons. Protection. Beatrice—I know this for a fact—Beatrice stood up to the gangs. She defied them and wouldn't get on board. She got on the wrong side of the wrong people. Broke their rules. So, it looks to me—and mind you, this is just my opinion; I have no proof. But maybe Walter's done that, too. Made the wrong people mad, I mean."

I shook my head.

"Look what happened to Gavin. He owed them. Word is he got in over his head. Bottom line, Beatrice got killed, same as Gavin. Question is, why? I think she was executed, just like Gavin." Stan studied my reaction. "You follow?"

I followed, but I didn't want to. "Maybe." I couldn't stop thinking of the betting forms stuffed down Beatrice's throat, of my father's history. If a local gang handled loans and drugs, did they also handle illegal gambling? Had my father and Beatrice made bets through these gangs? Lost? Owed more than they could pay? Oh, Lord. Had my father's gambling cost Beatrice her life?

I told myself that Stan didn't know anything for sure; he was just fishing. A nosy neighbor, trying to find out what I knew. I needed to leave, and I turned, starting toward the house, but Larry blocked my path.

"See, if I'm right . . ." Stan went on, casually. "Of course, maybe I'm not . . . But if I am, your father has some serious enemies. If he stands up to them, if he's into them for any sum of money, those people will do anything to get it, or to get even."

For a moment I stood silent, staring into Larry's eyes, absorbing the idea.

"The neighborhood isn't like it used to be," Stan went on. "Forget the genteel intellectual types, the professionals and academics. Undesirables are taking over. They blend in—a lot of them, they look like anybody else. These gang members aren't punks—they have day jobs like the rest of us, dress like the rest of us."

In madras shorts, gold chains and black-laced shoes?

"But see, they're not like the rest of us. They make their own rules. They'd kill you like a roach and then take their kids to a softball game. That's why I joined Town Watch, to keep an eye on what's going on. To get control."

I looked over my shoulder, back to the house, but Larry blocked my view. Stan kept talking, as if he had all day.

"Beatrice and I were partners. I miss her. She was a sweet old gal. I tell you, it's a shame, a terrible thing when a person can't stake their own claims. But this is America. It's a free country. Nobody's going to shut me in; even with Beatrice gone, I sure won't give up. I'll carry on what we started. I'm still here, and I'm not going anywhere."

Indeed, he seemed determined to stay. Stan stood too close to me, talked too intensely. His hair was slicked but untrimmed. He was too thin and his mustache needed trimming. His clothes didn't go together. He reminded me of some of my patients at the Institute, just a little bit off. It occurred to me that Stan might be imagining the gangs and their conspiracies; just because the man had a big dog didn't mean that what he said was true.

"Well, good luck, Mr. Addison."

"Call me Stan."

I smiled, trying to be pleasant. "Nice meeting you." I turned back toward the house.

"You need anything, you call." He held out a card.

I took it, thanked him and, giving Larry a final pat, tried to leave. But Larry sat on the path, unmoving. Stan didn't budge either. He stood still, blocking me in. I was surrounded, hemmed in by my father's shed, a strange man, a leash and a dog. The dog panted in the heat, his mouth dripping. If commanded, he could drop me in a heartbeat.

"You didn't mention your name." Stan waited.

I edged sideways into the weeds, feeling trapped and distrustful. "Oh, I'm Trish." Trish? The lie surprised me even as I said it. "Trish Hayes Wentworth. Pleased to meet you."

And, stumbling over roots and stems, I made my way around Larry, got back onto the path and hurried back to the house. I wasn't sure why I'd lied. Surely Stan, if he talked to Lettie, would find out my real name. How embarrassing. What would they think?

It doesn't matter what they think, I told myself. None of them had anything to do with me. I shoved Stan's card into the pocket of my jeans and kept going. Dogs were barking, and I heard Lettie calling commands, but I didn't turn her way. I held my head down and hurried back to the house. At the end of the path, when I looked back, Larry was still sitting there, and Stan was still watching.

TWENTY-SEVEN

I STOOD IN THE MUDROOM, THINKING ABOUT WHAT STAN HAD said. Gangs? Were local gangs actually taking over the area? Killing people? Had my father gotten involved with them? And who was Stan Addison? Was he a neighborhood crazy or a concerned citizen involved with Town Watch? I had no idea. In fact, I didn't want to know. My father's neighborhood was not my responsibility. Neither was his involvement in clubs or gangs, real or imaginary. His life was not my problem. I was here to clean the place and get him some clothes, nothing else.

In the kitchen, Susan was ferociously rustling plastic bags, clanking glass jars, deeply into clearing out an upper cabinet. She didn't notice me. So, glancing out the window to make sure Larry and Stan were gone, I went upstairs to pack up some clothes.

Of course, it wasn't that easy. At the top of the stairs, I faced the long dim corridor and a thousand shadows of the past sprang out, distracting me. At the far end of the hall, through the doorway to my bathroom, I could make out stark white tiles, a clawed foot under the bathtub, and my mind glimpsed slender, soapy arms reaching a cloth gently toward me through a cloud of scented bubbles. I could almost feel the steam. Keep walking, I told myself. Don't drift into the past. And don't even glance at your bedroom door. But why shouldn't I? What would the harm be? I stood there, forcing myself to look toward my room. See? I assured myself. Nothing was wrong. It was just a doorway down the hall. I started toward it, slowly. Maybe my old four-poster was still in there. Maybe the wallpaper with the birds . . . But out of nowhere, a vision whooshed past me. A wide-eyed, open-mouthed child, running into the bedroom, slamming the door behind her. Covering her ears. Hiding in her closet.

No, I insisted. Do not get swallowed up here. Do what you came to do and no more. Girding myself with a deep breath, I willed my feet to go no farther down the hall. I turned left to face my parents' room, and I opened the door.

The curtains in my father's room were open a crack, enough for a single beam of light to slice the shadows. Dust floated aimlessly there, without hurry. I opened the drapes, agitating the air, and the particles scattered, hiding in the must.

When I looked around, I was tempted to close the curtains again, sealing the place permanently. The room was a shambles of pathways carved among mounds of clutter. It smelled close and stale, held the odor of an unwashed man and unlaundered clothing. I waded through wadded clumps of T-shirts and shoes, extension cords, used cups and empty sacks, hangers, books. Several old televisions sat in random locations, towels hung over one, a lamp stood in front of another. I could trace my father's movements, his regular routes from the hall to the bathroom, the bathroom to the bed, the mattress barely visible under heaps of unfolded, probably unclean, linens and clothes.

How was this room possibly my father's? My father had always been dapper, dashing. Vain. A stickler for neatness and appearances. I pictured him again, his hair sparkling salt-and-pepper, his eyes flashing black, his stature tall and handsome in his dark pinstriped suit, a fresh handkerchief in his pocket. How could that man have lived in this sty? He's failing, I reminded myself. He's not the way he used to be. Just stick to business. This is not the time to get overwhelmed. Do not linger, analyze or reminisce. Do not even wonder. Just find some clean jackets and sweaters, a spare pair of pants, pack them up, and go. Leave the rest for another time. Do not consider how long it's been since the bed was made, let alone since the sheets were changed. Don't look into the mounds of clutter coating the floor.

Determined to be quick and efficient, I went to the dresser and opened a drawer, expecting boxer shorts. The scent hit me first, wafting out and embracing me like a spirit. My mother's scent, dusty but still distinct. The drawer held her lingerie, her potpourri. Her stockings, panties and bras. I blinked with disbelief and slammed the drawer shut, shaken. Why were my mother's clothes still here, decades after her death?

Tentatively, my fingers tried another drawer. This one held her sweaters. Cashmere and lamb's wool. I touched a pink cardigan, its pearl buttons. Did I remember it? Or the black one beside it? The camel cable-knit on the end? No. I didn't. Wouldn't.

My eyes burned. I closed the drawer, unsettled. My mother had been dead for thirty-five years. But her clothes were still here, untouched? I opened another drawer, bracing myself for nightgowns or sundries. But this drawer contained men's socks. Three of them. One black, one brown, one argyle. Other than that, the drawer was empty. Apparently, my father hadn't done laundry in a while. From the look of his room, his socks were well-worn and lying all over the floor.

The drawer beneath that one held a single undershirt. The bottom drawer contained odds and ends. I sifted through suspenders, belts. Handkerchiefs. A couple of old watches. Brand-new lined leather gloves, sunglasses, a rabbit's foot, dice, poker chips, an old wallet. Half of a two-dollar bill. A quarter with heads on both sides. A box containing cuff links and tie clips, a fraternity pin, a class ring. Under the box, a piece of manila paper, frayed at the edges. I unfolded it, saw the big lopsided heart colored with red crayon, the words in awkward, uneven print, all the *e*'s backward. "To Daddy. Be my Valentine. I love you XOXOX, Zoe."

I stared at the card, trying to remember making it, trying to picture the child I'd been. Amazed that my father had kept it all these years. And I looked around, curious. Was there anything else of me here? I stooped down, searching the drawer. Deep in the back of the drawer, behind cans of wax shoe polish, nail clippers and an IOU from a guy whose signature was illegible, I found birthday cards, Father's Day cards. Pictures I'd drawn, a scrawny self-portrait, a family of four. And photos. My mother, pushing a newborn in a pram. A skinny pigtailed girl with knocked knees and the sun in her eyes. A teenager wearing borrowed pearls, posing for her senior portrait. Or standing awkwardly in a formal gown next to tall and gangly Billy Monroe before the prom. My past, the girl I'd been, squinted at me from faded glossy paper.

My belly began to tighten, and I felt woozy. Bertram had shown me some relaxation techniques. Take deep breaths, I reminded myself. Let the tension out of your muscles. Inhaling, I looked around the messy room. How long had I been up there? Somehow, sucked into the room, engulfed by clutter, I'd lost my grasp of time. Put down the pictures, I told myself. Close the drawer. "Get his clothes," I said out loud, reminding myself why I was there.

I scanned the place. My father's usable clothing was lost in the piles around me. I wasn't about to sort it all, comb through his laundry, searching for a wearable shirt or a decent pair of black socks. Better to buy him a new wardrobe. I'd already bought him some basics. I could get him a few more golf shirts, some pajamas, a suit or two, underwear, shoes, a couple pairs of khakis. Socks. It would be worth the money not to have to sort through all this stuff. That's what I'd do. I'd toss all this stuff into Susan's bags and give it to charity. But not today. I drew long, slow breaths as my belly relaxed. Today, I'd done enough.

On my way out, I checked the closet. Maybe Dad had some suits in there. As I opened the door, I was assaulted by the smells of camphor, cedar and dust. I looked inside, but didn't see my father's clothes. On one side were clothes bags full of coats and dresses. Skirts. My mother's shoes sat neatly arranged on racks, as if she'd step into a pair in the morning. I walked into the closet and unzipped a bag, touching the tweed of a suit, the silk of a blouse. I looked at a terry-cloth robe in perfect condition. My mother's clothes waited for her, unaware that time had passed or that she was gone. Someone could use these things, I thought. I took out a black satin sheath, held it up, trying to remember my mother's size. It seemed a little tight at my hips, but not very. If I weren't pregnant, it might fit. I went through her clothes until suddenly, examining a loose flowery purple skirt, I had the sense that I was doing something wrong. It's okay, I told myself. She's dead. She doesn't care about her old clothes.

Even so, I had the feeling that her things weren't mine to dispose of, even to touch. They'd fit her form, still carried her scent. And, if I took her clothing, what of her would be left? What evidence that she'd ever lived? If I got rid of her possessions, in a way wouldn't I be killing her all over again? Maybe that was why my father hadn't discarded them. Maybe I should put everything back the way it was, leave it for now.

I began to replace the items. One by one, I hung each neatly inside the closet, arranging them as they'd been before I found them. When Susan came upstairs, I was about to zip up the last clothes bag.

"Zoe, hey—"

She startled me, and I jumped, pulling my hands behind my back as if I'd been caught pilfering. The sudden movement yanked the bag, dislodging a loose fold of plastic at the top. And a shower of tens and fives slipped out, sprinkling the shoulders and waistbands of my mother's old clothes.

TWENTY-EIGHT

"WHAT? MORE MONEY?" SUSAN HELPED ME GATHER UP ABOUT A hundred dollars. "Your parents didn't believe in banks?"

"It's my mother's closet. She probably just wanted to keep some cash around." Or to keep it from my father. I pictured her slipping bills into the seam of a clothes bag, taping it to the bottom of a drawer, hiding bits of cash here and there.

Susan didn't press the subject. "I guess we should be careful what we throw out. There might be a treasure in the tea bags."

A treasure? An image skittered through my mind. What was it? A box? A safe? I shook my head, not able to grasp it, letting it go.

"Anyway. There are dishes of food and water downstairs," Susan went on. "Does your father have a dog?"

A dog? Vaguely, I remembered seeing dishes filled with dog food the day Beatrice died. Did my father have a dog? I had no idea. "Maybe. If he has dishes, he must."

"So where is it? I haven't seen it, have you?"

No. And, if the food had been there all this time, why hadn't the dog eaten it? We wandered the halls, calling for a doggie, listening for a bark, a pant, a whimper, a growl, hearing nothing. Maybe he was hiding, frightened that my father was gone. Or, I realized with a sudden pang, maybe he hadn't eaten the food because he himself was gone. Who knew? Given the way my father had treated my mother's clothes, the dog could have died years ago.

Still, for a few minutes we wandered the halls and the stairs, looking for a dog that might have been dead for a decade. "Here, pup," "Here, doggie," we called, listening for a bark, a whimper, a growl, a yip, hearing nothing but floating dust.

We gave up, leaving the food and water in case there was an actual dog. In case he returned. Susan went back to work, tackling the refrigerator. I sat at the table watching her, my eyes drifting to the door to the basement. Maybe, it occurred to me, the dog was downstairs, unable to get its food because the door was shut. Oh, God. Maybe it was down there starving. Probably not. But maybe. After all, that's where the doggie door was.

"Man." Susan was wincing, holding up a container full of black fuzz. "Look at this. Label says cottage cheese."

"Looks about ripe." I went to the basement door, opened it. "Help yourself."

She grimaced. "Now I know where you got your culinary skills."

I turned on the light, looking down, my eyes straining in dim shadows. Something didn't smell right. I hadn't noticed such a strong odor a few days earlier, when Molly and I had been down there. Uh-oh.

"Doggie—" I took a step down, then another.

"Zoe? Where are you going? Wait . . . take this." She came after me, arms loaded with flashlights, testing them.

I waited until she found one with working batteries, holding my breath to avoid the smell of death. Halfway down the stairs, flashing the light ahead of me, I stopped.

Susan stood watching from the kitchen doorway. "What's the matter?"

I couldn't talk. I just pointed.

The answer lay at the bottom of the stairs. Emerging from a blanket of old newspapers was a limp rust-colored tail.

TWENTY-NINE

UNDER A WILLOW TREE WE FOUND A GOOD SPOT FOR A GRAVE. Quiet, undisturbed. Best of all, the earth was loose and soft, easy to shovel, and the tree provided some relief for the grave diggers from the hot sun. We began to dig, but as my blade struck earth, memories burst out at me, teasing, flittering too quickly for me to catch. Long-forgotten moments taunted me, dancing just out of reach. Maybe I'd dug in the mud here, playing near the creek as a child. Or maybe I'd planted stuff in the garden? I had no idea, and it was no use trying to recall; the images were gone. Instead of chasing them I thought of my mother, imagined her silhouette gliding through the house, hiding cash, squirreling it away in small bundles designated for school supplies or winter coats, for mortgage payments or dentist appointments, protecting it from the squandering hands of her husband. I wondered how she'd felt. Angry? Afraid? Desperate? What would it have been like, sneaking around, stashing a hundred here, two hundred there? Not trusting her husband at all? I thought of Nick. Of marriage. Of trust. There was a lot I didn't confide in Nick. Was I any different from my mother?

I stabbed the ground with my shovel and began to wedge out a clump of moist soil, wondering if I'd been responsible for the dog's death, if it had starved to death because I'd closed the door and shut it off from its water and food. Guilt ripped through me; I ripped at the earth.

"You know I love you, Zoe." Susan wiped sweat from her forehead, smearing it with dirt. "But I'll tell you what—grave-digging pushes the limit."

"Look. Dealing with my father's house is a grave responsibility."

"I'm serious," Susan grunted. "This is the last time I will ever dig a grave with you, no exceptions."

"That attitude"—I jabbed my shovel into the earth—"is hole-ly uncalled for."

"Ouch." She smirked, hefting another clump of soil. "I'll tell you this, though: Your family seems to have a lot of dirt to dig up."

"Yes. And plenty of mud to sling."

"I can dig it." And she did. Heaps of dirt flew off Susan's shovel. She was a dynamo, a human backhoe. We were working in rhythm, making progress, when suddenly the sweet smell of earth seemed cloying, sickening, and a sharp pang ripped through my gut. I stopped digging and drew a deep breath, waiting for the tightness to ease, wondering if the choke hold gripping my belly could simply be Braxton-Hicks. It was the second one that day. I put the shovel down and sat.

Susan stopped digging. "Zoe? Are you okay?"

I nodded, but I wasn't sure. The contraction was more defined than the earlier one. Not painful, exactly. But it made me feel light-headed. Maybe I should call the doctor. She'd said I should if they got worse. Was this "worse" enough? I hoped not; the threat of bed rest loomed ahead of me like a jail sentence. I'd better take it easy and forgo digging the grave.

"You all right? Maybe you shouldn't be doing this. Bending and lifting probably isn't a good idea."

I sat under the tree, not arguing. The doctor had told me to avoid doing anything strenuous, although she hadn't specifically cautioned against digging a grave.

Susan put down her shovel and knelt beside me. "Seriously. Are you all right? Should I get you some water?"

"I'll just sit a minute."

"Okay. Good. I'll sit, too."

She plopped down beside me, and we sat together under the willow tree beside the pathetic patch of dirt we'd dislodged, listening to the breeze gently rattling the leaves. Nearby, dogs were yapping.

Motors whirred. Life was going on as usual, but here, in the shade, Susan and I had a moment of stillness.

"It's weird, digging a grave." She leaned back on her elbows. "Makes you think about your own death."

Actually, I'd been thinking about early labor. Not to mention the dead dog and my father.

"Tim and I have burial plots at Memorial Park. Right near Tim's parents, beside a pond. We bought them when we buried his father. But tell you the truth, I don't want to use them."

"Why not?"

"I don't want to spend eternity lying in dirt. It gets cold and wet. And claustrophobic."

"You'll be dead, Susan. You won't know."

"Still. I want to be cremated. Scatter my ashes in the wind. Set me free. Tim's against it, though. He wants us to be together for all time." She paused. "What about you?"

Me? "I don't know. I haven't thought about it."

"Really? You ought to. If you wait, you might not have a choice."

"Susan. I'll be dead. I won't care."

"You never know. Think of your kids. You might want a place where the kids can visit you. I don't. I tell them to let me blow away. I'll be in the air."

I pictured Molly and the little stranger standing at a grave with my name. The breeze blew the leaves overhead, a ghostlike rustle. I eyed the hole in the ground, pictured my mother, her bones lying in the earth.

"Do you think there's any kind of afterlife, Susan?"

She blinked at me. "Like heaven and hell?"

"Maybe. Or just some kind of consciousness."

"Oh. Like ghosts?"

"Whatever." I was sorry I'd asked.

"I wish there were. It would be cool to think so. Tim's mother used to swear that her dead husband talked to her. She could hear his voice. We could hear her arguing with him."

I smiled. "So she still nagged her husband after death?"

"Nothing as trivial as death was going to stop her."

Go on, I told myself. Tell her about your dreams. "Sometimes lately, I have dreams about my mother. They're so vivid, it's like she's there with me. I wake up feeling that I've just seen her, as if she's trying to contact me."

"It's your own mind." Susan shook her head, dismissing the thought. "You're a therapist—you know that dreams are just pieces of your own experience, shuffled together. Some unresolved stuff, some random stuff all scrambled together."

She was right. My dreams were not messages from my dead mother. They were just dreams, resulting from my reunion with my father. My mind trying to resolve the past.

We were quiet for a while, two friends lost in thought, watching sunlight pierce through branches. Susan seemed deep in thought. "We need to go shopping," she concluded. "You need maternity clothes."

I supposed I did.

"Meantime, it's getting late. I better finish this hole." She reached for her shovel and stood.

I reached for mine, started to get up, too.

"Zoe, no way. Don't be stupid. Don't even think about doing this. Go inside, have a cold drink and lie down. I can finish this in no time."

I didn't argue. I simply thanked her and got up. Shaky and weak, I headed for the house.

THIRTY

BUT I DIDN'T MAKE IT THERE. AS I NEARED THE MUDROOM DOOR, I heard growling, then angry voices through the hedges. I stopped, listening. Lettie was still out there with her guard dogs. Shouting, "Dammit Craig, don't be a cretin. He's got to learn."

"Sorry, Miss Lettie. He'll do it next—"

"Don't give me sorry. I don't pay you for 'sorry.' He's got to perform, no hesitations, plain and simple."

I couldn't help it. Sweating and short of breath, I took a detour over to the hedges and peered through. Lettie was agitated, scolding one of the men. He was dark-skinned and twice her size, wearing a thick protective glove over one arm. At his feet, a large dog noticed me and lunged toward the bushes, snarling. Lettie's gaze followed.

"Zoe?" Her scowl inverted, became a smile. "Girl, is that you? Don't be shy—come on over. How're you doing?"

She was already at the hedges, grabbing the snarling dog by its collar. "What are you doing out here in the bushes? You know, I've been calling your house, but I get your voice mail. I don't leave messages, though. Don't believe in it. What's the point? To ask you to call me back? Give you one more thing to do when you're already too busy?" I could barely hear her over the growls of the dog. "No, I just wanted to check on you and your daddy, not to add to your problems."

Her face as parched and brown as the desert floor, Lettie studied me. Did she think I'd been spying on her?

I tried to excuse myself. "Lettie, I'm a little dizzy, so I was—"

"You're dizzy? Oh dear." The dog tugged violently at its collar, almost knocking Lettie over. "Craig—," she called. The dog yelped and growled, struggling to get free. "Come, take Walker."

The man rushed over, obeying.

"Take him downstairs. Work him with some bait. He's got to learn."

"He'll be fine, I swear." Craig led the dog away.

"I'm counting on it," she called after them. "We're training Walker, and he just won't attack. You can't have a guard dog that won't attack." Lettie shook her head. "Craig's a good trainer, but he's got to be more consistent. You want to train a dog, you got to be consistent. Now, come on over here and I'll get you a nice cold drink." Her gaze wandered over my shoulder, took in Susan digging under the tree. Lettie looked at me, confused.

"Lettie, did my dad have a dog?"

"You bet. Jackson's an old golden."

Jackson? I heard my father, insisting he had to go home; Jack was waiting for him. Now it made sense.

"Why?"

"I found a dog in the basement. Dead."

"Oh, damn. Jackson died? What a sin—I've been looking for him, meaning to take care of myself, now that your father's not here." Her eyes flitted back to Susan, rested there. "So that woman over there, she's digging his grave?"

I nodded, felt faint. "My friend. She's helping me."

"Well, no wonder you're feeling dizzy. Come on, girl. It's hot as hell out here. Let me get you a lemonade. And your friend, too." Lettie pushed the bushes apart, clearing a way for me to cross onto her property. "Poor old Jackson. Does your daddy know? He'll be devastated, you know. He loved that old dog."

Lettie took me by the arm into her kitchen, an expansive space painted yellow, full of eclectic flea-market furnishings, folk art and shelves of mismatched glassware, china, stoneware and teacups. A herd of a half-dozen puppies greeted us, swarming our ankles, yipping for attention. I knelt to pet them.

"No, don't do that, girlfriend." Lettie stopped me with a weathered hand. "See, these aren't house pets. These pups are bred special. They're pros. Working guard dogs. So you don't want to be too friendly to them; we don't want them to accept strangers."

"Even as puppies?" They were fluffy and playful, impossible to resist.

"Right from birth. They have to learn loyalty to just one master. "Hey—Jimmy? Hardy?" Her shout was jagged, grating. "Somebody, come get these fur balls out of here."

A freckled wirehaired man rushed into the kitchen, began herding the little dogs. Several escaped his notice, darting back into the kitchen. Lettie didn't seem to mind. She took a frosty pitcher of lemonade from the refrigerator and poured some into a purple plastic glass, set some pecan cookies onto a daisy-patterned platter. We sat on unmatched cushioned chairs at her big round wooden table, drank cool soothing lemonade and munched sweets while puppies scurried around the room, looking for mischief or affection, and feeling steadier, I struggled not to pet them.

"So, old Jackson's dead." Lettie shook her head. "But that says it all. You can see why I called you." Her voice scraped raw, like an emery board. "Walter's not right. Imagine. He left without tending to his dog."

"But you said Jackson was old. Maybe he died of old age." Why was I defending my father?

"Zoe, you and I don't have a lot of history yet, but as you get to know me, you'll find out I say what I think, straight out. And I'm telling you your father's just not all there anymore. Look, he doesn't even wash. His place is going to hell. He let Jackson die. And he cut off all his friends, especially poor dear Beatrice."

I knew about "poor Beatrice." I'd seen him cut her myself. Ouch. Surely, Lettie hadn't intended the pun. "So Beatrice and my father were . . . close?" The lemonade helped, but I was still sweating.

"Close?" Lettie brayed, her smile etching cracks into her parched cheeks. "You might say. Beatrice lives—well, she lived—across the alley." Lettie pointed at the wall facing the rear of the property. "Diagonal from here, right behind my place—our back-yards link up across the alley. She's been with your dad for, I don't know how long. A couple years."

"With him? So they were a couple?" I had no idea what my father's life was like. Or who'd been in it.

"A couple?" Lettie shook her head, cackling. "Lord. Nothing that formal. Beatrice was—what do you call it—Walter's squeeze?" I pictured Beatrice, her blood-soaked perm, lying dead on my father's kitchen floor. "They were on and off for years. Until, I don't know, maybe a month ago."

"They broke up?"

"No, not exactly." Lettie picked up a puppy. Her hands were rough and gnarly, nails short, polished iridescent pink. A bracelet dangled on her wrist, rhinestone dog charms of various sizes and breeds. "One day, Walter just dumped her. Poof, just like that, Beatrice was out. Yesterday's laundry. He tossed her off and had nothing more to do with her."

My mother floated to mind, crying as she was folding laundry.

"Now Beatrice, she was no angel. She got into some messes, from what I heard. Did things she shouldn't have. But without Walter, she fell apart. She was a mess." Lettie fingered her necklace. The golden head of a dog hanging from a chain. "But I guess she couldn't stay away from him. Look how she ended up. Look what he did. I told you he's not right—"

"He didn't kill her, Lettie," I began. "He was trying to save—"

"It's a tragedy." Lettie shook her head. "Walter isn't himself anymore. It's like he's gone. And Beatrice is gone, too. And now, so is old Jackson." She sighed. "My, all of this must be hard on you, walking into the middle of it. Have another cookie, girl. You're skinny; you can afford it." She thrust the plate at me. "So now that Walter's moved out, what'll you do—sell the place?"

Would I? I had no idea. "I'm not sure."

"Of course you're not. It's too soon. Well." She finished her lemonade and set the glass on the table. "When you're ready, talk to me before you put it on the market. I'm thinking of expanding my property, putting up kennels and dog runs. So I might make an offer on the place, save you the trouble. Make us both happy; that's what friends do, isn't it?" Her smile formed deep crevasses in both cheeks.

A muscle-bound man in a black T-shirt knocked at the back door. "Yo, Miss Lettie. You said to get you. They're ready."

"Okay, Hardy." Lettie sighed and squeezed my arm. "Well, girl, if you're feeling all right, I got to get back to work. Are you okay?"

"Much better, thanks." I stood to leave, but couldn't get out the door. Hardy was still standing there, as if waiting for a command. Somewhere close, dogs howled nonstop. The sound was grating but constant around the neighborhood; it had begun to blend into the background like the sounds of traffic or ocean surf.

"Oh, goodness, I haven't introduced you. This is Hardy, one of my boarders. Hardy, meet Zoe, Walter Hayes's daughter." As she chatted, Lettie's eyes locked with his, silently instructing him to step aside. "Craig, Jimmy and Hardy. They live here, help me out with the dogs. Believe me, I need the help, too. We've got Rottweilers. Bull mixes. These days, people are looking for protection, so business is booming." She opened the door; Hardy dodged out of her way. He was huge, bigger than Craig, towering over Lettie. His arms were purple murals of flowing tattoos. "Wait. Don't' forget the lemonade for your friend. And take Hardy. Hardy, go dig a grave for my friend Zoe, hear?"

Wordlessly, carrying a mug of icy lemonade, Hardy hulked after me to my father's property, crossing the hilly tree-covered yard to the willow tree. Susan wiped sweat off her forehead, grateful for the drink, and she gladly surrendered her shovel to Hardy. In no time, he'd finished a perfect rectangle, a yard long and at least as deep.

"Okay, miss?" Sweat dripped down his torso. His voice was polite. Soft.

"Perfect," I said, as Susan said, "Wonderful. Thank you."

Then, returning the shovel, Hardy nodded good-bye and left us alone under the tree beside the fresh empty grave.

THIRTY-ONE

"PURE SOLID U.S. GRADE-A BEEF," SUSAN WHISPERED. WE headed to the house to retrieve Jackson's body.

"Whoa, Susan. He doesn't actually speak. He grunts."

"Please. A man built like that does not need to speak. Better if he doesn't. Did you see his shoulders?"

"Did you see those bizarre tattoos?" He'd taken off his T-shirt as he dug, revealing raptors, snakes, skulls, flowers and naked women, all intertwined.

"Body art is cool now." We entered the mudroom. "Besides, the man has biceps wider than my thighs. No wonder the neighbor lady keeps him around."

We crossed the kitchen to the basement door. "So"—Susan sounded thoughtful—"do you think his job has benefits?"

Wow. What? Withered Lettie and buffed Hardy? Was she kidding? Susan hadn't met Lettie yet, so she couldn't share the image. I grabbed the flashlight and started down the steps, but Susan wouldn't drop the subject.

"He seems too obedient, too passive. I swear; it's not normal. There's something kinky going on. I just sense it. Wait . . . Think your dad's neighbor is a dominatrix?"

Oh, Lord. I pictured Lettie in black leather, cracking a whip. "Not likely."

"I bet I'm right. But never mind. She was nice, lending him to us. I was about to die out there."

"Sorry. I shouldn't have let you dig."

I continued down the steps, letting my eyes adjust to the dim light. The basement's clammy air chilled my sweat-dampened skin, and the smell of decay churned my stomach. But Susan was still fixated on Hardy's body parts.

"Seriously, did you watch his muscles ripple while he worked?"

"Susan, stop. Enough." Of course I'd watched his muscles. But I'd also watched the hole grow deep and wide, and I'd thought about the pet that would lie in it. I wondered if it had been my fault it died, trapped and hungry in the basement, and I worried how my father would react to its death. I hadn't known the dog, but I knew that it deserved better than to lie forgotten, rotting in the basement.

"Okay." Susan peered down the steps. "Where's the body?"

"Here." Ignoring shadows and the stink of death, I led her to the corpse, stopping beside the exposed tail. Again, I felt a tightening around my middle, and, closed in by dank air and hovering memories, I swayed, struggling to steady myself. That was the third contraction this afternoon; I'd have to call the doctor.

"Looks like the poor thing burrowed under those papers." She stared at the tail. "Well, here goes. Brace yourself for maggots." Susan stooped and, holding her breath, lifted the newspapers that covered Jackson's body. For a moment, neither of us moved. Then, as if in slow motion, I turned away, grabbing my stomach, and Susan recoiled, grimacing.

It wasn't maggots. It wasn't rot or decay. What stunned us was the ravaged meat and exposed bone where the golden retriever's eye had been. And the jagged hole ripped out of its throat.

THIRTY-TWO

I COULDN'T STAND UP. I PLOPPED DOWN RIGHT THERE ON THE steps, not necessarily by choice. My body insisted.

Susan recovered almost immediately, her forensic skills emerging. She knelt beside the body, examining the dog as if he'd been a murder victim in one of her cases.

"This dog was attacked by another animal."

Our eyes met. Were we both thinking of Lettie? Of the dogs next door? I recalled the way one had snarled at me, rabidly baring its teeth. "You think Jackson wandered onto Lettie's property? You think her guard dogs attacked him? You know, defending their property?"

Susan stood, shaking her head. "I don't know." She stared at the retriever, the place where his face should have been. She folded her arms, adopting an authoritative pose. "But the animal that did this is vicious. A real menace."

"So what do we do? Call the police? The SPCA?"

Susan frowned. "What would the cops do? Nobody can prove which animal did it."

"So it's just a coincidence that the woman next door trains her dogs to attack intruders?"

"I don't know. Maybe. But we can't be sure." Susan ran a grimy hand through sweat-dampened hair. "It's been a long day, Zoe."

"But we can't just leave him here."

Susan stared at the corpse. "Right."

We were both spent, silent. Finally Susan sighed. "I say we bury him and go home. There's no way to prove what happened."

And so, carefully, gently, we wrapped what was left of the dog's battered and decomposing body in a plastic trash bag, and Susan carried it up the stairs. I followed her through the weeds where she deposited it in the grave. She wouldn't let me help, insisting that I take it easy, and she began shoveling the piles of earth over the body. I watched, exhausted, grateful, wondering how I'd manage life without Susan. As she worked, I told her about Stan Addison and what he'd told me. About Gavin Broderick, and how his dogs had been killed days before his murder.

"That's scary." She grunted as she dug. "Think this is connected?"

I didn't know.

She wiped sweat off her forehead. "Pretty big coincidence, though. Dogs dying, people being killed." She looked around, as if expecting an ambush.

She was right, and suddenly I wanted to get out of there.

"Let's get this done and go, okay?"

Susan patted the ground, finished. Replacing the soil had taken much less time than digging it. "Want to say some words?"

Oh. Yes, of course. Somebody should say something. And I was the only one here who was in any way related to the deceased. But what was appropriate to say over a dead pet I hadn't even known? A dog who'd died terribly in a vicious, unspeakable attack.

Oh, God, what had happened to Jackson? I pictured hungry rats teeming, gnawing, ripping his skin and closed my eyes, chasing them away. Then, when Susan had finished the burying, I got up and stood by the grave.

"You were a fine dog, Jackson. You didn't deserve to suffer. Rest in peace." It didn't seem at all sufficient, but then, what would.

"Amen."

And with that, we headed back to the house, leaving the dog to his Master.

THIRTY-THREE

"How did it go at Walter's?" Nick stepped out of the shower into the bedroom. "Did you get much done?"

I'd taken a bath, soaking away the day's dirt and dust, trying to scrub away the whole experience. Lying down, I watched him towel off, focusing on his abs, his chest, his need for a haircut. Anything but the events of the day.

"It was overwhelming. There's so much to do there."

He lay down beside me, propped up on an elbow, resting a hand gently on my belly. His skin gleamed, clean and moist, and his shoulders towered over me, a protective wall. He smelled like soap. It seemed like forever since we'd spent time alone together. I had so much to tell him. About my father's dog. About Stan Addison, the other murder with the gutted dogs, the gangs. And, oh, yes. About my contractions. I'd called the doctor and made an earlier appointment, but Nick still didn't know. How had so much happened in just a few short days? How had we fallen so out of touch? I rested against Nick, my muscles gradually losing their tension. Secure in his arms, I was about to tell him everything, deciding where to start. But Nick spoke first.

"Zoe. I'm still going to be working late a lot for a while. Picking up as much overtime as I can."

He paused, his eyes studying the wall, then the floor. Darting. What was going on? Was he hiding something?

"And I've been thinking. I don't want you to work on Walter's house anymore. At least not by yourself."

What? "Why not?"

"Well, first of all, there's way too much for you to do."

"I'm not doing it alone—"

"But it isn't fair to ask so much of Susan—you can't expect her to clean out that whole place herself. And in your condition . . . frankly, it's too much for you."

Frankly, I didn't like him telling me what was too much for me.

"Besides, there are firms that do that. They go in, sort through, itemize and evaluate properties. They pack up what you want to keep, sell or give away what you decide to get rid of. They clean the place, too. I've already got the name of a reliable guy. He's bonded and everything. I talked to him, and he can start with a week's notice—"

What? "Wait. You already talked to him? Without talking to me first?"

"No, I was going to talk to you."

"But you didn't. You just went ahead—"

"Zoe, settle down. I didn't commit to anything. I haven't had a chance to talk to you. We haven't been in the same room long enough to exchange spit in the last few days. Anyhow, Greg Wyatt gave me this guy's number—"

"Greg Wyatt?" Greg Wyatt was one of the detectives Nick worked with. I'd met him a few times, but doubted if he'd recognize me; whenever we'd met, his eyes had remained firmly planted on my chest. "You discussed my business with Greg Wyatt?"

"I didn't discuss anything. I got a phone number. Look, Zoe. We need some help here."

He was right. The house was too much for me. But he should have asked me, not decided on his own.

"Look. We're in the middle of a high-risk pregnancy. You heard Dr. Martin. You should avoid stress and strain. Plus, you have a lot of demands on you: Your father. Molly. Your job."

No, my half job.

"You're already doing too much. That house puts you over the top. It's too much physical work."

"But it's still my responsibility." I sat up; my voice colder than I intended. I appreciated Nick's intentions, but I was upset. Did he think I had lost the authority to make my own decisions?

"Chill, Zoe." Nick sat up to face me. "I'm just trying to make things easy for you."

I knew that. "Thank you. I know that. But the thing is, I didn't ask you to."

He exhaled. "Look, I don't want to fight. I want to help. I just think you should take it easy until the baby comes."

"So what am I supposed to do? Lie around and eat bonbons?" Stop, I told myself. He's trying to help.

"If you want to, yes. Pamper yourself. Relax. Fix up the nursery. Knit booties. See a masseuse. Swim. Do anything stress-free. In fact, I wish you'd take a leave from work."

"Are you serious?" Suddenly I was on my feet, explaining in clear language that I was pregnant, not brain-dead. That I was capable of deciding what I could or couldn't do, what help I needed or didn't need. If I felt my piddling half a job and its responsibilities were too much, I'd say so. But I told Nick that I didn't want him to assume authority over my life or career or anything else of mine just because I was pregnant. My voice became louder and faster as I spoke. I vented, disturbed at my own temper.

When I stopped, Nick was still seated on the bed, completely relaxed. Unfazed. "Okay, Zoe. Okay. I get it. I hear you. You're right." His voice was patient, understanding. Infuriating.

"Damn it, Nick." How dare he agree with me? "Stop agreeing with me."

"Come here, Zoe." He was calm, oddly unaffected by my explosion. He stood, reaching for me.

I stood, still fuming, aware that I was overreacting, unable to stop. And how dare he look at me so tenderly, much less offer me a hug?

"I didn't mean to upset you."

"I know." His arms swaddled me.

"I love you. I know that you're stressed out. The wedding. Your father. His house. Molly. Me. Your job. The pregnancy."

The warmth of his body spread through me, comforting me. How could I have been so mad just a minute ago?

"And I know that you can't help it. Being pregnant, your moods are going to be erratic, but—"

Being pregnant, what? My moods were what?

"—believe me. I know what I'm saying. Walter's house is . . . well, it's just too much." He released me, put his hands on my shoulders. "I'm not trying to interfere with your independence. I'm not trying to control you. I'm merely trying to look after you and our baby. Maybe I'm clumsy about it, but that's my intent."

His eyes glowed blue, grabbing mine. I shrugged, acknowledging that I understood, calmed by his touch.

"So, promise me that you won't go work on Walter's house by yourself." His eyes held mine until, hesitantly, I nodded, giving in.

"You promise?" His eyes clung.

"Fine. I promise."

His arms enclosed me again, and I returned the embrace. When Nick let go and began to get dressed, I walked out of the room, still disturbed that Nick dismissed my moods and thoughts . . . just because I was pregnant? I knew he felt protective, but still, I was insulted. And I was afraid that if he knew about the contractions, he'd never let me out of the house. For the time being, I kept the contractions to myself, along with what had happened with Jackson and Stan Addison. And, most of all, that I thought his idea was great. The fact was, I'd be grateful as hell to have some help with my father's house.

THIRTY-FOUR

I BROKE MY PROMISE JUST HOURS LATER. MAYBE NOT PHYSICALLY, but mentally. In a dream, I spent the better part of the night wandering the halls of my father's house, once again opening closets and cabinets, riffling through crates in the basement. In a slow silent panic, I searched the shadowed attic, the abandoned bedrooms. My baby was there, somewhere, and I had to find him. My legs floated along dim stairways to layers of the house I'd never seen before. Long corridors with hidden rooms full of secrets. A kitchen overstocked with the leftovers of dinner parties; a full bar, glowing with dark blue light, surrounded by shadows and low, curving velvet divans. Each room tickled memories, threatening to distract me, but I kept moving, searching with agonizing slowness, finally finding a bunkerlike nursery filled with cradles; surely, my baby would be in one of them. I approached a crib and, thank God—there he was, wrapped in a blanket. I lifted him, relieved and full of joy, and gently lowered the blanket to kiss his face. But as I moved it, blood spurted onto my face, gushed onto my breasts, and I looked down at the baby in my arms to see not my child, but Jackson, my father's dog, his dead face ravaged and torn.

I woke Nick up with my thrashing. And he held me, talking softly into my ear about how safe I was, how everything was all right. How I should let my body drift back to sleep. He said all the reassuring things sleepy people say to someone who's just had a nightmare, and he kept trying to soothe me until, finally, he dozed off in the middle of a comforting phrase.

I lay still in his arms, not wanting to wake him. Nick was

breathing on my neck, and his arms became dead weight, pressing into my ribs. I ached to roll over, but I lay there, uncomfortable, marveling at Nick's ability to let go and sleep. How was it possible that we could lie together in the same bed, bodies tangled, and yet be in such different places? He was completely at ease, I was completely on edge. But then he hadn't entered those hidden rooms, hadn't been enchanted by their familiarity, their secrets. He hadn't had the shock of seeing a dead dog where our baby should have been, hadn't felt the warmth of its blood on his skin, and, surely, he didn't have the taste of its blood lingering in his mouth.

No, Nick and I were in different places. It was largely my fault. I had kept too many secrets. I hadn't wanted to talk, had kept my days, my experiences to myself. Why wasn't I letting Nick in? Why was I constantly bickering with him? Was it what Susan had said, that pregnant women always got irritated by their mates? Was I simply at the mercy of hormonal bouts of mood swings? Or was it something deeper? And why, lately, was Nick gone so much, finding reasons to work late? Was it really to earn the overtime? Or was he avoiding me? Hiding something? My mind kept spinning until, finally, Nick rolled over, releasing me. Exhausted, finally able to move without disturbing him, I slid away but extended an arm. Drifting off, I kept my hand against Nick's back. If I didn't, he might soon be out of reach.

THIRTY-FIVE

SUNDAY MORNING I AWOKE WITH TIGHTNESS IN MY BELLY EXpanding, sending waves up along my spine. I took deep breaths, worried, wondering how I'd get through the day, calling the doctor again, making an appointment for the next day. As soon as I hung up, the phone rang again.

"I've been thinking." Susan didn't bother to say "Hello." "Something bothers me about your dad's dog."

I made myself exhale before speaking. "What about him?" Besides the fact that his face had been missing.

"I keep wondering what attacked him. And how? Did he get killed in the house? And if so, how did the creature get in? Where is it now? Still in the house?"

I held my belly, closing my eyes, wishing I hadn't answered the phone. No. The creature wasn't, couldn't be in the house. "No, there's a doggie door downstairs. Animals can come and go that way." After all, I had many times. And, on one occasion, so had Molly.

"Oh." Susan was thinking fast. "So Jackson must have been attacked outside and crawled back home to die. That fits."

"Unless," I suggested, "the creature came in and left through that same door."

She dismissed the idea. "No. It wouldn't come inside. Not its territory."

She seemed certain. I lay back, resting. The contraction had finally completely passed.

"Okay, Zoe. I'm going say something but you're not going to like it. Ready?"

I waited.

"I think it might have been deliberate."

What?

"Think about it. You told me your father gambles, right? And you told me about his neighbor—what was his name? That guy who got killed?"

"Gavin Broderick."

"And you said his dogs got killed first. As a warning, because he owed a gang money."

Right. I'd told Susan what Stan Addison had said. Two dogs had been torn apart, and their owner had been killed, probably by a gang, probably because of unpaid debts.

"Think about it. It can't be a coincidence. Your father's dog was killed viciously, just like the neighbor's dogs. A guy was murdered after his dogs. Beatrice was murdered, probably soon after your father's dog."

I fidgeted, not liking where she was going.

"So, I'm guessing your father and Gavin might have owed the same people."

The idea was appalling. Unacceptable. Completely logical.

"So what exactly are you saying?"

"I don't know. Maybe your father placed bets with the gang. Maybe he lost and couldn't pay up, so they killed his dog to scare him. And maybe he still wouldn't pay, so they killed Beatrice as a final warning."

I didn't say anything. Stan Addison's voice echoed in my head, telling me that Susan could be right. After all, Gavin Broderick had apparently been killed for not paying the gang what he owed. I rubbed my temples, wishing that my head would stop pounding.

"Look—you're the one who said your father has a gambling problem—"

"My father would not deal with a gang." Why had I said that? How did I know what my father would or would not deal with?

"But you said yourself that he's addicted to gambling. You said he'd gambled everything he owned and lost it all. Isn't it possible that in his old age he might not be real particular about the people he places bets with?"

"He wouldn't deal with people like that." I pictured Beatrice's death grimace, her bulging eyes. Why was I resisting Susan? Hadn't I already had the same ideas myself?

"Because . . . ?"

"Because they're unspeakable. Because they torture animals and kill people. Because . . . you saw Jackson. Do you really think my father could be part of that?" And, by the way, did I?

Susan didn't answer. Molly galloped into the room, hopping onto the bed.

"Get off the phone, Mom."

"Hi, Molls." I collected myself, kissed her.

Molly tugged at my legs. "Get up. Nick's making waffles."

I nodded. "Susan . . . I got to go."

"Zoe, don't be so defensive. Look . . . I shouldn't have told you what I think. Clearly, you can't be objective about this."

"Of course I can." I held no illusions about my father's character. Molly kept pulling at me, repeating that breakfast was almost ready. "Give me a break," I told her.

"What?" Susan was confused.

"Mom, you've been talking for hours."

"One minute, Molls."

"Okay. One. I'm counting to sixty. One Mississippi. Two Mississippi." She darted out of the room. "But we won't save you any. First come, first served. Three Mississippi . . ."

My stomach rumbled; the baby wanted food. But Susan wasn't finished yet.

"All I'm saying," she went on, "is that we can't ignore the facts. Are you saying all these deaths are just coincidence? That they have nothing to do with each other?"

"Susan." I tried to hide my misgivings. "My father would not deal with violent street gangs. Gangsters, yes. Gangs, no way."

"Even with good odds?"

"Not funny."

She waited.

"No matter what the odds were. He wouldn't." The idea was too vile. Still, I'd wrestled with it for days.

"Fine, Zoe. I hope you're right. But I'm going to ask Ed to look into it, to see if he can find out what's going on." Ed was one of Susan's detective friends, her closest link to the police grapevine.

We were silent, breathing into the phone for a long uncomfortable moment, stewing the way we do when we disagree. Then, promising to talk later, we hung up. My stomach rumbled, demanding food. But I didn't rush downstairs for breakfast. I sat for a while thinking about dead dogs, violence, street gangs, my father's questionable ethics. And the possibility that, once again, his incorrigible gambling had cost lives.

THIRTY-SIX

SUNDAY AFTERNOON MOLLY WENT TO A BIRTHDAY PARTY FOR HER friend Serena, but I didn't stay to visit with the other moms. Instead I went to see my father. Nick insisted on coming along. I didn't argue, even though I wanted to see my father alone. I had serious questions for him. But Nick was trying to be supportive, and I appreciated his attention, if not his energy. He was all good cheer, talking about names again. Paige. Brooke. Kendall. Naomi. He went on, listing names for boys. Everything he said chafed my nerves. My mind wasn't on baby names; it was on my father and his old habits. So, by the time we got to Harrington Place, I was relieved to get out of the car.

We found my father in the lounge. He looked like a different man from the one who'd moved in days earlier. His silver hair was cut and groomed, his face clean-shaven. He wore a polo shirt and khaki pants—casual but sleek. And clean. He was still too thin, but his dark eyes beamed good humor and energy. When he grinned, his teeth sparkled like a movie star's. Oh, God. My pulse skipped a warning. My father was himself again.

Nick greeted him warmly, and the two of them stood smiling at each other, shaking hands, doing their male ritual.

"Good to see you. It's Nick, right? The cop?" He remembered Nick's name and job? Dad turned to me, held his arms out for a hug. My God. Who was this guy? And what had he done with the emaciated, disoriented old crank I'd fought with in his kitchen?

"Come in, come in. I'm glad you're here." He led us to his suite.

"Have a seat." He gestured, showing the space. "Not bad for an elder hostel, is it? I'm having quite a time here."

An elder hostel? "Dad, it's not a hostel. It's a retirement community."

"Fancy name. Same game. So what have you brought me?"

I handed him the box of crunchy nut toffee I'd been carrying. "I haven't been shopping yet. I'll bring you more clothes this week."

"No need. I'm fine. They have a laundry service here, and I don't need much."

"I'll bring it anyhow."

I sat on the sofa, Nick beside me, facing my dad in his easy chair.

"So, Walter. How is it here? You finding your way around?"

"Nice enough. They have a pool, a gym, a decent library, a barber. Even a gift shop. They show films. There's a lot to do. People are friendly. It's okay. Thanks. Thanks a lot. You must have spent a bundle for my spot."

"Not really, Dad . . . your insurance—"

"Don't worry about it." Nick interrupted. I blinked at him. Nick and my dad went on talking, deep in conversation. How had it happened that I was the outsider in this threesome?

I leaned back, pouting. Annoyed. Until I realized that they were talking about Beatrice.

"It was those damned gangbangers. Those slime," my father said. "They killed her."

"Who exactly? Can you give me names?"

"Names? Could be any one of them. Or the whole bunch."

I looked at Nick. But he nodded as if my father's answer made sense, even wrote a note on a pad of paper. "Anybody specific?"

"How should I know their names? They're everywhere, taking over the whole neighborhood. I told Beatrice. I warned her to keep her distance, and certainly not to cross them. But she didn't listen. She went ahead. Lord knows what she was thinking, and now she's dead. Tell you what, though. No matter what they do, nobody's going to drive me out of my house, no way. In fact . . . oh, say—that reminds me—can you give me a ride?" He started to get up, as if to leave. "I got to go back there and look after Jack."

Oh, God. He still didn't know about his dog.

"Don't worry, Dad. I found him."

"You don't say. Where was he?"

"In the basement." I hoped we could leave it at that. But he went on.

"In the basement?" He seemed bewildered.

"Jack," Nick repeated. He had no clue. "Who is Jack?"

Damn. How had it happened that I still hadn't told Nick?

Nick looked from me to my father, blank, waiting for an answer.

"Jackson," I began, but I couldn't deal with Nick's questions and my father's at the same time. Nick would have to wait. I took a deep breath and made my voice as gentle as possible. "I'm sorry, Dad. I got to tell you. Jack's dead."

"Dead? What are you talking about?" My father looked aghast. He stood, turned in a circle, sat back down. "He's dead? But I left him plenty of food. What happened?"

"Jackson's a pet?" Nick was catching on.

"His dog."

"Tell me," my father insisted.

I hesitated, trying to soften the facts. But then I thought about what Susan had said, that my father's gambling might have led to Jackson's, even to Beatrice's, death. In that case, I couldn't sugar-coat the truth. "He was torn apart, Dad. Attacked. His face was pretty much gone."

"His face was gone?" Nick asked, but my father talked at the same time.

"Damn them. Goddamn bastards." My father's hands covered his face.

"What happened, Dad?"

"Zoe, why didn't you tell me about this?" Nick's face had darkened. His eyes beamed trouble.

"Hell if I know." My father looked bereft. "I haven't seen him in a few days. I called him, but nothing. I thought he ran away. But it was those damned gangsters. Damn them to hell."

"Dad? Are you gambling again?"

He looked up suddenly, stunned. "What? Who said so?"

"Answer me. Are you placing bets with a gang, Dad? Do you owe them money? Is that why they killed your dog?"

"What?"

"Answer me, Dad."

"How can you even ask me that?"

"Zoe, what are you talking about?" Nick tried to break in.

"Tell me." I watched my father, wouldn't back down.

"No. I already told you." My father shook his head. "I haven't got a thing to do with any of this mess. Beatrice did whatever she did on her own. I'm damned if I know anything about any of it."

"Don't you?" I wasn't giving up; I knew how easily he lied. "How about the money, then? Why is money hidden all over the house?"

He blinked at me, the face of innocence. "Money?" His face was completely convincing. He hadn't lost his touch.

"I was over there, cleaning, and I found wads of cash. Hidden all over the place. Gambling stashes?"

"I don't know what you're talking about."

"Zoe, enough—" Nick tried to break in. "The man just found out his dog is dead. Lay off."

But it was no use; I couldn't stop myself.

"Dad, don't bullshit me. I think you're gambling again, and I think that's why you have money stashed everywhere. And you know what else? I think Jackson and Beatrice both got killed because of your gambling—"

"Now, just a minute." He raised his voice, pointed a finger. "What the hell were you doing in my house?"

"I was cleaning—"

"I don't remember saying I wanted you to clean my house."

"Well, somebody has to—"

"Listen here. Nobody's allowed in my house without my permission. Trespassing is illegal. You're all alike. Sneaking around, taking liberties, trying to drive me out—"

"Walter. Zoe. Settle down, both of you." Nick tried to take control.

We both ignored him. "Tell me about the money, Dad."

"What money?" Nick was still trying to follow us.

"The money," Dad repeated. He seemed puzzled. "The money's none of your business. I'm an American, aren't I? I can keep money anyplace on my own property that I want, can't I? Since when do I have to explain what I do with my money to you? Or anybody else?" Dad was angry now, fists clenched, half-standing.

"Just once, Dad, tell me the truth. Just once." I stared into his eyes. "Are you gambling?"

He glared directly back at me. "For the thousandth time: I don't gamble anymore. I'm a respectable man. Give me some peace, will you? Just trust me, Louise, and let it be."

Louise again.

Nick closed his hand around my arm. "Zoe, lighten up." His voice was low. A growl.

"No, I will not lighten up. And, dammit, Dad, I'm not Louise. I'm Zoe."

My father sat back, dejected. "Poor old Jackson," he sighed. "Dead."

"What exactly happened to his dog?" Nick still wasn't entirely sure.

"I found him in the basement."

"You didn't tell me." He seemed amazed.

"I know. I meant to. I just never got around to—"

"You said he was torn up?"

"His face and throat . . . his ear. He was mangled. A mess. Susan and I buried him."

Nick gaped at me in somber disbelief. "You and I have to talk."

THIRTY-SEVEN

WE DID HAVE TO TALK, BUT WE COULDN'T, NOT THERE, NOT then. Instead, Nick changed the subject, distracting my father from his loss, being deliberately cheerful and sociable, protecting my father from me. I couldn't sit there, listening while Nick fell prey to my father's manipulative charm, as if no murders or mangling whatsoever had occurred. My pulse was racing, and I was fed up with them both. I needed to breathe, so I got up and stormed out of the suite, almost knocking over my father's roommate, who'd been leaning against the door.

"Leonard?"

"I live here." He pretended that he hadn't been eavesdropping. "You're the daughter."

I nodded. His eyes shifted, and he adjusted the waist of his pants. "Are you all right, Leonard?"

"Sure, fine." He gazed down the hall. "So. Your father's going home soon?"

"No. He lives here now."

Leonard looked disappointed. "Because he says he's going home."

Of course he did. "No. He must have misunderstood."

"Well then, I guess it's going to be party party, all the time, day or night."

"Sorry?"

"Walter likes to entertain."

No surprise.

"And I mean all night. I can't get any sleep, living in the same apartment. Three o'clock in the morning, people are talking out loud, drinking . . . playing cards."

Playing cards? "I'll talk to him, Leonard." Especially about the cards.

"No. Don't. I don't want trouble. Besides, I shouldn't let it get to me. I'm not staying here much longer. When my son gets back, I'll be moving in with him." He reached into his pocket.

Oh, no, I thought. He's going for the itinerary again.

"Today, let's see, he's in Kenya. Next, he's going to South Africa."

Wait, weren't those the same places he went last week? "That's okay, Leonard. Let me speak with my father. I'm sorry he's bothering you."

"I don't want any trouble," he repeated, but I didn't hear the rest. I'd gone back into the room, where Nick and my father were chortling, deep in conversation, sharing stories like a pair of old drinking buddies.

I couldn't stand it. Avoiding them, I headed into my father's bedroom to check out his clothing. I opened his closet to count clean shirts but was distracted by a sparkle on the nightstand. I turned, curious. Beside my father's pillow, catching the sunlight, was a pair of light blue rhinestone earrings.

No question, Walter was thinner and older. Maybe he was subject to small strokes and his memory was failing; maybe he'd gotten deep into trouble with loan sharks or gangs. Maybe he was gambling again. But, no matter what else was true, one thing was certain: My father was back in the game.

THIRTY-EIGHT

DR. MARTIN'S HEAD REAPPEARED OVER THE SHEET COVERING MY knees. "You look fine. Baby's fine. I don't think you're having actual labor." Good news, but the doctor wasn't smiling. It was Monday morning. I'd called the Institute to cancel my first session, had gone for an exam.

"Still, I don't like the trend. It's early in the pregnancy yet. You've got four and a half months to go. And the contractions are coming more often and getting stronger. So, here's the plan. For now, if you have more than four of them in a day, or if you have more than two in an hour, call me. If any get really intense, call me."

"How intense is 'really intense'?"

She eyed me. "Oh, you'll know. Meantime, I'm going to give you some pills to calm down your uterus."

Pills?

"Brethine. Just a low dose. And listen. I want you to rest. Lie down with your feet up at least four hours a day."

Was she serious?

"If you can't do four hours, at least do two. Every time you can, lie down, even for ten minutes. Take it easy, Zoe. Give your body a break."

Half an hour later, I swallowed a pill as I knocked on Bertram's door, ten minutes late for my hypnosis session. Bertram opened his office door, frazzled, as if he'd slept in his clothes. His hair was greasy, his smell musky. He ushered me into his office, distracted, as if he'd forgotten I was coming by. The place was abnormally awry, papers scattered over the leather furniture.

"We can reschedule," I offered.

"Nonsense." Bertram took a stack of files off the leather chair. "I'm a little pressured, that's all. I've been writing grant applications, making calls, searching for new funding. The Institute is completely reneging on my contract. They claim we never finalized the terms. I ought to sue them. I might, too." He was pacing. The office was small, so he seemed to be spinning in circles, waving his arms.

"I should let you work." I started to leave. "I'll come back."

"No, I need to take a break and do something productive for a change. Sit." He moved a stack of papers off the chair.

I hesitated, but sat.

"So, how are you feeling? Are your contractions easing up? How's the half day going for you?"

He fired questions at me, waited for answers as I settled against the cushions. I described my work, told him about my patients. Due to the half day, mostly they'd seemed removed, as if holding back from the program and our relationship, not certain how long I'd be there.

"Could be that they're picking up on your attitude. Reacting to your feelings, mirroring them."

Could be.

"Or maybe they don't feel removed at all. Maybe you're projecting your feelings onto your patients, so you don't have to own them."

Could that be true?

"Either way, hypnosis and relaxation will help. So let's get to it. Breathe deeply."

I did, and then I closed my eyes. When I opened them again, Bertram was grinning. His mood seemed transformed, energized.

"Great session." He stood to walk me to the door. "Let's meet again as soon as we can. Tomorrow, if you want. Or Wednesday. Either one."

Why so soon? What was the urgency? "I'll check my calendar."

"Let's set up something, and you can call me later to confirm.

I think we're definitely on to something. Progressing. It's critical to continue."

I opened the door, thanked him. Bertram followed me into the hallway. "Don't forget," he insisted. "Call me later."

I nodded that I would. Of course I would. Hypnosis was good. It was necessary. It was helping me. I wouldn't think of dropping it now.

THIRTY-NINE

BEDTIME. MOLLY AND I WERE GOING TO READ TOGETHER. TRYing to climb onto my lap, she pressed herself against my belly. Not good. I felt like I'd explode.

"Molls," I groaned. "Ooof, not on my lap. Here. Sit next to me."

Frowning, she jumped off me and stood, eyeing my waistline. "You mean I can't sit on your lap anymore?"

"Well, maybe for a while. The baby's getting bigger, but my lap's not. It's not comfortable."

Her mouth dropped, speechless, as if it were unfathomable that my lap could be unavailable to her.

"Come sit with me." I reached for her, but she stood frozen, crestfallen.

Oh, Lord. Was she resenting the baby? Feeling that it had stolen her place? If she felt that way now, how would she react once the baby was born, taking up my attention, crying, needing to be held. Suddenly I was guilt-ridden. Was I betraying Molly by having another child? Was I stealing from her the time, love, loyalty I'd give to her sibling? And since Molly was adopted, would she wonder whether I loved her as much as a baby I gave birth to?

"Did I hurt Oliver when I sat on you?" She had named the baby a long time ago.

"No. Of course not." Oh my. Is that what she'd thought? "The baby's fine, Molls. It's just crowded on my lap."

She nodded soberly and ever so cautiously climbed beside me, resting her curls gently against my side, opening her book.

"Molls." I wanted to reassure her. "You know, when the baby

comes, lots of things will change. But not how much I love you. That will never change. Never ever."

"I know that, Mom." She sounded patient, as if my point were obvious. "Love's not a pie."

Okay.

"Miss Sarah said if someone gets a big piece of pie, there's less pie for everyone else. But with love, no matter how much one person gets, there's still plenty for everyone else. Because love's not a pie." She turned pages, picking a chapter.

Once again, Molly's wisdom took me by surprise. Apparently, her teacher was having a lot of influence on her. And on her reading skills. Molly read a whole chapter of *Mrs. Piggle-Wiggle* with almost no help. Miss Sarah said she was an excellent reader. Miss Sarah had her read aloud to the class. Miss Sarah told her she read like a fourth grader. I tucked her in, telling her how proud I was of her. Privately scolding myself for being jealous of how much Molly revered Miss Sarah, I kissed her and turned out the light.

I was almost out the door when Molly called me.

"Mom? Once the baby comes"—her voice was tiny—"can I sit on your lap again?"

I came back and hugged her, promising her a reserved seat. When I left, she was almost asleep, a smile on her face.

FORTY

THERE WAS NOTHING ON TELEVISION. I PUT ON A RERUN OF *LAW and Order* and put my feet up as Dr. Martin had instructed, waiting for Nick to come in. I needed to tell him about the contractions and the medicine, but I didn't want to tell him on the phone. I called his cell to see how late he'd be, got his voice mail, tried the Homicide Division at headquarters. Nobody there had seen him. Odd that no one seemed to know where he was. Doubt rumbled in my head, thoughts about where Nick might be. Maybe he wasn't really working. Maybe he was lying about that, cheating with somebody, having an affair. Stop it, I told myself. What's the matter with you? You're making up a whole scenario without cause. I called his cell again, heard his voice telling me to leave a message. Minutes passed, but Nick didn't call back.

I watched the clock, listening to sounds of the night, wondering how late he'd be, imagining where he was and how dangerous it might be, feeling overwhelmed and alone. Anymore, I was upset all the time, and thinking about that made me even more upset. Calm down, I told myself. Relax. Using Bertram's techniques, I lay on my side and gradually released the tension from my body, starting with my toes, moving up to my feet, my ankles, my calves . . .

When the fire alarm rang, I shoved Nick, who had somehow come home and been sleeping beside me, and leaped out of bed, heading for the hallway to grab Molly.

"It's the phone," Nick muttered. I was almost out of the room; he hadn't stirred at all.

Oh. It wasn't a fire alarm? It was the phone? I knew, even in my confusion, that he was right, so I reversed my steps and ran back to the nightstand to answer it. By then, Nick had rolled over, actually lifted an arm and picked it up.

"It's for you." Yawning, he held it out. I blinked at it, hesitating to take it, wondering who would call in the middle of the night, knowing it had to be someone with bad news. Oh, God. What had happened? Who'd died? Or been in a car accident? I braced myself to hear a catastrophe and answered the phone with a timid hello.

"Sorry to bother you, Ms. Hayes. This is Phyllis McHenry, an assisted living nurse at Harrington Place."

Oh, Lord. My father. "What's happened?" Had he had a heart attack? A stroke? Slit another woman's throat?

"What is it?" Nick sat up, repeating his question. "What, Zoe? What?"

I grabbed his arm. "It's about my dad."

"I don't mean to alarm you. It's just that yours is the phone number on Mr. Hayes's paperwork."

And? "Is he all right?"

Nick tried to wake up, rubbed his eyes.

"Well, to be blunt, I'm afraid he's gone."

Oh my God. "He died?"

Nurse McHenry and Nick spoke at the same time. "Walter's dead?" he asked, while she exclaimed, "Dead? Oh, no—at least, I don't think so. He's just gone. Nobody can find him. I was hoping he was with you."

With me? My brain tried to wake up and follow her, and Nick stared at me, his face asking questions.

"No, he's not here." I looked at the clock. Two thirty-seven. What could have happened? Where could he be? Rhinestone earrings sparkled, teasing in the darkness. Oh, of course. "Are you sure he's gone? Maybe he's just, you know, visiting somebody? Or playing a late card game?"

"Ms. Hayes. I wouldn't have phoned you if I weren't sure.

About five minutes ago, his roommate told me that Mr. Hayes had packed up his things and left the premises."

Oh goodness.

"His last words to Leonard Parks were, 'The party's over. It's time to go.' Phyllis McHenry remained silent, waiting for me to absorb the situation.

Nick nudged me. "Zoe? What's happening?"

"But it's almost three in the morning."

"Our residents don't always keep track of the time. Some don't sleep well. You know how it is."

I didn't, but I could imagine.

"At any rate, I hoped he was with you."

"No." But I knew where he'd gone.

"Well, in that case, we'll need to notify the authorities—"

"No, not yet." I pictured police cars hunting the streets for my father, his picture on the news, on flyers and milk cartons asking, "Have you seen this man?" "I might know where to find him."

I thanked her and ended the call, promising to call her back in a few hours. Then I grabbed a pair of baggy jeans and a sweat-shirt, telling Nick I had to go find my father.

Nick was on his feet. "What? Where? It's the middle of the night."

I zipped up the jeans. "He decided that his stay at the senior hostel is over." I stepped into a pair of sneakers. "I think he's gone home."

"He left?"

"With a packed bag. Remember? He thought it was a vacation spot? They said he checked out."

"So you're going to look for him?"

"Just at the house."

"Okay." Still half-asleep, he got up and began pulling on a pair of jeans.

"Don't get up, Nick. You're exhausted. Go back to bed. I'll be fine."

His foot fumbled with the leg hole, and he danced around,

hopping, until it found its way through. "You can't go alone—especially at this hour."

"Nick, it's okay. I can handle this."

"It's no problem." He was bleary-eyed. "I'll go with you—"

"And what about Molly? Are we going to wake her up and take her along, too? She has school tomorrow."

"So you stay here, and I'll go." He was clearly half-asleep.

"No. He's my father. It's my responsibility. Don't be overprotective. I'm going."

"Zoe, be reasonable. This is not about me being overprotective. It's about that it's the middle of the night, and your dad's house is not in the safest part of the city, and you're a pregnant woman—"

"Okay. I'll just do a drive-by, see if he's in there. If the lights are on, I'll know he's home; if they're not, I'll know he's not there and I'll come back. I have my cell phone. If there's a problem—anything at all—I'll call."

He frowned. "I don't like this. I should at least go—"

"No, Nick. It's okay. My father; my problem."

He was pouting. Pouting didn't look right on Nick. Incongruous. But it worked. I felt bad.

"Okay. Look, how's this? I won't even get out of the car. I'll just look for the lights. If he's there, I'll call you before I do anything else. Okay?" I kissed his lips gently and kept moving. "You're wiped. You need to sleep."

"Zoe, listen—"

"It's okay. I'll be fine." I looked back from the doorway.

Nick stood by the bed, his eyes strained and bloodshot from a week of sleepless nights. His jeans were hanging open, his hair was mussed, his chest bare. He fidgeted, uncertain. "I don't like this—promise me you won't get out of the car?"

"Go back to sleep. I'll be back before you know it." Before he could change his mind, I blew him another kiss and headed down the stairs. And I still hadn't told him about my contractions.

FORTY-ONE

THE MOON GLOWED LOW IN THE SKY, OUTLINING TREETOPS AND defining their shadows. Stillness draped my father's street. Nothing moved; no creatures chirped or stirred in the palpable silence of the night. I slowed the car, scanning the area, seeing no sign of life, telling myself that the hairs on my neck were standing up without cause. Stop it, I told myself. You've gotten yourself all worked up over nothing. Nobody's going to jump out of the bushes at your car. Just look, see if he's there; if not, just turn around and drive home.

Fine. Good plan. I approached the front of his house, slowing. Sure enough, a dim light shined through an upstairs window. Probably Dad was up in his bedroom, near the back of the house. Probably I was seeing the light from the stairway or the hall. At any rate, he was there, inside. My father had come home. I parked the car, started to get out.

Wait, a voice scolded. Not so fast. Aren't you supposed to call Nick?

Let him sleep, I told it. He's exhausted. I don't need to bother him. I'll just go get Dad and bring him back to Harrington Place.

I reached for the car door. But the voice continued. You promised Nick you wouldn't get out of the car. You said you'd just drive by.

It's all right, I assured it. Relax. This will just take a second.

And before the voice could speak up again, I opened the door and got out.

The air was chilly, thick with silence, and I hurried to the path, trying not to stumble over the overgrowth of weeds along the curb. Tree trunks surrounded me, motionless as if ready to close in, to ambush me from behind. I shivered, told myself to cut it out. This was not some slasher movie; it was the house that, with Hilda's starched laundry and beef stew, God help me, I'd grown up in. Still, I didn't dare look behind me, felt the clammy breath of the unknown on my back. I began to run, dashing the last few yards to the porch. There, the house blocked the moonlight, and I hit the stairs in darkness, but I knew the steps well, could climb them blind. So I flew, barely touching the banister, confident even in the shadows. Until my foot struck something lumpy and still warm, and I stumbled, sprawling forward, arms outstretched, to the ground.

FORTY-TWO

THE PROCESS OF FALLING SEEMED ENDLESS. FOR TIMELESS MOMENTS, my body sailed upward, unmindful of gravity, and my arms stroked frantically, swimming through air. Meanwhile, my mind grappled with decisions: how to cushion my landing and minimize damage, how to inform my body parts before it was too late. At the same time, it tried to define the object that had tripped me, reviewing the sensations of texture and shape, so that, by the time my hands and knees made contact with the porch, my mind had done massive amounts of work. It had concluded, for example, that I'd found my father. That I'd stumbled over him as he lay collapsed on his porch.

I landed with a howl, pain jolting through my limbs, reverberating along my spine. For a few seconds, I couldn't get up. I rolled onto my back, knees bent, trying to breathe.

"Dad," I panted. "Dad?" I reached for him, tugged on his shirt. A wave of tightness squeezed my middle, but I pushed myself up to a sitting position and nudged him. Oh, God. He didn't react. Didn't move or make a sound. Oh, God.

I shoved him harder. Still no response. Even as my belly contracted I yanked at his shoulders, trying to turn him, amazed that he was so heavy. He must be dead, I realized. That must be why he seemed so heavy. Didn't dead weight feel heavier than living? But I kept calling to him, refusing to accept that he could be dead. He couldn't be.

"Dad." I was gasping, contracting. "Dad? Daddy?" In a final grunting effort, I hefted his chest off the ground, twisting his shoulder up and around, turning him over onto his back. And then, with tightness strangling my midsection, I sank onto the floor beside him, closed my eyes and breathed through the contraction, trying to comprehend that my father, my handsome dandy irresponsible charming son-of-a-bitch father, was dead. I'd known as soon as I'd touched him; his body held the unmistakable stillness of death. I lay there, eyes closed, until the contraction peaked. Then, dreading what I would see, I opened them again.

It was dark and tears blurred my sight, so at first I thought my vision was distorted. I blinked a few times, smeared away the tears with the backs of my hands, and looked again. Nothing had changed. For sure, there was a corpse beside me, but it was not my father's.

Stan Addison, the guy from Town Watch, was still warm, but he was dead. His blood, still wet, oozed from a gaping hole in his throat.

Oh, God. Panting and trembling, I tried to stand, but couldn't. My legs were boneless, wouldn't support me. I sat staring at him and the darkness, holding my belly, telling myself not to panic, seeing the lights glowing next door in Lettie's upstairs window as if they were miles away. Oh, God. Think, I told myself. Call Nick. Right. I reached for my pocket to get my cell phone. It wasn't there. Of course it wasn't. It wouldn't be. After all, wasn't I in a nightmare? Wasn't this just another bad dream where people fall in slow motion and can't get up when they fall? Where invisible killers stalk, and even the night air is alive and menacing? All that was missing for complete terror was being late for a final exam I hadn't studied for in a school I didn't know in a hallway with too many doors where I'd forgotten my handbag and wasn't wearing any clothes.

Stop it, I scolded myself. Get your damned phone. It must have fallen out when I tripped. Tentatively, I felt around the porch for it, found only darkness. Maybe it was under Stan's body; after all, I'd moved him. My fingers slid underneath him through the puddle of clotting blood, probed under his trunk, and there it was, under his shoulder. I heard the bushes rustle beside the porch as my hand closed around the cell phone. Who was there? The person who'd killed Stan? Was he still there?

I ducked, hunkering down on the porch, and held still, listening. Cautiously I watched shadows, shivered, alert for a killer. Someone was out there. But hearing no one, seeing nothing, I slithered, slowly, low and lizardlike, to the front door. I'd be safe inside. I'd call Nick. And 9-1-1. I inched forward, silently, scraping bruised knees across splintered wooden slats, hiding from someone who might not be there.

Finally, I made it to the door and reached up for the knob. It wouldn't turn. I turned harder, forcing it. But no. It wouldn't budge. My thoughts were slow, muddled, and it took a moment to realize that, of course, the doorknob won't turn; the door was locked. I needed the key. Wait, I remembered. I had a key. I'd brought it with me. My fingers fumbled deep in the pocket of my jeans, finding it. Then, phone in one hand, key in the other, I shoved the key into the lock, turned it and swung the door open.

Light flashed in the hall; the air whooshed, and there was a harsh popping sound as the doorframe exploded above my head. Reflexively, I dropped to the floor and rolled away from the door, reacting before I understood that someone was shooting at me.

FORTY-THREE

"STOP RIGHT THERE." MY FATHER'S VOICE RUMBLED LOW AND dangerous.

I squinted, peering around the doorframe, trying to see him. "Dad—"

Before I could finish my sentence, he fired again. Something in the foyer shattered and fell to the floor. A vase? Part of the chandelier?

"Dad—"My mouth was dry, my voice hoarse. "Don't shoot. It's me. Zoe."

"The hell it is. Get out. You have to the count of five, then I shoot to kill—"

"Dad—whoa." I crouched, covering my head. Where had he gotten a gun?

"One . . . two . . ."

"Dammit. Will you stop counting and listen?"

"Three . . . Come on in. Think I won't shoot? What do you bet? Ten bucks? A hundred? How about your life? Four . . . five." Another flash of light and *bam*. I hit the ground and rolled sideways.

Oh, God. He was crazy. What had happened to him? Had he had another stroke? And where had the gun come from? I pictured Stan Addison lying outside on the porch, the hole ripped into his neck. Good Lord . . . had my father shot him?

He kept shouting. "Nobody's going to drive me out, you hear? Go tell your friends. Tell them I'll fight to the death, and believe you me, I'll take a bunch of you vermin with me."

He was sitting at the far end of the hall, ranting in the dark.

Dimly, I could make out his silhouette against the wall, seated in a dining room chair.

I sat still, catching my breath. "Dad," I called. "Listen. Will you please just listen for once?"

There was a pause. "Who's there?"

Was he kidding? "It's Zoe. I'm here to get you."

He didn't answer for a moment. "Zoe?" He sounded skeptical. Or confused?

"Your daughter."

"Zoe." He repeated. "What would she be doing up in the middle of the night?" He wasn't convinced.

Again I explained why I'd come and what I wanted. "Let me turn on the light. You can see for yourself." I stood up and flicked the switch.

Instantly, sparks flew and filaments sizzled from the chandelier, where a bullet had apparently ripped through the wiring. My father got up. "What the hell?" He walked over to examine the damage, staring up at the flickering fixture, the gun dangling from his hand. "Turn that switch off, will you? You'll start a fire."

I didn't. I stepped over to him and took the gun. He didn't resist, but when I touched him he looked up and stepped back, his eyes wide.

"Good Lord. It's you?"

Sparks popped over our heads.

"I swear." He kept staring. Gaping, actually. "I didn't know it was you."

His ogling made me uncomfortable. "Back off, Dad." I smelled booze on his breath. Bourbon? Wonderful. He'd gotten drunk and started shooting up the house, probably killed a guy.

"Louise? Where have you been? All this time?" He reached for my hand. I thought he might be going for the gun, so I tossed it into the dining room, heard it clatter to the floor, but he didn't seem to notice. He simply took my hand. "I've been so worried."

Oh. Not again. I opened my mouth to explain that I was his daughter, that Louise was my mother. That she'd been dead for decades. But I didn't. All that mattered was that my father had stopped shooting. If believing that my mother was back from the dead would keep him calm, then I certainly wasn't going to dispel the notion.

Besides, there was no point telling him the truth; he'd only get confused again. Dr. Habib had warned that Dad would have increasing periods of disorientation and confusion as the blood vessels in his brain slowly grew brittle and broke. So, suspecting that he'd had another small stroke or two, I let him hold my hand and squeezed his gently. His fingers felt bony and gnarled. If he thought I was my mother, what was the harm?

Holding hands, we went to the living room. "It's been so long," he repeated. We sat together on the sofa, and I didn't mention Stan Addison, didn't ask my father if he had shot him. Apparently he had already forgotten being holed up in his hallway, fighting off intruders with a gun. He sat rapt beside my mother, captivated, his hand closed around hers.

And slowly, so as not to disturb him, I used my free hand to pick up my cell phone and call home.

FORTY-FOUR

AGAIN POLICE CARS SWARMED AROUND MY FATHER'S HOUSE. I SAT with him in the living room while paramedics checked out my head and officers secured the crime scene. I gave a statement to the detective on duty, explaining my father's condition. My father sat quietly, withdrawn, his dark eyebrows knit, looking puzzled. Finally, Nick came in. I stood.

"What happened to not getting out of the car?" he greeted me. "What happened to just driving by and calling me if you saw a light on?"

I squirmed. He was right. I'd promised. "Sorry."

Nick seemed annoyed but not all that surprised. "You need to be more careful, Zoe. Think of the baby."

"I know. I'm sorry. Where's Molly?"

"At Susan's."

Oh. That's what took him so long to get here. "What did you tell her?"

"That we had to go see Grandpa. I told her he's okay, but he's having a problem with—"

My father interrupted, shaking Nick's hand and offering him a drink. "Scotch? Bourbon? Name it. Louise . . . get some ice, will you?"

Even if he was again confused about my identity, my father seemed very sure of Nick's. Nick was his friend, his guest. Someone he trusted and actually liked.

"So, what brings you here in the middle of the night, young man?"

Nick asked him to sit and talk. They faced each other like buddies, man to man. "Walter, I'm going to be straight with you, okay? And I want you to be honest with me."

"You got it."

"Good. Tell me what happened here tonight."

"Tonight?" My father glanced from me to the ceiling, searching the beams for an answer, stalling. Clearly he had no idea what Nick was referring to. Finally, he frowned. "Which part of tonight do you want to hear about?" He was covering up, too proud to admit he had a memory lapse.

"Well, start with Stan Addison."

"Who?"

"Stan Addison. Your neighbor?"

Dad just blinked.

"The Town Watch guy."

"Oh, him? He's an idiot. Trash. You say his name's Stan Addison? What about him?"

"Did you see him tonight?"

"No. Why would I? He doesn't come around here. He knows I don't suffer fools or hypocrites."

Nick leaned forward, rested his elbows on his knees. "Walter. Your daughter told me you had a gun tonight." He nodded toward the dining room, where detectives had bagged the weapon. "She says you were firing at her. You almost shot her."

"No, ridiculous. I wouldn't shoot at my daughter. I was chasing away those damned trespassing gangbangers. They're trying to take over and run me out of here. Those people will stop at nothing—"

"Walter, did you shoot at Stan Addison?"

"Why would I? I told you. I haven't seen him."

Nick sighed. "He's dead, Walter."

My father scowled. "Dead? Christ. Are you serious? That fool with the helmet and glow-in-the-dark vest? The flashlight? That's who we're talking about?" There was a pause. "You don't say."

"He's outside lying on the porch."

My father gaped at Nick. "He's what? Lying on the porch? My porch? They killed him, too?"

Nick watched my father's eyes. "What do you mean, 'they'?"

"The ones who killed Beatrice. And Jack. The same ones I've been telling you about—the gangs."

"Walter. Think for a minute. Is it possible that you shot Stan accidentally? Maybe mistaking him for an intruder? A gang member?"

"Me?"

"Well, you were shooting." Nick looked at the bullet hole near the front door, then at the burned-out chandelier. "Maybe you hit Stan. By accident."

"That's absurd." My father dismissed the idea.

"Maybe Stan saw a light on, and, since he knew you were away, since he was involved in Town Watch, he came by to see what was going on. Maybe you heard him out there and thought he was an intruder, so maybe you fired—just to scare him away. But maybe the bullet actually hit him. Unintentionally, I mean."

My father shook his head at each suggestion. "No. No. No and no. Never happened. He had no business here, and he knew it."

"Okay." Nick studied my father. "Tell me about Stan. How well did you know him?"

"Man's dead. I don't want to speak ill of him. Thinking he could pull wool over everybody's eyes. That community or Town Watch thing? They wanted everybody to ante up ten bucks for dues. Let's see, ten dollars times how many—maybe a hundred neighbors? But it was all a scam. A cover-up, a complete fraud. The guy was so dumb, afterward, he broke out on his own, trying to start his own deal, independently, on the side. I warned Beatrice, but she wouldn't listen. Stan Addison conned her into it, the stupid son of a bitch."

"Dad." I was appalled at his attitude. "Stan Addison died trying to protect your neighborhood."

"Really? What do you know about it?"

"I know what he told me. About the gangs taking over, and the violence—and that you were the only one who wouldn't join Town Watch—"

"Of course I wouldn't. Town Watch? Baloney. You know what that guy was really trying to sell? Protection. He was one of the—"

"Wait, back up. What did you say, Zoe?" Nick's eyes had narrowed, razorlike, slicing me with their gaze. "You knew the victim?"

Oh dear. More information that I hadn't shared with Nick. "Not really. I met him. Once."

"How? When?"

"The other day. I ran into him in the alley. He told me about Town Watch, that's all."

"What exactly did he say?"

"He was worried about gangs. He said they were taking over the neighborhood." I turned to my father. "He also said he thought my father might owe the gangs money. Is that true, Dad? Did you gamble their money and lose? How much do you owe?"

"Zoe." Nick's voice was a low rumble. "Cool it."

"Is that what Addison told you?" My father seemed astonished. "That I owe a gang? I told you he was a son of a bitch."

"Answer me, Dad." I avoided Nick's eyes and his questions. "Where did you get a gun? Who were you ready to shoot tonight? Gang members who might be coming to collect their money? People you placed bets with?" My voice was louder, higher, unstoppable. "Tell me. Are your debts why they killed Beatrice?"

"Zoe." Nick's voice glowered. "That's enough."

My father stared at air; I stared at him. I felt Nick staring at me. For a moment, nobody spoke.

"Dad," I insisted.

"Zoe," Nick persisted.

My father clenched a fist, his eyes flashing, resisting.

"Did Beatrice die because of you and your gambling?" I went on, couldn't stop. "Tell us. How many people have to die because of you? Let's see. Beatrice. Now Stan. Oh, yes. I almost forgot Mom. Who's next, Dad? Tell us. Who's it going to be?"

I stopped, eyes burning. Except for my furious heartbeat, the room was silent. Slowly, wordlessly, my father's thin frame lifted itself from the chair and hobbled to the front door. I watched him stand there, surveying the scene. The police, their cars. The flashing lights. The corpse on the porch. He ran a gnarled hand through his silver hair. He looked genuinely distraught. And fragile.

Suddenly I felt ashamed. Damn. Why did I feel guilty for speaking up? How could my father cause so much harm and still work his way into my heart? Why, after all this time, did I still simultaneously feel the urge to curse and embrace him?

"Zoe." Nick's voice slit like cold steel. "It's time we had a serious talk."

Warily I met his eyes. They were frosty and critical. And disappointed.

"Okay."

"What else haven't you bothered to mention?" His voice was a gravelly whisper.

"Nick, how could I mention any of this? How can I talk to you about anything when you're never around until the middle of the night? I simply haven't had a chance."

"You haven't had a chance? Zoe, there is a murder investigation going on. No—two murder investigations. You needed to find a chance."

He was right, of course. "Nick, I'm sorry."

"Let's continue this later." Abruptly Nick stood and started toward the doorway. "Walter," he called. "Come back inside. We have more to talk about."

Why? What did he want to talk to my father about? Oh dear. Was Nick going to have him arrested?

"Wait . . . Nick." I went after him. "You don't really think Dad shot him?"

He shrugged. "Ballistics will tell." He was trying to act detached, as if this case were impersonal, like any other. He was annoyed with me, but I couldn't let him take that out on my father.

"But think about it. If Dad shot him, it would only have been because he thought Stan was breaking in. Dad was barricaded in here, protecting his home. He didn't mean to kill anybody." Why was I defending my father?

Nick turned to me. His gaze chilled me, and I felt the need to keep talking, to thaw him. "So, even if he did shoot him, it would have been because he thought somebody was breaking in . . . And in that case—"

"Did I shoot him?" My father, dazed, went to sit on the sofa.

"Go home, Zoe." Nick was curt, impersonal. "We'll finish this later, after things are settled here."

I searched his eyes, saw sadness and anger, no affection. Nick led me out the kitchen door and walked me around the house, past Lettie silhouetted at her window, through tall weeds, past police cars and flashing lights, away from the howling of neighborhood dogs.

"You're sure you're okay to drive?" He held the door for me.

"I'm fine." If I weren't, he'd be even more upset.

As I was about to pull away, he leaned into my window. "Here, don't forget this." He held out my cell phone. "Not that you ever use it."

Then, without another word, he turned away and headed back to the house.

FORTY-FIVE

GUILT WAS ALL I COULD FEEL. IT SWELLED AND SWIRLED INSIDE me, sucking me into itself inch by inch, organ by organ. It poured over me as I showered away the shock of the night and the blood smears from falling onto Stan.

I felt guilt physically with every breath, hanging on my lungs, twisting my stomach, accusing, demanding answers. What kind of person are you? How unfeeling about the death of a man on your father's porch? How indifferent to your father, how insensitive to your daughter and your fiancé? How irresponsibly reckless with your unborn baby?

I stood at the bathroom mirror, toweling my hair, examining my face. My eyes looked back at me drawn and hollow, knowing they'd done wrong. Not sorry. Just guilty. Guilty of not being sorry? My head throbbed. I couldn't sort one feeling from another. One second I was angry, the next guilty about being angry, blaming myself for feeling what I felt, unsure what those feelings were. Whatever I did, thought, said or didn't say, I felt wrong. I glared at the mirror, wanting to jump from my body and run. Wondering how much I really looked like my mother. And the thought of her gave me chills, stirring up cold currents of more guilt.

In my way, after all, I'd let her down just as much as my father had. In fact, my anger at him was no greater than my anger at myself. If only I'd been a better child, if only I'd shown my mother how I loved her. Maybe if I'd helped her more . . . If I'd dried more dishes or kept my room clean. Or if I'd just stopped her from going downstairs . . . Oh, God. How many times through my childhood had I gone through the list of things I could or should have done to change the outcome? How many years had I spent blaming myself? How was it that guilt still consumed me, even though my adult self had learned, and my professional self had determined beyond any doubt that my mother's death had been beyond my control, had not been my fault?

I turned on the faucet, held a washcloth under cold water, pressed it against my face. Felt it cool my eyes, my temples. Slow down, I told myself. Breathe.

But the guilt stayed with me as I left the bathroom, churned in my abdomen as I went downstairs to make some mint tea. It was with me still as I sat on my purple velvet sofa sipping hot liquid, hoping the tea would steam away my failings before they erupted and spilled over—onto Nick, Molly, my unborn child.

And what about my father? Why did I feel guilty about him? He had destroyed my childhood and my mother's life. But somehow my anger at him seemed out of place; the man he'd been back then was gone. Now nobody else saw what I saw when they looked at him; nobody knew what I knew. Now my father was old. His shoulders were stooped, his mind confused. And although his age merely meant that he'd survived when others hadn't, it still felt wrong to be unkind to him. And so I was guilty again.

The tea had gone cold in the cup, and dawn had risen. When I finally heard Nick come in, I was still on the purple sofa, clinging to its cushions, riding a tidal wave.

•

FORTY-SIX

"YOUR FATHER'S BACK AT HARRINGTON, SAFE AND SOUND." NICK dropped his jacket on the back of the sofa.

"He wasn't arrested?" Thank God.

"Nope. We don't think Stan Addison was killed with his gun, and your father has a license to carry. For now, seems all he was doing was protecting his premises."

I waited, but that was all he said. I heard him walk back down the hall, mess around in the kitchen, make himself a sandwich. I stayed on the sofa, chewing my lip, tears brimming, not sure what to do or say.

"What are you doing down here? I thought you'd be in bed." When he came back into the living room his mouth was full of Swiss on rye. He held a Yuengling, and he looked disheveled, exhausted.

I shrugged, not able to form words.

"Apparently, your pop's got a girlfriend." He sat beside me, absorbed in his food. "At least one. Maybe more. His roommate—that guy Leonard—was up when we got back there, and he seemed pretty bent out of shape that Walter's such a chick magnet. When word got out that he'd left, women were banging on the door, going nuts. The roommate doesn't get it. Apparently, the ladies don't give Leonard the time of day."

I nodded, felt a smile emerging as I pictured tubby Leonard with his unbuckled belt and hiked-up, unbuttoned pants wondering why women preferred my slender, smooth-talking father.

"Did he tell you about his son?"

"The one traveling in Africa?" Half of Nick's face smiled sadly as he took a swig of beer. "Between you and me, I think that trip ended years ago. That son's in no hurry to let his father know he's back."

We sat, chatting tentatively on the sofa, each of us trying to act normally, as if nothing much had happened earlier. Each of us failing.

"Nick—," I began, and he said "Zoe—" at the same moment. We grinned, paused, began again, bumped each other again. "You start."

"No. Go ahead."

"You."

Okay. I would. "It's just . . . having my father back isn't easy. It brings up all kinds of issues. I haven't been myself."

He didn't say anything, just watched me and chewed his sandwich.

"To you, I know he seems like a charming old man, but it's not that simple."

"Meaning?"

What could I say that would make it clear? "He had a gun, Nick. Where did he get it?"

"Apparently, he's had it for a long time."

"Okay. But he was firing it at me."

"Zoe, he was confused. He didn't know who you were. Even now, he's not sure who you are."

"See that? You're defending him. That's what happens. People don't see him as he is. They forgive him—"

"Forgive him for what? You're accusing him without cause—"

"It's okay with you that he had a gun?"

"The gun's legal."

"But not to shoot it at people—"

"Like you said before, if he thought he was defending his life—"

"Nick, why are you standing up for him?"

"Why are you accusing him?"

I sputtered, frustrated. "Okay, forget the gun. It's only an example. Here's another one. He's got money hidden, wads of it, all over the house. Why?"

"Why not?"

Why not? "Nick, he's gambling again."

Nick shook his head, half-smirking.

"What? What are you smirking about?"

"You. You are so angry with him. You're irrational."

Irrational?

"He said it himself. It's not illegal to have money or hide wads of it in your own home. Besides, the money doesn't prove he's gambling."

I was exasperated. "You're not getting it. He's back to his old pattern. The weapon, the money, the women—they're typical behaviors. They're signals of his—"

"Zoe, your father is over twenty-one. He's able to have women in his life. His gun is legal. His money is his own business."

"And the gambling slips in Beatrice's throat are just coincidence?"

"No. They're not even coincidence. They're entirely separate. Your father is doing fine. Frankly, I'm more concerned with you than with him."

"Oh, really."

"Yes. Really. You're touchy and secretive. Withdrawn. Hypersensitive. You've taken crazy risks and shown a lack of judgment. Maybe it's just the pregnancy, but frankly, Zoe, I'm worried about you. I can't figure out what's going on."

I opened my mouth to defend myself, but closed it again. What was the point? I couldn't figure out what was going on either.

"Take Stan Addison. Why didn't you tell me you knew him?"

Oh, God. The interrogation was beginning again. "I'm tired, Nick."

"Answer me. Why didn't you tell me?"

"Like I said. I didn't really have a chance."

"Tell me now, then. What exactly did he tell you?"

I sank back against the cushions. Why couldn't I simply open up to Nick and tell him how out of control I felt? How worried I was about the contractions and the possibility of premature labor? How upset by fragmented memories and nightmares? Why couldn't I fall apart and sob in his arms until my fears and sadness drained? I eyed his shoulders, his chest, longing to crawl into his arms and nestle there. But I didn't move, didn't dare let on that I needed him. Instead, I bit my lip and answered his question.

"He told me why they founded Town Watch."

"Rising crime?"

I nodded. "And the first murder."

"First murder?" Nick sounded surprised.

"A guy named Gavin. I think his last name was Broderick. He owed money to a gang, so they killed his dogs, then him, apparently as an example to others."

Nick watched me for a while. "And you couldn't find time to tell me about that conversation?"

"Call me a dreamer, but I assumed the police would already know about that murder."

His eyes shifted. "Officially, I'm not on this case. I'll look into it."

"You mean they didn't know about it?"

"I didn't say that."

"So, you did know?"

Nick, as usual, revealed the absolute minimum. "I advised you not to hang around your father's neighborhood, didn't I? I told you it wasn't safe there."

To Nick, that was an answer. So he had known, but hadn't told me. And he was complaining that I'd been secretive? Once again I was bickering with him. I wanted to have some peace, to go upstairs and climb into bed. By myself. I stood up, but sudden tightness grabbed my middle. The contraction came fast, hit hard. I wobbled, held my belly, plopped down again. Alarm flashed on Nick's face; he reached out to steady me, held on to me even after I'd sat.

"What's wrong?"

"Nothing." I was panting. "It's okay." Actually, my middle was being strangled. Tell him, I thought. He needs to know.

"You look pale." Nick sat alert, eyes riveted on mine.

Oddly, as the contraction intensified, my feelings transformed, soared from annoyance to enchantment, aggravation to adoration. I reached out and clung to Nick, overcome with how much I loved him. What was going on? My emotions soared and plummeted every five seconds. Maybe it was pregnancy and hormones, but at that moment, I loved Nick from my soul. Totally. Without reservation.

As the contraction eased, I managed to speak again. "Nick, I'm sorry. I've been impossible."

"Well, not quite."

I let go of him and straightened up. Go on, I told myself. Get it over with. Tell him what just happened. I took a breath, held his hand, and before I could lose my nerve, I blurted it out. "I saw Dr. Martin again. I'm . . . I've been having some contractions." There. I'd done it.

Nick's skin went suddenly gray. "Contractions? What . . . Are you okay?"

"Yes. The baby's fine. I'm fine. It's nothing to worry about. I just have to take some pills and try not to lift any pianos. We'll be fine."

He wasn't convinced. "Zoe, it's only the fifth month—"

"I know. But this isn't uncommon. My doctor's watching me, and I'm taking medicine."

"You'll have to take it easy—"

"I know. I'll be careful."

Nick watched me with gentle melting blue eyes, and we held hands, our silence binding us more tightly than any words we might have said.

FORTY-SEVEN

FRIDAY, THE LAST DAY OF MY FIRST HALF-WEEK. BEFORE MY FIRST session, I had scheduled a hypnosis session with Bertram. I knocked but got no answer. Damn. I was early. He wasn't there yet. Breathing deeply, trying to ward off a contraction, the second that morning, I leaned against the door to Bertram's office, telling myself to relax. Picturing my happy place.

"Door's open."

The voice was so small that at first I didn't think it could be Bertram's. But it had to be; it came from inside his office. I opened the door a crack and smelled stale air. The place was worse than it had been on Monday. Wads of paper were crumpled all over the carpet; journals and files were strewn over chairs and the table. Half-empty Styrofoam cups of coffee dotted the desk, open bags of chips and pretzels spilled onto furniture. And at his desk, tie loosened, head bowed, Bertram sat motionless. His shirt was wrinkled and unwashed. He needed a shave, seemed edgy and distraught.

Okay, this wasn't a good time. Worse than last time, even. I began to back out. But Bertram glanced up. "Let's reschedule," I began.

"Zoe?" His eyes seemed to focus.

"Are you all right?"

His smile was twisted and pained. "Fine. Perfect."

Obviously, he wasn't either. The silence was awkward. I didn't know what to say.

"My wife split. So, it's perfect. First my job, now my wife. It's all gone to hell."

"I'm so sorry, Bertram—"

"No, don't be." He stared into space. "She hopped off a sinking ship, that's all. Who can blame her?"

"Bertram. You're no sinking ship. Your career's having a setback, but you have so much to offer—"

"Tell that to my wife." Bertram turned to me. "Come in, Zoe. Let's get started."

"Are you sure?" His skin was pale and clammy.

"Positive. Your pregnancy is far more promising than any of my worthless proposals. It seems that nobody wants to fund my research."

"That can't be true, Bertram—"

"Trust me, it's true."

"But your work is cutting-edge. It's daring and prestigious—"

"If you're so enthusiastic, maybe you want to fund it?"

I smiled. "Somebody will."

"Well, if that somebody doesn't show up soon, my days here are numbered. My sources have dried up, and I'm running out of funds. My wife, bless her heart, emptied our personal accounts. So I'm flat broke. It's maddening, actually." Tossing a stack of papers off his sofa, he took me by the hand and seated me, chuckling nervously. "But maybe that's the answer: If I go mad, maybe I can stay. Do you think they'll let me continue my research if I'm a patient?" His smile was disturbing.

"Something will come through for you. And your wife might be back." Why had I said that? How stupid. I was sorry I'd come. "Seriously, why don't I stop in later—"

"No." His voice was oddly urgent. "Sit." Dark circles underlined his eyes. "How are your contractions? Easier?"

I considered telling him that, no, they weren't. But Bertram didn't wait for an answer. He leaned forward, eyes intense, beginning the session.

"Go to your happy place." He moved his chair closer. "Get comfortable."

Get comfortable? How? His knees bumped mine; he was almost

in my lap. I smelled sour coffee when he exhaled. And he watched me almost hungrily.

I sat, eyes closed, hearing Bertram telling me to relax, assuring me that my visit was more important than anything else he had to do. I breathed deeply, waiting to be hypnotized, doubting as always that I would be. Focusing on Bertram's voice, I determined to remain consciously aware and to remember everything we said.

Except that the next thing I knew, tears were once again streaming down my face, and once again I didn't know why. Bertram was still seated opposite me, watching, his eyes gleaming. I wiped my cheeks.

"I was crying again."

He nodded.

"Why do I cry every time I come in here?"

He handed me a tissue. "You'll remember if you want to. There's nothing stopping you from remembering except your own will."

Ridiculous. Why wouldn't he tell me? "Is it about my mother? Am I crying about her dying?"

Bertram's face was a mask. A clammy, annoying mask, giving away nothing. "When you're ready to remember what's upsetting you, you will. Apparently, you're not ready to face those memories yet."

Damn. Bertram absolutely refused to share what he knew. Why? What harm could it do if he simply told me that I was—or was not—crying about my mother? I was an adult, a coworker, not one of his patients or a participant in some experiment.

"I'm not here to solve personal problems," I reminded him. "I'm here to ease my contractions. Any other topic that comes up during hypnosis—"

"—Is completely confidential. It never leaves this room, unless, of course, you yourself decide to talk about it elsewhere."

"I know that. I mean, I think I should be informed of any topics I discuss other than the contractions themselves."

Bertram smiled calmly, patronizingly. What had happened to him? How had he recovered from his despair? "Zoe. You're a professional. You know that the whole process of hypnosis is about trust. You need to trust me to keep what you say confidential—even from you. More important, you need to trust yourself to reveal to your conscious mind what it can manage, to conceal what it cannot. It's not my place to tell you what you talked about; it's yours."

Mumbo jumbo. As always, he refused to tell me a thing. Not a word. My eyes were red and swollen, my nose stuffed, my face streaked with mascara, and I had no clue why. Bertram peered into his computer, consulting his calendar, eagerly setting up our next session. Forty-five minutes had passed unaccounted for, and, somehow Bertram no longer seemed desolate about his plight.

For the rest of the day my body felt better, lighter, and I didn't have another contraction. Not one. I wasn't tired, either. The session troubled me; I strained in vain to remember why I'd been crying. But I had energy to deal with my patients, and I didn't worry, not about Nick, my father, the baby, Molly or my job. Not about anything. At one-thirty, when my day ended, I still wasn't tired. I felt energized, as if the day were just beginning. Actually, in a way, it was.

FORTY-EIGHT

THAT EVENING, AS WE ENTERED HARRINGTON PLACE, MOLLY held my hand, suddenly shy. She'd been asking for days to go visit her grandfather, but now that I'd made plans to have dinner with him, she clung to me, refusing to walk.

"What's the matter? Don't you want to see Grandpa?"

She looked up at me, whispering, "Everybody's old here."

Damn. How stupid of me; I hadn't prepared her for the realities of a retirement community. Molly had never been to one before, let alone to the assisted living section of a retirement community. She hadn't been around elderly people much, hadn't even had a grandparent until a few weeks ago. Suddenly she was surrounded by old people. For the first time, Molly was seeing people who used walkers and canes, who sat in wheelchairs, staring into their own memories, or who waited in hushed plush alcoves, looking out at us as we passed. I stopped walking and led her into a nearby reading room. A white-haired man sat by the window looking at his newspaper. I stooped to meet Molly's eyes.

Holding her hand, I explained as well as I could about the function of retirement homes. "As people get older," I told her, "they sometimes don't want to have to take care of a house or an apartment. And sometimes they have health problems or less energy than they used to. So they come to a place like this—"

"Is Grandpa going to die?"

The question took me by surprise. "Sooner or later, everybody dies, Molly."

"Don't baby me, Mom." Her tone was grave, sounding way older than her six years. "Tell me the truth. Is Grandpa dying?"

"What makes you think so?"

"Answer me. Is he?" Her voice was loud. I felt eyes on us, knew the man across the room was listening, concerned.

"No." I told myself that it wasn't really a lie. As far as I knew, my father would survive that day and the next. "He's here because his house is too big for him to take care of. And he has some medical problems. But don't worry. Grandpa's doing fine." I said this loud enough for the man across the room to hear. Somehow I wanted to reassure him, too.

Molly nodded, absorbing the information, and slowly we resumed our walk to my father's room. Molly ogled at residents as if at creatures in the zoo. Her honest and open amazement embarrassed me until she tugged at my hand with another question.

"Why is everyone staring at me?"

She was right. As we passed, people stared, studying her. A silver-haired woman wearing blue silk and large sparkly rings. Another in a pale green housecoat, her hair wrapped tightly in pink curlers. They stood still or spun their chairs our way and openly ogled. The old were eyeing Molly just as she was eyeing them. A heavyset woman with wispy thin hair gaped at her almost drooling, apparently fascinated.

"Maybe you remind them of their grandchildren. Or maybe they just think you're cute." But it was more. Pair after pair of eyes gaped at Molly, but seemed to be seeing something else, something lost or forgotten. Maybe youth?

But Molly came up with a more benign answer. "Maybe they're sad because nobody's here to visit them."

Maybe. Given that possibility, we made it a point to smile at everyone, to nod hello and good evening at all the people we passed. By the time we got to my father's suite a smile was frozen on my face, so I didn't have to force one. The door was open, but Molly knocked anyway.

"Dad?"

Nobody answered.

Molly peeked into the room, eager to see him. "Grandpa?"

We stood at the door, listening, realizing that Grandpa wasn't there.

Molly looked crushed, near tears. I knew how she felt, having myself been raised on my father's broken promises. But I told myself that he'd appear any moment. Maybe he'd gone for a walk. Or maybe he was in the gym or watching a movie. I refused to consider the idea that, once again, he might have left the premises, gone back to his house.

Molly complained. "You promised. You said we were going to eat dinner with him."

"He said he'd be here, Molls." What was I supposed to say? That it wasn't my fault if Grandpa broke his promises and couldn't keep his word? "And don't stamp your foot."

She let go of my hand, indignant. At opposite sides of the hall, we walked in tandem, looking for other residents, anyone who might know where Walter Hayes was. But we couldn't find anybody. Not a soul. The entire corridor was empty.

I was furious. How could my father disappoint Molly? It wasn't enough that he'd ruined my childhood; now he had to hurt my daughter, too? Why was I surprised? How foolish I'd been to let him near my child.

"Let's go, Molls." I took her hand, ready to exit and never come back. "I guess he's not here."

"Wait. Shh." She stood still, listening. "Do you hear that?"

Faintly, I heard men's voices swell and subside. Then silence. Molly had already scrambled toward them. At the end of the hall she turned right, disappearing through swinging double doors.

"Molly, wait." She didn't hear. Or, at least, didn't obey.

By the time I got through the double doors, she'd already scampered halfway down the hall. She glanced around to make sure I was coming before vanishing through another doorway.

The voices were louder now. And there were lots of them, a crowd. I ran to catch up with Molly, passing door after door, not sure which room she'd entered. I stopped, angry that she'd run ahead of me. Where was she? Which door should I open? I didn't have to wonder for long; laughter exploded behind the door to my left. High-pitched, shrill twittering and deep belly laughs. What was going on in there? What had Molly stumbled into? I opened the door, ready to pull her out of the room and scold her but couldn't find her. I faced a wall of backs. Dozens of people, facing away from me, staring at something in the center of the room. Stepping inside, I made my way deeper into the room. Where was Molly?

"Excuse me." I bumped into an elderly woman who stared ahead into the shoulders of the men in front of her.

"Watch yourself," she bristled. "We all want to see."

"See what?"

She eyed me with disapproval. "Who are you?"

I decided not to ask her about Molly. I kept moving, working my way around the throng. Finally, peering through a cluster of gray heads, I spotted Molly. She was standing in the center of the room, amid the flock of women who hovered over my father, who was seated at a table in the middle of the room. Several other men sat there, too. Holding cards. At the center of the table was a mountain of coins and paper money. Ones. Fives. A few tens. I almost keeled over, couldn't breathe. It was an old familiar feeling, catching my father in a lie.

"I'm out." One of the men put his cards down.

"Me, too." Another followed.

"Call."

The room hushed. Nobody moved. All eyes were riveted on the center of the room.

"Three tens."

The crowd murmured with anticipation.

"Two pair, jacks high."

Now it rustled, waiting, expectant.

"Fold."

Somebody sighed. "Damned bluffer," someone else muttered.

Nobody moved. Nobody as much as breathed. All eyes were on my father.

Slowly, silently, he laid out his hand. Five diamonds. "Flush." That was all he said.

Pandemonium broke out. Women were cheering, shoving one another to get close to my dad. Men were cursing or smiling, giving each other high fives, paying each other five dollars or ten, side bets on the game.

"I told you." A man held his hand out to collect his winnings. "The man cannot lose."

"Nobody wins that much." I recognized Leonard, my father's roommate. He grumbled as he handed over a twenty. "He's got to be cheating. There's no way he could win the way he does without cheating."

"You're just a sore loser." The other man pocketed his money. "Tell me how he's cheating. Otherwise, be quiet. Don't taint a man's honor."

Leonard leaned into the other man's face. "All I know is nobody wins ten hands in a row. Not unless they cheat. He got away with it so far. But he'll get his. What goes around comes around."

The other man walked away, ignoring him. Sputtering, glaring at my father, Leonard stomped out of the room. Except for the ladies adorning my father's shoulders, everyone was clearing out; I couldn't make my way through the crowd to get to the table. I stood against the wall, watching as Molly took a seat on my father's lap, as he deftly gathered up his winnings. The scene was so familiar that for a moment I had the sense that the child I was watching was not Molly, but myself. I knew the routine, could predict what would come next. I stood silently, seething, replaying a memory as my father demonstrated for Molly his flashy way of shuffling cards, as he deftly showed her a card trick.

"Pick a card." He held out the deck. I watched her baffled expression as he told her that she held the jack of spades. I almost recited his lines as, before he pocketed his money, he pulled a quarter from her ear. A regular magician.

"Bet you can't guess who this is for," he teased.

Molly giggled. "Bet I can."

"Okay. You're on. Who?"

"For me, Grandpa!" She shrieked with glee.

"Okay." My father sighed, feigning defeat. "You win the bet." He held out the coin.

I covered my belly before he suddenly jabbed to tickle hers; I tightened my fists before he let her grab the money. Who knows how long I stood there, watching my past, before I managed to reclaim my voice. Who knows what those straggling onlookers thought as a madwoman stormed across the room, shouting, demanding that the little girl give the money back.

Molly blinked reflexively, as stunned as if I'd struck her. "But, Mom—"

"What's the big fuss?" my father interrupted. "It's only a quarter."

"It's gambling money, Dad. You lied to me. You swore you weren't gambling anymore."

"What? It's a nickel-and-dime game. It's not real gambling." He lifted Molly off his lap and stood. "Let's go have some supper, why don't we?"

His teeth twinkled as he smiled, changing the subject, diverting attention from what he'd done. Molly clutched his hand with one fist, the quarter with the other. Together, they started for the door.

"A dollar says you can't guess what's for supper." Why was he persisting? Was he deliberately taunting me?

Molly glanced my way before answering. "Okay. I say I can." Her tone was gleeful and defiant. Oh, Lord. She was taking his side. Of course she was. He was fun.

Playfully the two of them started toward the dining room. I followed, seething. My father would never reform; he had no reason to. Why was I surprised that he'd lied to me about his gambling? He'd lied to my mother about it; probably he'd lied to Beatrice as well. Were there no limits to his lies? Was no price dear enough to get him to stop gambling? Of course not. He was addicted to it, completely at its mercy. Was there any game he wouldn't play?

Any moral lines he wouldn't cross? I wondered how involved he'd been with the gangs, whether he'd owed them money. He'd denied having any ties to them, but how could I believe him?

Women trailed along, and people swarmed around my father and Molly as they walked to dinner. "Walter, I hear you did it again!" "What's that—ten in a row?" "Who's that beautiful girl, Walter? Your good-luck charm?"

My father was his old sparkling self. Charming, waltzing his way through the dining room as through life. My daughter gazed at him, as enchanted with him as I had once been. "Do they have roast beef, Grandpa? Was I right? Did I win?"

He reached into his pocket for a single. "Yes. They do. You win!" He beamed as Molly grabbed the dollar, clapping, and he leaned over to whisper conspiratorially in her ear. I knew without hearing—I could remember what he would say: "Don't let your mother see this."

While my father and daughter got in line for a table, I shut my eyes and saw my mother, heartbroken, sneaking down the stairs, stashing away stacks of fives and tens to pay our grocery bills.

FORTY-NINE

SOMEHOW, I MADE IT THROUGH DINNER WITHOUT STRANGLING my father or even berating him further in front of Molly. I controlled my temper as he boasted about his social conquests and his latest winning streak, as he waved and nodded to admirers and fans. In just a short time, my father had become a celebrity at Harrington Place. In just a short time, he had become a hero to my daughter. And if I had to endure many more moments, I was going to choke from swallowing so many angry words.

Let it go, I told myself. What was the point of destroying Molly's image of her grandfather? What would I accomplish by pointing out his failings? He's an old man. She's a child. Let them enjoy each other. But as I listened to their happy banter, the cadence of my father's voice recalled my childhood. I could almost see my mother, almost touch her as she sat between us at the dinner table. My father and Molly ate roast beef and mashed potatoes as if she weren't there. He drank hot coffee and she a Shirley Temple, oblivious to the silent ghostly form beside them. He entertained her with humorous stories and number games, and I followed my mother, drifting to a dark place I couldn't quite remember and conversations I couldn't quite hear. I forced myself to chew and swallow, to feed the baby despite my lack of appetite. And when Molly finished the last of her chocolate sundae and Dad polished off his rice pudding, I whisked her away as soon as I could.

"It's not a bad spot for a vacation," my dad repeated as we walked him back to his suite. "They have lots of amenities. Nice people. But, fact is, I'm ready to go home."

Great. I'd have to explain it to him again. I searched for words to remind him that he was going to stay.

"But Grandpa, this is your home." Molly beat me to it.

He blinked at her, then at me. His mouth opened and closed. He seemed confused.

"Do you need anything to make you more comfortable?" I kept the conversation moving. "Is there anything you want me to bring?"

The man responsible for my mother's death looked at me, panic flitting through his eyes. "What's she talking about? Did she say I live here?"

"Yes, Dad." It was an awkward, painful moment when the information finally seemed to sink in. "But I can bring you whatever you want from the house."

His eyes aimed at me but looked inward, seeing his thoughts. "I suppose nothing matters there. Well, except Jackson."

"Jackson's taken care of, don't worry." I didn't know what else to say. Apparently he didn't remember that his dog was dead, and I didn't want to upset him.

"Oh, get me my slippers. You know the ones."

I didn't know, but I nodded anyway.

"And you might as well bring some of my pictures. Maybe that wedding picture—In the silver frame."

His wedding picture? Why would he want that? Then again, why had he kept all my mother's clothing for thirty-five years?

Molly grinned impishly. "Grandpa, I bet you a dollar you don't know what I've got for you."

Then, without giving him a chance to guess, she grabbed his waist and squeezed. "It's a hug, Grandpa. You couldn't guess! I won, didn't I?" She held her hand out for her winnings, and my father paid up.

FIFTY

It was only seven o'clock when we left. In the car, I thought about what to say to Molly. Should I warn her about the pitfalls of gambling? Scold her for unconditionally adoring her grandfather, for letting him enthrall her with his sparkling eyes and funny games? Anything I thought of saying sounded bitter and petty, even to myself. I drove in silence, practicing lectures, finally deciding to leave the topic of Grandpa alone for a while. But she wouldn't.

"Why are you so mean to Grandpa?" Her voice was petulant.

"I'm not mean to him."

"Mom. The whole world heard you yelling at him."

Oh, that. I'd already forgotten. "It's a long story, Molly. It goes back a long way. And you shouldn't take money from him."

"Why not? He's my grandpa."

"Just don't."

I felt her eyes boring into me as I turned onto Lincoln Drive, as I followed the curving road and stopped at a red light. I felt her studying me as I drove. She pouted but didn't say anything else until I parked. I looked out at the orange-and-red trees, wondering what about the street seemed altered. Was it my imagination? Or had the evening air suddenly cooled? Were the birds suddenly silent? Maybe it hadn't been wise to come here. Maybe we should go. But that would be ridiculous. I'd just have to come back again for Dad's things.

"Mom, don't take this wrong, okay?" Molly persisted. "I think you shouldn't be mean to him. Miss Sarah says everybody has goodness in them. So think about the good part of Grandpa and be nice. You don't want him to be sad, do you?"

I was distracted; it took a second to process her question. No, I assured her. I didn't want him to be sad. But I didn't want him to get himself into trouble, either. What was the matter with me? I wondered. Why was I so hesitant about going into the house? We were there simply to get my father's slippers—no big deal. And I hadn't broken my promise to Nick again; with Molly along, I hadn't gone there alone. We'd go in, find the picture and the slippers, grab them and leave.

"Mom." Molly was relentless. "Grandpa's not a kid, you know. He's a grown-up. If he gets into trouble, he'll deal with it."

I stared at her. She was so small; her sturdy little legs didn't even reach the floor. How did she know so much?

I kissed her forehead and thanked her for her advice. "Grandpa's lucky to have you for a granddaughter. How about we go get him the stuff he asked for." I opened the car door but stopped, looking up the street. The houses seemed off-balance, as if something intangible had shifted. Stop it, I told myself. It was the same street as always. The old house that had been Professor Hogan's. And the wrought-iron fence around what used to be Dr. Hennigsman's property. Lettie's front yard. But now it all seemed altered, palpably forbidding, as if daring anyone to come near. Absurd. What was wrong with me? I looked at my father's house, and it, too, seemed somehow different, off-balance. The windows seemed to sneer, and the eaves hung dark and sinister.

I told myself that I was being foolish. Nothing had changed. It was simply dusk. Under the fading light and in shadows, everything looked different. Still, I didn't get out of the car. I sat there, assuring myself that uneasiness was uncalled for. It was a remnant, a residual feeling left over from a miserable childhood. Or from the night I'd found Stan's body on the porch. Or from the day Beatrice had died. Or from the day I'd found Jackson's body. In fact, it could be left over from any of my visits; whenever I'd come near this house, something gruesome had occurred.

So? Don't you get it? I asked myself. How many hints do you need? Don't come back anymore. Leave. Start the car and go. But I didn't. I couldn't give in to groundless fears. Despite my instincts, regardless of my nerves, I was determined not to let the scars of my past dominate. The worst was over. The house was no longer a crime scene. There was nothing anymore to be afraid of. I was here to pick up my father's slippers, not to grapple with memories. And so deliberately, almost defiantly, I got out and helped Molly climb from the car. And for the second time in two weeks the two of us headed unsuspectingly up the narrow overgrown path to my father's door.

FIFTY-ONE

NOTHING'S GOING TO HAPPEN, I TOLD MYSELF AS I FELT SHADOWS close in around us. The streetlights dimmed faintly, and something chilly tickled the nape of my neck. I glanced around. Lettie's house seemed to tremble just slightly. No, that was me, shivering in the cool October air. We're fine, I insisted as we climbed the front steps. My fingers were unsteady, fumbling with the key as I unlocked the door, but we went inside, stopping in the foyer, since Dad had shot the lights out, to let our eyes get used to the dimness. There. See? Nothing happened. No corpse lay on the front steps. No body was splayed out in the front hall. No catastrophes greeted us.

When I could see well enough, I went into the dining room and turned on the lights. Looking around, my breathing was shallow, my fingers tightly clutching Molly's, my skin contracting in nervous gooseflesh. Stop it, I told myself. Relax. But I couldn't, felt tempted to run and hide in my childhood hiding place, the closet under the staircase.

"What's wrong now?" Molly released my hand and crossed her arms, sighing, impatient.

"Nothing." Except that the house was different. Disturbed.

"Where should we look?"

"What?"

"For Grandpa's stuff. Where should we look?"

Probably I was imagining things. After all, I'd just had dinner seated beside my dead mother; my imagination was in high gear.

Enough. I kicked into action, ignoring my instincts, and joined Molly in her search for my father's slippers and photograph.

"Let's sneak," Molly suggested. "Let's pretend we're on a spy mission."

We began sneaking in the dining room; moved stealthily into the living room. The wedding picture wasn't on the coffee table or the mantelpiece. It wasn't on the shelves, either. But something else was on the shelves. Or rather, not on them. I stared, trying to figure out what was wrong. And then I saw the clean spots, free of dust. Someone had been there, had removed—I didn't know what. Maybe a vase? A decanter? I wouldn't even have noticed the pieces were gone if not for the half inch of dust surrounding the imprints where they'd stood.

Damn. Someone definitely had been there and taken some of my grandmother's bric-a-brac. Or no—not taken it—the stuff was on the floor, beside the sofa. Just sitting there. A big old turquoise vase, a rather ugly green glass decanter, a floral-patterned china candy dish, a pair of pewter candlesticks.

Oh, God. What was going on? Would the police have moved this stuff? No. Why would they move a bunch of old keepsakes from a shelf to the floor? It made no sense. I grabbed Molly's hand and raced through the shadows of the house, aware that nothing that remained there was of much value, and that, amid my father's clutter, I probably wouldn't be able to tell if anything else had been moved. But I was angry. Incensed. Everywhere I saw evidence of an outsider. Someone had opened closet doors and dresser drawers and not closed them, had removed books from their shelves in the study, had tilted picture frames just slightly on the walls. A prowler had been here, had rearranged my father's luggage, tampered with the items on my mother's vanity. But, even stranger, nothing seemed to be missing. Things had been bothered, but not removed. The intruder had apparently come in, moved things around, and left. Why? Why would someone ransack a house and not rob it?

"I think I see them, Mom."

See what? Oh, Molly was still looking for my father's things. His slippers and wedding picture. She flew across my father's bedroom, reached under his bed and pulled out a pair of worn leather slippers.

"Great, Molls. Good job."

But she wasn't finished. She peeked behind a stack of magazines on the nightstand, and voilà: an ornately framed eight-by-ten wedding picture of my father and mother.

"Is this it? Did I find it?"

I reached for it and saw my parents in the peak of their romance. My father a debonair chap in his tuxedo. My mother a dark siren in a beaded, lacy gown. "This is it, Molls."

"Is this your mom?" She pointed.

"Yes."

"She's pretty. She looks like you. Exactly like you."

"You think so? Thank you."

"What happened to her?"

Oh, God. I didn't want to go into it. "She died."

"How?"

"Molls, it was a long time ago. An accident," I lied. But what was the point of burdening her with the truth?

Molly looked up at me. "How old were you?"

Oh dear. Was she afraid that I'd die young, too? "Around your age."

"Really? Poor you, Mom. That's so sad."

"It was. But I survived." Sort of.

She looked back at the picture. "I like her dress."

While Molly admired the wedding wardrobe, I looked around for more signs of the burglar. Wasn't the furniture out of place? Hadn't the bed been moved a little farther from the wall? The dresser edged a few inches away from the window?

"Mom." She was at the window, looking out. "Look."

Across the hedges, beyond the fence, in the moonlight, Lettie was running a small herd of puppies. "That's Lettie. She raises guard dogs."

"They're so cute. Can we go see them?"

Maybe. It was early. Why not? Lettie had said to come by anytime. Besides, I should update her on Dad and thank her for being so concerned and helpful, letting Hardy help us bury Jack. First, though, I thought I should call the police and report a burglary. But I couldn't even be sure that anything was missing, hadn't found a broken window or point of entry. The only proof that someone had been there were a couple of clean spots in an otherwise dirty house. For all I knew, Dad had moved the things himself during his visit home. There was no point, I decided, in calling. There was nothing, really, to say. And besides, I didn't want to deal with the police again. I'd tell Nick; that would be enough.

Yes, I told Molly. We could go.

And we started to. I stuffed the photo and slippers into my bag, and we descended the rear stairs, passing through the kitchen to the hallway. We didn't stop for anything, not even to find out why the door to the basement was ajar. Or why a bucket sat in the middle of the kitchen floor. At that point, I didn't dare to know. I just kept going, holding Molly's hand, until we were safely outside, heading for Lettie's house, feeling the evening breeze chill our skin.

That's when we looked down the street and, right in front of what used to be Dr. Hennigsman's yard, saw a crowd gathering at a gate.

FIFTY-TWO

MOLLY LOOKED AT ME WITH EAGER EYES. WITHOUT DISCUSSION, we walked hand in hand across the street to see what was going on. People were of mixed races, all ages, dressed casually in jeans and sweatshirts. Maybe it was a block party. Or a fund-raiser, a benefit of some kind. I pictured a backyard full of rock-climbing walls and trampolines. Face-painting. Music. Clowns. Molly would love that. We approached the crowd in front of the still stately property. The gate was open; people were lined up along the driveway, heading for the backyard fence.

"What is it, Mom?"

"Don't know. Maybe a block party."

"What's a block party?"

"It's where everyone on the block chips in and has a party."

She thought about that for an eyeblink. "Can we go?"

I didn't think so. We didn't live here, didn't know anyone.

"Please?" Molly made her pleading puppy face.

I looked around. The people were casual, seemed to be a bunch of couples and families hanging out together, some children and teens among the adults. Still, I wasn't sure we should stay. We didn't know what exactly was happening or even how much it would cost to get in. And, as an outsider, I felt awkward, hesitant to ask.

Curious, we drifted hand in hand to the crowd.

"Mom. Do you think it's a family-fun night? Like at school?"

"I don't know, Molls."

"Can we look?"

Okay. What would be the harm in that? We'd just peek in and see what was going on. It was still early. If we were welcomed and it seemed like fun, maybe we'd stay awhile. We went to the gate and looked onto the property.

"Ten minutes," a heavyset woman barked. "Ten-minute call. Ten minutes."

Suddenly, people on the street converged as if magnetized, closing us in. In a heartbeat the straggly line became a throng and we were sandwiched among a solid mass of bodies, unable to turn or edge our way out. I hung on to Molly, but she seemed unperturbed, striking up a conversation with a boy in line behind us. He was about two inches taller, older, probably around eight.

"No. But my grandpa does." I heard her tell him.

"Who's your grandpa? Because you have to live around here to get in."

"My grandpa lives here, but he's in assistant living." Molly pouted.

"Molls." I started to lead her away. "We ought to go. This seems to be a private party."

"Nonsense. Don't be silly." The boy's mother was about ten years younger than I was, and about fifty pounds heavier. Her rings dug into the flesh of her fingers, and her short hair was dyed an unnaturally bright shade of yellow. "Who's your grandpa, honey?"

"My dad lives down the block," I answered for Molly. "Let's go, Molls."

"Nonsense. I'll vouch for you. I'm Yvette Williams, and this is my son Brett."

Yvette and Brett? I blinked. "Zoe and Molly Hayes."

She offered her plump moist hand; I shook it. Brett and Molly were deep in conversation, like old friends.

"Thing is"—Yvette leaned over, speaking confidentially—"with all that trouble lately, you know, they're keeping security tight."

I nodded, as if I knew what she meant.

"But I'm a good judge of character. I can tell you're okay." She eyed me, then Molly, smiling coyly. "You are okay, aren't you?"

Okay how? "Sure we are. But look, we don't need to stay—"

"Of course you'll stay. No problem. You're with us." She slipped her hand through my arm, guiding me along, as Brett and Molly chatted.

The line moved forward, carrying us along with it, progressing through the gate where the ticket seller collected entrance fees. Unprepared, I faced him, an unshaven man wearing a purple bandanna around cornrows, a sleeveless sweatshirt. Scars of artistic carvings ran up his muscled arms and along his massive shoulders. He held his hand out for our admission fee.

"New neighbor?" He leered at me.

"It's okay, beefcakes, she's with me." Yvette stepped up and shoved him playfully. Familiarly.

"Hey, there." He grinned, revealing a gold front tooth. "Where you been, Yvette?"

"Nowhere you'd be." She gave a bawdy, suggestive laugh, and handing him a handful of cash, she leaned over to plant a sloppy kiss on his mouth.

When he could breathe again, he wiped his lips with his arm. "Okay. Let's keep it moving." He slapped her bottom as she passed. "Yo, Brett."

Brett gave him a high five as he passed. Behind him, an even larger man in a cowboy hat guided Yvette and Brett along toward the garage. Suddenly I wanted to leave. I felt trapped, panicky. The line pressed us forward, as eager and unstoppable as the tide; Molly had to cling to me to avoid being swept away. The man with the bandanna held his hand out, waiting for my cash. I fumbled inside my bag, fingers blocked by slippers and my parents' wedding picture, and I searched clumsily behind and under them for my wallet, finally pulling out a twenty.

The man rolled his eyes. "This all you got?"

Oh, God. Wasn't it enough? I had no idea.

"I got no singles." He handed me a five. "Next time bring exact." He smiled, revealing the gold tooth, resembling a pirate. I half-expected him to snarl, "Har, shiver me timbers." Gooseflesh rose on my arms. Who the hell was he? And what were we doing here?

Surrounded, bumped, pushed and jangled from all directions, we moved along with the crowd through the backyard into a huge five-car garage. We passed no entertainment on the way. No trampolines or face-painting or three-legged races. Someone was selling beer, and people smoked marijuana openly. But the great attraction was inside the massive garage, and it appeared to be a primitive sort of boxed-in plywood stage, mounted there like an arena. Maybe a hundred people crowded around it, shouting, shoving, chewing gum or sipping beers, a few holding kids on their shoulders. I looked around for Yvette, saw her standing with some other women on the other side of the stage. Brett had joined a bunch of older kids, teenagers. Molly held my arm with both hands, and she said something I couldn't hear. I leaned toward her so she could repeat it.

"Let's go." Her face was urgent.

She was right. Whatever was going on here felt wrong. The energy was too agitated. Disturbing. Slowly, trying not to attract attention, I led Molly back to the edge of the crowd, toward the side door. But tables were set up there, blocking the exit, and people scrambled around them, cash in hand. "Two large on Jangles." "Five on Ajax."

People were pushing to place their bets on whatever was about to happen. Okay. Time to go. I spun around, looking for a way out, slamming smack into a sweaty preppy-looking man with thick sandy hair, rough acne scars and tortoiseshell glasses.

"Christ Almighty. Can you watch out?" He stepped squarely on my foot, pushed Molly aside and rushed toward the tables. Wincing with pain, I was tempted to limp after him and share my thoughts about his behavior.

"Mom." Molly tugged at my hand. "Come on."

A woman with the skin color of cappuccino stood in our way, smiling as we tried to pass.

"Excuse us." I motioned toward the exit. "We're just leaving."

"But it's lockdown." Her smile faded; she tilted her head, eyeing us. "They're starting."

I nodded as if I knew and kept moving, trying not to draw attention, guiding Molly away from the platform.

The pirate and the man in the cowboy hat stood at the now locked garage door, blocking it. The crowd huddled around the arena, tense, hot, hungry. Brett and his buddies stood on tiptoes and craned their necks to see over the heads of adults. Oh, God. The first event was announced, and one by one, like heavyweight champions, dogs were introduced, led through the garage to the plywood structure.

Oh, God. The dogs—they were going to fight each other. That's what the arena was for. That's what people were betting on—the outcomes of the fights. How stupid was I? I should never have come in here. Incredibly, stupidly, I'd brought my six-year-old daughter to a dogfight. The dogs were released into the ring, ready to draw blood. The crowd swelled and hollered; the noise level peaked. I was sure Molly couldn't see over the others, but I covered her eyes anyway.

"Mom," she complained, "stop it."

"Hush, Molls."

"Mom, I can't see anything—"

"Shh."

I cupped my hands to make blinders, letting her see enough to stop her complaining but still limit her view, and I kept leading her slowly, inconspicuously away from the arena. As the fight began, I watched not the dogs but the crowd, their faces. What kind of people were these? Who would come to see dogs fight, let alone bring their families, their children? They looked ordinary, like folks you'd pass in the mall or the market. But as they watched their eyes grew bright, their skin flushed and thirsty. Their teeth gleamed; their bellies released howls and haunting bellows. The closed garage became airless, rank with the odors of tension, and, I was certain, fresh blood. And, even above the shouts of the crowd, I was sure I heard the soulful wails of wounded beings, the ripping of living flesh.

Keep moving, I told myself. Take Molly and get out of here. Casually, slowly, I edged her toward the door. We passed the coffee-toned woman, who now stood on a wooden crate in her Prada shoes, straining to see the fight. Her friend, wearing a diamond tennis bracelet and a brown ponytail, whispered something into her ear, and the two broke up laughing. We moved past the preppy guy again. Except for his rabid expression and dripping brow, he looked like an ordinary accountant; maybe he was one. His fists tightened around his betting slips and his jaw clenched; sweat beaded on his temples as he muttered a curse. Keep going, I told myself.

And we did. We kept moving until we were too far back to see the ring. And finally I took my hands away from Molly's eyes and led her to the door. The pirate and the cowboy blocked us.

I pointed to Molly. "Bathroom," I explained. I tried to seem annoyed, as if I resented having to leave the fight.

The men hesitated, assessing us.

Molly shifted from foot to foot, dancing impatiently. Maybe she really did need the bathroom.

"She's Yvette's friend," the pirate remarked.

The cowboy raised an eyebrow. "Then where's Yvette? Dammit. She knows the rules."

I shrugged, trying to seem apologetic. "We'll only be a minute." That would be about how long it would take us to run off the property.

Finally the pirate made up his mind and stepped aside.

"Your bag."

My bag?

The cowboy reached for my purse. "Leave it with us."

Damn. He wanted insurance to make sure we'd come back. I had no choice; I handed it over to him.

"Why's he taking your handbag, Mom?"

I squeezed her hand but didn't answer.

"Knock at the patio. Tell them Digger said to let you in." The pirate opened the door and switched on lights, illuminating the entire backyard. Before he could reconsider, I pulled Molly outside and we hurried away in the direction of the house.

FIFTY-THREE

BEHIND US, SPECTATORS ROARED.

"Mom? What is that place? Why did that man take your handbag?"

"Shsh." I pulled her across the yard. "I'll explain later. We have to be quiet."

"Why?" Her voice was loud. "Everyone else is shouting."

"Molls, shh."

"Mom. That boy, Brett? He said his mom's going to win ten thousand dollars in there tonight. Is she?"

I looked back, saw Digger talking into a cell phone, his eyes on us, so I steered Molly toward he house as if we were going to the bathroom. But as we walked I looked around, searching for a way out. The gate to the backyard was locked; a small battalion of bulky men stood guard. A tall wrought-iron fence blocked the perimeter of the yard. Think, I told myself. There's got to be a way.

Molly persisted. "Mom. Hello? Answer me."

I couldn't remember the question. "I don't know, Molls. Just come along with me, can you?"

"No. You're scaring me."

"It's okay. Don't be scared."

"Mom. You're not making sense."

"I'll explain later, okay?"

Digger was still watching as we knocked at the patio door. He was still watching as the door opened, and as I told the mustached, heavyset man who opened it that we had to use the bathroom. He gestured inside. When we were in the bathroom with the door locked, I knelt and spoke to Molly in a whisper.

"Molly, we have to get out of here. And we have to sneak."

"Why?" Her face said she thought I was crazy.

"Just trust me, will you? We're going around the corner of the house to sneak over the gate. But we have to be very quiet."

"Mom, why don't we just tell them we want to leave?"

"They won't let us."

"Why not? They have to. It's a free country—"

"They have the gates locked so nobody can come in or go out. Look, these people . . . What they're doing here is illegal."

"Really?" Molly's eyes widened. "So call Nick, Mom. He'll arrest them."

"Molls. I don't have my phone."

She paused, grasping the idea. "It's in your bag?"

It was, yes. As was the rest of my life—credit cards, driver's license, cash, house and car keys. Dad's wedding picture and slippers.

"So we can't leave." Molly was beginning to panic. "These people are bad guys. And that man has your stuff—"

"Don't worry about my stuff. Just act normal and come with me. I'll get us out of here. Okay?"

She bit her lip, nodding, and I kissed her forehead. Then, hand in hand, we left the bathroom, nodded to the mustached guy who didn't even look up as we went by, and began to head back to the garage. When I thought that no one was watching, I ducked with Molly behind the bushes near the fence and rushed her around the house, dodging the line of sight of the men at the gate, crouching under windows, edging our way silently toward the front of the house.

"I'm going to boost you up over the fence," I whispered. "Climb over the top, jump to the ground and run to Grandpa's."

She gaped as if what I said made no sense.

"Understand?"

"But what about you?"

What about me? I looked at the fence; it had smooth vertical bars that had to be eight or ten feet tall. No way I could climb it. But farther down, near the front of the house, I saw a magnolia tree. Its branches extended close to the top of the fence. Maybe I could climb it and shimmy along a branch, slide myself over the top. "I'll be right behind you."

"But—"

"No time to talk. Come on." And with that, I rushed Molly to the fence, stooped and held her around the waist. "Stand on my shoulders." One foot after another, she climbed up, and I leaned against the fence for balance. "On three, I'll stand, and you grab on to the fence and climb over."

I counted and, on three, pushed with my legs to a standing position. Molly hopped up and grabbed on to the top of the fence. Then she swung a leg up and over, shifted her weight and sat straddling the fence.

"Okay?" I whispered.

But she didn't answer. Still holding the fence, she lifted the other leg, and, facing away from me, without looking back, she leaped or fell eight feet down to the ground, letting out a loud involuntary shriek.

FIFTY-FOUR

"MOLLY? ARE YOU OKAY?" I KEPT MY VOICE LOW. "MOLLY?"

She didn't answer. She rolled on the ground, moaning. Oh, God. Was she hurt? I looked around, saw nobody. Maybe no one had heard her scream. With the tumult in the garage, maybe they wouldn't hear me call to her, either. "It's okay, Molls. I'll be right there."

Even as I ran for the magnolia tree, I felt the contraction begin. Damn. I had no time for a contraction now. Molly might be hurt. Holding my belly, breathing from my diaphragm, I scooted to the tree, found a low branch, stepped onto it, found a foothold in a higher one, then a higher one. Foliage blocked my view of Molly, and the contraction progressed, owning my body, making me dizzy. Oh, God. The baby—I needed to stop and keep still until the contraction peaked, but didn't dare. Instead I kept climbing, scratching my face and arms, twisting around branches to make my way up. Finally, when my feet were high enough, I grabbed hold of an overhead branch and edged out on a limb toward the top of the fence. The limb was thinner than I'd realized, and it swayed, sinking beneath my weight, threatening to snap. Lightheaded, swooning, I told myself to go slowly. Slowly was the only way I could go; the contraction tightened and held on to my torso. Don't faint, I ordered. Just keep moving. And then, just when I thought I was going to make it I heard a snap, and the branch beneath me was suddenly gone. Broken off. I was hanging by my hands, dangling from the sagging overhead limb. The contraction tightened. Hold on, I ordered myself. Just get over the fence. I kicked my legs out, banging my ankles against iron. Cursing, I looked around and saw the thug named Digger emerging from the garage, heading for the house. He was carrying my pocketbook, probably wondering where we were.

"Mom . . ." Molly's voice came from some bushes.

"Wait," I whispered; it was all I had the breath to say. I had to move; Digger was coming. My muscles screamed in protest as I tugged on the branch, lifting myself up, thrusting first my leg, then my body forward over the fence. Twisted, suspended at an angle, breathing through the peak of the contraction, I looked around to see if Digger had spotted me, and, just as his gaze turned my way, in one swift motion, I let go of the tree and swung forward, grabbing on to the fence, somersaulting, tumbling head over heels to the ground.

Oh, God, I thought. The baby. Not sure how many bones I'd broken, I lay on the ground in a fetal position, catching my breath, cradling my belly, praying I hadn't hurt the small being inside.

"Mom," Molly grabbed my hands and pulled. "Get up." She had a scrape on her cheek, and she was looking over the fence, at the backyard. "They're coming."

Panting, I followed her gaze and saw not just Digger, but several men in leather pointing guns and shouting, heading our way.

FIFTY-FIVE

SOMEHOW I GOT TO MY FEET AND HURRIED OFF WITH MOLLY. The lights were on at Lettie's, so we headed up her front path. Nobody would bother us there, not with all her guard dogs. Lettie would call Town Watch and the police, protect us from Digger. I rang the bell and banged on the door, but got no answer. Dogs howled and yipped, but no Lettie. None of her testosterone-loaded helpers. Nobody. Where was everyone? She'd been there just an hour earlier. I pounded on the door, but couldn't linger; any second Digger and his gangster posse would appear. So we hurried on to my father's place. And faced a locked door. My key, of course, was in my bag. I looked back down the street. We'd had a head start, but the men were moving more quickly than we were.

"Come on," I held on to Molly's hand and we ran toward the back of the house.

"Oh, no, Mom." She'd figured out where we were headed. "Please, can't we just go home?"

"No keys." I was out of breath, panting, sensing the onset of another contraction. Too soon.

"I can't go down there, Mom." It was a whine. "I can't. My knees." They were bleeding, scratched from her fall.

"Sorry, Molls. We have no choice." I pulled her across the lawn toward the back of the house.

"Why are they chasing us? What do they want?" She was out of breath, panting.

"Hurry."

"I'm scared. I want to go home." Her chin was quivering.

"It's okay." What was I saying? "Just hurry."

We scurried around back and flew down the slick basement steps, slipping silently through the doggie door. This time was easier than the last; this time, Molly didn't fight me. She scooted ahead, leaving me to squeeze my way through on my own. And I did. I lowered myself into the slime at the bottom of the stairwell, got down on my hands and knees, felt the cool muck slogging through my fingers.

"I can't take it anymore." The voice was desperate. Female.

"What?" I froze, crawling in sludge, realizing that the voice I'd heard hadn't been Molly's.

"You promised it would get better, Walter, but it isn't. It's worse. I can't live like this anymore."

I closed my eyes, recalled huddling in the basement, listening. Hearing my mother plead with my father. Crying. My father reassuring her. "Come upstairs." I saw him reaching for her hands. "Louise. Trust me. I promise. Believe me. It will get better."

What would get better? His gambling? His lies? The usual. But why was I remembering this now, while a gang of armed men were chasing us? And so vividly? I could almost see them, recall their words verbatim.

Are you crazy? I scolded myself. Stop dawdling. Get your butt inside before Digger gets here. And quickly, sloppily, I slithered through the swinging door and crawled into the basement, watching the shadows of my parents linger near the stairs, remembering their arguments, the way I'd listened from the shadows of secret places.

"They saw us, Mom." Molly snapped me back to the moment. "Those men know we're here." She looked gaunt, terrified. In the dim light I hugged her, examined her with slimy hands. Her face was smudged, her cheek scraped raw, and her curls tangled. Her knees and the heel of one hand were bleeding a little, covered with muck from the stairwell.

"Let's go wash up." I took her hand and started for the stairs.

"Mom." Near tears, she enunciated carefully, as if her mother were slow to comprehend. "Are you crazy? They saw us. Those men? They're following us. Call the police, would you?"

Right. Of course, I would call the police. But I was no longer in a hurry. Calmly, I led Molly up to the kitchen and called Nick on my father's phone. Then I washed our hands and dampened a cloth to clean Molly's scrapes. And by the time we heard the men banging on the front door and scratching at the windows, we were hidden away, safe in a place only I knew, where no one could find us.

FIFTY-SIX

"YOU USED TO PLAY HERE?"

It was dark, and Molly's whisper was so soft I almost couldn't hear it. "It was my very secret place. Nobody's ever been here but me, and now, you." Sliding through the doggie door, remembering the tension between my parents, I'd seen myself retreating into it again, and I'd known instantly what we were going to do.

"It's so cool. Was this your doll?" She'd found my old Tiny Tears. The baby doll could drink water from a bottle, cry and wet its diaper.

"Mama!" Its cry was loud, catlike.

"Shh. Put her down, Molls." I thought the men were still out on the porch, but we needed to keep quiet. "I used to pretend I'd found her. That she'd been abandoned." And now, she had been.

"So you pretended to adopt her. Like me."

Maybe. I kissed her head. "Never like you."

She leaned against me, her body alert, listening, and we snuggled in the tiny storage closet hidden under the front stairway. For a child, the spot had been perfect: a cozy triangle wedged under the steps, its door camouflaged, concealed in the wooden paneling. Without a flashlight the place was pitch-dark. When I closed the door, blackness swallowed us.

"Mom, it's too dark."

"The police will be here in a few minutes. It's just until then." Meantime, we'd be safe.

"I don't like it here." She held on to me, her body rigid.

"Molls, try to be quiet."

"But I have to sneeze."

"Go ahead."

A pause while she tried. "It's gone. I can't."

We waited, listening, and in the darkness, if not for the steady warmth of Molly's body, I might have been five or six years old again, hiding there. I could almost hear the voices in the hall.

"Give it to me, Louise," my father was pleading.

"I can't. I don't have it."

"I need the money. I've got to pay up."

"I told you, I don't have it."

"What did you do with it?"

"Nothing. It's gone. I don't know. Maybe I paid the phone bill."

"No, you didn't. It's here in the house. Think. Where did you put it?"

"Forget about it, Walter. You'll never find it."

The voices echoed in my head. Why was I remembering them? Why now? Damn. It had to be Bertram, his damned hypnosis. I must have talked about my parents while I was under. He had said I'd remember what I wanted to when I was ready. But I didn't want to and I wasn't ready. So why was I remembering? I never should have let him hypnotize me. My memories were better buried. Block them out again, I told myself. Sing to yourself. Or count the seconds. How many would pass before the sirens began to wail? How many minutes? Eight, tops, I thought. Less, since I'd called Nick on the house phone, and he'd called it in himself. So, maybe five. Or four. No way Digger and his friends would find us before that; my parents had lived with the closet in their house and they'd never been able to find me. Of course, I wasn't absolutely sure they'd been looking.

"Zoe Hayes? Hello?"

Oh, God. I hadn't heard them come inside. Molly jumped and clung to me, startled to hear their voices. Were they in the hallway? I wrapped my arms tighter around Molly, felt her heart beating quickly, birdlike, and we held perfectly, absolutely still, not daring to breathe.

"Yo—Zoe Hayes?" Oh, God. How did they know my name? "We know you're in here, Zoe Hayes. We saw you going up the path."

Silence. My heart was jumping, shaking the wall; surely they'd feel the vibrations. More footsteps, soft, prowling. "Come on out here, Zoe. We won't hurt you. We just want to talk."

Another voice. "We want to give you back your purse."

Oh, right. My purse. Of course—my license was in it; that was how they knew my name. They also had found my father's keys. Molly wiggled, rubbing her nose. I touched her arm, reminding her to be quiet.

"Come on, Zoe Hayes. You got guests. Be hospitable."

Suddenly, Molly stiffened in my arms, took a deep breath and grabbed her nose. Oh, no. The dust was getting to her; she had to sneeze again.

"Come and get your purse. We'll sit down and talk." On the other side of the paneling we heard slow, heavy steps. Old wood, creaking under the weight of strangers. Men prowling through the house. Whispers. Silence. Did they know their way around? Or had they been there before, moving vases off the living room shelves, moving my father's luggage, rearranging furniture? I wondered. Keep counting, I told myself. How long had it been now? A minute? More? In darkness and danger, time distorted. Moments merged with eons, indistinguishable. I stroked Molly's head, mostly to comfort myself.

A few feet away, a door opened. Oh, God. Someone was stepping into the hallway powder room, adjacent to our hiding spot. Skin prickling, unable to breathe, I turned so that my body would shield Molly in case they found the closet door. Would they use their weapons? I wondered. I thought of Gavin and Beatrice. Of Stan. Damn, we could be killed here. Once again, I'd endangered my children. I wasn't fit to be a parent, didn't deserve kids. What had I done? I pictured Digger standing just inches away from us, holding a gun. Any second he might notice the unsealed panel under the steps. Would he reach out and touch it, releasing the spring that opened it—

"Huh—huh—" Molly's back arched. Oh, God, she was going to sneeze. I grabbed at her face, fumbling in the darkness, covering her hands and nose with my hands, trying to stifle the sound.

"Shh," I breathed into her ear. "Don't sneeze."

She stiffened and squeezed her nostrils tighter, trying not to.

"Think about something else. Think about puppies." Puppies? Of course, cute and furry, ripping each other's throats out.

"Anything?" The voice was hoarse.

Close by, the powder room door closed. With all our four hands clamped onto her face, Molly held her breath.

"Nothing." The voice seemed farther away. Thank God. Slowly, cautiously, I exhaled.

"They gotta be here somewhere."

"This fucking place is so full of nooks and crannies, they could be anywhere. Right in front of us."

The men had moved away, but were still close enough for us to hear them. And for them to hear us.

"Breathe through your mouth," I whispered. Molly clung to her nose, her eyes glowing in the dark. "Stay calm." I held her, trying to slow my heartbeat, picturing men with guns tramping through the house, opening closets, looking under beds. I closed my eyes, recalled another man searching, frantically opening drawers, feeling under cushions.

"If we don't pay," he wailed, "do you know what will happen? Do you have any idea? Louise, don't you see the trouble we're in?"

"It's not my fault, Walter."

"I know that. I didn't say it was your fault."

"It's your fault. I warned you, didn't I? I told you what I'd do. You shouldn't have married me, Walter. It was all wrong, and you knew it. You knew how it would be."

"Louise. Cut it out. Just tell me where the money is. Where is it?"

My mother shook her head, tears soaking her cheeks. "I can't tell you. It's gone."

My father stormed through the house, tearing rooms apart, looking for loose floorboards, under cushions. My mother watched him stomp away as, in despair, she wandered toward the basement steps. And I huddled in the closet under the staircase, hiding from them both.

"Zoe, where are you? Zoe?"

For a moment, swathed in darkness, I clutched Molly, not sure who was calling. Was it my father? Digger? Was the voice past or present, imagined or real? How long had we been there? And where were the police? "Zoe?"

I sat perfectly still in a timeless void, deprived of light, feeling the past and present merge, not daring to breathe, holding Molly's head against my belly to stifle her sneeze.

"Zoe?" My name rattled the floorboards, echoed through decades, disguised to trick me. Suddenly, Molly pushed me away and let out a blustering " 'Choo!" Then another. And a third, each louder, more powerful than the last.

Oh, no. Surely, they'd heard. I held her, my body curved over hers, pressed against the wall, waiting for men to raid the closet. But nobody threw the door open; no one yanked us out by the hair. Instead, Molly rolled off my lap, calling, "In here—here we are!"

"Molly—" I grabbed at her.

But she loosened the hinge, slipping from my grasp, scampering through the paneling into the light.

"Molly—there's my girl!" Nick? Was he really here? "Are you okay? Where's your mom?"

"In there."

Easily, without guilt or hesitation, Molly exposed my secret spot. But I didn't come out, couldn't move yet. Exhausted, I closed my eyes and glimpsed my father running toward the basement steps, calling my mother's name. Enough, I insisted. No more remembering. Despite Bertram's guarantee that I'd recall only what

I wanted, I didn't dare to face more. I sat in the closet under the steps, replaying that moment, watching my father run to the door again and again, not moving even when I heard sirens wailing outside, even when I saw Nick reaching through the wood paneling, repeating my name.

FIFTY-SEVEN

NOBODY WAS THERE. NOT A SOUL. NOT A SIGN OF THE CROWD which, less than an hour before, had surrounded the arena. In fact, the arena was gone, too. The gates to the property had been locked, but as we stood there the gardener pulled up in a pickup truck. Lono, a Polynesian man who spoke little English, seemed both concerned and confused by the police presence. When he'd seen the badges, he'd let us in, allowed us to wander freely about as if there were nothing to hide. I'd scanned the ground for any sign of a crowd, found nothing. Not a single beer can; not even any cigarette butts. Lono turned on all the outside lights and tagged along as Molly and I led Nick and the other officers back to the garage, which he'd willingly unlocked, gesturing for us to step inside. I'd told Molly to wait outside and followed Nick, bracing myself to face a hideous scene of gore and maimed animals.

But the garage was clean. Perfectly, completely spotless. No bloody footprints on the floor. No ripped-up betting slips or receipts. Instead, a gleaming white Lexus was parked beside a shiny black Range Rover, with an antique Oldsmobile against the wall.

"I swear they were here." I was stunned, blathering. "At least a hundred people. A woman named Yvette and her son Brett. And a redheaded woman. And . . . some preppy guy with glasses. The betting tables were right there, against the wall. And the fights were in the middle, where the cars are. The first dogs—I think they were pit bulls—"

"Zoe, slow down. You're hyperventilating." Nick was frowning.

I looked at the other cops, saw doubt on their faces. Didn't they believe me?

I went to the door and pulled Molly inside. "Tell them what was in here before. What did you see?"

Molly paused, thinking. "You mean that kid, Brett?"

"That's right. Tell them."

"He was a liar." She paused, looking up at the circle of adults watching her.

"Why? What did he say?"

"He said dogs were going to fight in here. He said they'd even kill each other. What a liar."

There. I wasn't crazy. I met Nick's eyes with confidence as Molly went on. "Oh . . . Mom . . . Did you tell them about Digger? Nick . . . There was this big ugly guy, and that was his name. Digger. He took Mom's purse."

Nick scowled at me. "You gave him your purse?"

"It was collateral—I took Molly to the bathroom so we could get out. Digger took my bag to make sure we'd come back. That's how they got my dad's house keys."

"You say his name was Digger?"

"And he looked like this." Molly sneered, puffing her nostrils and curling her upper lip, not a bad impression.

Nick patted her head. "That's good information, Molly." Then he crossed the garage, peering behind the cars, examining the floors, the corners, the walls. "Where's the owner? Whose place is this?"

One of the officers checked his notepad. "According to Lono, their name is Fairfax. Eugene and Evelyn. Apparently, they're off on a cruise."

The gardener nodded, as if eager to be of help. "In Medirranean. Back on twenty-nine."

"So tell us, Lono"—Nick turned to the gardener—"who was here a while ago?"

"No one." Lono shrugged. "I think nobody was here. I just got here and I didn't see nobody but you here."

"Who else has keys to the property?"

"Fairfax sons, Alex and Jeffrey. But they away in school. In college."

The officer took down the boys' names and schools.

"Anyone else?"

Lono shook his head. "Nobody." We stood in silence, looking around.

"Oh, wait. Sure. Maybe other people have keys. Town Watch people, for security. You know, they watch the house. Also, maybe a lady from Mrs. Fairfax club. Mrs. Fairfax have good friend in her club."

Nick asked the woman's name, but Lono didn't know it. He knew only that Mrs. Fairfax was an officer in the club and that meetings were often held in the house.

A contraction started, and I grabbed Nick's arm.

He squinted at me. "Are you all right?"

I nodded, deciding that this was not the moment to tell him about falling off the fence. "Fine."

"You look like hell."

I smoothed my hair, self-consciously covered my stitches with my fingers.

"And Molly's knees are all banged up. You need to go home."

He was right. Again.

"I'll drive you and have one of the cops take our car. I've got the key."

"No. It's okay. I'm okay to drive." Why had I said that? I wasn't.

Nick sighed. I could almost hear his thoughts. He was exasperated, wondering why I kept getting into scrapes, what the hell I'd been doing here, how I'd managed to take Molly to a dogfight. He was dumbfounded that, once again, I'd put not just myself, but also Molly and the baby in harm's way.

I wanted to explain, but had no explanation. All I could do was apologize.

"Nick—" I began.

But he cut me off. "There isn't a speck of evidence here." He crossed his arms, deep in thought, gazing across the garage. Apparently, I'd been wrong about his thoughts. "I don't see a single hair or drop of blood. Amazing. How could they clean up so fast? These guys are pros."

"Detective Stiles?" A police officer gestured for him to follow.

Nick guided us outside and we stood on the grass, waiting as they took a walk around the outside of the garage.

Molly pulled on my arm. "Can we go?"

"As soon as Nick gets back."

"What's he looking for?"

"Evidence."

She looked at me, the question still hanging unanswered.

"He's looking for signs that those people were here."

"Why?"

Why. Obviously I had some explaining to do. I knelt beside her and tried to figure out what to say. "Molls, the people who were here—they were criminals."

Her eyebrows furrowed. "That kid Brett was a criminal?"

"Well, Brett's mom was."

"Mom. Is it against the law for dogs to fight with each other?"

"Yes, you bet it is—"

"So Brett wasn't lying? Those dogs were really here to fight?" Her eyes widened with disbelief.

I couldn't lie to her. I nodded. "Yes, they were."

"Like—how do they fight? Do they jump? Do they bite each other?"

I touched her face, kissed her forehead, sorry that she had to contemplate such ideas.

"Where are the dogs now, Mom? Are they hurt?"

"I don't know. Nick is trying to find out."

"But why do they fight?"

"I guess they're trained to." I thought about dogs and how driven they must be to serve their owners. Lettie Kinkaid's dogs served her by guarding and protecting; others served their masters by attacking and killing.

"But why would somebody want their dog to fight? It could get hurt."

She wasn't going to stop asking questions, and I had no answers, no energy to think.

"Mom." She tugged at me. "Answer me."

"I don't know, Molly." That seemed to be my standard reply. "Some people are just mean. Maybe their dogs learn to be mean like them."

That seemed to satisfy her. She stopped hammering me with questions and, deep in thought, wandered onto the lawn. I leaned back against the garage wall and closed my eyes, fatigue washing through me. I was exhausted, but I knew I shouldn't have been so abrupt with Molly. I'd need to talk to her more carefully about the dogs, to help her understand. I didn't want her to be afraid of them. But what should I say about something I didn't understand myself? And, although I didn't want to lie, I couldn't bear to present her with so ugly a truth. Wearily, I took a deep breath and started to join her beside a cluster of bushes.

"Zoe." Nick gestured for me to join him. "Think you're strong enough to look at something?"

I told Molly I'd be right back and followed Nick around to the back of the garage, where several policemen stood in a row, staring at the ground. A detective crouched on the ground, examining something; just beyond him I glimpsed feet wearing dark sneakers.

Nick took my arm, led me forward, past the police. "It's a body." His whisper was raw. I braced myself, gulping air.

"Do you know this guy?" Nick waited for me to look.

I started at his feet, saw the gun lying next to him, expected him to be one of the thugs from the dogfight. I scanned his jeans, his black zippered sweatshirt bearing a glow-in-the-dark Town Watch logo. Finally, my gaze reached his face.

Even with his head half blown away, yes, I recognized Hardy, the muscle-bound hunk who worked for Lettie.

FIFTY-EIGHT

NICK WALKED MOLLY AND ME BACK TO MY FATHER'S. POLICE cars lit our way, and neighbors watched out windows or from curbs as we passed. Lettie was among them, standing outside, watching. Was she looking for Hardy? Oh, God. What would we say to her? Were we going to be the ones to tell her he was dead? What had happened to him? I hadn't seen him at the dogfight. When had he come? And why? Had Hardy been gambling on the fights? Not possible.

I couldn't imagine that a man who worked with dogs, who trained them to guard people, would also enjoy watching them tear each other apart. Besides, Lettie wouldn't hire someone like that. Lettie was devoted to her dogs. And she was committed to protecting her community from violence. Then it hit me: Hardy had been wearing a Town Watch sweatshirt. He must have been on duty, patrolling the neighborhood and, just as I had, walked in on the event. Maybe he'd approached Digger or his friends, trying to shut down the fight. Maybe he'd even threatened to call the cops. Maybe that was why they'd shot him.

Lettie saw us coming, and wrapping her cardigan tighter around her, headed toward us. "What the hell?" She hugged herself, probably cold in the night air. "What's going on down there?"

I introduced her to Nick, hoping he'd keep walking, letting Molly and me escape. But he couldn't help himself; he began questioning her right away. Did Hardy work for her? How long? What was his last name? Did she know what he'd have been doing up the street? Did she know why anyone would shoot him?

Lettie was stunned. She grabbed me for support, her bony fingers digging into my arm.

"Who's shot?" Molly wanted to know. "Mom? Tell me." She tugged on me, wanting an answer, while Lettie recovered her balance and began spewing questions directly into my face.

"What were they running up there? A dogfight? What happened? Who shot Hardy? Did you see it—"

"Why would you ask about a dogfight?" Nick interrupted. "Did you know about it?"

Lettie eyed him harshly. "What else would it be? They're all over the place nowadays. Dogs are about the fastest-growing sport there is around here."

Sport?

"You know who's running them?"

She scoffed. "You want to know? Check out the cars."

"The cars?" I looked up the street.

"Those fights bring big money. Heavy betting. The winnings buy fancy wheels. Among other things." She gazed up the street. "So now they killed Hardy. Lord. They're taking over. What next?" She shook her head, hugging herself, shaking.

"Lettie," I suggested. "Why don't we go inside? You need to sit down." So did I.

She didn't seem to hear me. "Where's Craig? Was he shot, too? Or Jimmy?"

"We didn't see them." Nick frowned when I answered; I explained that Craig and Jimmy worked for Lettie.

Molly kept interrupting, asking what had happened, tugging on me, begging to go home.

"Soon," I promised.

"You always say 'soon,' but you don't mean it."

"In a minute."

"Okay. Sixty seconds." She began counting, "One Mississippi, two Mississippi . . ."

"They were together, you see," Lettie was saying. "All three of them. On patrol."

"Patrol?" Nick didn't follow.

"For Town Watch." Lettie looked up the street, as if trying to find Craig. "It was, you know, their turn."

That was why Hardy had been wearing a Town Watch sweatshirt. "When did you last see them?" Nick asked.

Lettie fretted. "About seven. When they set out. We take turns patrolling." She turned to me suddenly. "Who'd you say was running that fight?"

"I don't know."

"Some guy named Digger," Molly said. "He looked like this." Again, she curled her lip.

"You know him?" Nick asked.

"No, no. I don't know anyone like that." Lettie closed her eyes, set her jaw. "He's a new one."

Stan Addison flashed to mind. What had he said? I heard his voice warn about gangs taking over the neighborhood.

She stiffened, her jaw set. "But they've gone too far this time, these newcomers. Now they're not just intimidating us. Now they're killing us. Killing Town Watch people. Well, forget that. We were here first. This is our neighborhood, our home turf, and Town Watch won't stand for it."

Nick was on the phone, calling for detectives to come interview Lettie. Molly kept asking questions, wanting to know who was killed and who killed him, when we could go home, whether the dogs had been saved. I answered her vaguely, indefinitely. Finally, we walked Lettie up the long narrow path to her house. Dogs barked wildly. Inside, several meaty Rottweilers salivated at us from behind a hallway fence. Lettie scolded them and they settled down, sitting silent but alert, guarding her.

Police officers arrived. While Nick talked with them, I asked if Lettie was all right, if I could get her some tea or anything.

Her hands folded on her lap, Lettie clenched her teeth

and shook her head. Then she answered, "It's too late for tea, dear."

It wasn't that late. Not even nine o'clock. "Not really. I don't mind—"

"They took Hardy. Hardy is gone." She closed her eyes. "So this is the big time. This is war."

FIFTY-NINE

At Nick's request, a police car followed us and Carla Hollingsworth used Nick's keys to drive our car and unlock the house, taking us safely inside. My contractions didn't start again until Molly was getting into bed. They continued as I dealt with her never-ending questions about the dogfight, Lettie, Brett and Hardy. They got worse after that. Stronger, more frequent.

Call Dr. Martin, I thought. You've had more than four today. More than two big ones in an hour. But I knew she would want me to come to the hospital and be examined, and I couldn't imagine going anywhere. I was completely spent, lacking the energy to do anything, much less go into labor, so I told myself that the contractions weren't really that bad. That if I'd relax, they'd let up. If they didn't in an hour, I'd call the doctor, wake Molly and go to the emergency room. But first I'd rest. Nothing much could happen in an hour. I lay down and closed my eyes, following Bertram's hypnosis techniques. Breathe from the diaphragm, I heard him say. And relax your body, letting yourself sink into the mattress. Let the tension out part by part. I began with my toes. Moved on to my feet. My ankles. My calves. But when I released the tension from my thigh muscles, I felt myself lose my balance, falling, not safely into the mattress, but uncontrollably through empty air, toppling again off a fence toward hard, unforgiving ground.

Allow that memory, Bertram's voice whispered. Allow it and then set it free. Keep breathing. Inhale deeply. Exhale slowly. Envision yourself in your happy place on the lake. But despite his soothing voice, the skies I pictured grew dark, and bloodthirsty faces swarmed around me with gleaming eyes. Salivating dogs snarled, baring their fangs, and they leaped at each other, tearing through fur and skin. Stop it. I opened my eyes and sat up. But Bertram's voice persisted, urging me to get rid of the dogfight and everything else that happened today. To let go of all of those images and start over.

Okay. Why not? Once more, I lay back against soft pillows, hearing Bertram's voice in my head, letting him command me to breathe, to relax, to suggest to my uterus that it calm itself down.

Maybe it worked. It must have. Because the contractions didn't bother me as I lay there. I floated, unaware of my body, relaxed but doubting that I was hypnotized, and followed a path of memories that had begun earlier. I was a child, playing in my hiding place under the stairs. Voices rose in the hall, and I peeked through the paneling to see my parents.

"For God's sakes, Louise," my father pleaded. "Tell me."

"It's gone." My mother shook her head, bereft. Her hair was tied back in a long loose braid. "It's nowhere."

"It's not gone. You've hidden it." He sounded desperate. "Tell me where."

My mother didn't respond.

"If I don't pay, do you know what will happen? Not just to me. To all of us."

She stared at him, her shoulders slumped. "You knew better than to marry me. You knew how it would be."

"Don't start that again, Lou," he barked. "Just tell me where you put it."

My mother stood and looked at him, shaking her head.

And now I wasn't in my hiding place. I was invisible, following my parents, as in a dream. Watching my father rip the house apart, yanking pots out of kitchen cabinets, pulling drawers out of dressers, spilling flowerpots, checking the ledges along the tops of the walls. Meantime, unnoticed, my mother drifted toward the basement stairs, and I didn't want to remember any more. I tried to stop the images, but I couldn't; I was trapped, watching events unfold. But maybe this time I could do something about them. Maybe this time I could run after her—maybe even stop her.

Mom, I tried to shout. Don't go down there. Mom . . . But she drifted away, as if washed by some invisible tide. I turned to my father. Dad, I tried to scream. Stop her. Don't let her go. But he was caught in his own torrent of commotion, cursing, ripping through closets, tearing at coats and hatboxes, slamming doors.

She didn't stop when I hollered, so I ran to the basement steps, my feet pedaling air, arms flailing frantically as I realized I was too late; she was already out of sight, gone down into the darkness. I stood motionless, dreading, knowing better than to go down. Open your eyes, I told myself. Do not go on. But my eyes wouldn't open. I was stuck at the top of the steps, unable to escape, knowing that an awful, unbearable event was about to happen.

Except that it didn't. As I stood there mouthing silent screams, my mother came back up the steps. Seeing me, she smiled. Relieved and amazed, I stepped back to let her through the door, and she reached out for a hug.

Mom? I tried to say, but made no sound.

Her arms were slender and white, her eyes familiar. She wore a sleeveless pink nightgown, a ring of lace around the neck, and she continued toward me slowly, smiling gently. Was it really my mom? Had she come back? I waited for her embrace, ached for it.

Mom, I tried again. It had been so long. I closed my eyes, anticipating her touch, letting myself fall into her arms, and so I was surprised at the impact on my belly, the snarls, the sharp clawing nails—or maybe teeth—that dug into my flesh, trying to tear the baby from my womb.

SIXTY

A CONTRACTION, I TOLD MYSELF. THAT'S ALL IT WAS. I'D FALLEN asleep, and my dream had been interrupted by a sharp, sudden contraction, and, in the logic of a sleeping mind, I'd worked the contraction into the story of my dream. The ghost of my mother had not reappeared or ripped at my abdomen. Still, I put a hand on my belly, feeling it to make sure it was intact. No wounds. No pain. See that? It had only been a dream. I glanced at the clock: twenty after eleven. A couple of hours had passed since I'd lain down. Suddenly I was hungry. Actually not just hungry. Ravenous. And not for just anything. For peanut butter. Inexplicably, desperately, I wanted peanut butter. I flew downstairs, praying that we had some, that I hadn't used the last bit on some sandwich for Molly's lunch. In the kitchen I threw open the cupboard door and scanned the shelf, found the jar, grabbed it and, fumbling to open it, dropped the lid, let it clatter to the floor as I pulled a spoon from the dish rack. Finally, without shame or hesitation, I attacked.

Yes. No bread was necessary. No crackers, either. I shoveled up sticky moist mouthfuls and savored them straight off the spoon, wondering only vaguely at my sudden yearning. I'd never paid much attention to peanut butter before. Why now? Who cared? It didn't matter why. I had to concentrate on peanut butter. I licked the spoon clean, dug it in again, closing my eyes while sucking on the comforting glob. And, unbidden, the image of my mother reappeared to me, her face so vivid I could see the fine creases around her eyes, and she was smiling, her arms reaching out for a hug. A wave of fear passed through me, recalling the dream. What had it meant? Why had she attacked me?

Stop, I scolded myself. Dreams don't always have symbolic meaning; sometimes, they merely present a hodgepodge of impressions, a tossed salad of experience. My dream had obviously been just that. It reflected elements of real life: revisiting my childhood hiding place; seeing my mother's face again in her wedding picture; finding myself at a dogfight; being terrified by Digger and his pals. No doubt my mind had been trying to sort itself out, jumbling pieces of reality together. Still, I couldn't shake the image of my mother reaching for me, or the surprise and betrayal of sharp talons.

Okay, so I'd had a bad dream. I needed to get over it. I poured a glass of orange juice and headed for the comfort of the living room, my purple velvet sofa, my arms loaded with the jumbo jar, the full glass, some napkins and my spoon. But in the dark hallway I stumbled over something, splashing juice onto the floor. Dammit. What had Molly left in the middle of the floor? Sneakers? Her backpack? Cursing, I turned back to the kitchen, set the OJ and peanut butter down on the counter, grabbed some paper towels and turned on the hall light so I could clean up the juice. And stiffened, suddenly unable to move, as I saw what I'd tripped on.

My handbag. The one that Digger had taken. It was there. On the floor in the hallway.

For an endless moment, I stood blinking at it, trying to make sense of it. Unwilling to touch it, I watched it, suspicious, certain that it couldn't actually be there. And then, in a jolt of comprehension, I took off, spinning around in panicky circles, ducking into the kitchen, peering down the hall, realizing that whoever had left my bag in the hall had to have been in the house. Might still be there. Lord—

Without another thought, I scurried up the steps, first to check on Molly, and then to find a phone.

SIXTY-ONE

Officer Carla came back to search the house, and she'd stayed with us as a courtesy until Nick came home after midnight. When Carla left, he double-checked every inch of the house, finally announcing what I already knew. "Nobody's here. Molly's safe and sound asleep, snoring."

He joined me at the small kitchen table, my pocketbook between us. Nick looked worn out, bedraggled. I thought he'd lost weight. Even the blue of his eyes seemed faded, outlined in pink. The only feature that seemed vigorous and tight was the scar across his cheek. Probably he'd been working too much, hadn't adjusted well to overtime and late-night hours, had fallen behind in his sleep. Which, lately, with daily crises, I'd been interrupting. I told myself to let up. Nick needed some nurturing.

He lifted my purse. "Let's see what's inside. May I?"

I nodded, trying to breathe normally, as if I weren't having another contraction. It was after twelve; technically, it was a new day. The first one of the day. No need to call the doctor yet.

He unzipped it and turned the leather sack upside down, spilling the contents onto the kitchen table. I leaned back, grateful that Nick was momentarily distracted so that he wouldn't see me exhaling, wouldn't notice me holding my belly, waiting for the peak. He was busy, eyeing my scattered possessions. My father's slippers and parents' wedding picture were the largest, surrounded by my compact, hairbrush, lipstick. Headache pills. Contraction pills. Stash of M&Ms and chewing gum. A bag of trail mix. A pen. Tissues. My bulging overstuffed calendar. My cell phone. Various receipts and coupons, clipped together. My Institute ID. My keys, and my dad's. Nick opened my wallet, faced a photo I'd taken of him and Molly, found a couple of twenties, a five, and some change. Diver's license and credit cards were all there, intact.

"Go through it. What did they take?"

"Nothing." The tightness intensified. I almost couldn't speak. "I can't remember anything else."

"Good. At least you didn't lose anything."

I managed a nod, and as the contraction eased, I wondered why they hadn't taken the cash.

"These guys don't consider forty-five dollars worth taking." Wait, had I asked that aloud? Or was Nick answering my thoughts? He rubbed his eyes. "Let's be sure to call the locksmith in the morning. They probably copied the keys."

Oh, God. Of course they had. With their own keys, they could come back whenever they wanted. "You think they'll come back?"

"Let's not encourage them, okay?"

"But why did they come? What did they want?"

Nick watched me, spoke simply, as if to a child. "Probably they wanted to let you know that they'd been here. That they know who you are and where you live, and that they can get to you anytime."

I pictured Digger and his friends in my kitchen, walking down the hall. I wanted to fumigate the place. Nick took my hand and waited for me to digest what he'd said.

"They're trying to scare me? Why? So I won't talk about what I saw?"

He sighed. "These aren't nice people, Zoe. This was a serious warning."

A warning? I thought of Gavin's warning, the gutted dogs on his porch. Of Stan, lying dead on my father's front steps. Had Stan been warned, too? Had Beatrice? Oh, God. Was I next?

"I don't want you and Molly staying here alone at night."

Oh, Lord. Neither did I. But we were only alone because he

was out. I studied his eyes for the presence of a secret. With Nick, there were always secrets. Was overtime the real reason he was gone so much? "Nick, can you switch back to days?"

He closed his eyes and sighed, releasing my hand. I guessed that didn't mean "Of course."

"Can't you at least try? Just for a while—"

"Zoe, I'll do what I can. In the meantime, I'll get somebody to stay with you." He took out his phone, made a call, got up and walked into the hall.

I didn't argue. I didn't want to be alone with Digger and his friends prowling around, threatening us. I sat in the kitchen, an open jar of peanut butter staring at me, accusing me. Oh, God. Look what I'd done. My entire family was in danger because of me. How had this happened? Why? As if in response, my father's face appeared in my mind. Of course. It all came back to Walter. If I hadn't been at his house, Molly and I would never have seen the crowd, would never have chanced upon the dogfight. It was his fault. Again I saw my mother, refusing to give him money to pay his debts, regretting that they'd ever married. He'd ruined her life; now he was ruining ours. Because of him, killers and gangsters were after us. Because of him, my life was upside down.

Nick handed me the phone. "It's Susan."

Susan? In the middle of the night?

"She's coming over."

That's whom he'd just called? Susan? Was Nick crazy? What good would Susan be against thugs like Digger?

I took the phone. "Susan—"

"I'm on my way." It wasn't an offer; it was a fact. "Ten minutes."

"But it's after midnight—what about your kids?"

"Zoe, this is an emergency. Besides, Tim's here."

"But you don't need to—"

"Are you kidding? I'm not letting you be alone tonight—"

"So what are you going to do if they come back? Scold them? Give them a time-out?"

"Don't be cute, Zoe. You're on their radar, and you better be careful. These guys don't mess around. Don't argue. I'm on my way." She hung up.

I was furious. Why hadn't Nick asked if I wanted Susan to come over? "That's genius, Nick," I began. "Now, not only Molly and I will be in danger, but Susan will be, too. What a great idea."

Nick didn't defend himself; he just asked me to sit down. I met his eyes, saw exhaustion there. I sat.

"They won't be back tonight." He sounded certain. "They left their warning, but they didn't expect that you'd find it until morning."

So then why was Susan coming?

Again he answered my unspoken thoughts. "You're high-risk, Zoe. All this stress can't be good for you or the baby. Someone needs to be here, just in case your contractions start up."

Oh. It wasn't the burglars he was worried about; it was the baby. I looked away. Did he know the contractions had already started up? How could he? Either way, shouldn't he have asked if I wanted Susan to come? Why was he so controlling?

"I know. You're pissed. You think I'm controlling because I called Susan without asking you. But if I'd asked, you wouldn't have let me call."

Was the man reading my mind? How come he kept answering what I was thinking?

"So? Maybe you shouldn't have—"

"Damn it, Zoe. I'm worried about you and the baby. You're a pregnant woman over forty who is having early contractions and is under a huge amount of stress. For once, can you—" He stopped, exhaled, slowed himself down. "Can you try to let me take care of you both, just for a while?"

He looked wounded. I wanted to hug him. To have him take me in his arms and carry me to bed. I wanted to fall asleep with my head on his chest, feeling his skin, hearing his heart. But he was going back out, leaving me with Susan. Was that his way of taking care of me? And what about tomorrow night? Who would stay with us then? And the night after that?

"Tomorrow, I'll get you a real bodyguard. But for tonight, Susan should be fine."

How was he doing that? Were my thoughts so transparent and predictable that I didn't even have to speak?

Nick took my hand and led me to the living room sofa, covered me with an afghan. Then he went back to the kitchen and puttered around, reappearing moments later with glasses of milk and peanut butter sandwiches. I swallowed carefully, sickened at the smell of peanuts, alarmed once more at how suddenly, how drastically my passions could change.

SIXTY-TWO

SOMETIME AFTER ONE, SUSAN ARRIVED WITH A COUPLE OF homemade black-and-white milk shakes. More food. While Nick went back to work, we sat on my sofa sucking thick vanilla-and-chocolate cream through thin straws.

"When I was pregnant, I lived on these." Susan licked her lips. "They were my lunch. A banana and a shake. That's where I got these hips."

I sipped. The shake was sweet and smooth. Soothing. "Thanks, Susan."

"Don't thank me. Explain. How could you do that?" Her lips returned to her straw.

"Do what?"

"Go to a dogfight?"

Oh, that.

"And with Molly? Are you insane?"

Maybe. Probably. I sucked thick sweet shake.

"What were you thinking?"

"I wasn't thinking anything—I didn't intend to go."

She shook her head. "That makes no sense."

"I didn't know what it was. There were families, a mix of people, all sizes, shapes and colors. A few of the kids were even younger than Molly. Who'd have thought it was a dogfight?"

She wasn't listening to my explanation; she'd moved on to another issue. "But you didn't call me. Why not? Why did Nick have to call?"

"I was going to call you in the morning. I didn't want to bother you—"

"Bother? It's no bother. You know you can call me anytime, even the middle of the night—"

"I was tired, Susan. I thought it could wait." Lord. Did I have to defend every detail of every moment in my life?

"Well, thank God Nick called. You shouldn't be alone. Not in your condition, not with all the stuff that's going on."

I leaned my head back against the cushion, sucking on the straw. I didn't feel like talking.

"What? You don't feel like talking?"

What? First Nick, now Susan was answering my thoughts. Were my brain waves being broadcast, beamed from my forehead?

"Sorry. I'm real tired."

She frowned. "But otherwise, are you all right?"

"Fine." Except that every inch of my body ached. Old wounds that hadn't yet healed. New bruises that I hadn't been aware of, bumps from toppling off the fence were beginning to throb. Contractions surged through my body every time I began to relax. I wished I could have a glass of wine, closed my eyes and fantasized about something red and dry gliding down my throat, loosening my muscles. Susan's voice drifted around me like a melody, lyrics undefined.

"That's why it took me so long."

I had no idea what she was talking about.

"Are you too tired to hear what he had to say?"

I shook my head, no. Of course I wasn't. Whoever he was.

"He wasn't all that surprised. In fact, Ed says local gangs are popping up all over."

Oh, Ed. Susan's cop friend, her pipeline to the police blotter.

"These gangs may be local, but that doesn't make them small-time. They deal drugs, illegal weapons, prostitutes, loan-sharking, protection, gambling. And a particular kind of gambling is on the rise. Guess what it is?"

I blinked.

"Dogfights." She sounded proud of herself. "He says dogfights are actually the fastest-growing gang activity not just here—in the whole country."

I didn't say anything.

"And he said that, until this latest murder, the cops have been treating the Mount Airy cases—Beatrice and Stan and that guy Gavin—like gang-related executions. Which translates to: The cases have not been overlooked, but they also have not been the district attorney's top priorities."

I didn't follow.

"Wait, you're saying that the police think the victims were involved in the gangs? Beatrice?" I pictured her. Her pillowy torso, her pinkish perm. Not my image of a gangster.

"They think so, yes. You don't have to be a tattooed thug to take bets."

I saw her on my father's kitchen floor, betting forms shoved down her throat, imagined her working at a dogfight. But she'd been active in Town Watch. Hadn't Stan said she was his patrol partner? No, Beatrice hadn't been in a gang. It wasn't possible.

"Anyhow, gang killings are tough to solve. They involve a lot of layers. The actual killers, if they get caught, are usually just grunts who don't even know the top guys who ordered the killings. Fact is, for better or worse, these kinds of murders often go unsolved and unpunished."

I still didn't quite get it.

"So the police are giving up? The murderers get a pass? Gangs can do whatever they want?" I put my milk shake down, disgusted.

"No, they aren't giving up, not at all." Susan sounded defensive. "The cops are doing what they can, but the DA's office isn't pushing. Realistically, if the cops pick up a guy or two, the DA doubts they can get a conviction. And even if they did, it wouldn't affect the overall operation of the organization."

I still didn't get it. If they could arrest gang members, why wouldn't they? Maybe they could cut deals with them, like on television. Get the bad guys to testify against their bosses. "A killer is a killer. And killers should go to jail."

"Zoe, why is it that you can't accept reality? You like things clear-cut, black or white. Right or wrong. The world doesn't operate like that."

"So in the real world a gang murder is not as urgent to solve as—what? A murder of passion? Or revenge? Or greed?"

"Look, Zoe. It's not about urgent. It's about solvable. Gang activities like these dogfights are big business involving gobs of money and lots of invisible but powerful people. It takes time and manpower figuring out who did what. The cops are on it, but for now the DA's office wants them to focus on other cases—cases they can win in court."

I sat up, picked up my milk shake. "Fine. So people get away with torturing animals—and oh, by the way, with multiple murders."

"Dammit, Zoe. Horrible stuff goes on every day, all around us. The police are working literally hundreds of open murder cases, and these are among them. But Ed says the DA isn't content to just go after the little guys. The cops are being advised to keep a low profile until they can get the kingpins—"

The "kingpins"?

"—and that takes time. Nobody's saying that dogfights aren't horrendous. Frankly, I agree with you. The DA's position pisses me off. I'm just repeating what Ed told me."

I thought of the dogs in the arena. I pictured Jackson, ripped up in my father's basement. Hardy's face, half blown away.

Susan was still talking; again I'd missed what she'd said.

". . . but they're beyond saving anyhow before they're even in a fight. Most of them are doomed from birth."

Who was doomed from birth?

"Those dogs are bred to fight; they're genetically predisposed, primed for aggression. And, trust me, you don't want to hear how they're trained."

No, I didn't. But I knew she was going to tell me. I leaned back, adjusted the afghan, waiting.

"It's sickening."

I waited, in no hurry to hear the grisly details, knowing there was no stopping her.

"To begin with, the breeders mate only the most aggressive dogs to make sure that genetically the puppies have fighting dispositions. Then, when they get old enough to train, their trainers withhold food to keep them hungry, almost starving. Then they get a live rabbit or a puppy. Maybe they find a stray cat or steal a neighbor's pet. They dangle these animals in front of the dogs like bait. Can you imagine what a pack of starving dogs can do to a little kitten?"

She waited for me to respond. I didn't. I wouldn't. I closed my eyes and tried to breathe, to visit my happy place.

"They rip those helpless animals to bits, and they get rewarded. These dogs are trained to attack and kill from the time they're puppies. The only affection they get is for being aggressive. Their only rewards are for drawing blood."

She was right; it was sickening.

"I bet your dad's dog Jackson came up against one of them. A normal pet wouldn't hurt him that way. Against a fighting dog, Jackson didn't stand a chance."

I couldn't listen anymore. Didn't want to. I picked up my milk shake and sucked until it was gone, kept on sucking, making loud noises pulling air through the straw to drown out Susan's voice.

". . . cops want the top dog. They aren't just going to nip at the heels of this operation. They want to take a real bite out of crime."

I groaned. "Please, Susan. No puns, not now."

"The cops want to collar these guys, believe me. But the DA doesn't want to waste time barking up the wrong tree."

She wasn't going to stop. When she couldn't deal with something, Susan made jokes, the worse the better. It was her defensive mode. In her law practice, Susan dealt with murders on a daily basis. But there, the victims were human, not tamed, defenseless pets. Despite her bravado, Susan was having trouble dealing with violence against animals.

"It's a dog-eat-dog world—"

"Good God, Susan."

"What? Got a bone to pick with me, Zoe? A pet peeve? Are you trying to muzzle me?"

"Doggone it, Susan. Curb it, will you?" There.

"Sorry." She stopped, thank God. "So. It's late. We better get some sleep. We want to be bright-eyed and bushy-tailed Monday morning."

We did? "Why?"

Susan leaned forward, elbows on her knees, head extended, body contracted like a tiger about to pounce. "This gang stuff—I agree with you. It's gone too far. We've got to do something about it."

What could we do?

"Ed said the DA isn't pushing these cases. We want that to change. So we're going straight to the top. Right to the DA."

Wait. What? "We're going to the district attorney?"

"You bet. First thing Monday morning."

"Monday? I have to work." And I had a hypnosis session with Bertram.

"Call in. Say you'll be late."

"So we're just dropping in? And the DA's going to see us why?"

"Are you serious? What's going on in your father's neighborhood is absurd. Unconscionable. Multiple murders. Animal mutilations. Organized crime. Illegal gambling. Dogfights. And among this bubbling hotbed of crime, what single element is spectacularly absent? I'll tell you what—an arrest. So far, there hasn't been a single one. Not a solitary suspect. And you know why? Because, according to Ed, the DA's office has been letting these cases slide. So we're going to tell the DA that we want . . . no—we demand—to know why."

Indeed. "But detectives were on the scene when I left, Susan. They're working on it."

"The cops do their work, but the DA doesn't follow up. We need to press him to make this priority. Maybe threaten to get the press involved." She sat up, crossing her arms.

Susan had made up her mind. I knew her well enough not to argue. She was determined. Whether I wanted to or not, we were going to visit the district attorney. Still, I offered a comment. "Susan, you can't just barge in—"

"Of course I can. I work with that clown. I beat his ass in court on a regular basis. They know me there, and they know better than to mess with me." She smiled, looking evil. "And think about the richness of the situation. Here I am, a criminal defense attorney—a defense attorney, complaining that the prosecutors are too lenient. That the DA's office isn't being tough on crime? That, basically, they suck at their jobs? They ought to be mortified. That opportunity, that scene—actually, it's a reward in itself."

Her eyes were shining. Her skin was aglow. She reached for her milk shake and sucked hard on the straw, draining the cup. Then she took a legal pad out of her bag.

"I know you're tired." She searched for a pen. "But before we go to bed, while they're still fresh, I just need to jot down the basic facts. Tell me about the dogfight. What you saw, exactly. Where it was. How many people were there—and how many minors. How you happened to be there. What happened when you left. Tell me about Hardy and his body. And who got ahold of your purse and keys to your house. Just briefly."

Was she kidding? I could barely sit up; I was exhausted. Still, if it would help apprehend the "kingpins," I had no choice. Tired as I was, I ran through the events of the day. And as I talked I realized that, once I sifted out my conflicts about my father, my fears about the early contractions, my tensions with Nick and the emerging memories of my mother, there wasn't much to say. With those elements omitted, the day's events had still been frightening. But compared to all the rumbling emotions and the darkness in my mind, frightening didn't seem that bad.

SIXTY-THREE

FIRST THING MONDAY, WE ARRIVED AT THE WIDENER BUILDING across from city hall just before 9 A.M., but District Attorney J. Foster Blaine wasn't in.

Susan knew his secretary by her first name: Lois. Apparently, Lois and Susan were old pals. Short, square, powerful, her reading glasses dangling on a beaded chain, her extended fingernails painted shimmering white and decorated with rhinestones, Lois stood when she saw Susan, greeting her with a warm hug, and the two immediately began catching up, swapping gossip, whispering loudly about one lawyer's divorce and another's scandalous disbarment. I shifted my weight from leg to leg, finally took a seat without being asked to. Nobody noticed. They talked on, breaking into occasional fits of laughter, until finally Susan asked when the DA would be back and learned that he had meetings all day, something she had apparently failed to anticipate.

"Well, that's a shame. Tell him I stopped by, would you?"

"Sure. He'll be sorry he missed you. Next time you're around, give me a buzz first. I'll put you on his calendar."

"And we'll have lunch." Susan turned, ready to go. I stood, still nameless without an introduction. "By the way, Lois, do you happen to know which ADA handles animal cruelty cases?"

"Animal cruelty?" She frowned. "No. Wait a second." She punched a few buttons on her computer. "That would be Bill Frazier's office. Why? Do you have a case?"

"Me? No. This lady might, though." She pointed to me as if I were a casual stranger. Or a potted plant. "Where's his office?"

Before I knew it, we were headed for the office of William B. Frazier III, the assistant district attorney in charge of animal cruelty cases. Susan didn't apologize or explain her behavior, and trailing along with her through the halls of the old office building, I realized I was not with Susan my friend. I was with Susan the attorney, someone I'd never met before. This Susan didn't bother to ask the secretary if William B. Frazier III was available. She saw the door to his office open and marched right past the secretary, surprising him, introducing herself but, again, not me.

The ADA was a young man in his thirties. His hair was thinning and dark, his forehead shiny, his mustache well trimmed. His shirtsleeves were rolled up, his striped tie loosened. Susan's sudden arrival startled him. Ruffled, he pushed his chair away from his desk and jumped to his feet, as if ready to fend off barbarians. "Excuse me. You are?"

Susan stood still, waiting a beat. "I'm Susan Cummings."

She paused, allowing him to process what she'd said. When he did, it was apparent. His facial expression changed. His scowl became an uneasy smile. He stepped forward to shake her hand.

"Well, well. Susan Cummings." He repeated her name while holding on to her hand, as if trying to figure out what she wanted, what he should say next. "I've heard of you. I'm Bill Frazier. Please, call me Bill."

Bill was awkward, eyeing Susan warily. Why? Was she so formidable an attorney? Was her name enough to terrorize prosecutors?

"Okay, Bill." Susan released his hand and pulled up a chair, placing it directly beside his, invading his space. "Can we sit down, Bill?" She was already sitting. "Let me tell you why we're here."

As Susan talked about the dogfight situation in Mount Airy, I breathed through a contraction and looked around the office, noting the family photos on the desk, the diplomas on the wall, the palm tree in the corner, the trappings of a professional man. I noticed, too, how his eyes darted, how his fingers tapped his desk as she spoke. Halfway through, he tried to stop her.

"Actually, we have an ADA assigned to those very cases. He's working closely with the police, I believe. But you must understand that we need to have solid evidence before we can prosecute, and that's difficult with organized crime—and make no mistake, that's what you're talking about here. Organized crime. These gangs are local, but surprisingly sophisticated. The actual perpetrators are often the lowest guys on the totem pole, far removed from the people at the top. Often, even if we can identify the little guys, they have no idea who's at the top with all the layers of involvement and responsibility. We might jeopardize a whole investigation if we make an arrest too early, tipping our hand, so to speak. Because, as you well know, Susan, if the police don't have enough to make an arrest, we don't have enough to get a conviction."

"Don't put this on the cops, Bill—they're not the ones lagging here. If dogfights were a political priority for the DA, the cops would push these cases."

Bill smirked and leaned forward, elbows on his desk. "What planet do you live on, Susan? Let's talk about politics and priorities. The fact is we're overloaded here. My office handles animal cruelty, but guess what? We also handle rape and sex crimes. Hundreds of cases each year. We're always backed up, and we have to triage. How do you think the public would react if we let rape and child molestation cases get buried in order to prosecute some guy who raises pit bulls? Face it; animal crimes and illegal gambling don't arouse the public. If they're mentioned in the paper at all, they get a small paragraph on page twenty-nine. The DA is elected. We use our resources the way the public wants us to, or we're out. It's really that simple." His voice was gruff, defensive, and his skin pasty. The room smelled of his soggy aftershave.

Susan waited for him to finish. Her voice was patient, adamant. "Sorry, no. It's not that simple, Bill. These fights are linked to a string of homicides."

"Homicides aren't really my area—"

"Fine. Then let's stick to the dogfights. How do you think the public will react when the media report that the DA allows man's best friend to be routinely brutalized and mutilated or puppies to be tortured—"

"Okay, cool down." He grabbed his phone and made a call. "Morrison. Come in my office for a minute, can you?" When he hung up, he seemed more relaxed. "ADA Morrison is assigned to these cases. He'll be right in."

"I know him." Susan sounded unimpressed.

"Good. And since he heads up prosecutions of our animal cases, he should be in on this conversation." Bill leaned back, exhaling, loosening up, smiling, pleased to be passing the buck. "Would either of you like some coffee? Tea? A soda?"

I was thirsty, craved a ginger ale, but before I could answer, Susan offered a definitive "No, thank you." The pause grew awkward while we waited; Bill tried to fill it by turning to me. "So. Do you work with Ms. Cummings?"

Again, Susan answered before I could open my mouth. "No, actually, this is Zoe Hayes. She's a witness."

Bill raised an eyebrow. "A witness? To what, exactly?"

"Among other things," Susan replied for me, "Ms. Hayes was present at a Mount Airy dogfight Friday night where a man was murdered."

Bill blinked rapidly as he looked from Susan to me.

"She is also the woman who found the body of a man named Stan Addison in that same neighborhood."

"Wait, no. That wasn't gang-related. Didn't some senile old man shoot that guy?"

"No." My voice surprised me; I hadn't heard it all morning, and now I was correcting the ADA. "They don't know who killed him."

Bill's voice was condescending. "As I recall, the victim was found on the old man's porch, and the geezer still had the gun in his hand. At any rate, that death was not related to animal cruelty or dogfights—"

"You wanted me, Bill?"

Bill's gaze moved over my head, focusing on someone behind me. "Come in, Morrison. You two have met."

"Oh, yes. Doug and I go way back." By her tone, I knew that Susan wasn't a fan.

"My oh my. Susan Cummings. What brings you here? It can't be that piddling client you've been harassing me about—what's his name?"

"His name's Hiram George, and no, I'm not here about him, but—"

"What then? Raising money for the old alma mater? Need a check for the alumni fund?"

Oh. They'd gone to law school together. I turned, curious to see Susan's smarmy classmate. And immediately, almost fell off my chair. He was in a suit now, not khakis and a polo shirt. But there was no doubt. The man had the same sandy hair, rough acne scars, tortoiseshell glasses. The same preppy demeanor.

No question. ADA Doug Morrison was the man I'd bumped into at the dogfight.

Oh dear. My throat tightened, cutting off my breath. Pretend not to recognize him, I told myself. Act like you've never seen him before. Ignore him. Oh, God. Did he recognize me? Did he remember that Molly and I had been the reason that the fight had shut down early? He must, I thought. After all, Susan and I were there to complain about dogfights and related violent crimes. And he'd seen me a few nights ago. Stepped on my foot. Exchanged words. Of course he knew who I was. Oh, man.

Okay, I told myself. Don't let on that you remember him. Pretend. If he thinks you don't know him, it might still be okay. So, while Susan talked, I concentrated on her, keeping my face clueless and blank. I didn't utter a word or as much as glance at Douglas Morrison for the rest of the meeting. I barely took a breath. When we said good-bye, I looked at Bill. When Susan and I walked to the elevator I felt wobbly, but kept on moving, staring straight ahead.

I had no idea what went on at the meeting, how it ended. In my panic I couldn't hear a word. And I knew, as Susan and I entered the elevator, that it hadn't mattered whether or not I'd avoided looking at ADA Doug Morrison. I'd felt his eyes on me the whole time.

SIXTY-FOUR

I LOOKED FROM SUSAN TO NICK, NICK TO SUSAN, AND SAW twins. Identical expressions of doubt and concern.

We sat at a table at the Fifth Street Deli, having lunch. I couldn't touch my chicken salad. I was too nervous to eat, queasy with fear. As soon as we'd left the DA's offices, I'd taken Susan into the ladies' room and frantically told her about Doug Morrison. She'd listened but dismissed what I said, insisting that it couldn't be true. She'd defended him, not because she knew he hadn't been at the dogfight, but because she'd known him since law school. Sputtering mad, frustrated with Susan, I called Nick and told him I needed to talk to him. Even though he hadn't slept yet, he'd come right over, met us for lunch. I repeated for him what I'd told Susan.

"He was at the dogfight."

Nick blinked at me, half his face wincing. "Are you sure?"

"I can tell you what he was wearing."

More eyeblinks.

"Look, he pushed Molly and me out of the way so he could place a bet. He practically knocked us over, he was in such a hurry; the fight was about to start."

They both stopped eating and sat still, watching me with furrowed eyebrows and tilted heads. Why? Didn't they believe me?

"What? You don't believe me? He was there—"

Susan shook her head, doubtful. "Are you sure it wasn't just someone who looks like Doug? I mean, Doug's always been an asshole, but dogfights? I can't imagine—"

"Susan. He was there. And if I recognized him, you can be sure he recognized me. He must know that I was the infiltrator who caused the fight to shut down early. He definitely knows that I was there. And that I know that he was there."

Silence. What was the matter with them? Didn't they see the danger?

Finally, Nick turned to Susan. "Well, if Zoe's right, it would explain—"

"Wait—," I cut him off. "What do you mean, 'if'?" Aha. I'd caught him. "If" meant that he doubted my word.

"Huh?" He seemed confused. "Please don't go semantic on me, Zoe."

"It's not semantics if you don't believe me."

"I didn't say I didn't believe you—"

"Well, do you believe me?"

He looked away, sighing. "Oh, Mother of God." He pushed his plate away and leaned his elbows on the table. "What are you talking about? What's the problem here?"

"The problem is that you doubted what I said." I was hurt, wanting to lash out and hurt him back. "And you know what? If a man can't believe a woman, maybe he shouldn't marry her—"

"Zoe—," Susan gasped.

"Oh, Christ." Nick grabbed my hand and met my eyes. "Zoe, what the hell? Look. I understand that you're strung out. I get it. I know that you're upset. But can't you accept that maybe—just maybe—the entire world isn't against you? Maybe you're hypersensitive?"

"Stop right there, Nick." I withdrew my hand from his. "Stop blaming everything I say or do on my pregnancy. I know what I saw."

"I never said you didn't. I merely suggested that you're overreacting—"

"Lord Almighty, will you two stop?" Susan put her hands up, a gesture of peace, but I wasn't pacified. I glared at Nick, who looked right back at me, eyes unwavering.

"Zoe, let me finish what I was about to say before you interrupted. *If* you are right, it would explain what's been hindering the dogfight investigations. I wasn't doubting your word, I was just—"

"—doubting my word," I finished his sentence for him, steaming. "If" was not merely an introductory word. It was a disclaimer.

"Guys, please," Susan pleaded. "Zoe, stifle it. You're not being fair."

"You know what, Zoe?" Nick reached for his plate, picked up his corned beef sandwich. "Think whatever you want. I'm not going to debate with you about how I phrased my sentence."

"Fine." I crossed my arms and sat sulking and childlike, resenting them both. For a few minutes they ate in silence. I watched the door for dogfight club members to barge in and shoot at me, saw two young mothers with preschoolers waiting for a booth. The gunmen would probably not make it past them. Safe for a while, I stared at my chicken salad sandwich, determined not to eat. But as I watched, it began to beckon me, luring me with tender white meat and crisp celery. Okay, I thought. I'll just take a nibble. I reached for it, took a bite of pure flavorful creaminess on rye. And suddenly the rest of the deli disappeared, and so did all coherent thought. I was completely absorbed in the act of devouring my sandwich, chewing, tasting, feeling, smelling. And, swallowing mouthfuls, I was overwhelmed with a craving for quantities of mayonnaise. I looked around, searching for sources of mayo, dug my fork into Nick's potato salad and helped myself to a healthy wad. Then another. Delicious. Smooth. Mayonnaise, I thought, was an underrated substance. I'd have to buy some on the way home, wondered why people didn't eat it plain, by the spoonful.

"So please, just be patient." Oh. Nick was talking. Apparently, I'd missed the first part, engrossed in condiment appreciation. "Even with your statement, we can't prove anything yet. And if this guy's involved and thinks you recognized him—"

"If?" Nick had balls, using that word again. I snapped back to reality. To the danger my life was in.

"Dammit, Zoe. Can I finish what I'm saying?"

"Jesus God." Susan shook her head, sick of us both.

"If—and, yes, I mean *if*—he thinks you recognized him, we've got trouble. Fact is, even if he didn't recognize you, we've already got trouble from your friend Digger. So, here's what we're going to do."

He waited for me to protest, but I didn't. Finally, he was addressing the danger I was in.

"First, I'm getting you that bodyguard. Don't argue about it. It's not negotiable. I want somebody to be around you whenever I'm not."

I didn't argue. A bodyguard sounded fantastic.

"And, beyond that, I think you should take a leave from work." Before I could open my mouth, he put his hand up to stop me from responding. "Hear me out before you respond. You're having contractions. Dr. Martin's advised you to take it easy. But your job—even half-time—is demanding and stressful. And with your father and his house, and Molly, and—if I haven't blown it by pissing you off—the wedding . . ."

He kept on talking, but I wasn't listening. I was studying his face. His eyes were bloodshot, his scar too purple, his skin too pale. Nick's rugged features seemed hangdog and haggard. He needed to take a leave more than I did.

"Okay. I'll think about it." I already had been thinking about it. The half-day schedule wasn't working for me; basically, it meant doing a whole day's work in half the time. In a few months, I'd be on maternity leave; I'd begun to think about starting it early. Nick's eyes widened, surprised that I wasn't arguing with him. I took his hand, smiling at him.

". . . just forget it." Susan nudged my arm for emphasis. "You won't have a minute to yourself." I'd lost track of the conversation again. Susan had said something that I'd missed. What was the matter with me? Why couldn't I stay focused? "You should grab every chance to rest now, while you can."

Was she crazy? "How am I supposed to rest with Digger and Doug and the whole dogfight community coming after me?"

Susan closed her mouth and turned to Nick; Nick turned to me. "If this ADA is corrupt, Zoe, he's going down. So are the dog-fights and the people who run them. In the meantime, you're not alone. We're going to take care of you."

I nodded. I didn't bother to point out that, once again, Nick had prefaced his statement about the ADA with "if." We all knew that it wasn't just my imagination or my hormones. Doug had recognized me and knew I meant trouble. I was in real danger. Whether or not Nick and Susan wanted to admit it, they knew that, too. Otherwise, Susan wouldn't have come running to stay with me in the middle of the night. And Nick wouldn't have jumped to hire a bodyguard. I could count on Nick and Susan. I loved them both. Suddenly I went all sappy, overcome with affection for the two people at the table with me. Tears swelled in my eyes. Oh, Lord. What was the matter with me? One minute I was cursing them, the next I was ready to slobber them with kisses. Nick was right. I was a bundle of confused, fluctuating hormones.

Susan was agreeing with Nick, urging me to pamper myself, get massages, take naps. When my cell phone rang, I was grateful. It gave me a chance to look away before they could see me cry.

SIXTY-FIVE

THE PHONE CALL WAS FROM HARRINGTON PLACE. MY FATHER had gone missing again. Not for the first time, he'd apparently wandered off the premises without signing out, and the administrator who called was not amused. My father hadn't been seen since the night before; his bed hadn't been slept in when Leonard looked for him at breakfast time.

Okay, I thought. Maybe he'd slept out. Maybe this time he was with a lady friend.

But he hadn't shown up for his dental appointment, either.

So what, I thought. He was having fun. What man wanted to go to the dentist when he could hang out with a babe?

And he'd not shown up to meet several men friends for a card game.

Now I knew it was serious. Dad had gone missing. Oh, God. Had the people who'd killed Beatrice and Stan gotten to my father?

In minutes, Nick had paid the check and popped the three of us into his unmarked police car. He put the light on the roof and, siren blaring, we went searching for my dad, finding him at the first place we looked.

He was in his kitchen, going through cabinets. When we walked in he looked surprised.

"Where were you?" he asked me. "I was worried."

Oh, God. He'd slipped again; he thought I was my mother.

"We've been worried about you, too, Dad. Nobody knew where you went."

"Me? I was on vacation. It was nice, but enough is enough. Time to come home."

Lord. What could I say to him that would make him understand?

"Walter." Nick stood beside Dad, leaned on a counter. "What are you doing?"

"Somebody's been in the house while I was gone. Damned thieves and punks in this neighborhood. I'm checking, figuring out what all they took."

"I've been here, Dad. My friend and I have been cleaning the place."

"You? You emptied out the kitchen? What the hell for?"

Susan tried to look innocent, as if she hadn't the slightest idea why his cupboards were bare.

Again, Nick stepped in. "Your doctors want you to move, Walter. They want you to stay at Harrington Place where you can get medical attention when you need it."

My father gaped at him. "What?"

"It's not just a vacation spot. It's where you live."

My father's lips trembled. "Hell if it is. This is my place."

Nick tried to explain that he'd pulled strings, helping Dad avoid legal entanglements regarding the deaths of Beatrice and Stan by placing Dad in an assisted living unit for his medical conditions. As I listened, though, tightness grabbed my abdomen, and I actually swooned.

Susan grabbed my arm. "Are you okay?"

I held on to her, steadying myself, sitting down at the table, unable to talk.

Dad was unimpressed by Nick's comments. "Those bastards." He shook his fists. "They think they can run me out? Hell if they can. I'm not going. They've been in the house, dammit." He headed out of the kitchen into the study across the hall. "Look—I'll show you. They've gone through my desk." His voice trailed after him, as did Nick and Susan. "The bastards have drilled holes in the walls and pulled up the flooring. I know how to protect myself, though. I've got plenty of tricks of my own."

"Nick?" Susan's voice was soft, urgent. "Zoe might need some attention."

While my father droned on about his house and what had been done to it in his absence, Nick left him in the study and came back to me, knelt beside me, putting a tender hand on my cheek.

"Zoe? Are you all right?"

I nodded, exhaling slowly through my mouth, waiting for the contraction to run its course.

"Oh, Jesus—a contraction? Can you get in the car? I'll take you to the hospital." His face blanched. I shook my head, telling Nick and myself that it was all right; I'd only had two other contractions that day, while across the hall my father cursed his neighbors and shuffled through his desk drawers, growing more angry and agitated.

Susan stood at the doorway, halfway between crises, watching my father on one side, Nick and me on the other. I couldn't get any air. I grabbed Nick's hand and watched Susan's face. "It's really all right," I managed.

Maybe it's not all right, I thought. Admit it. This one was more intense than the others. "Actually, I think . . . ," I began.

I was about to say, "we should go to the hospital," but I was interrupted by a loud explosive bang.

Instantly, we all ran to my father. He was in his study, seated at his desk, gripping a shiny, still-smoking handgun.

SIXTY-SIX

MY FATHER SEEMED AS STARTLED AS WE WERE AT THE NOISE. He put the gun down as if it were burning his fingers. "So? What are you looking at?" he scolded us. "It's old. I wanted to know if it still worked."

"Walter, exactly how many guns do you have?" Nick was obviously concerned.

My father shrugged. "A man's allowed to have firearms." That was all he would say. Nick locked the gun in its box, replacing it, for now, in the locked bottom drawer of the desk, keeping the key. By the time I'd assured Nick and Susan that I was better and that, if I had another contraction that day, I'd call the doctor immediately, Dad had finished surveying his study, and he accompanied us without resistance out of the house. Somehow by the time Molly came home from school, we'd delivered Dad safely back to his suite at Harrington Place, where he was welcomed like a returning celebrity.

Somehow the day passed without further upheaval. After the monster contraction that I'd had at my father's, my body quieted down. Nick and Susan made a fuss, but for some reason I was confident I didn't need to rush to the doctor. I insisted that the baby and I were fine, and repeated the promise that I'd call Dr. Martin if the contractions began again. But they didn't, not that night. For the first time in weeks I went twenty-four hours without gasping and cramping and contracting, and I couldn't help wondering what had happened, if anything was wrong.

The next morning, soon after Molly's school bus left, while Susan and I were sipping coffee, six-foot-five-inch Rudo Bachek reported for work, ready to guard my body. He was a burly, hairy Eastern European who spoke little English but knew his job. I couldn't open a door without him checking first what was on the other side, couldn't even drive a car or open my own mail. At work, as I conducted therapy sessions, he positioned himself so that he could see the windows as well as the door, and he wouldn't leave my side even to go to the bathroom while he was on duty.

Rudo's presence, of course, did not go unnoticed among patients. Some were bothered, others merely curious. Finally I gave him an easel and a stick of charcoal as camouflage, making him seem like a new patient. Besides, if he got bored, he could pass the time by drawing. Even so, with Rudo there, the dynamic was different.

In my morning group, Hank Dennis was disturbed at the introduction of a new person. He paced, wringing his hands, fretting that the balance was off, that there was now an odd number of people in the room, that Rudo was infringing on his share of personal space. Kimberly Gilbert, however, seemed delighted with Rudo; to her, he was a new surface to decorate, and she began dabbing her acrylic vermilion onto Rudo's arm or pant leg whenever she could. After four or five dabs, Rudo, irate, jumped up, cursed, and dragged his easel away. Kimberly followed, and, before I could intervene, he growled at her, teeth bared, eyes bulging, and grabbed the brush from her hand. Hank was mortified, gaping at Rudo as if face-to-face with his greatest fear. Samantha Glenn ran from her own easel to cower behind Frank DiMarco, coyly nuzzling her breasts against his back. Only Jeremy Wallace seemed unfazed, only vaguely aware of his own behavior, much less anyone else's. Finally, I moved Kimberly to the other side of the studio, where her paintbrush drifted off her paper onto the wall and the closet door instead of onto people.

During my private session, Rudo's presence seemed even more intrusive. Evie Kraus refused to draw or participate at all, and I assumed she was reacting to Rudo. It took a while for me to realize that Rudo wasn't the problem, that, in fact, Evie had taken no notice of him, had taken no notice of anyone. I finally understood that Evie was slipping away again into her catatonia, not talking, not singing, not drawing or responding. I talked to her softly, touching her hands and arms, but she gazed past me into space with unfocused eyes.

I tried to reach her. "Evie. Don't drift away. Come back. Be with us."

I put a CD on, playing music I knew she liked. Jack Johnson. I sat with her, singing along. "Please please please don't pass me, please please please don't pass me by . . ." But Evie didn't blink. She sat expressionless, a hollow hull. For whatever reasons, at least for now, Evie was gone; her spirit had clearly abandoned ship.

Evie was on my mind during my lunch break. Absorbed in thought, I was startled when Bertram landed at my table with his egg salad platter. Wearing an incongruously rumpled Armani suit, he sat beside Rudo, breathing quickly, even more intense and desperate than usual. When I asked how he was, he complained that research funding had almost run out and that he still hadn't been able to find a new source, even temporarily. Besides that, his wife had made it clear that money was the reason she'd left and, if he could only make more of it, she'd consider coming back. Bertram gazed sadly at the saltshaker, then, suddenly changing the subject, he asked how I was doing and suggested conducting a hypnosis session with me that afternoon. I declined, saying I had plans, but he became oddly persistent. "But you need to. You have to continue and keep up the rhythm of sessions or you could have more problems. No question, Zoe. For your own sake, come by. I can do one or two o'clock." His voice seemed shrill and a little frantic.

I wasn't in the mood to be hypnotized, didn't want to wake up crying without knowing why, and I didn't want to explain myself to Bertram, either. But Bertram wouldn't give up. He urged me to come by, almost insisting, even stating that if I didn't let him hypnotize me, if I stopped at this stage, something awful could happen to me. With that, Rudo stood to his full height and, glaring down at Bertram, asked me, "Is problem here?"

Bertram hadn't paid attention to Rudo until then. His neck craned, taking him in. "Who's he?"

"He's with me." I felt kind of smug.

Taking his tray of egg salad with him, Bertram slunk away, muttering that he was only trying to help, and that nobody better blame him if my pregnancy ended badly. Rudo sat down, beaming, pleased with himself. He'd guarded me successfully.

The week passed without major incident. Molly went to school and swim club and gymnastics. I went to see Dr. Martin, who proclaimed the baby healthy, reminded me to take it easy and count contractions, and increased my dosage of medicine. Rudo tailed after me like a silent shadow on steroids, but to his credit, when he was around I felt safe.

Nick left in the evening and came in early in the morning, crossing my path only for dinners, which were his breakfasts, and breakfasts, which were his dinners. We talked more on the phone than in person and seemed to avoid topics that were stressful or, for that matter, important.

I didn't visit my father for a few days, but I received two more phone calls about him. He was still insisting that he was merely on vacation, going home soon for good, and twice more he was stopped while trying to leave with a full suitcase.

Susan did some research on ADA Douglas Morrison and found that he was newly divorced and deeply in debt, information not inconsistent with his involvement in gambling and dogfights. She was beginning, finally, to believe me.

And despite Rudo's presence, Bertram continued to nag me, sending e-mails and leaving phone messages, seeming too interested, too eager to continue our hypnosis sessions. Nevertheless, I wanted to do whatever I could to minimize the contractions, so I finally relented, meeting him in his office on Thursday afternoon while Rudo waited in the hall. As in earlier sessions, I had the sense that I was there for only a few minutes, but when we finished an hour had passed of which I'd been unaware. I wasn't crying this time, but I was drained. Depleted, as if I'd run a marathon. When I asked why, as always Bertram assured me that I'd remember as much of the session as I wanted to whenever I was ready.

The week passed without more burglary, murder or tortured animals. But, day after day, I felt more removed from my life, distant from everyone. Molly was in first grade. She was in school all day now, had her own activities and friends. She was developing her own life, away from me. And Nick was gone most of the time, too. My professional contacts had been reduced, might soon disappear altogether. In the uneasy calm following the recent upheaval I felt lost, unsure of my identity and purpose. I didn't return phone calls, didn't want to talk to friends or hear chatter about daily events. I was surviving tentatively, hanging on to a routine that was about to end, following a dead-end path.

Increasingly, though, even when I was alone, I felt the presence of another person with me. The baby. A stranger, unknown yet already familiar, growing within my body, fluttering around behind my belly button, riding me like a bus to life on earth. A few times a day, I tried hypnotizing myself, not only for the contractions, but also to relax. I closed my eyes and pictured the baby's cells dividing: two became four; four became eight and so on, and I listened, straining to hear them multiplying behind the rush of my blood and the beating of our two hearts. Let your muscles float, I told myself, hoping that by relaxing my body I might relax its passenger as well. At night, alone in bed, I'd think about the baby, tried to imagine who it was, what life would be like after it arrived. And inevitably, thinking of the baby and parenting, my mind would wander to my own childhood. How handsome, how clever and slick my father had been. How troubled, how desperate my mother. And, drifting off, I'd wonder about Nick and me, and, years from now, what memories of us would haunt Molly and our fluttering, precious, still unborn child.

SIXTY-SEVEN

MOLLY GAVE ME A BUTTERFLY KISS AND FLITTED OFF INTO THE back of Susan's car to join Emily on a trip to Lenape Farms for a fall apple-picking excursion. I watched them pull away, waving, and turned to face my day. Rudo Bachek sat in my kitchen, taking up too much space. His hulking back hunched, he leaned onto the counter over his coffee cup, looking bored, waiting to accompany me to the supermarket.

But I couldn't focus on making a grocery list. I was unsettled, inexplicably jittery. I felt compelled to get out of the house, but not to do my Saturday chores.

"Come on, Rudo," I said. "It's a beautiful day; we're going for a drive." At first, I didn't think about where we were headed. Maybe we'd ride out to the Main Line where we could explore winding roads and look at elegant homes in which nothing nefarious ever happened. Or the countryside. Maybe up to Bucks County—to flea markets and antiques shops in New Hope. Or out to Valley Forge. We could walk the trails there, look at the fall foliage and the tiny log cabins where George Washington's soldiers slept.

Fact was I didn't give a hoot where we went. I just wanted to get away. Rudo didn't comment, but apparently he was as glad as I was to be moving. He seated me in his '02 blue Taurus, got behind the wheel, started the engine and pulled out of the parking spot without even asking where we were heading. And that was fine. We drove silently west through Center City toward the art museum. From there, I guided him onto Kelly Drive, and suddenly I was clear about where I wanted to go. Once again—like a lemming to the shore or a moth to the flame—I was going back to my father's house.

I told myself that it was important not to abandon the place. I'd just stop in briefly. Check on the property. Clean up a little; throw out another bag of trash or two. But the truth was, I had no idea why I wanted to go there. I just needed to. Rudo accompanied me up the front walk, stepping inside before me, making sure it was safe, and gesturing for me to come inside. As soon as I stepped over the threshold, though, I knew that, once again, someone had been there. There was no question this time. I told myself that it must have been my father. When he'd wandered home, he'd probably rearranged chairs and moved the end tables. But I wasn't convinced by that explanation. This time, the living room sofa had been moved. Instead of sitting neatly beside the fireplace, it sat sideways, at an awkward angle. Why would my father move the sofa? He wouldn't, even if he'd been strong enough. I grabbed Rudo's arm, partly to get his attention, mostly to steady myself.

"Rudo." I didn't know if he'd understand me. "Somebody's been here."

Rudo brightened; he had something to do. "Okay." He patted my hand. "I will check house. Sit here. Don't you to move." He put a hand on his holster and, surprisingly quiet for so large a man, crept down the hall, beginning his search.

I sat on the crooked sofa, waiting, looking around. Noticing the chairs. They were too close together. And the coffee table was off center. All the furniture, not just the sofa, had been moved, cushions turned. I couldn't sit there anymore, got up and wandered into the dining room. The hutch had been shoved several inches from the wall. Who had moved it? And why? Rudo slunk down the stairs to check the basement, then headed upstairs to the bedrooms. Curious to see what else had been moved, I went to investigate the part of the house he'd just secured. I stepped into the kitchen, headed down the basement steps. As always, I steered clear of the cedar closet, avoiding that corner. Wandering through chill air and damp shadows, I passed the stacks of packing boxes and trunks of old linens and clothes. The clutter seemed intact, untouched. The furnace, the workbench. The shelves laden with soup pots and cracked coffee mugs. So much stuff. Bulky old cushions, damaged kitchen chairs. And, in the far dark corner, a flicker of my mother, stashing valuables under the linoleum flooring or behind the loose brick in the wall.

Wait a second. Until that moment, I had forgotten all about that brick. But where was it? I closed my eyes, envisioning the wall, and in my mind I saw the spot clearly. It was at eye level, behind a pipe. I remembered it vividly now. A brick that came loose, concealing a cigar box full of valuables. Slowly, squinting in the dim light, I scanned the perimeter of the basement, examining the walls near pipes. And there it was, on the wall opposite the staircase, near the washing machine. I'd found it. It was real. I hadn't been just dreaming or recalling a childhood fantasy; the brick was there, just as I'd pictured it. Suddenly, all around me, other memories flickered, coming alive. The basement teemed with hiding places and secrets, all of them clamoring, fighting for attention. "Look over here," I heard them whisper. "Remember what happened?" "See what I've got?"

I looked around, making sure that the taunts I heard were only in my head, the voices of lost memories, struggling to break free. But I didn't follow any of them. I remained where I was, standing by the wall beside a loose brick. It wasn't at eye level, though; it was chest-high. I'd been shorter when I'd last looked at it. Still, I didn't dare to touch the thing. I stood there, staring at it, rubbing goose bumps off my arms, reminding myself that I was safe. Rudo had checked. Nobody was down here, lurking in the shadows. There was nothing to be afraid of; it was only a brick. Whatever was behind it couldn't hurt me. Slowly, I extended an arm and touched it, fingering the dark gaps around its edges. Then, tentatively, I pulled at it, but couldn't get a grip; the brick was wedged tight. Leave it, I told myself. Go find Rudo. But I didn't go. I stayed where I was, couldn't stop picking at the brick. I broke a fingernail, then another. I scraped a knuckle. I jiggled it, dug and tugged. Still, it wouldn't budge.

Get a tool, a voice in my head suggested. Look on the workbench. I crossed the basement and riffled through my father's tools, finding duct tape, screwdrivers, hammers, wrenches. A saw. A file. A file? I took it, slid it into the wall alongside the brick, working the brick loose until finally it came out far enough to grip. Then I tugged. Finally, easily, the brick came out, leaving a dark hole in the wall. I stared at it, wondering what was inside. I saw my mother tiptoeing down the stairs, hiding something under her robe. And I saw myself following, crouching on the steps, watching, wondering what she was holding. More than thirty years had passed. And now I could finally find out. I bit my lip, took a deep breath. Then I stuck my hand into the space, feeling for the box.

But nothing was there. No cigar box. Not even a spiderweb. Nothing but crumbled cement and dust. No sign that anything had ever been hidden there. I closed my eyes, replaying the memory. I knew the box had been there. I could picture it clearly, the big letters on the front, the insignia. Coronas? But it wasn't there. Probably my father had found it, sold the valuables and gambled away the money. At any rate, it was gone. As if it had never been there.

A wave of sadness washed over me, taking me by surprise. Stop it, I told myself. Nothing happened. There's no reason to feel anything at all. Still, I was overcome, as if I'd discovered a tragedy or lost something irreplaceable. Why? What was wrong with me? I stared at the brick, hoping it would answer, but it lay still and silent, and the only sounds I heard were the hushed echoes of my past and my rapid breathing. And the footsteps creaking on the floor above me.

I spun around, expecting to see Rudo standing at the top of the basement steps. But nobody was there. You're imagining things, I told myself. You're spending too much time in a dusty old house.

"Rudo?" I stood still, waiting for him to answer.

But he didn't. The floor creaked again. He probably hadn't heard me calling, must be looking for me.

"Rudo—" This time, I shouted louder. "I'm down here. Rudo?"

Still, Rudo didn't answer. But over my head, old wood creaked as somebody slowly crossed the kitchen floor. And silently, cautiously, opened the basement door.

SIXTY-EIGHT

OH, GOD. SOMEONE WAS IN THE HOUSE. SOMEONE WHO WASN'T Rudo was coming downstairs to the basement. Oh, God. Where was Rudo? Why hadn't he seen them?

Quickly, silently, I skedaddled across the basement, huddling behind stacks of crates and luggage, scooting when I got close to the door. Without looking back, I dropped to my knees and slithered through the doggie door into the mud, and as fast as I could I flew up the stairs, leaping through weeds and overgrown grass, trying not to stumble on roots and stones. I didn't know where I was going. Rudo's car was out front, but I didn't have the keys. Think, I told myself. Call somebody. But my bag, my phone were in the house. Okay, go to Lettie's. She'll call for help. You'll be safe there, with Lettie and Craig and all the dogs. I ran across the path, and through overgrown grass dived into the hedges that divided the properties, separating bushes with my outstretched arms, and tripping over a stump, sprawled into sharp branches that scratched my skin but broke my fall.

I lay still for a moment, panting, stroking my belly, listening for someone following me, but Lettie's dogs had sensed my approach, and I couldn't hear anything but their barking. Branches were above, beside, beneath and beyond me. They jabbed my back, arms, face and thighs. All I could see were leaves, dirt and rough bark. When I finally caught my breath, cautiously, I attempted to get up. My knees, then my feet made contact with the ground, and squatting in the hedges, I pushed foliage aside to peer out toward my father's house. Everything seemed quiet. No one was following me, not even my so-called bodyguard. Why didn't he know I'd left the house? Where the hell was he?

Pushing hair out of my eyes, I managed to stand and tried to regain some composure. It was possible, I admitted, that nothing at all had happened. It may have been Rudo I'd heard in the house. Maybe he hadn't heard me calling. Or maybe I hadn't heard him answer. Maybe I'd panicked and run for no reason except my overactive nerves and overworked imagination.

I stood in the middle of the hedges, looking at Lettie's place, then back at my father's, wondering where I should go. Maybe I should go find Rudo before I made a huge fool of myself. Probably, yes, that's what I should do. I started out of the hedges, going back in the direction from which I had come. And again, I tripped. This time, though, I caught myself, regaining my balance before I fell. Glancing down to see what I had tripped over, seeing a leg.

SIXTY-NINE

RUDO BACHEK'S LEG. OH, GOD. MY EYES FOLLOWED THE LEG TO the rest of him. Through the dense cluster of bushes I could barely see his body or find his face, but I could see the carnage at his throat, and now I felt woozy, smelling blood.

Dizzy, frantic, I whirled around, tore through the scraping hedges, sped past Lettie's dog agility course, raced across her backyard, not stopping until I reached her back porch. I was about to shout her name and pound on the door when I glanced around and saw Craig behind the picket fence of her side yard. Lettie was out there, too, the top of her head barely visible above the fence. Side by side, they were out there training dogs.

I called her name, but dogs were barking wildly, and she didn't seem to hear me. I ran off the porch, mouth dry, heart pounding, midriff tightening, contraction beginning. "Lettie," I called again. Again, my voice was lost in the yelping of dogs.

And the contraction intensified. Slow down, I told myself. Take your time. Breathe through it. Dr. Martin had said the baby was okay, but she also had reminded me that I was still in danger of going into early labor. Oh, God. Was that what this was? I was only halfway through the fifth month—was I about to lose the baby? Stop it, I told myself. You're panicking. This is no different from any other contraction you've had. Sit down and rest. Nothing will help Rudo anymore; wait until the contraction passes and you can move again. So, holding on to my belly, I stopped running and shouting and hoped for the stranglehold around my middle to ease. But Rudo Bachek's eyes were watching me through the branches, warning me to move. Slowly I made my way toward the gate to the side yard. Light-headed, I stumbled forward, one foot following the other. At the gate, I stopped to breathe through the peak of the contraction, leaning for support against the wooden fence, staring at the blurry latch with unfocused eyes.

When the contraction finally eased, I reached out to open the gate, peeking over the top of the fence to make sure no loose guard dogs would greet me. Two immense beefy Rottweilers met my eyes, growling with bared teeth, their muzzles moist and dripping red. They were right behind the gate, standing on hind legs, jumping, snarling, leaping to reach me.

I waved across the yard, hoping to get Lettie's attention, but she didn't notice, absorbed in what she was doing. She wore a bulky glove that covered her lower arm; Craig wore an entire outfit of protective gear. They stood together under a tree alongside a third man—maybe the one named Jimmy?—all facing away from me. I couldn't see what they were looking at; the tree was in the way. But I couldn't get their attention. The Rottweilers grew more excited, began slamming their bodies against the gate, trying to get to me.

"Good doggies." I tried a smile but, unimpressed by the sturdy fence, they leaped toward my throat, dripping pink foamy saliva. "Lett—" I started again, but the man beside her took a step, turning to talk into her ear, and I saw part of his face, and I stopped calling mid-syllable. Oh, God. I shut my eyes and opened them again, making sure I was seeing right. The man with Lettie—could he be the ADA . . . the one in charge of dogfight cases? It was. Definitely, Doug Morrison. But what was he doing here? How did he know Lettie?

Instinctively I ducked, crouching behind the fence so they couldn't see me. Why had I done that? What did I care if the ADA saw me? But there I was, hiding. The dogs, though, were not fooled. Smelling me or maybe my fear, they continued to bark and attack the wooden planks.

"Yo—quiet down." Lettie's voice was a low growl. "Bruno.

Dahmer. Down." The barking reluctantly waned, became yelping, and finally subsided as Lettie ordered them to be silent. "Settle down, you two. You did good, but it's over." She paused, maybe looking around. "Nobody else is out there, is there? Probably it's a damned squirrel. I don't see anything. Hush up, boys."

The dogs whimpered and grew mum. Whew. In the quiet that followed, I drew a deep breath and warily stood, peeking over the fence across the yard. Lettie and the men stood together beside a tree, blocking my view of whatever they were riveted on. A dog barked, scampering away from the tree, probably learning to obey command words. Of course. Training dogs was what Lettie did. Maybe the ADA was buying a guard dog. It didn't matter—I needed help. I reached for the latch and was about to call out to Lettie again, but just then Craig shifted his weight, moving a step away from the others, revealing what they were looking at. Standing at the gate I froze, my hand outstretched in the air, my mouth open, aborting its shout.

I blinked, absorbing what I saw. The dog sat at attention, staring at a rope that was hanging from a branch of the tree. And suspended from that rope, a small animal—a kitten? Or no, a rabbit. It was hard to tell from what was left of it.

Lettie called, "Now!" And the dog tore at the animal, snarling and ripping as Lettie, Jimmy, Craig and ADA Morrison watched. Lettie commanded, "Down," and the dog cowered on the ground, salivating, until she gave another order. When she said, "Now," it bounced up again and attacked, locking its teeth into the twitching, bleeding body dangling from a rope.

SEVENTY

I SANK TO MY KNEES, RECALLING ANOTHER BODY HANGING FROM a rope. Whose was it? Where? But it didn't matter, and I didn't know. Right now, I had to get away from here. Rudo Bachek was dead in the hedges, and Lettie was training fighting dogs. I couldn't believe what I was seeing. Lettie was involved in dogfights? And why was ADA Morrison there? Maybe he was investigating the dogfights, going undercover. No. That wasn't it—the man had gambled on dogfights; I'd seen him there. Maybe he was also involved in training the dogs. Maybe he owned some.

My mind was reeling. I backed against the fence, trying to grasp what I was seeing. Who had killed Rudo? Maybe he'd followed my intruder to the hedges and the intruder had killed him there. Lettie and the others might not be involved; certainly, if they'd known there was a dead man in the bushes, they'd have moved him. My mind was whirling. Crawl back to the hedges, I told myself. Go back to your father's house. Don't let Lettie see you here.

But Lettie was telling Craig to take the dog inside. "Hose him off but don't feed him yet. We want him hungry. Then clean up that mess."

There was some growling and barking as Lettie called to Dahmer and Bruno, who were still trying to announce my presence. But Lettie wasn't interested in what her dogs were trying to say; she was talking to Doug Morrison, walking him to the gate. I crouched, trapped, trying to hear over the whimpering of the dogs.

"He's going to win big." She sounded pleased. "If Craig doesn't spoil him."

"All your dogs are winners, Lettie."

"You should have thought about that before you went and did business with those sons of bitches. They killed Hardy, Doug. And I'll see all of them dead."

"Come on, Lettie. You're not afraid of that scraggly bunch, are you? Nobody can touch Town Watch."

There was a pause before Lettie replied. I imagined her pulling on a cigarette. "Listen, Dougie. You know, with Hardy gone, I got to look at my friends. I value loyalty, and I appreciate how long you've been with me. You know me. You know that to me, friendship is everything. It's for life. Nothing is more important. So, you and me, we're cool. It's a free country. You can go with those traitors if you want. No problem. Town Watch will survive. Do what you want."

"Lettie, you mean that?" Doug sounded baffled. "Thank you. You're right about our friendship, too. It means the world to me."

"Oh, I know that." She paused to inhale a cigarette. "And by the way, if you ever place a single dollar on even one event with even one of their dogs, you'll have to forget about me covering you."

What was she talking about? There was a pause. "Lettie, it was just one time." Doug was whining. "Give me a break."

"Sorry, pal. Can't. No breaks. You know the rules."

"You can break the rules. You're the one who made them."

They'd arrived at the opposite side of the fence from me, beside the gate. Not two feet away from me. I hunkered down, not daring to breathe.

"That's exactly right. I made the rules. You knew that. Which is why you had no business supporting those amateurs—"

"Look, Lettie. I made a mistake. I gave them a chance. Sorry. I screwed up. But you need me. Face it. If not for me, you'd have been in jail years ago. Probably for the rest of your life."

"Dougie, please. Don't try to scare me. Don't act tough. You just can't do it. You come off sorry and pitiful."

"Dammit, Lettie, you need me—"

"Oh, save it. We both know that the only way I go to jail is if you go with me. Not likely you'll want to do that. You'll have to come up with the money, love."

"You're not thinking clearly, Lettie. I'm your only legal protection. What I do for you is worth a fortune—much more than the paltry amount I'm in for."

"You owe me what—seventy-three grand? No, it's more now, isn't it? Eighty-something?"

"What I do for you is worth a lot more than that. All I'm asking is some fair consideration for my services. I'm worth it—"

"Doug, listen. You're very precious to me. If you weren't, you wouldn't be standing here. Dahmer and Bruno would have had you for lunch. I mean that sincerely."

"Now you're threatening me?"

"You disappointed me deeply. You went to my competition, Doug."

"Once—big deal. I'll never bet with them again—"

"I believe you. After all, they won't be around long. With the two main partners dead, they're all but out of business—"

"Lettie, give me a break. I had no choice; I had to help them out. Stan was family. My brother-in-law's cousin—"

Stan? Stan Addison? Wait. Dead Stan? Stan from Town Watch? Oh, God. What were they saying? That Stan had been running dogfights? I closed my eyes, sorting out what I was hearing. Doug went on, giving excuses for betting with Stan instead of Town Watch. So Town Watch was a front? A fake organization that sounded legitimate but covered up illegal gambling and dogfighting? And Lettie ran it. I pictured Stan, a middle-aged man wearing madras shorts and white socks, complaining that gangs were taking over the neighborhood. All that had been an act. He had been out on the street not to protect it, but to protect the gang's interests, and then to keep an eye on Lettie's gambling business so he could start up his own.

My back was beginning to ache from crouching, but I didn't

dare move, dreading what would happen if Lettie opened the gate and saw me hiding there. I prayed that they'd walk away. But they neither opened the gate nor walked away. They stood right where they were, talking.

"The way I see it, Doug, I've carried you for years. How many now? Four?"

"No. Less. Not even three—"

"Whatever. You're mine. Stan knew that. So did Beatrice."

Beatrice? Dad's Beatrice? Lord. The betting forms in her throat. Beatrice had been involved with the dogfights, along with Stan.

"This is America, Lettie. It's capitalism. Stan and Beatrice were little guys. Besides, a little competition never hurt any—"

"Stuff it. Those two cheated me. They betrayed me. They pretended to be part of Town Watch the whole time they were running their own paltry operation. That's why they went down. And I'll tell you what, the sorry assholes who worked for them and killed Hardy are hamburger. This neighborhood's spoken for. It's mine. It's my home base, and nobody gets an inch of it. In fact, I'm going to expand."

"You're what?" Doug's voice was an octave too high.

"I'm adding on. Business is booming—"

"Lettie, are you kidding? Not now. Don't do anything to draw attention to the business right now—"

"Opportunity knocks, Doug. I've been ready to expand for years. The place next door'll be available soon. That stubborn old fart. You know the one. Nothing—not Hardy and the dogs, not Gavin, not even what happened to Beatrice—could persuade him. But he's finally moved out. Old goat's in a nursing home. Lucky for him, too. He was about to have an accident."

An accident? Lettie had been planning to kill my father?

"Listen to me. You need to keep a low profile."

"Forget it. I've got to buy that place while I have the chance. More kennel space, more runs and training yards—"

I finally understood. Lettie had played the caring, good-hearted neighbor only to get rid of Dad. She'd called me, feigning concern, only to make sure to get rid of him. She'd had a hand in Beatrice's death. No wonder Dad had ranted about the gangs terrorizing his neighborhood. He was right. He'd stood up to Lettie and her helpers, and I'd unwittingly cooperated with her by moving him away. Oh, Lord. I was livid, wanted to leap across the fence and throttle her. Instead, I crouched in her side yard, alongside her fence, wishing that the pair of them would walk away, take a stroll toward her house. My muscles were stiff from huddling, but Doug and Lettie didn't move. Doug continued pleading with her to forgive his debt, reasoning that if she was flush enough to buy her neighbor's land, she must not really need his money.

But Lettie was unmoved. "I gave you a pass, Doug. You're still in one piece because of what you do for me and the business. But make no mistake; you're going to pay me what you owe. Plus interest."

"Lettie, technically I don't owe you this last twenty grand."

"Oh, yes, you do. I've taken over Town Watch. I own Stan and Bea's operation. Which means their dogs are mine; their events are mine; their bets are mine. You owe me every penny you lost to them. Plus what you owed me already."

There was an audible sigh. "You know I don't have it."

"Too bad." Lettie seemed unimpressed.

"I'm serious. I can't come up with it." He whined, pathetic.

"You'll manage. I know you will."

"Please, Lettie—"

"Oh, I almost forgot, Doug. How's your little boy? Stevie, right? How old is he now, five?"

Doug didn't answer.

"Doesn't he have a puppy?"

"Lettie, don't even go there."

"It's a golden Lab, isn't it? That's sweet. Every little boy should have a puppy dog."

"My family isn't involved—"

"Wouldn't it be a shame if, one morning, little Stevie opened the door—"

"I swear, Lettie—"

"—and found his doggie on his porch. I should say, all over his porch, you know—"

"If you even go near—"

"Guts spilled all over the steps? That would be a shame."

"You don't want to do that, Lettie." Doug was steaming. "I swear you don't."

"Of course I don't." Lettie's voice was sweet, chilling. "But business is business. Rules are rules. I know you'll find my money, Doug. I have complete faith in you. Now, come have some lemon cake. I baked it this morning."

There was silence for a moment; then, as Lettie chatted about zest of fresh lemons and payment schedules, the voices began to recede. Finally, they were walking away. I exhaled, relieved, listening, estimating their distance from the gate. When I could barely hear their words, I began to crawl away from the fence, keeping my head down so that if they looked in my direction, they wouldn't see me. As I moved, the dogs began barking again, slamming their bodies against the fence, but Lettie didn't seem to notice. At least she didn't return. I kept on, racing on hands and knees across the grass toward the hedges and Rudo Bachek's body, not noticing Craig until I bumped into his boots.

SEVENTY-ONE

SLOWLY I TILTED MY HEAD UP, NOTING THAT HE'D TAKEN OFF HIS training suit. He wore work boots, jeans. A scruffy flannel shirt. His chin was unshaven. Craig's eyes laughed as he stooped beside me and, in no rush, lifted me to my feet. Neither of us spoke. There was nothing to say. Panicking, I looked around for help, but saw only trees and hedges. And Rudo Bachek's body.

Rudo had been dragged out of the hedges. Oh, God. His face and throat were blood-soaked, torn wide open. By Lettie's dogs? Is that why they'd been so excited? From just killing a man? Craig had pulled him onto Lettie's property, ready to dispose of him.

Now Craig carried me back to Lettie's house. Along the way it occurred to me to fight. I began to kick and squirm, but Craig didn't seem to mind. He held me, my back against his torso, one massive arm encircling me and squashing my breasts, his free hand gripping my wrists so I couldn't scratch or slap at him. Bodies entangled, we crossed the yard engaged in a wordless struggle until, without a word, he kicked in the yard door to Lettie's basement and hefted me inside. Dogs were barking, and the air smelled of their breath, stale and musky. In the dim light I saw cages stacked around the perimeter. Hungry eyes glared out, teeth gleaming, flashing in a ferocious din. Dogs surrounded us. Pit bulls and Rottweilers. Mixed breeds. I couldn't see very well. A half-dozen cages, more. Oh, God. Lettie's fighting dogs. The kind she'd abused and starved to keep them aggressive. The kind that had killed Rudo.

I tried to break away and run, but Craig tightened his grip around my chest; I almost couldn't breathe. Effortlessly he carried me to the far wall of the basement, pinning me on a table with his knee, and, without releasing his hold on me for an instant, somehow managed to bind my wrists. I twisted and resisted, but Craig squeezed my nostrils until I opened my mouth to breathe. When I did, he shoved a kerchief into my mouth, gagging me. When he was sure I was unable to move, he took out his cell phone and made a call. Within seconds Lettie appeared at the top of the stairs. She didn't come down.

I gazed up at her, my eyes pleading. Surely she'd greet me, command him to take out the gag so I could explain and talk my way out of there. But Lettie looked down at us, frowning. "Damn it to hell, Craig. What next?"

Craig shrugged.

"Look, I can't deal with this right now. You take care of it, but keep her here till after the fight."

He nodded.

I grunted and wiggled, but Lettie didn't seem to notice. She turned and left without even addressing me, closing the basement door.

Craig picked up the end of a long rope, attached it to the ones binding my hands. Then he swung me over his shoulder and carried me to the center of the basement, where I saw that the long rope descended from the ceiling, from a pulley fastened among some pipes. Oh, God. Craig was going to hang me by my wrists.

Okay. Time to beg. I tried to talk through the gag. Please, I tried to say. Let me go. I won't tell anyone. I promise. I'll even gamble on your fights. But everything came out the same, a guttural gargle of unintelligible sounds. Craig wasn't listening anyhow. He checked to make sure my wrists were secured to the rope and pulled the slack rope dangling from the pulley, lifting me by the arms until my feet were about a yard off the floor. I kicked, I moaned, I pleaded for myself and my unborn child. But Craig didn't pause. He didn't even glance at me. He went around the room to the cages, unlocking doors. At the top of the stairs, he paused to say one word: "Now." Then he left.

Pain tore through me. My arms seared as if they were being torn from my shoulders. Another contraction grabbed my midsection, so sudden and powerful that I couldn't breathe, couldn't even see. I thought that, for sure, I was losing the baby. But in an eyeblink I realized that pain and contractions were the smallest of my problems. From all directions, dogs burst from their cages and lunged at me. Snarling and growling, they circled my legs with bared, dripping fangs while I hung, kicking and swinging, spinning in the air, as helpless as the mangled rabbit in the backyard.

SEVENTY-TWO

THE RABBIT, THOUGH, HAD HAD BETTER ODDS. IT HAD BEEN attacked by just one dog; I was facing about eight. Legs flailing, I dodged gnashing teeth, my muffled shouts lost in the din of barking and snarling. I contorted and twitched, too panicked to think. My shoulders screamed as my own weight seemed to tear my arms from their sockets, and for a never-ending moment the dogs and the room faded, bleached white, the color of my pain.

This was it. I was going to die. My baby would never be born. I would be chewed to pieces. I saw my corpse, pieces of my face missing, teeth marks in my legs, chunks gone from my neck and stomach. I wasn't afraid; I had no time for fear or any emotion. Not regret. Not sadness. I didn't think about Molly, Nick or even our unborn child. My life did not pass before me. I was about to be torn apart by starving, blood-hungry fighting dogs; that was all I knew.

Thoughts became irrelevant, burdensome. A deeper, more primal force took over, and my paralyzed, useless mind followed events sluggishly, as if from a great distance. Dodging the dogs, I saw myself kick and twist, thrusting my body forward and back, pumping the air until I began to swing. My heel accidentally collided with a dog's skull, adding momentum, and soon I was crossing the floor like a pendulum, legs tucked up to my belly to keep out of the reach of snapping jaws. I couldn't maintain that position for long, didn't have the strength. My legs weighed tons, and lightning pain flashed through my shoulders, sapping my energy. I looked down, faced starving eyes and savage teeth; looked up, saw ceiling beams and pipes. And suddenly, energy surged through me. Adrenaline flooded my veins, and I began swinging with both legs extended out, then up, higher and higher. Once, twice, again and again, yanking my torn, agonized shoulders against the ropes for leverage until, finally, my right foot reached high enough to touch, then to rest against, then to twist over and lodge an ankle above a beam. I hung there, inverted, working my right foot over the beam, turning it inward to secure its hold. Then, I lifted the left leg, struggling to pull the leaden thing up, realizing how heavy my left thigh was, becoming vaguely aware that I was having repeated contractions and that my midair leg lifts were making them worse. But it didn't matter. I had to get that second foot onto and over the beam. Beneath me, hungry dogs barked and chomped at empty air, salivating, reaching for my flesh. My left foot hit the beam, nearly making it over the top but slipping, nearly dislodging my right foot with its weight as it dropped. Immediately searing pain sliced the side of my heel as it grazed a dog's fang. Open jaws tried to close on it, tugging at me, almost yanking me from the ceiling.

"No!" I finally spat out the gag and tried to scream, but the barks of maddened animals drowned out my voice. With all my might I yanked my leg up, ripping it from the dog's mouth, leaving a chunk of flesh behind. Driven by pain, determined not to die as dog food, I thrust my left leg up with so much force that it rose well above the beam, allowing me to push it forward and land not my wounded heel, but my lower calf there. Great. Now I was crooked, hanging from my right ankle and left calf. My left heel was gushing blood, dripping it onto the floor, where half-starved ferocious dogs lapped it up. I couldn't stay in this position long, needed to shift my weight so I could balance. Pressing on my right ankle, I pushed my body up, shoved the left leg forward an inch, then another, until, magically, my left knee enfolded the beam. With it holding me securely in place, I shimmied the right leg forward until I was hanging from my wrists and knees, head dangling. The dogs watched me, no longer jumping, and they circled, waiting, not yet convinced that I was out of reach.

But I was. My shoulders throbbed, but the pressure on them had been relieved. My arms, still tied together, extended out over my head, and at first I couldn't move or feel them. Gradually, with my legs raised, the blood returned to them and they came back to life. Slowly I began to work the rope, squeezing my wrists, wiggling them until finally, painfully, I managed to work my right thumb down and out of the loop of rope. Somehow, throbbing, the rest of my right hand followed.

Exhausted, I stopped to assess my situation. My right thumb, probably dislocated, was now useless and pounding with pain; my foot was torn and bleeding, my contractions were increasing, my body running on adrenaline and agony. But at least, for the moment, gravity was working in my favor. With my head hanging below my body, blood was flooding my brain, allowing it to think again. Untie yourself, it advised. I arched my back and craned my neck to locate the knot around my left wrist. Then, reaching, straining, I worked the four fingers of my right hand, managing slowly to free the left. But, with my arms free, my upper body dropped and I hung upside down, dangling from my knees, arms folded at my chest. I waited, knees aching, staring at upside-down dog fangs, until a strong contraction peaked and ebbed. When it passed, I swung forward, lifting my torso toward the ceiling, reaching up and grabbing ahold of a pipe. Great. Progress. I was untied, hanging like a monkey from a pipe in Lettie's basement ceiling. And, for an eternity, that was where I stayed.

Beneath me, the dogs grew bored. When I'd bled onto the floor, they'd gone wild. But with my leg raised above my body, the bleeding had abated. When I'd been swinging from a rope, twitching like a pet in their training sessions, they'd been ready to kill me. But now I was motionless and beyond their reach. Gradually they quieted down, yelping or snarling occasionally. A few lay down, giving up. Now and then one would pass beneath me, pacing lion-like, hungry and impatient. Once a couple of them wrangled with each other, wrestling and biting until one retreated into its cage. I clung to the pipe, struggling to catch my breath and think.

The dog attacks might have stopped, but my contractions hadn't. One came after another, dizzying and only minutes apart. I scolded myself, hating myself for getting into this mess. I needed to go to the hospital, should have done so days ago. Now it might be too late. What if the contractions didn't let up? Would I miscarry, giving birth prematurely right there, in the ceiling? No, I wouldn't. I couldn't. Gripping the pipe, knees draping the beam, I told myself to relax, then realized that if I relaxed too much I'd fall and become a doggie treat. Tightening my grasp, I breathed, counting the seconds between contractions, replaying Bertram's calming voice in my head. "Imagine your happy place. Go there in your mind."

Eyes closed, suspended like a bat, I imagined myself safe at home in bed with Nick, Molly snuggling between us. My legs were numb from a lack of circulation, and the rest of my body throbbed, reminding me that I wasn't home safe in bed, that I might never be there again. I stifled a sob. Cut it out, I told myself. Keep breathing. Stop feeling sorry for yourself and think of a way to get out of here.

First, I had to deal with the contractions. I made myself count and breathe, breathe and count. In between, I tried to calm down and think. But before I could come up with even one idea for escape, the basement door opened. Craig paused, looking down, no doubt expecting to see my gruesome remains hanging shredded from the rope. When he didn't, he must have panicked. Without stopping to think, he came bounding, charging down the steps.

Lettie's half-starved dogs leaped to greet him. I wasn't sure if they'd obey my voice or if it was actually the right command. But for good measure, I forced a single syllable from my raw throat, shouting as clearly as I could the attack command I'd heard him yell earlier: "Now!"

SEVENTY-THREE

"DOWN!" CRAIG SHOUTED, BUT TOO LATE. AFTER THAT, HIS cries were shrill and soprano, but they didn't last long. The dogs ripped at his throat before he could make much noise. I stared into the ceiling, my eyes drilling through the wood over my head. I tried not to imagine the bloodbath beneath me, but I heard bodies thumping, blood spurting, dogs grunting and snarling, and I smelled the reek of terror and gore. I remained still, trying not to gag, not to faint, and I waited, not daring to look down, knowing that the horror that was happening to Craig was supposed to have happened to me. The worst sound was the quiet that came when the struggle was over. The soft ripping of flesh, the wet chewing as the half-starved dogs chomped, jaws smacking on fresh meat.

Who knows how long I hung there, frozen with dread, too sickened to move?

At some point, the dogs were sated and they lay around, bellies full, sleeping, snoring. It was time to go. Dreading what I would see, I turned my head and looked down at the basement floor, eyes darting away from the bloody mass near the steps, finding a safe landing spot beneath me. And slowly, trembling and weak, I grabbed the pipe with both hands. Then I lifted first my right, then my pulsing left foot over the beam, letting them drop, intending to catch myself, hang from my arms and hop gently to the floor. My shoulder muscles, though, were too sore, too wounded to support any weight at all. As my legs dropped, hot pain shot through my shoulders and arms. I wailed; my hands involuntarily released the pipe, and I fell the final yard or so, landing on my gaping wound, howling, slipping in my own blood to the floor. Around me, a few dogs looked up, bored or curious, but no longer vicious. None of them attacked. None of them even stood up.

Panting and trembling, refusing to look at Craig, I limped as fast as I could through a sea of dogs and cages toward the basement door. When I got there, I paused, listening before I opened it a crack and peeked out. I saw nobody, no people or dogs. But from upstairs, I heard Lettie's voice, and I froze, not daring to move.

"Craig?"

Oh, God. She was looking for him.

"Craig—you ready?"

The basement door opened.

"Craig? Where the hell is he? Yo—you seen him?"

A male voice said something. Jimmy? Another of Lettie's studs? Or maybe Doug Morrison. Maybe the ADA was still there.

Footsteps started down the basement steps. Holding my breath, I plunged out the door to the yard and, frantic and breathless, contracting repeatedly, I hobbled back through the hedges where I'd found Rudo Bachek's body and back to my father's house.

SEVENTY-FOUR

I RAN IN THROUGH THE KITCHEN DOOR, REMEMBERING ONLY AFter I'd shut and locked it behind me that it had been closed when I'd left the house. Someone else had opened it. I told myself that the prowler had undoubtedly left, that whoever it was would not be as great a threat as the people chasing me from next door. Still, I looked around for a weapon, opened a kitchen drawer, cursed myself and Susan for packing up all the kitchen utensils. I couldn't find a single carving knife, not one skillet or rolling pin. Get your cell phone, I told myself. Call for help. Watching the windows for Lettie or Jimmy, I searched for my purse, trying to remember where the hell I'd left it, replaying my arrival at the house. Had I left it in the living room?

Trembling, gulping air, I made it to the living room and collapsed onto the sofa. The contraction was blinding, overpowering; I couldn't keep moving around, couldn't even inhale. I lay back against the cushions, closing my eyes, waiting for it to ease. But it kept tightening, choking my spine, strangling my organs. What was it doing to the baby? I wondered. Could the baby feel the pressure? Bertram's voice echoed in my mind. Relax, he told me. Visit your happy place. Screw you, I told him. He had no idea what a contraction felt like. Who was he to tell me what to do? I lay there, my foot bleeding on the rug, feeling defenseless, noticing my purse on the floor beside a chair. Great. I had to get up again. It seemed impossible, out of the question. Go on, I scolded myself. Do it. For a moment I considered it. Maybe it would be better to die right there, to let Lettie or Jimmy or ADA Morrison find me than it would be to muster the energy required to pull myself to a standing position and walk the few steps to my cell phone. Every centimeter of my body was in pain. My thumb throbbed; my shoulder sockets burned. My heel was a searing, gory mess. And my uterus was a hard, tight knot, threatening to expel my baby. Death, for the moment, seemed like a viable alternative. A relief.

But some voice in my head nagged me to get up one more time. Get the damned purse, it kept saying. Take out your cell phone. Make the call. Then you can collapse. Grimacing, unable actually to stand, I rolled off the sofa and crawled toward my pocketbook. I was halfway there when a dining room window smashed. I looked across the hall, saw a shape at the window, an arm reaching through to unlock it. Oh, God. They'd found me. I couldn't run anymore. I kept low to the floor and grabbed my bag, dumped the contents onto the carpet, picked up my cell phone while watching the window lifting, Jimmy's beefy bulk climbing into the house. Lettie followed, then Doug Morrison. I crouched behind the chair, waiting for them to spot me. But they didn't come toward me into the living room. Jimmy went to the stairway; Lettie and the ADA headed for the kitchen. And as they swung the door open, I heard a howl, then a dull *thwack,* like the sound of a cracking skull.

I had no idea what had happened. All I knew was that I had a chance to bolt. Cell phone in hand, I hobbled to the front door, only vaguely aware of my body and my pain. All I could think about was escaping. I threw the door open and took a step, then froze. Dahmer and Bruno growled, jaws dripping, ready to attack. The gash on my foot came to life again, urging me to back into the house. Slowly, whispering curses at them, I backed inside and closed the door, expecting to see Lettie and her entourage waiting for me.

Instead, I saw my father. His cane was raised over his shoulder like a baseball bat, ready to swing. The ADA lay limp in the kitchen doorway, and Lettie was backing up, cowering, arms raised to fend off a blow.

SEVENTY-FIVE

OH, GOD. MY FATHER HAD COME HOME AGAIN, STILL NOT grasping that he lived elsewhere. He swung his cane again, swishing it through the air. "Out. Out. Get out, all of you. I told you—I want nothing to do with you leeches—"

Lettie, meantime, was yelling back. "Settle down, Walter. Stop swinging that thing—"

"You no-good trollop. You killed Beatrice—" The cane made a whooshing sound as it missed Lettie's head.

"Walter, stop—"

"I ought to smash your worthless skull in."

Doug Morrison lifted his head and tried to get up but, dazed, sank back to the floor. My father kept swinging, moving around the dining room toward the hutch. Deftly, he opened a cabinet and, an eye on Lettie, reached inside, behind a stack of saucers. Lettie waited until he was off-balance, then lunged, grabbed his cane, raised it over his head, ready to strike.

"No! Stop—" I bellowed, limping, running to tackle her. She glanced my way, hesitating for just a heartbeat, long enough for my father to extract the thing he'd been reaching for. A gun? Another one? I'd never seen a gun in our house, had no idea he'd had one, let alone a whole collection hidden away. But there it was. Silvery and cold, aimed at Lettie's chest.

She dropped the cane. It clattered onto the floor.

"Get the hell out." Dad's voice shook ominously.

"Walter, you're not well." Lettie adopted her soothing tone, acting the caring neighbor. “Put the gun away before you get in trouble. You’re losing your—”

The shot shook the walls, shattered the remaining glass in the already broken window. I jumped, ears ringing. Doug Morrison twitched to life in the kitchen doorway. Wobbling, he hurried to his feet, a purple welt rising on his temple. For a moment the four of us stood silent, stunned and waiting. And I remembered—the third man, Jimmy. He’d gone upstairs, must have heard the shot. I looked into the hall, expecting to see him creeping toward us, but he wasn’t there. Where was he? What was he up to?

Dad motioned with his gun, herding Lettie and Doug to the door. “Get out. If you ever set foot on my property again, I’ll kill you.”

Lettie opened her mouth to say something, and Dad fired the gun again. Again I jumped involuntarily. Splinters flew from the foyer wall, leaving a gaping white hole in the flowered wallpaper. I felt like I was going deaf.

Dad kept coming; Lettie and the ADA kept backing away until they were out the front door, where the dogs waited, barking and ferocious. My father fired through the doorway, and the snapping and snarling of the dogs became whining and wailing. Apparently at least one of them had been hit.

Lettie cursed, shaking a fist at my dad. He stood on the porch grinning, shooting at the bushes, and she, Doug and the whimpering dogs fled toward her house. My ears were ringing, and I didn’t notice the sirens until after I’d seen the flashing lights. I was puzzled at first. I remembered getting my phone, but after all the commotion, I couldn’t remember actually having spoken to 9-1-1. Obviously, though, I must have; the police had arrived, responding to the call.

SEVENTY-SIX

DAD'S SKIN WAS WAXY AND WASHED OUT. HE SAT DOWN, DEflated. But when Nick walked in, my father's eyes lit up, alert.

"The press is outside." Nick frowned.

Of course they were. The ongoing dogfights and related crimes hadn't interested them; even the murders of Beatrice and Stan hadn't made headlines. But the involvement of an assistant district attorney in such sordid crimes was a big story, bound to draw lights, cameras and TV crews.

"You're not talking to them. I'll have someone take you home and drive the car around back so you can avoid them." Nick was angry. He felt blindsided. Ambushed. His pregnant spouse-to-be had once again endangered herself and their child. The man he'd hired to protect her was dead. And his soon-to-be father-in-law had brained an ADA and shot up the neighborhood.

I didn't have the energy to deal with his feelings, though. I was spent. Hurting and exhausted. I wanted Nick to comfort me, but he was seething. I didn't dare look at him, much less climb into his arms.

While I'd waited for Nick, the police went to work. The dogs next door and the bodies—Craig and Rudo Bachek—were removed. Lettie and Doug Morrison were arrested, the latter taken away in an ambulance with a skull fracture and dog bites on his legs. And though I'd told the police about him and they'd searched my father's house, Jimmy had not been found.

"Walter, you're going back to your place, and Zoe, you're going to the hospital."

I didn't argue. I'd had about ten more contractions since the police had arrived and the EMT who'd treated me had said I'd need stitches to reconnect the torn pieces of my temporarily bandaged heel.

Nick headed outside to shoo away the media, but I stopped him. "Nick, wait—"

"What?" The expression on his face stopped me.

I fumbled for something to say, a reason for him to stay with me. "What about Molly? I mean, I was supposed to pick her up at Susan's—"

"Don't worry. I called. It's fine for Molly to stay there."

More blame. More guilt. I was a terrible irresponsible parent, not even remembering to pick up my child, too busy getting eaten alive by slobbering canines.

"Thank you," I managed. But he was already gone.

I sat opposite my father in his living room; he was on a wing-back chair, I slumped on the sofa.

"What the hell were you doing here, anyway?" my father growled.

"Sorry?"

"In my house. What were you doing here?"

I didn't answer, didn't know what to tell him.

"Somebody's been in here, taking my stuff. Was it you? My kitchen's empty—it's all gone."

I felt my face heat up, guilty again. I'd have to explain once more that he didn't live here anymore, that Susan and I had been cleaning the place out. "Dad," I began. "We have to—"

But he interrupted, his eyes sharp, mind lucid. "Somebody moved everything around. Look at this chair. It's out of place. And who moved the couch? What the hell's going on? That damned Lettie—she acts like she's everybody's favorite aunt, but trust me, she's evil. It's Lettie who got Beatrice into that vile business with the dogs."

"The fights? Beatrice was betting on them?"

"Betting?" My father scowled, shaking his head. "It was a hell of a situation. Beatrice got in bed with the Devil. A while back, she borrowed a bundle from Lettie, and to pay it off she started working for them, helping Lettie run the fights. But then Stan the genius—he had an idea, and Beatrice and Stan put their sorry brains together and decided to start up their own operation."

"But Stan was part of Town Watch. Wasn't that Lettie's group?"

Dad snorted with disdain. "Town Watch. Sounds like a legitimate oufit, doesn't it? Like they care about the community. It's a scam. Nothing but a cover. You join or they watch you. You join, and you get allowed into the fights. You get credit for your bets. You get hooked up with drugs or loans or whatever the hell you want. I don't even know what all. I want no part of it."

"So that's who killed Beatrice? Town Watch?"

"Beatrice made decent lasagne. But she was a stupid woman. She and that dunderhead Stan." Apparently he thought he'd explained everything. He pushed the coffee table, moved it about three inches, lost his breath. "This doesn't belong here."

"Leave it, Dad. Nick will help."

He sat down again, breathless. It was just as Lettie had said. Beatrice and Stan had been part of Town Watch, Lettie's gambling organization. But after a while they'd decided to develop their own dogfights, competing with Lettie's.

"Dad." I needed to know. "Did you gamble with Beatrice?"

"Do I look crazy to you? They came to me, those two. 'Join in with us, get in on the ground floor.' That's what they said to me. 'There's lots of money to be made in this business.' Can you imagine? The woman thought I'd be a part of that? I wanted none of it, and I said so. I told her not to do it, too. But Beatrice was stupid. She wouldn't listen. She thought she'd get rich."

"Did she?"

"Who knows. I broke off with her, didn't want anything to do with a woman who'd be part of something like that. But then she turned up at my house, choking. It was Lettie who killed her, too.

Maybe not with her own hands, but she was behind it. No doubt about it. Lettie found out what the two of them were doing and put a stop to it."

By having the betting slips shoved down Beatrice's throat and having Stan shot.

Dad picked up his cane, waved it like a wand. Or a scepter. "But now she thinks she can come in here and invade my home. Lettie and her thugs. No, there are limits, and my house, well, that's the limit."

My father didn't seem to grasp that Lettie and her friends were gone, but he was acutely aware of what they'd been up to. But I couldn't help wondering . . . If he'd known how violent they were, why hadn't he done something to stop them sooner? Why hadn't he called the police? But then I realized what a ridiculous question that was. Walter Hayes was a man who'd never turn down a bet. For all I knew, he'd been involved with the gambling, maybe even betting on the dogfights. Even if he hadn't, his former girlfriend had been. Maybe his relationship with Beatrice had been the reason he hadn't gone to the authorities. Or maybe he'd feared for his own life.

"It's a sorry thing"—my father was still talking—"when a man's home isn't private. When he finds gangsters and punks and half his neighborhood raiding the place."

"Nobody was raiding it, Dad."

"Says you."

A question occurred to me. "Why were you here, Dad?"

"What are you talking about?"

"Why did you come home?"

"Does a man need a reason to come into his own house?"

"How'd you get here?"

He looked confused. Didn't he remember? His eyes shifted, avoiding the question. "I came to get some cash. I need some spending money."

"For what? Everything's paid for—your food, all the activities—" Somewhere in my mind, I heard my parents, arguing about money. "It's gambling. You lost again, didn't you. You're over your head." My mother's accusation came out of my mouth.

"No. Who said that?"

"Dad, don't lie to me—"

"Just nickel-and-dime. Some cards. Social. I bet a guy on a baseball game. The pennant."

"Dad, you promised—"

"This is nothing. It's just social. Friendly games."

I shook my head. There was no point debating semantics; Dad wasn't going to change. "How much? How are you going to pay?"

"Relax. I have plenty of cash here in the house."

Of course he did. Hidden money. I'd found some of it with Susan. I took a deep breath, thinking of Dad's secret guns. I remembered my mother stashing away cash and valuables, burying treasure in holes in the basement wall, under the floor. For all I knew, a fortune might be concealed in the house.

"Anyhow, I owe a guy, name's Norton. Or Morton. I owe him fifty bucks, okay? Is that so bad? I came home to get some cash. Which, by the way, I have plenty of, and you don't need to know where it is."

In the walls? Near the cedar closet? Under a drawer? Behind a pipe? I shivered, images tickling the edges of my memory.

"And, for your information, Miss Smarty-pants, a taxicab."

He was glaring at my eyes, pleased with himself.

"I took a cab. That's how I got here."

Nick came back from the dining room. "Okay. Let's go." He reached a hand out for me, and I tried to stand but my legs were limp. I couldn't use my left foot, the rest of me wasn't strong enough to get up. Nick's arms enclosed me, lifting me, carrying me. I leaned against him, smelling fading soap and aftershave, exhaustion and stress. I closed my eyes, stretching out the contact, feeling his firm muscles, his body heat. I ached for him to whisper something private, maybe that he loved me, and I looked up hopefully. Nick's lips parted, ready to speak. "Come on, Walter. You ready?"

That was all he said. I hung on, glommed onto him as he supported my weight. There was tenderness in his touch; that was enough for now.

"Walter?" He was impatient, peeved. "Let's go. Now."

"I need a moment. One moment." My father used his cane and shuffled into the hall, watching us until we left. "I'll be right out."

"Hurry it up. Before the press sniffs us out."

Nick hefted me into an unmarked car idling in the overgrowth outside the kitchen door. A moment later, even before I could tell Nick that I was sorry, my father joined us, a wad of twenties in his fist.

SEVENTY-SEVEN

My foot had been stitched up and bandaged, and I spent the night in the hospital. An IV was wired to my arm, delivering medications that would slow my contractions and dull my mind. After the surgery, Dr. Martin came into my room, scolding me for not calling her about the contractions and coming to the hospital earlier, reminding me—as if it might have slipped my mind—that the baby's life was at stake.

Nick stood there listening, alarmed. He hadn't been aware that I'd been having such severe contractions. I was sure that he'd never trust me again. Oh, God. I'd messed up big-time. Who could blame him if he couldn't forgive me? I'd almost killed our baby. What if he didn't want to marry me anymore? I needed to talk to him, to explain, to go home. I was desperate to see Molly. But I was drowsy, drugged. My eyes yearned to close and my mind felt hazy, couldn't process thoughts. Drifting, I heard Dr. Martin talking to Nick, saying I should stay in the hospital for the duration of the pregnancy. They were walking away, or maybe I was falling asleep. As their voices faded I tried to figure out how long she meant, to calculate how long the 'duration of the pregnancy' was. I was nearing the end of my fifth month, had another four to go. But that couldn't be right; nobody could be expected to stay in a hospital that long. Besides, I couldn't stay, had to go home. I had to take care of Molly. Had to work. Had to—I knew there was more, but too sleepy to think of it, I let myself float into a medicated slumber, assuring myself that Nick would explain to

Dr. Martin that I couldn't possibly stay in the hospital for four whole months. The idea was out of the question.

Drifting, I watched, unnoticed, as my mother sat in the bedroom in a rocking chair, not rocking. Her cheeks glistened with tears. Her arms were loaded with treasure, and my father was there, begging her to give it to him.

"Louise, let go," he pleaded, trying to take it from her.

He tugged at it, but she held tight, wouldn't release it. Her eyes glowed wide and furious, resisting.

"Louise—" My father kept trying to take it from her, and she kept clinging to it, tightening her grasp.

"This is no good, Louise. Let go—"

My mother didn't answer; defiant, she clutched the treasure to her breast. For a while my father stayed beside her, waiting for a chance to grab. Then he was gone and my mother was alone, gliding through the house with full arms and hollow eyes. When she began to float down the basement stairs, I knew as I always did in these dreams, that something awful was about to happen.

"No! Mom, don't go down there!" I called, but my shouts were futile, without sound.

My mother was already down in the basement, hiding the treasure; I could see her, picking up loose flooring beside the cedar closet, digging a hole. I had to stop her, and I ran to the steps, dreading what was coming next. I swam through air, making no progress, shouting to her as she buried the treasure in the basement, knowing that, once she finished hiding it, it would be too late.

"Mom . . . Please," I screamed. "Stop . . . Mom! Mom . . ."

"Mom?"

I opened my eyes.

"Mom? Are you okay?"

Molly stood beside me, shaking me, looking worried. "You were yelling in your sleep."

I blinked, focusing, and overjoyed to see her, reached out for a hug. "Molly. Oh my goodness. Come here." It had only been a day since I'd seen her, but it felt much longer, and I squeezed her clumsily, encumbered by the IV tube.

"I miss you, Mom. Can you come home now? Please?" Her eyes were large and troubled.

"I hope so." I still wasn't completely awake, had only just remembered where I was. I held Molly's hands and looked around, saw Nick standing in the doorway, talking to Dr. Martin.

"Why are you in the hospital, Mom? Is Oliver going to be born?"

Oliver. She seemed certain of the baby's name. And, apparently, of the gender. "No, it's not time for the baby, Molls. I just needed to rest."

She frowned, obviously doubting me. "But what happened to your foot?" She stared at the massive bandage.

"Oh. I got bit by a dog."

"You did?" Her mouth dropped. "How? Whose dog was it? And what's this?" She pointed to the IV tube.

Her questions kept coming. I answered as well as I could, but I couldn't stop staring at her. My eyes drank her image; I couldn't get enough. Molly looked stressed, less rosy than usual. Her socks were unmatched and her blond curls, unbrushed and tangled, were bound up in sorry, uneven pigtails. Obviously, Nick had done her hair.

"What's with your socks?" I changed the subject.

"We couldn't find the partners. Please come home, Mom." Her eyes begged and pouted, puppylike. "Nick's great. But, honestly? Without you, he doesn't know what he's doing."

I didn't know what to tell her. I ached to come home, claustrophobic in the hospital. My body itched from feeling closed in. After just one night, I longed for the freedom to open a window or change my clothes at will. I wanted the damned tubes out of my arm and the chance to look at something other than a bedside commode, an overhead television, pale green walls and an insipid still life of orange chrysanthemums. One night had been enough for me. And seeing Molly close to tears made my own eyes fill.

"Come here, Molls." I helped her up onto the hospital bed beside me, showed her the control buttons. Together, we rode the bed, giggling and cuddling as Molly raised and lowered the back and the foot, separately and together, until Nick and Dr. Martin joined us, and the conference began.

In the end I was allowed to go home on certain conditions. I had to measure my contractions with a contraption that would transmit the results to the hospital four times a day. I had to stay on heavy doses of medication. I was not to drive, had to avoid all exertion and stay in bed for at least the rest of the week. And if the contractions continued, I had to agree to go on bed rest, possibly in the hospital, for the duration of the pregnancy.

I listened to the conditions, nodding and promising, but truthfully, I'd have agreed to anything just to get home.

SEVENTY-EIGHT

IT WAS A WEEK BEFORE I WENT BACK TO MY FATHER'S HOUSE. I spent the week healing and trying to reconcile with my fiancé. Fortunately, Nick's anger with me was outweighed by his concern. He reassured me of his commitment repeatedly and I tried to believe him; somehow, we managed to shove our conflicts aside in the interests of stress reduction and the baby's health. Still, no matter how much he declared his devotion, I had doubts. Nick worked more hours than he had to, seemed evasive, and I was sure he was hiding something. I suspected that he was sticking it out, staying with me only because of the baby; after it was born, when he didn't have to coddle me anymore, I thought that he might leave. I tried to dismiss those thoughts, telling myself that Nick wasn't necessarily hiding anything, that he'd always seemed secretive. That openness didn't come to him naturally. That it wasn't too late to save our relationship if I proved my devotion to him and the baby.

So, during the week, I rested. I took my medication and stayed home, mostly in bed. My contractions dissipated; I felt better than I had during the entire pregnancy. Staying home from work, I spent more time with Molly. While I lay in bed, she read to me, did her spelling and arithmetic homework beside me, carried trays of juice and cookies for us to share.

But in the morning exactly seven days after my release from the hospital, I woke up from another dream about my mother, more vivid than the others. Once again, I'd watched her descend weightlessly into the basement to hide a treasure downstairs. More urgently than ever, I felt compelled to go back to the house, to figure out the dream. So, when Susan called about driving Molly and Emily to gymnastics, I asked her to take me for a drive.

"No. Absolutely not."

"Susan, I've got to get out of the house. I'm going crazy."

"I'll bring you a DVD and some bonbons. How about *When Harry Met Sally*?"

"Come on, Susan. I can't stay here."

"You're supposed to stay in bed—"

"I did. For seven whole days. Now I feel fine. Really. As long as I don't exert myself, I can go out."

"Yeah? What about your foot?"

My foot was still a problem, healing slowly, throbbing whenever I stood on it. "So I won't walk far. Just from the house to your car. I'll use a cane."

"What does Nick say?"

I was exasperated. "Do I need a note?"

She was silent for a minute. "Okay. We'll go for a drive. But you are to do nothing—I mean nothing."

And so, after we dropped off the girls, we started out on our drive.

"Where to? Anyplace special?"

I didn't dare tell her where I wanted to go; I knew she'd refuse to take me. "How about Kelly Drive? We can see if the leaves are turning."

She liked that idea, so we followed Kelly Drive, admiring fall foliage, watching people jog, row, skate or ride bikes along the Schuylkill River. I was quiet, replaying my dream; Susan chatted most of the time, commenting on the press coverage of the dogfights and the tumult in the ADA's office, in the same breath updating me on Tim's business travels, her new living room upholstery, Lisa's grades, Julie's cheerleading exploits, Emily's growth spurt, her desire to leave her criminal law practice and open an antiques store or a bakery. We moved from Kelly Drive onto Lincoln Drive while Susan continued her stream of consciousness to which I gradually stopped paying attention. Instead, I directed her to turn into my father's neighborhood, and then onto his street.

"Why?" Susan eyed me suspiciously.

"As long as we're so close, we might as well drive by."

Susan drove on, silent now, obviously disturbed. "You're not going in."

"Susan, I'm fine, really."

"Zoe, I swear, I'll turn around right now—"

"Okay, I won't go in. Just let's drive by the house."

"Why?"

Why? "I should make sure it's locked up. After all, there were a lot of people here when I left. I don't know why. I just want to see it."

That part was true. I didn't know why. But the house had been drawing me back, whether in dreams or wakefulness. It had been on my mind constantly for weeks. Susan was displeased, and she drove in petulant silence until we arrived at my father's curb, where she stopped and put the car in park.

"Okay. You're here. Satisfied? Because we're leaving when I count to three. One . . . two . . ."

But I didn't hear her say "three"; I was out the door, limping up the path, leaning on a cane.

"Zoe—" Susan was screaming my name, furious. The car door slammed and she caught up to me, grabbing my arm. "What the hell are you doing? You promised—"

"It doesn't count. I was under duress. You insisted." I removed her hand from my arm.

"Your doctor said—"

"I know what the doctor said. And, excuse me, but you don't. You weren't there. I'm actually allowed to move around a little."

She sputtered, furious. I continued my hobble, keeping the weight off my left foot, awkwardly making my way up the front steps.

"I'm calling Nick."

I stopped on the porch and watched her dig in her purse for

her cell phone. What the hell was this? Was I a prisoner? Was she my guard? Was Nick?

"Susan, I'm not on house arrest. My contractions are under control. And Nick's not my keeper."

"Well, he should be. Somebody should be. I don't know if it's hormones or what, but you're not yourself. You're not rational."

"Because I want to go into my father's house?"

She gaped at me as if I'd said, "Because I want to chop my head off and use it as a punch bowl?"

"Why are you acting like this, Zoe?"

Pulling the key from my pocket, I unlocked the front door. Susan stood at the threshold.

"I can't be part of this." She held the cell phone in her hand, but she didn't make the call.

"Part of what? What the hell is the matter with you, Susan? Ever since I've been pregnant, you've changed—"

"Oh, really? *I've* changed?"

"Yes, you've changed. And so has Nick. Both of you have become controlling and overbearing, and neither of you can mind your own damned business—"

"It doesn't occur to you that maybe it's you who's changed? Maybe your behavior has caused some concern among people who care about you—"

"Stop putting it on me, Susan. I'm pregnant, not psychotic. I don't need you to tell me what I can or can't do."

"Oh, so you're saying that you think you've been making good decisions lately? Chasing murdering dogfighters? Getting yourself and your bodyguard eaten alive?"

"You're missing the point."

"Am I? What point would that be?" Her nostrils were flaring.

"The point is that it's not your place to judge my decisions or my behavior. Good or bad, right or wrong, my life is my business. Not Nick's. Not yours. Mine. Stop bossing me around—"

"Fine. I get it. I won't boss you around. Now, get in the car."

"Back the hell off, Susan."

Our eyes met. For a moment, time froze. Nobody breathed. Susan blinked first. She looked away.

"Okay. Fine. If that's how you want it." She turned around and stomped down the steps. "I'm outta here. You want a ride home? I'll be out here for exactly three minutes. After that, you can call a damned cab."

I didn't worry. I knew she'd wait. I opened the door and stepped inside, trembling for reasons I couldn't identify, following an impulse I didn't understand.

SEVENTY-NINE

INSIDE THE HOUSE, MY DAMAGED HEEL BEGAN TO PULSE WITH pain; I'd been standing up too long, and gravity was pooling the blood in my foot. But I couldn't stop myself, couldn't wait anymore. I was drawn to the house, had to figure out my dream. I limped through the foyer, the dining room, the kitchen, stopping at the door to the basement as if I'd suddenly woken up. What the hell was I doing? Why was I so compelled to follow the path of a recurring dream? What was wrong with me? Susan was right; I was irrational. I should be home, resting, drinking a milk shake, not acting out a scene from a nightmare by climbing down cellar steps and digging up the floor. And certainly, given my history, I shouldn't be digging it up alone.

Oh, cut the drama, I told myself. Lettie and her vicious gang are gone. You're perfectly safe now. Something about that basement has been nagging at you for decades; you need to go see what it is. Go on down. Get it over with.

I stood at the top of the basement steps, debating with myself, replaying the scene from my dream, seeing my mother float downstairs, wanting to stop her, calling out to her, knowing that something awful was about to happen as I saw her kneeling on the basement floor . . . I heard a *thwack*.

I stiffened, stood still, telling myself that the sound had been my imagination. I listened, deciding that there must be an animal downstairs. Maybe one of Lettie's dogs had managed to escape the animal control officers. Or maybe it was just a squirrel. I waited, heard nothing, almost managed to convince myself that the sound had never happened. It was okay to go downstairs. I opened the door cautiously, silently, and started down. Holding my cane in one hand, the banister in the other, I lowered myself onto my right foot. One step. Another. A third. A fourth. Then I heard it again.

EIGHTY

THWACK.

I froze. The sound was not my imagination. It was a definite noise, and it didn't sound at all like a dog or a squirrel. *Thwack. Thwack.* It was dense and scratchy. Like a shovel.

Oh, God. Someone was definitely down there. Maybe Lettie's assistant, Jimmy—no one had seen him since Lettie's arrest. I stood there, heart racing, mouth dry, unable to move. Get out of here, I told myself. Turn around and go back up the steps. But I couldn't. Not yet. I needed to see who was there, what they were doing, and I bent down low enough to see deep into the basement. And I froze.

There, across the dark expanse, in the shadows beside the cedar closet, I saw something impossible, the exact image of my dream. I blinked. I shook my head. But the image didn't disappear. Someone stood right where my mother had stood, digging where she'd buried her treasure in my dreams. As I watched, the figure lifted a pick and brought it down again, shattering old tiles and loosening the concrete beneath. *Thwack.* Again. *Thwack.* What I was seeing made no sense. But immediately, without seeing his face, I knew who was digging in the shadows: my father. Obviously, he'd taken another cab ride and come back again to raid yet another secret stash from the house, the one buried by my mother. He needed more gambling money.

I almost called out to him. But at the last moment I hesitated, uncertain. The man seemed too steady, too agile to be my father. I squinted to see more clearly. Holding on to the banister, bending forward with my weight on my right leg, I peered into the darkness at the man near the cedar closet. As if he could feel my gaze, he stopped digging and looked over his shoulder toward the stairs, exposing his face.

He wasn't my father. He wasn't Jimmy or Digger or any of the other guys from the dogfight. Bertram Haggerty, the shrink, gazed at me across the darkness, his eyes startled, his pick poised to strike another *thwack*.

EIGHTY-ONE

"BERTRAM?"

His knees bent, his eyes darted around for an escape. I lowered myself step by step.

"What are you doing?" It was a challenge more than a question. I knew damned well what he was doing. Clearly, I'd told him about my dream while under hypnosis. No wonder he wouldn't tell me what I'd talked about; I'd talked about the buried treasure. Probably, I'd subconsciously remembered all the details. Probably, I'd told him where all the family valuables had been hidden, and in the guise of helping me, he'd gathered all the information, coming here to collect the loot. He'd betrayed my confidence and all his professional ethics, not to mention the law. And he'd dug an impressive hole in the basement floor.

"Zoe." He stuttered, stalling for time, still holding on to the pick. "Oh. Okay. I didn't, well, I didn't expect to see you here."

He babbled on, saying anything that came to mind, trying to think of what to do. Meantime, I made it to the bottom of the steps and started toward him, unafraid.

"How could you, Bertram? I trusted you."

He stopped talking and eyed my bandaged foot, watched me hobble toward him on my cane.

"W-what happened to your foot?"

For a moment he was the old Bertram. Helpful, concerned. "No, Bertram. What happened to *you?* You used me. You used what I told you under hypnosis—"

"What? Listen to me, Zoe. You know I'd never—"

"Bullshit. Why would you be here otherwise? You betrayed my trust—" I was almost an arm's length away from him now. Or a pick's length. Or a cane's.

"Okay. Yes. You're right. I betrayed your trust. But I would never have done it if I weren't desperate. I had no choice. Can we talk about it? Please, Zoe? Just let me explain."

He squirmed, trying to excuse his behavior. He told me again how funding for his research had been cut, how he had no money left, no credit, either. Over the past few years, he and his wife had overspent the equity in their house, maxed out their credit cards. Borrowed from his parents until they'd turned him down. Then, under hypnosis, I'd mentioned my father and the money and fortune in valuables hidden throughout the house. At first it hadn't occurred to him to search for it. But one day, he'd found himself prowling through the house, seeking stashes of cash or objects of value. And when I'd told him of the treasure my mother had buried near the closet, he thought that no one would ever miss it. And it might help him save his marriage and his research, might see him through his financial crisis. He'd pay me back in time. His research depended on my decision. He seemed to think his actions, sneaking in and robbing the house, were justified.

And gradually I began to accept his viewpoint. His cadence was relaxing, assuring, and his voice gave familiar cues. "Don't be upset, Zoe. Breathe deeply. Relax. Listen to me." The rhythm of his voice seemed to caress me, and I felt less tense. Maybe I was being too harsh. His program had been cut, his funding withdrawn. What was the poor man supposed to do? Forget about his patients? Abandon his life's work? Discontinue his vital research? He was only looking for the treasure in order to help others and make a lasting contribution to psychiatry. Maybe I should let him dig. After all, wasn't it my dream about my mother that had brought both of us here? If he found the treasure, wouldn't that answer my questions? Wouldn't we both be better off? Besides, I owed him. He'd helped me when I'd needed it, easing my contractions, taking time out of his hectic schedule whenever I needed him.

Bertram was a gifted, generous man. Wasn't it actually a privilege just to know him? Shouldn't I do whatever I could to promote his work?

A shrill voice penetrated my haze, and I blinked, disoriented. I was sitting on a crate, facing Bertram, who'd turned toward the stairs, blinking rapidly. Obviously, I'd missed something, couldn't remember sitting down.

"Pay no attention; the only sound you hear is my voice," Bertram urged. But he was too late; I'd already heard something else.

"I swear, Zoe. This is your last chance. I'm leaving—"

Oh, it was Susan. She was up in the kitchen. "Susan?" I called to her, confused.

"Focus, Zoe. Relax. Listen only to my voice." Bertram reached for my chin, turned it back to face his. Wait . . . he was trying to hypnotize me? I resisted, turning away, realizing too late that he must have already done so. When? For how long? I had no idea. But he was nervous now. Trembling, trying to sound calm. "Look at me, Zoe. Look at me."

"What are you doing down here?" Susan thundered down the steps, slowing when she saw us.

Bertram jumped to his feet, his pick raised over my head like a weapon. "Don't come any closer."

"Who the hell is this?" Susan asked, undaunted, slowing her pace but not stopping.

"Stop there—" Bertram ordered.

"Dr. Bertram Haggerty, meet Susan Cummings, attorney at law."

Bertram looked from me to Susan, Susan to me. "Stay away," he said. "I don't want to hurt anybody." He danced around, nervous, not sure how to look threatening.

"Nice to meet you." Susan stepped closer, as if about to shake hands, and as Bertram flustered, I swung my cane up suddenly, knocking the pick from his hands. It clattered to the floor and he leaped after it, but Susan was faster, pouncing on him, landing on his back. She held him down as I hobbled over and joined her, and we sat on him, planted comfortably until he quieted down.

"I told you not to come here." Susan took out her cell phone, ready to call 9-1-1.

"It's a good thing I did. He'd have dug up the whole basement."

"Wait . . . please. Don't call the police."

Bertram whined so pathetically that Susan hesitated, looking at me. "Want me to call?"

I shrugged, uncertain. "What else are we going to do with him?"

"You could let me go," Bertram pleaded. "Please."

"Is he kidding?" Susan looked baffled. "Who the hell is this guy?"

I was about to tell her, but Bertram spoke first, breathless from our combined weight on his back. "I'm not a thief. Zoe, tell her. You know I'm not. Tell her I'm a psychiatrist. Tell her who I am. I'm not a criminal; I'm just desperate. It's all been too much. My whole life's come apart. Have some compassion . . . look at me, what I've been reduced to. I'm so desperate for cash I'm digging in a basement for buried treasure? I'm a zero. An absolute joke—"

"What's he talking about? Is he nuts?" Susan whispered, as if not to offend him.

"If you let me go, I swear, I'll never do anything like this again. Ever. I'll live in the street before I rob anyone." Bertram's voice was wobbly, as if he was about to cry. "I only did this for my patients. For their sake." He dissolved into tears, not a pretty sound. "Please don't call the police. Please. I'll do anything."

Susan blinked, baffled. "What should we do?"

"Hold on a sec." I needed to think. Bertram had betrayed my trust, and, moments ago, he'd tried to hypnotize me to get away. But he was pathetic, and I knew, as he insisted, that he wasn't really a thief. No doubt, after this he'd never attempt another criminal act. And actually he'd saved me some trouble by digging that hole.

Beneath our butts, Bertram's body shook, sobbing. "I'm begging you, Zoe."

"Okay," I decided. "We'll let you go on one condition."

"Anything." He stopped crying.

"You tell me everything."

"What do you mean?" The question was a duet; Susan and Bertram asked it together.

"I want to know everything I told you under hypnosis. Including why I cried during every session."

Bertram was quiet for a moment. Why? A minute ago, he'd been begging for freedom; now he was hesitating?

"Deal?" I asked.

He remained silent, struggling to breathe.

"Or we can call the cops."

"No . . . don't."

"Fine. Tell me. All of it."

"Zoe, think about it. The only reason you don't consciously remember on your own is that you don't want to. There are reasons for that. I can't be responsible for what happens—"

"Okay, your choice. Go ahead, Susan. Call—"

"No. Okay. I'll tell you. Just don't blame me afterward. I'm doing this under duress."

EIGHTY-TWO

Of course we had to let him up first so he could breathe. Then, mussed up from our tussle, Bertram sat on the basement floor and gave a list of disclaimers. He didn't know for sure that anything he was about to say was true. After all, the events he was about to describe had been told to him by the voice of a child. Under hypnosis, I had revealed what I'd seen when I'd been young and unsophisticated. The truth may have been colored by emotion, distorted by time. Et cetera. Finally, though, he began.

I listened as he reviewed my parents' repeated arguments, my mother's frustrations with my father's gambling. Bertram knew that she'd stashed away money and valuables, protecting them from his gaming so that she could pay the electric bill or the grocery. But, apparently, money wasn't the only thing my mother hid.

"According to what you said, I think your mother had a form of OCD."

"OCD?" Susan echoed.

"Obsessive compulsive disorder." My mother?

"That's right." Bertram nodded too enthusiastically. "She hid things, all sorts of things, not just money. Apparently, she felt compelled to protect all kinds of possessions, concealing them. Protecting them."

"I told you that?"

"Not in those words. You told me what you saw her hiding. Sometimes it was jewelry or cash. Sometimes it was a box of laundry detergent." He pointed to the floor. To a soiled and crushed box of Tide that he'd unearthed.

Tide?

"Your father couldn't understand her behavior," he went on. "So tensions built. Your parents fought, and you saw their fights. Nothing was secret from you. You watched your mother sneaking around, hiding her shoes, jars of peanut butter, family heirlooms, wads of cash. Like most children, you knew what went on in that house better than anyone else. But, like most children, you lacked context and maturity to understand its significance. So, in your mind, you linked two behaviors, trying to make sense of them. Mommy was mad at Daddy for gambling; that must be why Mommy hid money and other things from him. That idea was how you made sense of your world. But, in reality, I think your father gambled, and your mother hid things. The two behaviors became entangled in your mind, but actually occurred independently of each other."

What? My father gambled, and my mother hid things. My mother had obsessive compulsive disorder? I saw her again, sneaking down through the hallways, tiptoeing down the stairs, hiding bundles.

"Louise," I heard my father pleading. "Where is the money?"

"You'll never find it."

"Think, Louise. Try to remember. There are bills to pay."

My mother shrugged with hopeless eyes. "You knew it would be like this, Walter. You shouldn't have married me."

All these years, I'd thought that comment had been my mother blaming my father. Had she in fact been lamenting her own compulsive behavior?

Susan was confused. "Why exactly are you digging up the floor?" Susan gawked, struggling to understand what was going on.

"Go ahead, Bertram. Explain." I was balanced on the edge of a crate, waiting for pieces of a puzzle I hadn't been able finish on my own.

Finally, he rubbed his eyes and caved. His voice carried me back, repeating what I'd told him, showing me what I'd seen and tried to forget. I saw my mother, crying, holding a precious treasure, more valuable than anything else she owned. My father tried to take it from her, just as in my dream. They fought over it. My father tried to grab it; my mother wouldn't let go. Frustrated, pleading with her in vain, my father stomped out of the room empty-handed. My mother sat for a while, holding the bundle, then went downstairs. I'd watched her go, followed her, saw her hide the treasure in the basement, near the cedar closet.

It was that treasure that Bertram now sought. He hadn't found it.

"That's it?" I wasn't convinced. "The whole story?"

Bertram nodded, avoiding my eyes. Was he lying?

I got up and, hopping over to the hole, removed chunks of linoleum, sifted through the bits of displaced cement and dirt, digging with my fingers.

"What was it?" Susan followed me, stooped beside me, watching. "Your mom's big treasure . . . Was it diamonds? Coins?"

No. It wasn't diamonds or coins. It was something far more valuable. And I'd found it. I scooped out a few handfuls of dirt and suddenly, there it was. Hidden in a fragment of worn flannel, a tiny, fragile piece of the treasure.

Susan yelped in shock. Bertram gaped. And, in a jolt, I remembered. Everything.

EIGHTY-THREE

My mother sang and rocked, but the treasure remained cold. It didn't move or make a sound. It didn't even cry. My father begged my mother to let go, but she wouldn't. He tried to take the bundle from her, but she clutched it more tightly. They argued.

When he finally gave up and left the room, my mother carried the baby downstairs. I followed, watching from the stairs as she buried him. There was no cement or tile yet. No cedar closet or clutter. The basement had been an empty expanse with a dirt floor then, and she dug a hole and buried the dead, swaddled baby.

Now I held his tiny skull in the palm of my hand, tears streaming down my cheeks.

"Oh, man," Susan kept repeating. "A buried baby?"

"That's the treasure?" Bertram gawked. "The treasure was a dead baby?"

He began walking in circles, running his hands through what was left of his hair, laughing too wildly, chanting. "That's just great. It was a baby. A fucking dead baby."

Susan tried to sort out facts. "Who is it?"

"My baby brother." Why had I said that? I didn't remember; I just knew. "My mother called him her precious little treasure."

Behind us, Bertram wailed. "Oh, God. I'm a genius. What was I thinking? Taking a five-year-old at her word. Looking for her treasure. A moron, I'm a goddamn moron."

"How old were you when he was born?"

I didn't know. "Four or five." I stared at the little skull, trying to put a face on him. Or a name.

"Do you know how he died?"

I didn't know that, either. "I think he just stopped breathing."

"Maybe crib death," Susan suggested. "SIDS."

"Maybe not." Bertram stopped walking. "I think your mother had postpartum depression. I think she might have killed him."

"But then, you're a moron." Susan glared at him.

I cupped the skull in my hands, trying to remember the baby. Had I held him? Had I helped feed him a bottle or give him a bath? I strained, closing my eyes, coming up with nothing. Then I saw a blue room with soft clouds painted on the ceiling, a white crib in the middle of the floor. A rocking horse in the corner near the window. And outside, on the porch, a huge black pram with shiny silver wheels. I saw myself standing beside it, reaching inside, feeling a strong little hand wrap itself around my finger. Were these memories or imagination? I didn't know. But my forefinger twitched away from the skull, as if releasing itself from the tightness of a tiny grip.

Susan was still asking questions, wanting to know his name, to figure out when he was born, to understand why nobody had missed him in all the years, to comprehend how I had survived a childhood that was so confusing and dark. And Bertram kept lamenting his lost marriage and career, his final lost hope. I closed my hands around the skull of my dead baby brother and drifted into my own thoughts, piecing together images, beginning to understand the meaning of my recurring dream. Much of it had actually, literally happened. My mother had really buried a bundle downstairs, just as she had in my dreams. But what about the rest? Why was I terrified of her? Why in dreams did she reach for my belly, arms clawing, legs chasing, floating through the air? There was more to the dream than just the treasure, and Bertram had deliberately omitted it.

"Sit down, Bertram." I was furious. Even now, he was hiding something from me. "You're not done."

"What?" He tried to look innocent, failed miserably. "What are you talking about? There's nothing else. Nothing substantive, anyway."

Susan looked from him to me. "You mean there's more?"

I got up, gently replaced the skull in the hole and stood by the cedar closet, my mouth becoming dry, pulse accelerating. Something had happened right here in this spot. There was a reason I dreaded that closet. What was it? I closed my eyes, tried to remember. And saw my mother's face. My mother? What about her? "Dammit, Bertram. Tell me."

He sighed. He paced. He turned, faced me, opened and closed his mouth.

"I'm counting. At three, Susan is making the 9-1-1 call. One . . . two—"

"Fine." He spun around, snapping. "You want to know? You want to deal with it? Okay. Here it is: You found her. You were five years old, and you found your mother here."

I found her? So? Bertram watched me, waiting for his words to sink in. And, yes, they did. I saw her, right there where we stood. Floating above the ground, just as in my dream. Her feet hovered in the air, right in front of my eyes, and her lacy nightgown was soiled. Her head was cocked at an odd angle, her hair draped forward, hiding her face. She didn't answer when I called. She ignored me, didn't come down to the ground. I reached up, tapped her on the leg. And she swung. Back and forth, toward me and away, like a yo-yo on a string. Her arms dangled, limp, and I stood, frozen and bug-eyed, swallowed by the black shadow of her swaying form.

I took off. I ran across the basement, up the steps. I flew, unable to breathe or to scream, afraid to look back, certain that she was behind me, coming after me, reaching and clawing and gliding through the air, her feet not reaching the floor.

EIGHTY-FOUR

"OKAY. YOU CAN GO, BERTRAM."

Bertram didn't leave. He stood there, studying me. "You can see why I didn't want to tell you. You weren't ready to remember, and it's a lot to digest. Are you okay?"

No, but that was not his concern. "We made a deal. You kept your end. Thank you. And good-bye."

"But, about this . . ." He gestured at the hole in the floor. "About what happened here . . . We're cool?" He sounded shaky and repentant.

"Completely cool. Very cool." What could be cooler? My mother had buried my brother and killed herself, and I'd found her hanging from the basement ceiling. Bertram had known about her suicide and that I'd buried the memory, and he'd exploited me, hypnotizing me not so much to ease my contractions as to find my mother's buried "treasure." He was pitiful and repulsive, and I wanted him to leave. I'd have said anything to get him to go, even that we were cool.

"Anyway, for what it's worth . . ." He looked away. "I'm sorry."

Susan pointed at the stairs. "You can find your own way out."

Bertram began to say something else, but thought better of it and scooted up the steps, leaving his pickax behind.

For a while I sat, glued to the crate, silently replaying what he'd said, trying to absorb the implications.

Remembering my mother, I ached. I was consumed by loss and grief. And by nagging questions. How could she kill herself? How could she leave a five-year-old child? I thought of Molly and how nothing—no power in the world—could force me to abandon her. Hot rage surged through me, first at my mother for leaving me, then at myself for allowing her to go. I could have stopped her . . . If only I hadn't gone upstairs and left her down there bereft and alone, maybe she wouldn't have died.

I reminded myself that I'd been only five years old. I'd been jealous and resentful because, all day, she'd ignored me, paying attention only to her "precious little treasure." I'd thought that, now that he was buried, she'd stop crying and forget about him. Maybe she'd spend more time with me, coloring pictures and baking banana bread, as before the baby had come. I sneaked upstairs and waited for her to come up and look for me, but she didn't. Finally, I gave up and went downstairs. And found her near the baby's grave, in the spot where there was now a cedar closet.

I remembered all of it. Clearly. As if no time had passed. As if I were reliving it. Susan handed me a tissue, and I smeared tears off my face.

"Can I do anything?" She sat beside me on my crate, thigh-to-thigh, watching me, a hand on my back.

I shook my head. "I'm all right."

Not even close to true. I was dizzy, unbalanced. In the space of half an hour my mind had become a kaleidoscope of memories. Childhood rhymes singsonged in my head, and whispers retold jumbled secrets. I saw myself playing alone, making up games of pretend, hiding in secret places from invisible seekers. I watched my childhood self playing dress-up in my mother's clothes, painting my mouth with her lipstick, wobbling around in her high heels, pretending to be just like her. Fresh tears poured down my face. For the first time in decades I recalled my mother's patient face, her deep-violet eyes. How I'd worshipped her, pestered for her attention, copying her, pretending to do whatever she did, attaching myself to her like an appendage, emulating her movements, imitating her while she cooked dinner, washed dishes, folded laundry, unpacked groceries, hid money and random sundries from my father.

Even that. I'd watched her planting wads of money, pearl necklaces, crocheted tablecloths, pieces of silverware under cushions, inside linings, behind loose bricks or under floorboards. And, oh my God. I'd copied her. I remembered now. There was a treasure, a real treasure. And I knew exactly where it was.

EIGHTY-FIVE

I BOUNCED UP OFF THE CRATE AND MY CANE AND I HOBBLED across the basement.

"Where are you going?" Susan was at my heels. "Zoe, don't run. You'll be back on bed rest—"

But I didn't listen. I scuttled up the steps, heading for my hiding place under the staircase. I opened the door to the little closet and stooped, ready to climb in.

"Stop right there." Susan stepped between me and the door. "Tell me right now what you're doing."

"Okay." I was breathless, felt a contraction coming on. "There really was a treasure here. And I just remembered where."

She didn't look convinced. "A treasure."

I nodded, wiping my face. "I think it's still there."

"It better be rare coins or diamonds. If it's another of your relatives, I'm done." Sighing, she crouched, looking inside the closet, making sure the space was clear.

Slowly, on my knees, I entered the cavelike niche, squatting to estimate how tall I'd been at about five years old. Taller than Molly had been. Maybe as high as the fourth step? I felt along the underside of the step to the end where a wooden support board formed a small triangular enclosure. It was empty. My hands moved a step higher, then another.

And, yes. There it was. I pulled out the small tin box and crawled out of the closet.

"You have it? Oh, God . . . Let's see . . . What is it?" Susan could barely contain herself. "Please tell me it's emeralds."

"Even better." The box seemed to swirl in my hands, timeless and magical. And when I opened it, I was breathless, overcome. New tears spilled. I couldn't speak.

Susan stared, silent.

"Aren't they beautiful?" My voice hushed, choking on a sob.

"Zoe? They're buttons."

I supposed they were, mostly. Some were shiny pieces of glass. And a few were marbles. But, to me, as a child, they'd been a prized collection, my secret treasure. Something metallic peeked out among the colors. I reached for it, but just before I saw it, I remembered. It was a tiny silver rattle, engraved "LWH," for Lukas Walter Hayes. My brother.

EIGHTY-SIX

SUSAN TALKED ALL THE WAY HOME, REMARKING ON MY TRAUMATIC childhood and the odd character we'd just banished from the basement. "What a weenie. I can't believe you let him go. He should be locked up, never allowed to practice psychiatry again."

I didn't answer, didn't even pay attention to her words. But I hung on to her voice as it ran on, soothing and rhythmic, rooting me in the present.

She brought me home and walked me inside, clucking like a mother hen, asking me if I was really all right, until I had to shoo her away. And, once she was gone, when I was alone, I took my tin box upstairs, depositing it safely in my nightstand drawer. Then I climbed into bed and lay there awake under the covers, trying not to think or remember, until Molly and Nick came home carrying pizza.

Over the next few days, memories flooded back to me. No matter where I was or what I was doing, pieces of my childhood assaulted me. I knew now that my mother had been unstable; maybe, as Bertram had said, she suffered from postpartum depression. Most certainly, she'd had a compulsive disorder, constantly hiding things, mostly money, but also seemingly random, unpredictable objects. After the baby was born, she stayed in her rocking chair, unwilling to talk or eat, staring at some private darkness, and I'd watched her, waiting for her old self to emerge. But, despite Bertram's suspicions, I knew that my mother had not, could never have killed her baby. Little Luke had to have died of some natural cause; his death had pushed my already delicate and acutely depressed mother over the edge. I was certain that she had hanged herself out of sheer unbearable grief.

Most of my memories, though, weren't of events. Mostly, they were of feelings. They erupted suddenly, unexpectedly, and I struggled to define and endure them. Putting dishes into a cabinet, I'd see my mother secretly hiding bracelets, squirreling away jars of coins, and, instantly, without warning, I'd be overcome with loss. Tears would gush from my eyes. In the bathtub, resting my hand on my swollen tummy, I'd picture my mother's sad, vacant eyes and be terrified that I'd become like her, losing myself to depression after my baby's birth. And, reading with Molly or tucking her into bed, I'd see shadows of myself with my mother and become paralyzed, almost speechless with grief, enough so that Molly would notice and ask what was wrong.

Worst of all was nighttime. Trying to fall asleep, I tossed, unsettled, haunted by guilt. I told myself that her death had not been my fault. I'd been a young child, and my mother's suicide had been beyond anything I could control. My guilt was irrational, childish.

But the little girl who'd been hiding in my mind still felt responsible for my mother's death. Little Zoe blamed herself, insisting that if only she'd stayed downstairs, if only she'd been there, she could have prevented the suicide. My adult mind assured her that she was not at fault. It explained that, even if she'd interrupted Mom that day, she'd have no doubt killed herself at another time. I reasoned that Mom had been deeply disturbed, too sick to survive. But the child remained unconvinced. Petulant, she insisted that if only she'd been a good-enough girl, if only she'd have made her mother happier, there would have been no suicide. Her mother would not have wanted to die. The little girl still living in my head knew beyond any doubt that the death was all her fault.

You're a therapist, I reminded myself. Stop this hysterical guilt trip. You know better; your mother's death was not because of you. But the confusion and secrets my mind had contained all these years burst out, overpowering my rational thoughts, spouting guilt and self-blame, spewing unresolved pain and confusion. Even if my adult self had studied psychology, a five-year-old child was cowering at the back of my mind, frozen in the basement, staring at swinging feet.

I told myself that it would take time to recover. I had to reacquaint myself with my childhood, absorb these emerging memories. Not certain what to say, I kept the process close and private, not discussing it with Susan, not even with Nick. I was too raw, not able to put my feelings into words, not ready to expose the tender child I'd been to the scrutiny of others, even those who loved me. For now, I hid her away, kept her as protected and quiet as I could, bracing myself for her tantrums, trying to cope with the intensity of her sudden revelations.

And at night, when she was too troubled and restless to let me sleep, I took the tin box from my nightstand and calmed her by holding colored glass buttons up to the lamplight, marveling at the magic of their glow.

EIGHTY-SEVEN

MY MEDICATIONS SEEMED TO BE WORKING; THE CONTRACTIONS had increased, averaging six an hour, but they were mostly mild. Although I still couldn't go back to work, Dr. Martin said that I could resume some of my normal activities, even, with reservations, moderate driving. I felt like a bird released from a cage, couldn't wait to go someplace. Anywhere. Even to the grocery store. Molly had a different idea. She wanted to visit her grandfather. And so my very first outdoor trip in weeks was to see my dad.

When we got to Harrington Place, he was in the lounge, playing poker. What a surprise.

"We're almost done here," he welcomed us. "Have a seat. Watch some television. I'll just finish cleaning these guys' clocks and call it a day."

"I wouldn't count my winnings yet, if I were you." The man to my father's left was tall and mustached, elegant in his posture.

"Will you fellows stop jawing and play the game?" Leonard complained. From what I'd seen, Leonard was always complaining.

"What's your hurry, Leonard?" The tall man grinned. "You got a train to catch?"

"No," my father jabbed. "He's expecting his son. Any minute, he expects him to walk in from . . . Where is he, Leonard? Tasmania?"

There were chuckles all around while Leonard bristled. "Is that supposed to be funny?" He sat up straight, piqued. "Don't make comments about my son."

"Forget about it, Leonard," the tall man advised. "I'm raising a dollar."

"What's raising a dollar, Mom?"

I wasn't sure. "They play for money." Maybe that made sense.

"Anyway, what did he say about my son?"

"Leonard, wait. No kidding—you have a son?" Dad teased, merciless, throwing his dollar in the pot. "Tell us about him. What's he up to these days?"

"Cut it out, Walter—don't egg him on." A man with thick white hair and glasses chewed an unlit cigar and tossed in his dollar. "Call." He waited for the tall man to show his cards.

"You know I have a son, Walter." Leonard reminded him. "I told you—"

"Forget about it, Leonard," Arthur called. "Put your damn dollar in." The tall man turned to my father. "You can't help yourself, can you, Walter?"

My father grinned. "Of course I can. And usually, I do. But do I get credit for those times? No."

"Guys." Arthur shook his head. "I called. Are we playing cards or what? What have you got, Moe?"

Molly had wandered over to my dad and climbed onto his lap. "What are you playing, Grandpa?"

"Poker. Shh. You can't talk until we're done."

"Why?"

"People will think we're cheating."

So Molly sat perfectly quiet while they finished. As my dad collected the pot, she cheered and threw her arms around his neck. "You won! Grandpa won—"

She stopped mid-sentence, seeing my face.

"Your mother doesn't like me to gamble. She worries that I'll lose."

"Lose? Him? Not likely." Moe, the man with the mustache, told Molly. "He beats everybody. Your grandpa's what they call a card shark, young lady. If he teaches you half of what he knows, you can get rich."

Okay, I thought. That's enough about the benefits of gambling. "Molly, let Grandpa get up so we can go get some lunch."

We started for the dining room, Molly fascinated by my father's winnings, marveling at all the singles and the pile of change he'd pulled in. "If your mother lets me, I'll teach you to play gin."

"What's gin?"

"Oh, it's fun—after lunch, I'll show you."

"Dad—"

"—I said, 'If your mom lets me.' "

Molly turned to me, begging, and I changed the subject, commenting about my father's new friends. Dad replied that he, Moe and Arthur were buddies, playing cards almost daily, arranging bimonthly Saturday-night bus trips to Atlantic City. I simmered, remembering his fights with my mother. But before I said a word about it, he promised that his gambling was under control, limiting his bets to petty cash.

The hostess greeted us, showed us to our table. As we passed, women of various sizes, shapes and hair shades greeted my father with a dazzling array of smiles and blushes. A wave of "Hello, Walter" seemed to ripple through the dining room, but my father didn't seem to notice. The hostess smiled and handed us menus.

"Don't open it yet," my father told Molly. "Bet you a dollar you can't guess what the soup of the day is."

Oh, Lord. "Dad—"

"Bet I can." Molly closed her eyes and thought. "Chicken noodle?"

My father's jaw dropped. "How did you know that?"

Molly beamed, thrilled. I watched her, saw myself at her age, two little girls completely enthralled by the same man.

"I can't believe it. You got it right. I got to give you a dollar." He reached for his wallet. "Tell me how you knew."

Molly beamed with pride, palm out to take the cash. "That lady." She pointed to a stout red-haired woman at the next table who was sipping a cup of chicken noodle.

"Dad. Molly," I barked. "No more gambling." The man was incorrigible.

"Why not?" Molly had no idea.

"Relax. It's only a dollar. Leave us alone, we're fine."

"It's a waste of time and money."

"It's fun, Mom. I won a dollar."

"You were lucky this time. How would you feel if you lost a dollar?"

She looked confused. "But I didn't—"

"Let the kid have some fun, would you?"

I didn't want to fight with him in front of Molly. Besides, he'd already given her the dollar; it was best to let it pass. I picked up the menu, trying to think about something else. Maybe chicken salad. Or no. I wanted red meat—roast beef? I was considering a rare cheeseburger when, without warning, the air was crushed from my lungs. Light flashed in my head, and my ribs began to cave in.

The contraction was worse than any I'd had or even imagined, and for its duration I was aware of nothing else.

EIGHTY-EIGHT

AS SOON AS IT PASSED, I KNEW I HAD TO CALL DR. MARTIN. BUT my father and Molly were watching me, four wide eyes, alarmed.

"What's wrong, Mom? Is it the baby again?"

"The baby?" My father hadn't known that I was having a difficult pregnancy. "What's she talking about? Is something wrong with the baby?" He seemed to lose color.

"It's all right." But I knew it wasn't. This contraction had been serious. Stabbing. Oh, God. Was I going to lose the baby? I grabbed my belly. Stay calm, I told myself; don't panic. But I wasn't calm, and I didn't have the energy to panic. My body was damp and shaky, my brain sluggish.

"What's wrong with the baby?" my father asked again.

"Nothing," I breathed. "Don't worry."

"Mom? Are you having the baby now? Should I call?" Molly was on her feet, digging into my pocketbook. "Where's your cell phone?"

Oh. Right. My cell phone. "It's okay, Molly. I'll call Nick."

She stood beside me, supervising as I took out the phone.

My father watched me, frowning.

"I'm all right, Dad. Don't worry."

The waitress came for our orders.

"Hi, there, Mr. Hayes. What can I get you folks?"

"Sally, this is my family." Dad's eyes didn't leave me; he was concerned.

"Your family? Well, it's nice to meet you. You have a charming guy here." Sally smiled sweetly, fondly patting my dad on the shoulder, reminding me yet again of his way with women.

Still shaky, phone in hand, I smiled back at her. "Go sit down, Molls. I'm okay now. Order some lunch."

Reluctantly Molly sat, leaving me holding the phone, figuring out which call to make. Should I call Nick first, then the doctor? Or the doctor first, then Nick?

"Mom." Molly was talking to me. "You need to order."

Sally was waiting; my father was watching me. I couldn't think about food.

"Need some more time? Should I come back?"

"No. I'll just have some tea."

"How about something with that?" She talked in singsong, as if to a small child. "A nice banana nut muffin—"

"No—just tea," I snapped, wanting her to go away, feeling another contraction rumbling through my middle. So soon? I took a deep breath, shut my eyes, waiting for it to pass.

When I tuned in again, Sally was gone. My father was shifting in his chair, agitated, muttering.

"Mom. You need to call."

I began to, but my father leaned forward, upset about the baby. "Just remember, you're the important one. No matter what, you come first. You can always have another baby, but there's only one you."

What? Oh my God. "Dad. Stop it—"

Molly sucked her bottom lip, her skin ashen.

"Sometimes these things happen. Babies don't always make it—"

"Dad, stop. The baby isn't dying. Please just let me call the doctor."

My father was distraught. Maybe confused, recalling the loss of his own baby boy. He wouldn't quiet down. He kept talking, acting as if the baby was going to be lost, and I had to cover my free ear in order to hear Nick's, then the doctor's voices. Before I got off the phone, though, another monster contraction began, much worse than the last, and I sat, afraid to speak or move, counting its duration, trying to breathe, waiting for Nick to arrive and take me to the hospital.

When the contraction finally abated, it did so gradually, and it was a while until I could see straight. My father and Molly were deep in conversation.

"You have to be patient with her." He put his hand on her arm. "She can't help it. It's how the world looks to her."

Molly shook her head. "But, Grandpa, Mom's not like that—"

"It's hard for you to understand, Zoe."

"But I'm Molly."

Oh, God. He'd slipped again, confusing me with Molly, my mom with me.

"Listen to me. Your mother imagines things. She's always been a little different. She sees trouble everywhere, so she tries to keep everything safe, to protect us." He sighed. "I probably should put her in a hospital, but, well, the truth is I can't bear to."

What had happened? Half an hour ago, he'd been completely oriented, winning at poker. Was it my contraction? Had his concern for my baby transported him to his past?

"Your mother doesn't trust a single living soul. Even her friends. Remember Edith? Or Helen? You must remember Roslyn."

"I don't know any of them—"

"Well, you used to. Roslyn used to paint your fingernails and cut your hair. But you forgot them because they don't call anymore. And why don't they call? Because your mother has accused them—each one of them—of stealing from her. It's very sad."

"You're wrong, Grandpa." Molly was defiant. "Mommy's not like that."

"Listen. You hear her when she yells at me for gambling. When she says I lose our money at poker and God knows what all. Zoe, I swear. None of it's true."

It wasn't?

"None of it. Oh, I like some penny-ante poker now and then, but I'm no big-time gambler. Your mom imagines that I gamble away the roof over our heads. Or that thieves will come in the night and take her pearls and sterling. She imagines that people are out to take whatever she has, whatever she values—"

Wait. She imagined it? What? I tried to process what he was saying, couldn't keep up.

". . . so she hides everything. I find money behind drawers or under the rug. You have no idea how many places she's hidden stuff in that house."

So, what Bertram said was true?

"And she's bought guns—"

"Uh-uh. My mom does not have a gun—"

"She does. I ought to know, Zoe—"

"Grandpa, I told you." Molly's voice was patient. "Remember? I'm Molly."

But my father wasn't deterred. "Listen to me, young lady. If you find a gun hidden somewhere, don't you touch it, you hear me? She has real bullets in it. You could get hurt."

The guns? How many were there? I tried to count. There was the gun. Dad had used the one in his desk to chase off the dog-fighters. And the gun he'd fired the night I'd found Stan Addison. Were there others? I felt dizzy, unable to speak. I watched them talk as if I weren't there.

"She was always nervous, even before we were married. In fact, she warned me not to marry her. But I didn't listen, didn't believe her. I mean, even after you were born, she was fine. It wasn't until later, after your brother . . . that she just . . . Well." My father choked up and cleared his throat, waiting for his voice to steady.

"You all right, Grandpa?" Molly had been leaning on her elbows, watching him. Now she reached out, touched his arm. He patted her hand, collecting himself.

"You need to understand. Since the baby, your mother hasn't been the same. The doctor says it will pass, but she's in bad shape, Zoe. I know it's been hard on you, but you're my big girl, and I need you to be strong. Maybe, between us, we can convince her that it's not the end of the world. Even if the baby dies."

Molly's mouth dropped. "The baby could die?" She turned to me, her face an unspeakable question.

"Dad, stop. You're scaring her. Molly, no. Don't worry. The baby's fine." I hoped.

My father closed his mouth and stared at me with glazed, sorry eyes. Their pain astonished and confused me. For decades, I'd been angry with him, convinced that he'd been an unrepentant gambler and neglectful, indifferent husband and father. I'd never considered other possibilities, never thought about how the deaths of his son and wife might have affected him. His comments had rattled me, shaken my foundations.

"Chocolate milk, coffee and tea." Sally delivered our beverages. "Your meals will be out in a jiffy, Mr. Hayes."

My father cleared his throat, suddenly brightening. "See that?" He turned to me. "Lunch will be here in a second, Louise. Eat. You'll feel better. We'll all feel better. Everything will be fine."

Lunch arrived before Nick did. My father quieted down to eat his broiled flounder. Molly put aside her worries long enough to chomp down on her hamburger special. Between increasingly rapid contractions, I stared at a pot of black tea, puzzling over my parents and my memories, trying to grab on to ephemeral images and piece together the jagged shards of my past.

EIGHTY-NINE

Dr. Martin met us at the hospital. I was beyond listening to the procedure she was going to follow. Molly was there, gaunt and staunchly holding on to my hand, reassuring me as if we'd suddenly reversed roles. I watched Nick's face for signs of sadness or hope, reading my prognosis from his expressions, somehow forgetting that Nick never showed emotion, never gave his thoughts away. I studied him, read his blank face as a positive sign until my vision blurred. The medicine they pumped into my veins slowed the contractions but made my head hammer unbearably and gave me unfocused double vision. Nick and Molly disappeared. The doctor was gone. I lay alone on a gurney among double white curtains and double bare walls, writhing, convinced that I was dying, having a stroke. The pain in my head was surely a sign of exploding, hemorrhaging vessels, and no one seemed to hear when I moaned for help.

It seemed like hours, but might have only been minutes before they removed the IV bag, replacing it with another. A nurse with two heads and two bodies explained that I was having a reaction to the medication. They were going to try something else. I asked for Nick and Molly. I asked for the doctor. I have no idea what I was told. I remember the harsh skull-cracking pain and split images, waiting for time to pass.

And, slowly, time did pass. The medicine washed out of my veins. The pain in my skull let up. My vision returned to normal. The contractions were under control, and the baby was unharmed. But this time, Dr. Martin said, I was to remain on bed rest, probably for the duration of the pregnancy. If I couldn't manage it at home, I'd have to stay in the hospital. But I was not to return to work. There would be no more trips to visit my father or his house, not even to the park or to Molly's school. No driving. No lunch dates or shopping trips with friends. No dinners out with Nick, not that he'd been around for dinner lately. No anything. Just bed, for the next approximately four months.

Actually, I didn't care. I was so medicated, so tired that bed seemed a good place to live. I don't remember how it happened, but somebody hired a practical nurse, a bosomy older woman named Darla, to come in daily and make sure I got bathed and fed. My contractions were still monitored remotely, four times daily, by a computerized contraption. Susan and Karen organized a car pool with other moms to take Molly to soccer and gymnastics, her after-school activities, and they invited her over, making sure her life went on as normally as possible. And Nick came and went as usual. Mostly, he went. He was home less and less, usually only to sleep. When I had energy, I thought about our future, and I knew the wedding was off. Probably Nick was just waiting until the baby was born to tell me, not wanting to stress me further during the pregnancy. I wondered how I'd deal with it, couldn't imagine. Couldn't focus long enough to face it.

During the day, unable to concentrate, too woozy to be bored, I watched talk shows and soap operas. I floated in my mind, dozing, drifting through shadowed corridors in dreams filled with fighting dogs and hanged women, of a cold baby, crying under the floor. Awake, I muddled through medicated thoughts of my parents, wondering how my personality had been shaped by my mother's compulsive disorder and paranoid imagination. I worried that I would inherit her illness. My mother hadn't trusted my father, just as I doubted Nick. Was Nick really as uncaring, as secretive, as I thought? What was real, what imagined? I didn't know anymore, couldn't sort it out. My thoughts were scattered, out of sequence, groggily peppered with ravaged animals, with Craig's screams and Bertram's pleas. I saw my patients in my sleep, their drawings of the secrets buried in the walls of their minds. I worried about Molly, how she would be affected by my months in bed, by the arrival of a sibling. And I thought about the baby, whether it would be born too early, whether it would survive. I wondered if, like my mother, I'd suffer postpartum depression. If I'd be driven to desperation, wanting life to end.

I lay in bed day after day, dozing through a timeless and isolated haze, waiting for interruptions by Darla or increasingly rare phone calls from friends. Daytimes, I'd stare at the pages of magazines or try to follow the story lines of television soap operas. In the evenings, Molly would bring her homework into the bedroom and cuddle beside me, adding or practicing her cursive. Often, we'd have dinner in my bed and read together before Darla ran her bath.

Gradually, though, day and night became seamless, interchangeable. I'd wait for Nick to come in, wanting to talk. But his hours were irregular, and when he came home he seemed distracted, kept our conversations superficial. "Can I get you anything?" he'd ask. Or "How do you feel?" "Boy, I'm bushed" was also big. A few times I tried to talk, but his eyes put up walls, making him unreachable. He claimed he was too tired to talk. Or dodged, apologizing for not being more attentive, explaining that he had a lot on his mind, that his work was taking over his life, that he would try to do better. He'd hold me with loose, passive arms and fall instantly asleep, returning the next day to his attitude of removed indifference.

One Friday morning, about three weeks into my bed rest, near the end of my sixth month of pregnancy, Susan stopped by with homemade scones. Darla served them with a pot of decaf, blackberry jam and butter. When Darla was out of hearing range, for the first time I gathered the nerve to say out loud what I'd been thinking for weeks. I told Susan that Nick had lost interest in me.

"You're crazy." She didn't even look at me. She slathered butter onto a scone.

"He's never home, Susan. And when he is, he spends all his time with Molly. We never talk. We never have a meal together. We never . . . anything."

"He's working hard, Zoe." She bit into the scone, closing her eyes to savor it. "Fact is you're very needy right now. But so is Molly. Her world is upside down with you in bed all the time. You should be grateful that Nick's trying to pick up the slack—"

Why was she sticking up for him? "Yes. It's very nice of him."

"It proves he's devoted to you—" She poured cream into her coffee.

"It proves he'd rather do anything than spend time with me. Molly's just an excuse."

"You're too sensitive. Have a scone." She took another bite. "Man, I really am a good cook." She broke off a piece of scone and spread jam onto it, held it out for me. I ignored it. Or tried to. Fact was the scones were calling to me, begging to be devoured.

"Nick's different, Susan. He's secretive—"

"Hello? Zoe? Nick's always been secretive. It's part of his charisma."

I sighed, accepting the piece of scone, shoving it into my mouth, feeling it melt sweetly away. Why didn't Susan believe me?

"Something's changed. He's . . . I don't know. Even when he's here, he's gone." I had to stop. I was out of breath.

"Stop this, Zoe. You're going to make yourself upset and you'll go into labor. You have to trust—"

"I think Nick's having an affair."

Her mouth dropped. She stared at me. Then she laughed out loud.

"You find it funny? What if Tim were cheating? Would that be funny, too?"

"Please. Tim couldn't cheat. Who'd want him?"

I wasn't amused. "I'm serious."

"I know. But you're being ridiculous."

"Then tell me. Why is he never here, even when he's not working? Where is he? Why is he too tired to talk? Why doesn't he mention the wedding anymore?"

"Hold on," she interrupted. "I know you're on medications that scramble your brain. But try to follow me for a minute, will you?"

She had an annoying, know-it-all look on her face.

"You're not going to like what I'm about to say."

I waited. "So?"

"You've been through a lot, Zoe, and as a result you've become very focused on yourself. But guess what? You aren't the only one who's been through a tough time here."

What was she saying? That I was selfish? "Meaning?"

"Meaning that you should think about things from Nick's point of view. Can you? He might be just a little stressed out. Just a tad nervous. His fiancée is on bed rest, having a difficult pregnancy, in danger of losing their child. She's almost gotten herself killed a half a dozen times in a month. The guy he hired to protect her is dead. In addition to these mundane factors, he's facing marriage. For the first time since his disaster with his first wife, he's making a commitment to someone. He's never been a father before; now he'll—poof—have two kids. Nick's facing a lot of changes and he's understandably not at the top of his act. You're not the only one having to cope."

I listened, wanting to strangle Susan. Oh, poor Nick. She made me want to cry for him. I was the one lying here day after day, contracting eight times every hour. I hadn't made myself pregnant; I hadn't been the one to propose marriage, either. He'd created this whole mess. I had no sympathy for him. But Susan wasn't finished.

"Worst of all, Nick can't fix things for you."

I blinked at her. "I never asked him to."

"Trust me, I know this about men: If there's a problem, men want to fix it. If they can't fix it, they don't know what to do. They get frustrated. They say and do bizarre, even random things. It doesn't mean they don't care. It means they don't know what to do, so they do something stupid. So you're having trouble with the pregnancy. Nick can't fix it. So what does he do? He hides. He says inappropriate things or avoids talking altogether. He acts clumsy. It doesn't mean he doesn't love you or want to marry you. It means he's a man and he can't handle being powerless."

She smiled smugly, impressed with her own insight.

I was more impressed by the fact that, no matter what I said, Susan stood up for Nick, making excuses for his absences, explaining away his distance, trying to make him sound shy and vulnerable. Shy? Vulnerable? Those words fit Nick like his kid brother's suit. At the end of the conversation I was more upset than ever. Doubts lingered, festered in my mind. In fact, I found myself distrusting Susan, wondering what she knew. Why had she been so adamant in her defense of Nick? Was she hiding something? Trying to protect me from some awful truth? I told myself that the medication was muddling my thoughts, that I was overly sensitive, that my confinement to bed rest had skewed my perspective. But the fact remained that the only way I would find peace was to talk directly to Nick. Nothing Susan said, nothing I told myself would appease me; I needed to confront him.

Once I made my mind up, I couldn't wait anymore. I had to act. And so, after Susan left, I called Nick and found out that he'd be home by noon. Then I planned my speech. I would regain my dignity. I would refuse to be passive and dependent. I would ask him directly if he was with me simply out of guilt or sympathy. I would tell him that if he wanted out of the relationship, he needed to go. Not after the baby was born. Now.

As soon as I'd planned what I was going to say, I felt better. Lighter. All that was left was to say it to Nick. I wondered how he'd respond. Would he try to dodge? Would he leave? All morning that Friday, lying in bed, I waited to hear Nick come in, apprehensive about the confrontation, dreading the knowledge it would bring.

NINETY

Sometime later, I woke up to see Nick sitting on the side of the bed, watching me.

"Hi." Half his face smiled. But he was hiding something, trying to act as if nothing were wrong.

"Hi." I rearranged myself, accepting his perfunctory kiss. On the forehead.

"So? How are you feeling?"

I shrugged. How did he think I was feeling? I'd been in my damned bed for weeks, faced another two and a half months there. I was lonely and contracting and missing my fiancé, who probably wanted to leave me. I was miserable. "Fine. You?"

"Tired. Up to my eyes at work."

Of course. I knew that.

"I've got some stuff to do and I need to catch some sleep. But you said you wanted to talk. What's up?"

Go ahead, I told myself. That's your cue. "What do you have to do?"

His eyes shifted. "Is that what you wanted to talk about?"

No. I was just being a coward. "No. I want to talk about us." There. I'd started.

"Us?" He looked blank. "What about us?"

I watched him. "Exactly. What about us?"

His eyebrows furrowed. "I don't understand. Can you be more specific?"

Words weren't coming as I'd planned them. And Nick wasn't

making it easy. Go on, I scolded myself. Talk. "You seem, I don't know. Far away. Like you're hiding something."

"You think I'm hiding something."

"Are you?"

He took my hand, played absently with my fingers. "I might as well tell you. Yes. I've been hiding something. But I guess secrecy isn't good for either one of us. I guess it's gone on long enough."

Oh, God. I'd thought I'd been prepared, that I could take the truth, but I was wrong. My heart clogged my throat. The blood drained from my brain. I couldn't speak.

"I have a secret. I thought it was best not to tell you. Given your situation, you didn't need more stress. But maybe I was wrong. I mean, you have a right to know."

So? What the hell was the secret? A woman? Had to be. What else would he need to hide from me? I wondered how long it had been going on. If I knew her. If she had children. Molly stuck her head in the doorway, asking if she could come in. I wondered why she was home so early from school. Was she sick? And suddenly, it hit me—oh, poor Molly. She really loved Nick. She'd be heartbroken to find out the news.

I tried to look at him but couldn't. Didn't dare. I'd fall apart. I told myself not to cry in front of him. Not to let him know how much I needed him, how I couldn't imagine life without him. A contraction strangled my abdomen. I felt drained, as if my head would fly away.

Molly came in and sat on the bed, interrupting us. The three of us sat there like a family. Like old times. I wanted to ask Molly why she was home so early, if she was okay, but I still didn't dare try to talk. My voice would be a sobbing pitiful wail. Besides, Molly was telling me about a surprise for me, probably something she'd made in art class.

"But first, you have to close your eyes." She waited, watching me. "Close them."

I obeyed. To make sure I wouldn't peek, she climbed up beside me and covered my eyelids with her hands. Apparently, she didn't notice the tears that leaked out; at least she didn't comment.

"Now, count to ten. No peeking."

I lay there, stifling sobs, my heart not just broken, but torn to shreds, counting slowly along with Molly. "One Mississippi, two Mississippi, three . . ."

It occurred to me that, at ten, Nick would be gone. Or worse, he wouldn't be. He'd be waiting to finish our conversation. What would happen afterward? Would he pack up and move out today? Could our relationship end so quickly?

"Nine Mississippi, ten Mississippi." Molly removed her hands. "Open your eyes, Mom."

Go ahead, I told myself. Make a big deal over her project, whatever it is.

"Zoe?" Nick's voice was gentle. "Open your eyes."

Okay. Might as well. I took a deep breath and braved it. I opened them.

And the room exploded.

NINETY-ONE

"SURPRISE!"

A chorus of shouts, my bedroom erupted in noise and color. Balloons, words, faces. Right away, I saw Susan in a crowd. I blinked. Then I saw my father, grinning at me. Then Karen and Sandie. Liz, Ileana and Davinder. My college roommates, Helene and Leslie were there. And, oh my God—my oldest friend, Juree—she'd moved to San Diego, and I hadn't seen her in years. There was a stack of gifts . . . And a shiny blue pram near the closet. A wooden high chair by the bathroom door.

"It's your baby shower, Mom!" Molly beamed. "Nick and I kept the secret."

"You did a great job, Molly." Nick half-smiled, kissed her curls. "But your mom's sharp. She suspected something."

"Did you, Mom?"

Nick took my hand. "I was afraid you'd figure it out. I kept avoiding you so I wouldn't let anything on. Susan would have killed me if I let the secret slip."

The secret? The baby shower? That was his secret? Thank you, God, I thought, and I grabbed some tissues to soak up the latest flood of tears washing my cheeks.

"It wasn't easy, hiding it from you. You always know when something's up." Nick leaned over and kissed me. On the lips.

"Hey, you two—cool it," Sandie interrupted. "This isn't that kind of party."

More voices. From all sides. "Zoe, were you surprised?"

"How are you feeling? Are the contractions any better?"

"You look great; bed rest must agree with you."

"When's your due date? How long do you have to lie here?"

Suddenly, while I'd counted to ten, my bedroom had been converted into a cozy café, complete with cloth-covered tables, flowers and a catered lunch. Friends chattered all around me, eating and laughing. I was surrounded by beautiful women, a golden child, a surprising man. The party went on, but I didn't talk for a while. My throat felt swollen, choked up. But this time, it was okay; I was choking on humility. And a mouthful of sheer joy.

NINETY-TWO

LATER, AFTER MY FRIENDS HAD GONE, AFTER THE CATERER HAD cleaned up, I stared at the stack of gifts. The pram and the high chair, towels and blankets, an oversized bear, tiny playsuits with snaps at the bottom, a unicorn mobile to hang above the crib, a silver spoon, a huge carton filled with disposable diapers. The room still glowed with the warmth of friendship, and I basked listening to the echoes of loving voices.

Surveying the gifts, I felt the clear presence of the small being in my body. Who was it? I tried to imagine the baby riding in the shiny buggy, smearing cereal on the new high chair. Who would wear those tiny garments; whose diapers were those? The person who owned them was already here with me, hidden from view. The evidence was all around me, possessions waiting to be claimed. I found myself talking to the baby now. Listing the gifts, naming the givers. Saying something about each one out loud. I realized, as I talked, that lying in bed for the next ten weeks, I shouldn't feel lonely. After all, I wouldn't be alone.

From down the hall I heard Nick and Molly laughing. A day ago, I'd have found fault with that. I'd have felt left out, abandoned. Now I knew better. My doubts about Nick had been due to his secrecy about the shower. Nothing else. As a contraction began, I lay back against the down pillows, minimizing it through self-hypnosis, counting my blessings along with my breaths.

When it passed, with another ten minutes or so until the next one, I gazed out the window at the fading sun. The days were getting shorter. Thanksgiving was almost here. A man in leather crossed the street, walking a pony-sized dog. A mastiff? My pulse quickened reflexively. Cut it out, I told myself. It's nothing. A man and his pet. Not every dog was trained to fight. But my pulse wasn't convinced; it sped, only too aware that even if Lettie's operation had been shut down, others hadn't. Somewhere not far from us, dogs were being forced to rip each other apart. I closed my eyes, dismissed images of sharp teeth chomping at my feet.

Stop, I told myself. I looked away from the man and his dog, making myself focus on the teddy bear, on memories of my day. I drifted, dozing, into a dream of a sunny morning. My mother and I were at a playground; she was pushing me on a swing. Then we were swinging together, side by side, flying back and forth, and when I looked I saw her smiling, a riot of loose dark hair bursting free, framing her face. The swing shook suddenly, and my mother fell away.

Replaced by Molly. She'd jumped onto the bed and was telling me something with great urgency. "So? Can we? Please?"

Apparently, I'd missed most of her question.

Nick came in, scowling. "Molly, I told you not to wake your mom up."

"But it's important—Davinder's going to give them all away."

"Give what away?"

Molly rolled her eyes, as if the answer were obvious. "The puppies."

Puppies? What? I closed my eyes, saw Lettie's little Rottweilers tearing the skin off a hanging rabbit.

"I just told you. Davinder and Hari's corgi, Lucy? She had puppies, Mom. Four of them. And Davinder said we could have first pick. Nick says it's okay with him if it's okay with you. Please, Mom. Can we get one? Please?"

Molly's eyes begged, puppylike. She folded her hands as if in prayer. Nick shrugged, signaling that the decision was up to me. The air in the room tightened with tension, ready to snap at the next sound. Four eyes watched me, waiting for a response.

What the hell, I thought. It was only a puppy. How bad could it be?